PASSION'S CHALLENGE

Lorelei snatched up the parasol and held it out before her as a fencer would wield an épée. "Stand back," she threatened. "Don't you dare come near me."

Holt had intended to leave, but he couldn't resist that daring challenge. He grinned, then grabbed the end of the parasol and gave the thing a jerk.

Caught off guard, Lorelei didn't have time to release the handle, and she found herself in Holt's arms. It felt perfect. It felt right. It was . . . insane. What was she doing? She had vowed to stay away from this man. He devastated her good sense with one quirk of his lips. He was dangerous.

"Kiss me, Lori. Please."

Please. That did it. If he hadn't sounded so desperate, or so sincere, she wouldn't have turned her face up to his. She would not have wrapped her arms about his neck so that he couldn't pull away.

Just this one last time, she told herself. She needed to have this to remember. . . .

THE TIMELESS PASSION OF HISTORICAL ROMANCES

FOREVER AND BEYOND (3115, $4.95)
by Penelope Neri

Newly divorced and badly in need of a change, Kelly Michaels traveled to Arizona to forget her troubles and put her life in order again. But instead of letting go of her past, Kelly was haunted by visions of a raven-haired Indian warrior who drove her troubles away with long, lingering kisses and powerful embraces. Kelly knew this was no phantom, and he was calling her back to another time, to a place where they would find a chance to love again.

To the proud Commanche warrior White Wolf, it seemed that a hundred years had passed since the spirit of his wife had taken flight to another world. But now, the spirits had granted him the power to reclaim her from the world of tomorrow, and White Wolf vowed to hold her in his arms again, to bring her back to the place where their love would last forever.

TIGER ROSE (3116, $4.95)
by Sonya T. Pelton

Promised in wedlock to a British aristocrat, sheltered Daniella Rose Wingate accompanied the elegant stranger down the aisle, determined to forget the swashbuckling adventurer who had kissed her in the woodland grove and awakened her maidenly passions. The South Carolina beauty never imagined that underneath her bridegroom's wig and elegant clothing, Lord Steven Landaker was none other than her own piratical Sebastian—known as The Tiger! She vowed never to forgive the deception—until she found herself his captive on the high seas, lost in the passionate embrace of the golden-eyed captor and lover.

MONTANA MOONFIRE (3263, $4.95)
by Carol Finch

Chicago debutante had no choice: she had to marry the stuffy Hubert Carrington Frazier II, the mate her socially ambitious mother had chosen for her. Yet when the ceremony was about to begin, the suntanned, towering preacher swung her over his shoulder, dumped her in his wagon and headed West! She felt degraded by this ordeal, until the "preacher" silenced her protests with a scorching kiss.

Dru Sullivan owed his wealth and very life to his mining partner Caleb Flemming, so he could hardly refuse when the oldtimer asked him to rescue his citified daughter and bring her home to Montana. Dru dreaded having to cater to some prissy city miss—until he found himself completely alone with the violet-eyed beauty. One kiss convinced the rugged rancher not to deny Tori the wedding-night bliss that he was sure she would never forget!

Available wherever paperbacks are sold, or order direct from the Publisher. Send cover price plus 50¢ per copy for mailing and handling to Zebra Books, Dept. 3406, 475 Park Avenue South, New York, N.Y. 10016. Residents of New York, New Jersey and Pennsylvania must include sales tax. DO NOT SEND CASH.

ZEBRA BOOKS
KENSINGTON PUBLISHING CORP.

To my dear friends,
Freda and Sissy

ZEBRA BOOKS

are published by

Kensington Publishing Corp.
475 Park Avenue South
New York, NY 10016

First printing: May, 1991

Printed in the United States of America

Prologue

Boston, late summer, 1881

Clifton Abbott's gnarled fingers gripped the gilt-edged frame until he winced with pain. The grimace became a scowl as he stared at the gamine face smiling back at him. Light hair surrounded his daughter's head and shoulders like a shimmering halo in the sepia-tone photograph. He shook his head. *Halo? Ha!*

"Enders! Enders, come in here, right away!" The call resounded throughout the richly appointed library and echoed down a long, dark corridor.

A tall, scrawny man suddenly appeared before the carved mahogany desk. Clifton started. "Damn it, Enders, I've warned you before. It's hard on my heart when you sneak up on me like that."

A grin quirked the corners of Enders' mouth, causing his cheeks to wrinkle in folds, resembling old, scuffed leather. He ran a finger under the collar of his starched white shirt and tugged. "Yes, sir. You needed me, sir?"

One of the twinkling black eyes in the photograph suddenly appeared to wink. The full, pouting lips gnawed at Clifton's heart, and he harrumphed. "Need you? That's an understatement. My head-strong fool of a daughter is determined to go to Colorado Territory."

He laid the picture face down on the polished surface of the desk and wiped a crisp handkerchief across his forehead. "I don't understand what got into my brother to leave Lorelei that albatross of a store in the first place. She's a *woman,* for God's sake! I'd give anything to be able to wring his dear, departed old neck."

Enders' thin lips twitched. He stood quietly, waiting.

Clifton sagged farther into his chair. "I'm glad you're back during this trying time, my friend. I couldn't trust anyone else for this assignment. Follow her. Keep me informed of her every move." He sighed and rubbed his red-rimmed eyes. "If I know my daughter, she'll tire of her new toy within the month and come running home to Daddy to recuperate before trying out her next hair-brained adventure."

Enders nodded.

The older man steepled his fingers and rested his chins atop manicured nails. His dark eyes glittered with hard determination. "See to it that no harm befalls her. Do you hear me?"

Again the tall man nodded and snapped his shoulders back. "I understand. You need have no worries about her safety."

Clifton Abbott's smile was ruthless. "I've always been able to depend on you."

Bowing stiffly at the waist, Enders backed toward the door. "I shall prepare to leave immediately, sir. Is there anything else?"

Clifton reached into the top drawer and pulled out a thick envelope. He laid it on the corner of the desk. "Pick this up before you leave. It's her travel diary, and enough cash to take care of any . . . emergencies . . . expected, or otherwise."

"Thank you, sir. I'll handle whatever arises."

"Never had a doubt. Never a one. I want my daughter back, Enders."

"Yes, sir!"

Chapter One

Where is the damned bull?

Holt Dolan walked briskly along the line of empty stock cars. The Denver and Rio Grande train had just pulled into the Durango depot, and the tall, lithe cowboy was beside himself with frustration because the valuable addition to his herd was not amongst the cargo.

When he reached the first pullman, he stopped and massaged the back of his neck. Wasted. Two days wasted already this week. And now he would be trapped in town even longer. Damn! He had been looking forward to heading back to the ranch today, prize bull in tow.

He hunched his broad shoulders and started toward the depot. With each step his pace quickened. He would get to the bottom of this delay, one way or the other.

"Ouch! Well . . . I beg your pardon, sir."

The husky feminine voice did more to stop Holt's forward progress than the sudden collision. But one careful, considering look at the woman was all he needed. Rich. Immaculate. Snob. She appeared to represent everything he had grown to despise in a woman.

He looked toward the busy depot and back to her incredibly beautiful features. Even with her mouth slightly agape, the pouting lips invited exploration. But it was her eyes from which he could not tear his gaze. They were a striking black; yet, her hair was the color of summer wheat. The gorgeous locks were nearly hidden, though, beneath a garden of flowers perched at a precarious angle atop her head.

Holt frowned. He recognized what could happen here and came close to shuddering. Oh, no, this curvy little piece was *not* going to distract him from his business.

His voice was deep and gruff as he stepped gingerly past her, like he would avoid tromping in a pile of cow manure. "Uh, sorry, lady."

Lorelei Abbott slowly recovered her composure. She clasped her hand about her throat and muttered, "Of all the rude . . ."

The tall cowboy swung around to stare at her with a look on his face reminiscent of someone who'd just caught a pesky mosquito annoying his person. His pale gray eyes flashed the color of hot steel before he turned again and stomped from her presence.

Lorelei huffed out her breath at his brusque dismissal, then quickly stepped from the path of the rest of the disembarking passengers. She stood with her hands on her hips, staring after the tall, broad-shouldered brute. Disjointed images registered in her bemused mind: Black. Black clothes. And hair. Long, flowing stride. Gracefully dodged the crowds. Handsome. Extremely.

At twenty-one, she had seen a lot of men and experienced their strange dispositions, but this one had to be the crudest, the most boorish, exceptional . . . A smile curved her sensuous lips. There was an excitement about the man that set her own nerves to tingling. From the determined way he moved, he was a man with important things on his mind.

She sighed. As did she, Lorelei mused, and it was a waste of time to stand around. Her attention quickly reverted to the area about the depot. She wiped soot and ashes from her face and eyes as the little train's engine loosed a cloud of steam.

Where were her bags? And the porters? Why, back home, a person could hardly make a move without at least two uniformed men haggling over which one would carry the baggage.

While looking for someone, anyone, to help her, people in a great hurry to get to heaven only knew where jostled her first one way, then another. Finally, she lifted the hem of her skirt out of the dust and stepped up on the depot platform.

From her elevated position, she had her first good view of Durango. Her uncle John had described a town that was just becoming settled with the arrival of the Denver and Rio Grande Railroad the first of the year. Therefore, she had expected a small, quiet place.

She was pleasantly surprised. Durango was a thriving community with two- and three-story buildings, banks, a newspaper, churches and homes of every conceivable style of architecture, all situated in a peaceful mountain valley alongside a beautiful, rushing river. It could be fun living here. Living here? For a long time? Home?

Lorelei inhaled a deep, calming breath as the enormity of her situation settled over her. She had nearly had to run away from home. And though she knew she had done the right thing by coming to claim the mercantile she had inherited from her late uncle, her mantle of confidence had suffered a few rips and tears on the long trip to Colorado Territory. It seemed to have evaporated, or turned to dust in the dry, thin mountain air.

This was her first time to venture so far from home, away from her father's supervision and influence. She rubbed her suddenly scratchy eyes, then sniffed and glared in the direction the cowboy had taken. Her shoulders stiffened. Her change of mood was all his fault. He had completely ruined her arrival by upsetting her so. There was no sign of him, and it was a good thing. She felt tempted to charge after him and give him a good piece of her mind.

She inhaled deeply and let the air out in a long breath. Yes, she felt better now. Much better.

Holt Dolan shook his head. Shaggy strands of coal-black hair curled beneath the collar of his light-blue shirt and black leather vest. "Damn it, Tony, when's my cargo goin' to get here?"

The young man squirmed behind the long counter and ran his eyes over the schedule for the tenth time in five minutes. His Adam's apple bobbed up and down like a piece of driftwood caught in a fast current.

"Uh, wish I could help ya, Mr. Dolan. It don't say

here that it was due today."

Holt slammed his fist onto the hard wood, then lifted his hand, too casually, tenderly. "I've been waitin' for two days. Does it say *anywhere* on that sheet when it *might* be expected?"

"No-o, sir. It shore don't. I done looked, several times. Surely it'll be here in another . . . uh, day or . . . so, if they done told ya it would arrive this week. Don't ya think?"

The lean, ominous-looking man turned away with a dark scowl etched into his clean-shaven features. "Yeah, one would *think.*"

Holt heard Tony sigh with relief. The kid probably figured he would get lucky, thinking that mean ole Mr. Dolan would leave the building today, instead of standing around the depot like he had yesterday, glowering at all the Denver and Rio Grande customers. Well, he could just keep hoping.

When Holt suddenly swung back around, the boy's eyes widened. "Uh, is there somethin' else I c-can do for ya, s-sir?"

"Does the train come in at the same time tomorrow?"

"S-sure does."

"I'll be back."

The boy's lips curved in a sickly sort of smile. "Uh, that's fine, Mr. Dolan. S-see ya then."

As Holt shouldered his way through the constantly opening and closing door, he stepped to the side and leaned back against the wall. There was still an odor of fresh-cut wood and new paint hanging about the building, as the depot was barely a year old.

He pushed his black Stetson to the back of his head and surveyed the bustling city as he looked north, up

Main Avenue. God, he hated these useless delays. He had just settled on his ranch, stocking it with longhorns he and some friends had driven up from Texas.

The new Hereford bull would be a good cross with the longhorns. The calves would carry more meat, but still have the long legs necessary to walk long distances for forage or water. He could hardly wait to get his new purchase home and start working on the corrals.

It had surely been a stroke of good luck for all of the ranchers and farmers in the area when the railroad bypassed Animas City and settled on Durango for the next stop on the line. It was like shipping from his own back door.

Scratching a match down the seam of his denims, he lit a long, thin cigar. The bull wasn't here. He might as well resign himself to the reality of remaining in town indefinitely.

Wincing at loud shouts and the sound of gunfire, he walked toward the Mother Lode Saloon. With all of the good things in a new town, also came the bad. Durango had sprung up so quickly that little thought had been given to the need to keep law and order. So, it was up to the individual to protect himself.

Holt jerked around when a heated feminine voice rose above the noise. At first, all he could see was what looked like a bouquet of flowers incongruously bobbing amongst sweat-stained felt hats.

Then a fashionably dressed young woman, swinging a parasol with all the aplomb of a Comanche hefting a hatchet, emerged from the center of a group of scruffy miners.

Holt's eyes narrowed. Two of the more belligerent individuals followed in her wake, hurrying to block her path. His stride lengthened as he headed in that direction.

The grimiest of the two grabbed hold of the woman's arm. "C'mon, little lady, we've got money."

"Yeah, what'sa matter? Think yore too good fer us, or somethin'?"

"I beg your pardon, lout. Take your filthy hand from my sleeve, immediately."

Holt almost hesitated when he heard the smooth-as-silk voice. It was oddly familiar. However, with a sickening lurch in the pit of his stomach, he lunged forward. The stupid woman. Didn't she realize she was making matters worse with her condescending attitude?

"Didjya hear that, Smiley? I'm a lout. Whassa lout?"

The man called Smiley hiccupped with laughter. "An' ya got dirty hands, Thornton. Whadaya think a that? Haw! Haw!"

Before the woman could open her mouth again and stuff it full of her sandy shoe, Holt stepped in front of her, breaking the frowning Smiley's hold. "Oh, s'cuse me. Wasn't watchin' where I was goin'. You folks all right?" He looked back at a young boy wheeling an overloaded barrow and motioned him on to the hotel.

Unaware that the latest arrival upon the nightmarish scene had gallantly come to her assistance, Lorelei stared with open-mouthed hostility at the blundering trio. The moment she had heard the newcomer's deep trebled growl and felt the hard body shove against her, she'd known who it was.

Of all the luck! Not only had she been unfortunate enough to be accosted by a pair of hard-headed ruffians, but now that oaf mauled her again.

Disgusted with the entire situation, she stammered, "I-I should have known. Of all the rude . . ."

Quickly bored by the conversation, or lack of it, Smiley licked his lips, shrugged his bony shoulders and stuck his thumbs under the straps of his suspenders. "Fiesty bitch, ain't she, Thornton? C'mon, we kin find easier pickin's some'eres else. I ain't got no hankerin' ta cuddle up ta no porky-pine ta'night."

The two men threw their arms across each others' shoulders and staggered into the street. A wagon nearly ran them over, and Lorelei blushed profusely at the language rained upon them from the driver's box.

When she looked back around, the tall cowboy stood spraddle-legged, his hands splayed across his hips, glowering at *her*. She cocked her head and said, "Well?"

His eyes flashed the color of flint as a muscle jerked in his cheek. "Well, what?" The words literally ground from between his clenched teeth.

She sniffed and pointed her nose in the direction of a sign swinging in the breeze above their heads. "I am waiting for your apology."

Holt's weather-roughened features paled before turning a similar color to some red dirt she had seen in several locales during her trip across the country. For a moment, she was afraid he was having some sort of fit.

As if to confirm her fear, Holt coughed and sputtered, "Ap-apology! From me? *You* think *I* should apologize? What in hell *for?*" Holt had been caught off guard. Was the idiot woman really naive enough not to have recognized her danger? Who had been so stupid as to turn this . . . person . . . loose, unattended? She honestly didn't know he had saved her neck.

Lorelei instinctively took a step backward, then another. She should have known better than to think the cowboy could react in a civilized manner.

"Why, sir"—she emphasized the "sir" with a slight sneer on her full, pink lips—"that was the second time today that you have careened into my person. That is uncommonly boorish, even for a person of your . . . ilk."

"And just what is my 'ilk'?" he asked too politely, stepping forward, clenching and unclenching his fist.

Lorelei gulped but refused to be intimidated. "I am certain that a lady, such as myself, daren't to say."

She drew in a breath, thinking it best to walk away from this embarrassing encounter, especially since it didn't appear she would receive her apology.

That was when she noticed the sign across the street: ABBOTT FAMILY MERCANTILE—John Abbott, Proprietor. When she hesitated, the cowboy's large body loomed before her, blocking her vision.

Her head tilted back as she looked up the line of gold buttons on his vest. His hard-set square jaw and firm lips, which were now slanted in a sour-looking grimace, caused a queasy fluttering in her stomach. But it was the glint in his cold gray eyes that stilled her movement.

Holt found himself speechless for the first time in years. Surely she wasn't as ignorant as she seemed. Or was she *that* confident and sure of herself? If that were the case, someone needed to pound a little sense, or fear, into her thick head. "Lady, the next time a bunch of drunks mistake you for a whore, I'm goin' to enjoy watchin' the show. Hell, I might even take me a turn."

Lorelei's black eyes rounded with horror. Her mouth

gaped open at the same time her heart threatened to pound a hole through her chest. She sputtered, but nothing came out.

It wouldn't have done any good, anyway. Once again, he had vanished.

Lorelei went straight to the hotel. She couldn't be sure her trembling knees would support her through an inspection of the mercantile. Though she hated to admit it, she had been terrified when those two men had stopped her. If it hadn't been for the cowboy, why, who knew what could have happened? She probably did owe him an apology, and a lot more.

Once inside her room, removed from more gawking stares and curious glances, she collapsed into the only chair and stretched out her legs in a quite undignified, and definitely unladylike, sprawl. It felt so-o good.

She rubbed at her burning eyes. For days on end during the long trip, she had kept at bay the emotions that threatened to overwhelm her by concentrating on the scenery or visiting with the other passengers. Now that she had reached her destination, and was safely behind a locked door and out of view, the loneliness of being away from home and family clogged her throat until she could hardly breathe.

She had purposely ignored her father's wishes. And now, doubt about her capability to protect herself, let alone a business, weighed heavily upon her fragile shoulders. She slumped beneath a tide of self-pity.

Tears threatened to streak her sooty cheeks when she recalled her last confrontation with Clifton Abbott. Upon entering his private domain, a huge library, lined with walls of endless copies of brightly bound books and smelling of cigars, old leather and dusty paper, she'd had to stop for a moment and soak up the completely male atmosphere. What a wonderful place, her father's room.

Then she had noticed her photograph lying flat on the desk. The pain in her chest had been unbearable. Her father had always been the one stable factor in her life. To think that he was so upset that he couldn't even look at her. . . .

Now that she'd had time to think about it, though, there had been a calmness to his features that day, almost a sad acceptance, or so she had imagined, until his words belied his visage. He had shouted at her before she'd had a chance to open her mouth. "Damn it, young woman, I won't stand for it. For the last time, I forbid you to leave this house."

Clifton Abbott had settled his bulky frame behind the gleaming mahogany desk and pushed his spectacles back up the bridge of his long nose.

Desperation had prodded her. She had felt trapped, as though life passed her by while she continued in the same staid tradition of most women before her—get married, have children, look after the household. But she had dreams of being more, doing more with her life. Later, of course, she hoped to find a good man and raise a family, but the important word was "later."

She had pleaded, "Father, you know how I hate to argue with you. Can't—?"

"Couldn't tell it lately," Clifton had grumped.

"Well, I do, but I'm twenty-one years old, of an age where I can, and must, do what *I* think is best." Then she had suddenly choked, indignation flooding her being. She had felt ten feet tall when she had righteously announced, "I will go!"

Her father had twiddled his thumbs and stared. She had fidgeted like a young girl guilty of some unspoken crime, but still guilty, nonetheless.

Finally, he had nodded. She had sighed and walked, with all of the dignity she could muster, over to kiss his florid cheek. It had taken a lot for her father to give in to her wishes, and she had been grateful, and ecstatic. "Oh, thank you, Father. I'll make you proud of me. Honest, I will."

"Darling girl, you'll be home within the month."

She had straightened her spine, knowing he referred to her inability to complete a task, and responded, "It will be different this time, Father. Uncle John must have had faith in me, or he would not have named me to inherit."

Drawing in her breath, she had puffed out her chest and stated quite regally, and naively, "I will accept this challenge, and I will make a success of my life."

Lorelei shifted in the uncomfortable chair, breaking the spell of her daydream. She groaned. Yes, those had been her exact words, and she was determined to make them come true.

"Damn her to hell!" Holt grumbled to himself as he shoved through the batwing doors of the Mother Lode. What had gotten into him? When would he learn to leave a woman be? It was a wonder the damned firebrand hadn't accused him of interfering with her handling of the fiasco.

A grin slowly curved his lips. Several patrons lined

along the bar cast him curious glances, and he smiled, really smiled.

Now he remembered her. She had stumbled off the train and practically run him down. And she blamed him for *that,* too?

Her snapping black eyes glittered in his mind, along with that gorgeous pile of blond hair. She was an attractive woman, he'd give her that. But her temper rivaled that of an overdue pregnant sow.

For the first time in days, he felt lighthearted and glad to be in town. He slapped the man next to him on the back, causing the fellow to blow a spray of beer over the already sticky counter.

Whistling along with the piano player, he wondered what time the *lady* would attack the unwitting streets of Durango tomorrow.

Chapter Two

Lorelei stomped across the main thoroughfare of Durango, scuffing pebbles and small clouds of dust in every direction. Ever since she had left the hotel after a few moment's rest, thoughts of her awful encounters with the cowboy surged through her mind. The nerve of the man! She certainly hadn't asked him to come barging to her side like some . . . some . . . hero on a white horse. She was perfectly able to handle—

She tamped down the remainder of her mental tirade. Her arm throbbed where the drunkard had grabbed her. Rubbing the tender area, she stopped and looked up the street in time to see a tall figure in a light-blue shirt, black vest and denim trousers shove his way into a noisy saloon.

A shiver quaked down her spine. She might as well be honest and admit it—he had rescued her. He had gallantly foiled a situation that had gone beyond her control. She had been scared and unable to think rationally. And how had she repaid his kindness? By hiding her fear and anxiety beneath an outburst of childish temper.

She sighed, wishing she could have the last hour or so back. Well, the next time she saw him, she would swallow her embarrassment and tell him how grateful she was for his help.

Stepping up onto the walkway in front of the mercantile, she cupped her hands around her cheeks and peered inside the dark store. From her reflection in the glass, she gratefully acknowledged that her dress was still fresh-looking. The buttons were hooked; her hair, neat and tidy.

Well, she couldn't stand outside all day. Taking a deep breath, she stepped through the archway to what she hoped would be a wonderful new beginning.

A bell tinkled merrily when she hesitantly pushed open the door. The welcoming sound gave her renewed confidence, and her shoulders straightened. Then astonishment widened her eyes. The store was nearly empty.

Several tables scattered about the large room, and rows of shelves lining the walls, were almost bare. Dustmotes swirled and hung suspended in the dank air with her every step.

She frowned. Why was the mercantile empty? Where were the people who should be wandering the aisles, fingering bolts of material, sampling candy from huge glass jars?

"Good afternoon. May I help you with something?"

Lorelei started, but turned to look into the pleasant features of an elderly woman with round, pink cheeks and twinkling eyes. The woman was short and frumpy, but possessed a smile that literally illuminated the dreary room.

Lorelei stammered, "Uhm, I don't know. I mean, I hope so."

"My goodness, young lady, you look absolutely exhausted. No wonder you're confused. There's a chair by the stove. Sit down for a minute, and then tell me what brings you to Abbott's Mercantile." The woman fussed until Lorelei was comfortably seated.

"Thank you, very much. I did just arrive, and it was a long trip. But I am fine, really. It is just . . ." She looked around the mercantile, at the warped, worn floor—evidence of heavy use, though the building was nearly new—and smelled the musty odors of tobacco and flour, even though none of the items were visible. A lump caught in her throat. There was still that lived-in, cozy atmosphere, and it reminded her so much of Uncle John.

Lorelei jumped when the other woman touched her arm. "I'd be glad to help if I can."

A weak smile curved Lorelei's lips. "Thank you, uhm, Mrs. . . . ?"

The pink cheeks blushed to deep red. "Oh, my goodness. Where are my manners? I'm Minnie Westfield." She hesitated, as if afraid to seem too personal. "And you are . . . ?"

Lorelei held out her hand. "Lorelei Abbott."

"Abbott! Abbott?"

"The late Mr. Abbott was my uncle. I guess you could say that I am the new owner of Abbott Family Mercantile." She felt awkward, unsure about flatly announcing that she had come to secure something over which Mrs. Westfield might have proprietary feelings.

Her anxiety went for naught when the older lady smiled and clapped her hands together. "Oh, thank goodness. I was beginning to wonder what would become of the place."

Lorelei looked around and asked, "Where is everything? I thought this was supposed to be a profitable business." When Mrs. Westfield's face fell, Lorelei quickly added, "I—I do not mean to presume . . . I am sure you . . ." She spread her hands and shrugged helplessly. "I don't know what I mean, exactly. This just is not at all what I expected."

Minnie took one of Lorelei's hands and patted it. "I understand, dear. And I don't blame you for having questions, lots of them. Before your uncle was murd—passed away, he had the inventory replenished. But the town keeps growing so quickly that it didn't take long to go through everything we had on hand."

"And there is nothing more? Anywhere?"

Minnie frowned. "The bank refused to let me order or restock until they knew what would happen with the store, who would replace John, er, Mr. Abbott, or whether it would be sold. I kept it open for John's sake, as his dying wish."

When moisture filled Minnie's eyes, Lorelei instinctively sensed that Mrs. Westfield must have had a special relationship with her uncle, to have so devotedly followed his wishes.

Looking quickly out the front window, Lorelei frowned. "It looks as if it is too late to go to the bank today. Tomorrow morning, I will stop by and get everything settled. I really need to have the mercantile operating again as soon as possible."

"I'm happy to hear you say that, Miss Abbott."

"Please, call me Lorelei."

"Very well, Lorelei. And now that you're here, I'll gladly relinquish responsibility and give you the keys."

The woman sounded so relieved that Lorelei hesitated to ask, but did, anyway. "Mrs. Westfield, Minnie, would you mind staying on awhile? I could really use some help when the supplies start coming in again."

"My dear, I would be delighted to help you." She cleared her throat. "But, just part-time, mind you. I do have a house to look after and all."

The mention of a house reminded Lorelei. "Are there living quarters with the store?"

"We-el-l, not really. But there is a large storeroom, and John, your uncle, built on a privy not six months ago. Said he'd be damned—" Minnie winked. "He said that, he did. That he'd be *damned* if he'd traipse outside in a bloomin' blizzard anymore."

Lorelei smiled. Yes, that sounded like Uncle John. He and her father had been alike in so many ways. "Perhaps, then, I will be able to turn the back of the store into something quite liveable."

Mrs. Westfield shrugged into her coat. "I'm sure you will, dear. There's already a cot, too. Now, when you decide you need me, just give a yell. I live on Third Avenue, in the two-story white house with gables."

The bell jingled as the door opened and closed. Lorelei wrapped her arms about her waist and turned slowly around. She had made it. She finally stood in the midst of her own store.

There would be a lot to do, but she could already imagine the shelves full and people shopping for goods of every kind. Women would want items to help them look pretty and smell good. Men would be more concerned about necessities. How fun it would be, deciding what to order.

She looked out of the window at the darkening sky. It was later than she thought. She was preparing to leave, making a mental list of canned goods, bolts of cloth, ready-to-wear dresses, hats and perfumes, when the door opened again.

"I am sorry, but the mercantile is closed." She turned and looked into twinkling blue eyes.

A young man tipped the brim of his hat and looked her over very slowly, very carefully, from the tilted flowers on her hat to the laces on her kid shoes. His brows raised appreciatively. "I'm plumb sorry to hear that, ma'am."

Lorelei blushed profusely beneath the intense scrutiny. She nervously twisted a dangling tassel on her handbag. She wondered if all western men were as brazen, and suddenly recalled the cowboy and the drunkards who had accosted her on the street not a half hour after her arrival. Perhaps she would just have to get used to it. She tightened her grip on her parasol. Or, perhaps not.

She cleared her throat. "Maybe you did not understand. I—"

The man, several inches taller than she, in high-heeled boots and silver spurs that clanked with each movement, stepped forward. A day's growth of dark whiskers stubbled his cheeks and chin. "Please, I promise not to take much of your time."

His smile was totally disarming, and Lorelei found herself warming to him, despite her sometimes overly cautious instincts. He was quite good-looking, in a naughty-boy sort of way. His moustache curled in a dastardly manner, setting off his straight white teeth, which had flashed engagingly at her since his arrival.

"Well, all right. But a minute is all I can spare." When he laughed mischievously, watching her expectantly, she stammered, "Uhm, pardon me. Did you say something?"

His eyes sparkled. "I said today was my lucky day, runnin' into such a pretty lady." He swept off his hat and covered the area of his heart with the wide crown. "Name's Chad. You stayin' long 'round these parts?"

Her eyes widened. "How did you know I'm a stranger to Durango?"

"Oh, I take it real personal, keepin' an eye on all the pretty ladies. Don't remember seein' you before."

Lorelei's face became exceedingly warm. "Then, you must be the town flirt."

"Yes, ma'am, and proud of it." He leaned against the nearest table and hooked his thumbs under a pair of bright red suspenders. "You aren't married, or engaged, are you?"

She clasped her hands together and laughed. It felt good. It seemed ages had passed since she had teased with a man, and such a charming one, at that. "No, I am neither married, nor engaged."

"Good. Now, how about tellin' me *your* name, an' then chowin' down with me tonight? There's a place that burns the best steak an' beans you ever—"

"Wait just a minute . . . uhm . . . Chad? Just because I am not spoken for, directly, does not mean that I am available."

His pleasant expression faded. For a moment she was afraid she had angered him, until he pleaded, "Please, ma'am, hope you don't reckon I meant to take unfair advantage. Why, I was just fixin' to eat a lonely meal, an' just assumed *you* were by yore lonesome, too. Hopin' for company, was all."

She tucked the strings to her purse more securely into the crook of her arm. Sure, his invitation had been innocent enough, but she couldn't help remembering her father's warnings about a woman alone in a strange town. She had to admit, though, it was tempting to spend her first evening in Durango with a friendly face. "No harm done."

Then she happened to glance out of the window again. It was dark. "I am sorry, but I really must go. Perhaps you can come back another time?"

His blue eyes bored into her. "Yes'm, pretty lady, I'll surely do that."

She returned his smile, then sighed when she found herself alone. It came to her all of a sudden that he never did get around to telling her why he came into the store in the first place.

Her heart fluttered as she grabbed her cloak. And she hadn't even told him her name.

It was almost noon the next day before Lorelei finished her business at the bank. The mercantile was irrefutably hers, all accounts changed to her name.

However, she felt a trifle uneasy about some of the things she had learned.

She tugged her bonnet over her forehead and headed resolutely across the street. Butterflies beat against her rib cage as she entered the store and cast baleful glances about the dim interior. Would she be able to do it? She plunked down onto the lone chair. Even with the money she had, combined with what her uncle had left, it added up to precious little.

Maybe it would be enough to restock at least once, but what would happen if the customers who were now doing business elsewhere decided not to come back to the Abbott Family Mercantile? She would own a store full of goods with no one to purchase them.

Taking a deep breath, she dragged herself off the chair and over to the window. She watched the people passing until one face began to run into another. What did they all need? So many people. So many nationalities. So many livelihoods.

She wrapped her arms around her waist and sighed. Even nice Mrs. Westfield had deserted her—already. As she had left the hotel this morning, the desk clerk had given her a message. Mrs. Westfield had taken a trip to Denver to visit an ailing sister and wouldn't be back for three or four weeks.

She didn't dare reveal to Mr. Trundell, the president of the bank, that she hadn't the foggiest notion of how to run a mercantile, and that her only means of help was out of town. There was still a mortgage on the store for over two thousand dollars, and it was important that he have confidence in her ability to pay the remainder of the debt.

A frown puckered her brow. It was especially vital, since he didn't seem at all pleased that the new proprietor was a *woman.* She seethed even now when she thought about his condescending attitude.

She was about to turn away from the window, when she focused on a tall, very thin man lounging in the shade of a vacant building across the street. There was nothing particularly outstanding about him. His clothes were nondescript, his face hidden beneath a wide-brimmed hat. There was nothing really sinister about him, either. Then another figure drew her attention, and her back stiffened. She pressed her face to the glass to get a better view.

It was that rude cowboy. He wore the same black attire, except the shirt was now beige, rather than light blue. The added contrast was startling. Her breathing quickened. His blue-black hair and dark, tanned skin against that light color set off his virile good looks to the extent that she experienced a fluttering in her stomach that had been missing since her fiancé—

Her eyes strayed to the holster strapped about the cowboy's narrow hips. She shuddered. It had been a long time since she had thought about Frank. He had been killed in a senseless hunting accident only two days before they were to be married. Guns! Why did men think they were somehow less than whole without a firearm somewhere near their person? She was afraid of guns—scared silly that a weapon would take away another loved one.

The cowboy's stride faltered, and Lorelei regained her senses in time to duck back into the dark room. Sure enough, he turned and stared directly into the window where she had stood only moments before. The hair on the nape of her neck tingled until he shrugged and continued on his way.

She stepped forward again. There was something very arresting about the man—something she couldn't quite put a name to.

Perhaps it was his unusual western garb, or the grace and confidence with which he carried himself. Then again, his rugged handsomeness could have quite a lot to do with her more than casual observance. She tapped a fingernail against the glass. One thing for certain, he was absolutely pleasing to her eyes.

She sniffed and turned away, uncomfortable with the sensations taking place within her body, consoling herself that he *could* be nice to look at *if* one didn't have to bear witness to his surly disposition and arrogant speeches.

The bell above the door jangled, and Lorelei spun about, halfway expecting to see the cowboy standing before her. However, she soon relaxed and smiled. "Hello, Mr. . . . Chad." She couldn't remember. Had he mentioned his last name?

"Afternoon, pretty lady. Another lucky day."

"Oh, really?"

"Yeah. I wasn't expectin' to find you here again. In fact, after I vamoosed the other night, I got to thinkin' I was dreamin'. Some old lady usually waits on me." Then, as if he needed to explain his reason for being there, he added, "I always get my chaw—tobacco—here. Only place in town sells it. One of my men, uh, buddies, said he thought the new owner was in town, so I come ta see if he'd order me some. Ah, he around?"

She walked over to lean against the counter, a thoughtful expression on her face. "Yes, the owner is here. Only I am afraid that *he* is a she."

Chad took off his hat and flashed her a shame-faced grin. "Uh oh. Guess I stomped in it this time, didn't I?"

"Not at all. How could you have known?"

He sidled closer. "Well, after findin' you here the other evenin', reckon I should have suspected. Hope ya ain't aimin' ta hold it against me."

She shook her head. "Of course not."

He looked about the empty store. "What're ya goin' to do with the outfit?"

"Oh, I will reopen. It might take a week or so, but I plan to get it going again."

There was such intensity to her voice that he responded, "I just bet ya will. And since I know the boss, reckon *she*'d place a special order for a *friend?*"

Lorelei pretended to consider the request. "Well-l-l, it is an Abbott Family Mercantile policy to please the customer."

Chad's relaxed stance shifted slightly. "Abbott family? You related to the old geezer who ran the outfit?"

She smiled. *Old geezer?* Her father would have a fit. "He was my uncle."

"Sorry."

She wondered why his merry eyes had suddenly shattered. They were such a pretty shade of blue when he laughed and teased, set off by his dark brown hair and long moustache.

He stammered, "Too bad, 'bout his . . . death. You must miss him."

"Oh, yes, but it had been ages since I had seen him."

He quickly changed the subject. "Did you really mean it?"

She blinked, confused. "Really mean what?"

"What you said, 'bout pleasin' the customers?"

The sparkle was back in his eyes, and she felt a twinge of excitement. "Maybe." Good heavens, she was flirting again. Cold, willful Lorelei Abbott was batting her long lashes at the fellow.

He leaned over and whispered, "It'd *please* me if ya'd step out with me for lunch."

Her hands fluttered over the dust on the counter. "I couldn't, really. There is so much to do."

"Ya got ta go for grub sometime, don't ya?"

She hid a smile. He was so quaint—the epitome of what she imagined the western man to be. "Well, I guess I do."

"C'mon. The food's good, an' the company even better."

She looked around the cold, lonely room. She was tired of being by herself, with no friends, no one to talk to. The work would still be there when she returned. Besides, Chad was fun and nice, and she liked him. He made her feel feminine and pretty. "All right, all right. I would love to have lunch with you."

As they walked along the busy street, Chad kept her entertained with stories of early Durango. He was charming, and she thoroughly enjoyed herself.

And she marveled at the deference shown Chad by the townspeople. It was wonderful that a man so young, and seemingly uneducated, would be accorded nods and greetings from men twice his age. Of course, her father had friends who, with little formal learning, were the brains and brawn of huge, money-making companies.

She was about to ask what it was that Chad did for a living, when he guided her into the restaurant. "Here we are." He led her toward a table in the far corner, near a window facing the street. She hesitated when two gentlemen in front of them headed for the same space. Chad never faltered, but gave her a slight nudge forward.

The first man took a chair with his back to the room. The other was about to sit when he looked up and saw Chad and Lorelei. He suddenly straightened and mumbled a few words to his companion, who shot up so quickly that he nearly sent his chair through the glass.

It was that same chair that Chad caught and held out for Lorelei, who was still gaping after the two retreating figures. "I wonder why they left?"

Chad had taken his seat and was looking nonchalantly at the large menu. "Yeah, strange, huh? Lucky for us, though. That's the best table in the house."

She wanted to ask more questions, but a buxom woman with frizzy red hair and a gray-stained apron hurried over. Chad looked askance at Lorelei, then ordered for them both. Turning his full attention to her, he said, "Now, tell me 'bout the Abbott Family Mercantile."

By dusk, Lorelei was bone tired. Limp strands of

long blond hair hung in damp, dusty tendrils down her neck and back. Her hands were red and chapped. Brown smudges colored her sunken cheeks. The skirt of her expensively tailored dress was covered with dirt where she had, at times, gotten down on her hands and knees to clean.

Several kerosene lanterns lent the room an eerie glow. Shadows loomed and receded in the corners and far reaches with every flicker of her movement. She laid aside the cloth she had used to wipe the tables and took a deep breath.

A fit of coughing loosened the dust she had breathed all afternoon. Sneezes shook her slender body. More hair sifted down to her shoulders. She admonished herself for thinking that she could do all of the work and save a little money.

Money? It was something she had never given a thought to before. Why, all she'd had to do was ask her father, and her every wish had been granted.

Hysterical laughter bubbled forth as she recalled her energetic conversation with Chad during lunch. How easy she had made it sound. Had thought that it *would* be. Flipping a coil of hair away from her face, she allowed her shoulders to sag.

It was time to quit, to go back to her room, to rest and soak in a nice, warm bath. She extinguished the lamps, pulled on her cloak and barely stopped long enough to lock the door behind her. Thoughts of sinking her aching muscles into a steaming tub lent speed to her protesting feet.

She turned and stepped onto the walkway. A loud curse sounded to her right. She felt the presence of a tall form and turned to see a teetering body trying valiantly to avoid running into her. "Ouch!" she exclaimed, as a large foot tromped on her toe.

"Damn!" Holt Dolan rubbed his ribs where he'd been gouged by her elbow. His head cocked to the side as he looked down into a decidedly familiar face. The same tilted nose was pointed right at him, only tonight it was smudged with dust. Her thick mane of honey-gold hair fell in loose tendrils around her face. She sneezed, and puffs of dust scattered with the slight breeze. He grinned.

"You! I should have known." Lorelei seemed to forget that she had intended to apologize the next time she met up with the cowboy.

Holt sucked in his breath. God, the throaty huskiness of her voice vibrated throughout his body. He almost lost his concentration; but her shrewish temper was in fine fettle, and his escalated to match it. "Lady, you're dangerous."

Lorelei gasped. "Oh, you . . . you—"

"Of rude, boorish ilk?" he supplied.

Her eyes flashed. All evidence of exhaustion vanished. Her lips twitched suspiciously. "Why, yes, I believe that says it quite nicely."

The color of Holt's eyes darkened remarkably as he watched her back stiffen. She was tall for a woman, taller than he usually found attractive. But she *was* damned attractive. He sighed. Too bad she had that hair-trigger temper. He might have been tempted to give her a tumble.

"Look, mister, why don't you—"

He shrugged and started to move around her. "Holt.

Holt Dolan."

Lorelei's heart skipped a beat, or several. The man had actually curved his lips into a slight grin. Even that little bit of movement had transformed his hard, chiseled features. For a moment, she forgot to breathe.

"And just who are *you,* lady? Seems if we're goin' to keep meetin' this way, I oughta know *your* name, too, don't you think?"

Before she could answer, a man staggered backward from the saloon down the block. He drew his gun and fired through the swinging door. Glass shattered. Women screamed. Flames flickered eerily.

Holt found his arms full of voluptuous woman.

Chapter Three

With the trembling female body pressed full against him, Holt swallowed, hard, and gently put his arms around her shoulders. His hands rested flat on her back. It took all the power he possessed to resist running his fingers down her sides and over her rounded hips. His chest swelled beneath the long-forgotten desire to hold and protect.

She shuddered and gulped back sobs, and Holt ground his teeth. He felt awkward and helpless. What did one do with a terrified female? Temper he could handle. Tears were entirely another matter.

Holt looked around the nearly empty street. Gunfire and loud noises were such a common occurrence that no one even bothered to crowd around and see what was happening anymore. But he could see where it would be upsetting to a stranger, especially such a soft, sensitive stranger.

Maybe if he could take her mind from the ruckus at the saloon, she would calm down. "This is real friendly an' all, lady, but I thought we were goin' to trade names first."

Lorelei gulped and sniffed. Her fingers clutched the soft leather of his vest as if it were a lifeline. She drew in several shuddering breaths until she could concentrate on what he had said. The innuendo in his voice hadn't been lost on her, but she felt much too secure to bother with an immediate response. She was safe and protected for the first time since she'd left New York. Heat radiated from the tip of her nose down to her kneecaps, wherever her body and his made contact, and she reveled in the warmth.

He was so big and strong, yet his arms offered solace to a perfectly abominable woman who had done nothing but berate him from the moment they met.

Although loath to do so, she finally raised her head and pushed away. The evening breeze chilled the portions of her body that had touched him. Shyly, she glanced into his face, only to observe that *his* gaze was concentrated below her chin.

She looked down. Her cloak was open, her taut nipples clearly defined by the soft clinging material of her day dress. A hot flush crept up her neck and flamed in her cheeks as she snatched her wrap closed. Her voice crackled with embarrassment. "M-my name is Lorelei Abbott."

Holt gulped. He should have known she'd have a beautiful name, too. *Lorelei. Lorelei.* He repeated it over and over in his mind. His voice was deep and husky as he said, "Well, Miss Abbott, it's a pure pleasure to make your acquaintance." His hand ran up and down his chest in an effort to brush away the sparks that her touch had ignited.

He looked toward the saloon and shook his head. "That's somethin' you're goin' to have to get used to around here. Durango's still a wild town."

Using the time while his eyes were directed elsewhere to regain her composure, she took a deep breath and replied, "I'll *never* get used to guns. The loathsome weapons are good for nothing but death and destruction. I *hate* them."

He swung his gaze back to her impassioned features. "Maybe so, but they also save a lot of good lives."

Her teeth clicked as she snapped her jaws closed. She had found out through many such conversations that arguing served no purpose. So, she smoothed a wrinkle in her rumpled cloak and lowered her eyes. There was something else, more important, that she needed to say. "I apologize for throwing myself at you so shamelessly. It won't happen again."

"Aw, shucks."

She glanced up to see his incredible eyes dancing with merriment. His teeth were straight and even as he dazzled her with his most astounding smile yet. Her stomach muscles fluttered. She shyly grinned back at him.

Holt tugged at the knot in his bandana. "Reckon I sort of owe you an apology, too."

"Me? Whatever for?"

"The other day. I was angry and shouldn't have taken it out on you. Gave you a sorry introduction to our fair city."

Lorelei couldn't believe her ears. She had already discovered he wasn't such a callous oaf as she had imagined, and now he was making amends for his horrid behavior. "Your apology is accepted, Mr. . . .

Dolan, wasn't it? It just took me by surprise when you ran into me, twice."

"I ran into *you?"* Holt swallowed the rest of what he was tempted to shout. After all, he had vowed to tell her he was sorry. There was no sense in starting her on another rampage.

Then he latched on to something else she had said. "Abbott? You said your name was Abbott. Are, were, you related—"

Lorelei smiled. "Yes, he was my uncle."

Holt's eyes narrowed. A muscle jerked along his jaw. "Damned shame. John was a fine man."

"Y-you knew my uncle?"

His fists clenched. "Yeah. Did all my business with him."

The thought that Holt Dolan and her uncle John were friends gave Lorelei a warm feeling inside. "Then, you could probably tell me a lot about him. I hadn't seen him in ages."

Before she could ask any questions, he grabbed one of her hands and placed it on his arm. His fingers covered her soft skin, but when he found himself enjoying the sensation, he jerked his hand away. "It's too dark for a lady to be out on the streets alone. Where are you stayin'?"

He winced slightly when she gave him a curious look, but he had no desire to talk about John Abbott. Every time he thought of how the old gentleman had been shot down, it made him angry as hell. One day, he would settle with the man who had murdered the storekeeper. One day soon.

All Lorelei knew was that the cowboy seemed to have returned to his surly self again. What had happened to the kind man of a few moments ago? She had never seen anyone change moods so quickly.

She eased her hand away and started walking without deigning to answer his question, and also ignored the sudden rush of blood to the tips of her fingers. They still tingled with the indelible impression of a hard, corded forearm. Tossing her head, she decided that if he wanted to know where she stayed, he could follow along and find out, if not . . .

Holt's eyes widened at her abrupt departure. What had he done now? But he had to admit, he surely admired the way she stalked down the boardwalk, her little nose in the air, her hips swaying back and forth. It was enough to drive a red-blooded man crazy, and *he* was definitely red-blooded.

He caught up with her, walking on the outside nearest the street, just in case more drunks decided to take potshots at anything that moved. As he fell into step beside her, he found himself wondering what she was doing in Durango and how long she might stay. In fact, the more he thought about it, the more he hoped—

He shook his head, reminding himself that whatever she did, she was not here for his pleasure. Lorelei Abbott was too much a lady, too beautiful, feisty, and much too independent. Definitely a woman to avoid. "Miss, you mind if I call you Lorelei?" Ah, the name seemed to trip off his tongue.

She shook her head and kept walking.

"What's going to happen to the mercantile?"

"I'm going to reopen it, of course."

He grumped, "Oh, of course. Now, why didn't I know that?" Though he pretended to be sarcastic and unaffected, deep down an excitement began to build that he hadn't felt in years.

Lorelei smiled in spite of herself. Butterflies fluttered against her rib cage. They had reached the hotel, but she hesitated outside. Part of her demanded she stay and talk with her handsome escort; but another part, the part that turned suddenly jittery and dry-mouthed, won her over. In an effort to mask her ambivalence, she told Holt, "Thank you for seeing me home. Good evening, Mr. Dolan."

She disappeared through the lobby door, leaving a bemused Holt in her wake. He couldn't help but think those miners had been right. She was prickly as a "porky-pine." And damned if that didn't make her all the more intriguing.

Once inside her room, Lorelei sat on the edge of the bed to relieve her shaky legs. What was it about that infuriating man that could make her angry one moment, yet cause her to feel all warm and queasy the next? Most of all, she didn't appreciate the tingly sensation that coursed through her insides every time she looked at him.

Even after she crawled wearily between the covers, she couldn't get the tall cowboy out of her mind. She pictured him wearing many different faces. His features changed dramatically with every nuance of his personality—whether he was being polite and enthralling, or arrogant and rude.

And she sensed something even deeper underlying those expressions he presented publicly, something very . . . dangerous.

She tossed and turned, unable to fall asleep. The covers twisted about her body. And then, to top off the miserable night, her neighbors on either side decided they had better things to do than sleep.

To the left, she heard mumbling male voices and the unmistakable sound of a deck of cards being shuffled. She grimaced. No telling how long their game would last.

Lorelei rolled over and pulled a pillow on top of her head. No sooner had she dozed, albeit fitfully, than a loud giggle from the opposite wall raised her droopy eyelids. A man's voice echoed clearly and distinctly, "Aw, c'mon, sweety. Take off the rest. Don't tease ole Harry. Cain't ya see I'm ready fer ya right now?"

Lorelei's eyes blinked open, all trace of drowsiness wiped away with a swipe of her knuckles. She jerked straight up when the giggle came again. Then she heard the squeak of rusty bedsprings. Groaning, she slunk down and buried herself beneath the covers *and* the pillows. It didn't help. Bump. Squeal. Thump. Squeak. Giggle.

When moans and gasps overrode the springs, Lorelei thought she would die of embarrassment. How dare they carry on so, advertising their depravity to the world? Why, if she weren't a woman alone, in a town dominated by men, she'd march right over and pound on the wall until they stopped their . . . their . . . Oooh! She couldn't bring herself to even *think* of what they were doing.

Suddenly, as if imagining the sound caused it to happen, someone from the card game banged on *her* wall. "Hey, you over there. Keep it down, will ya?"

The skin on Lorelei's body literally crawled with humiliation. Dear Lord, did they believe those ghastly noises came from *her* room, *her* person? Her black eyes glittered with apprehension. What if they came to make certain the commotion stopped. What if . . .

In a moment of rational thought, she realized the other room was now quiet. No more squeaks and grunts. No more thumps and vibrations as their bed rocked against the thin partition passing itself off as a wall.

She sighed and started to crawl back under the covers, but her gaze kept returning to the far wall. In fact, it bothered her so much that she couldn't relax, or even try to sleep. Finally, she dragged herself from bed to tiptoe, barefooted, over to straighten the tin-type that had been recently slanted askew.

That done, she flipped her long braid defiantly over her shoulder and slowly returned to bed to slip meekly between the sheets. Still she couldn't sleep. She rubbed her damp palms on the blanket and turned very carefully onto her stomach, then rolled onto her back, praying that her own springs wouldn't betray her restlessness.

It was stifling hot. Her body was slick with perspiration. Every once in a while, images of a tall, smiling cowboy reached out to her.

A curse welled in her throat, but she swallowed it back. She was overly sensitive, that was all. The events of the evening had conspired to wreak havoc upon her emotions. She took a deep breath and exhaled it slowly, then repeated the action over and over.

Everything would be all right. She would sleep now.

She would. And she was moving out of the blasted hotel with all possible haste.

The next morning, Lorelei skipped breakfast and went straight to the mercantile. She ducked her head and focused on the ground, hoping against hope that she wouldn't "run into" anyone today.

Pride and vanity. She had seen herself in the tiny mirror above the wash basin. Her eyes were red and puffy. Dark circles accentuated every imperfection. She hadn't gotten one wink of sleep last night. Not one wink.

Her lack of rest was evident as she dragged herself through the first few chores of the day. At least she had nearly finished cleaning the storeroom yesterday, and all she had left to do was to shake out the blankets on the cot. It might not be the best bed around, but the store would certainly be a quieter place to *sleep* than the hotel. The privy and lavatory were clean. She had everything she needed right here.

Straightening her back, she groaned and reached around to massage a sore muscle. *Several* sore muscles became a more accurate description with the movement.

Another important matter came to mind as she worked. What would she do when the crates of supplies began arriving? She couldn't handle the heavy boxes alone, and Mrs. Westfield shouldn't lift anything.

She wandered to the front of the store and looked out of the window. It was a pastime she never seemed to tire of—watching the crowds pass by, wondering where they came from, where they went, if they were married, where they worked and lived.

Pressing closer to the glass, she saw that poor thin man again. He was in almost the same spot every day—across the street, lounging against a wall, or walking back and forth in front of the vacant building.

She tapped her chin. An idea formed. She backed into the middle of the room and stared at the high shelves she'd been unable to reach, and the large expanse of floor that had yet to be swept. Perhaps, just perhaps, she had a solution to several problems. Quickly exiting the store before she had a chance to reason herself out of taking the chance, she strode purposefully across the busy street.

For a moment, when the man saw she headed straight toward him, Lorelei was afraid he would run. She hesitated, mentally rechecking her articles of clothing and haggard appearance. Surely she didn't appear *that* threatening, or frightening. But the fellow drew himself up and stood, waiting, a defensive expression on his features.

"Excuse me, sir, but may I have a few moments of your time?"

He stared, then nodded. She shifted uncomfortably. She'd never approached a stranger quite this brazenly before, and prayed she wasn't making a huge mistake. At least he didn't *appear* to be a depraved desperado. Clearing her throat, she explained, "Ah, I've noticed you hanging about for the past several days."

A muscle jerked in his jaw as he pushed his hands into the pockets of his baggy trousers. She sighed. He wasn't going to make it any easier for her. "Yes, well, I wondered if you, perchance, needed a job?"

The man's eyes shifted from the ground to her face,

filled with very real surprise. "A job?"

She nodded, and held herself stiffly erect.

"What kind of job?" There was a hint of suspicion in his gravelly voice.

"I need part-time help. Over at the mercantile. Someone to do the heavier cleaning, and to move and unpack supplies as they arrive. I can't pay a lot, but it would buy you a decent meal every day and be better than your standing on a corner in the cold."

She thought that he certainly couldn't fault her reasoning. Though the weather had been sunny since she had arrived, the fall days were quite chilly in this high altitude. A slight shiver caused her to wish she had brought along her cloak.

Her eyes drifted away from the fellow's frail-looking form, but not before she noted the fierce scowl around his narrow lips and sunken cheeks. She'd never seen skin that looked so rough and weather beaten. Why, it appeared to be as tough as leather.

She started when he answered, "I'll take it."

"Y-you will?"

"Yes. And thank you . . . madam."

"Ah, it's miss. Miss Lorelei Abbott. And what may I call you, sir?" When the man chuckled, she assumed it was over her use of the term, *sir*. Poor fellow, he was probably unused to someone treating him with manners and respect.

"Call me End . . . er . . . Endsley. Robert Endsley."

"All right, then, Mr. Endsley, I'll see you tomorrow morning. About ten o'clock? Oh, do you have a way . . . ?"

"Don't worry, Miss Abbott, I'll be on time."

There was definite amusement in his voice, and she

darted him a quizzical look. "Well, good." She backed up a step and nearly toppled off a cracked board. "See you tomorrow."

Mr. Endsley nodded. She turned and hurried back to the store. Once inside, she stood in the shadows, watching as the man, his hands still stuffed in his pockets, sauntered casually up the street.

She sighed and hoped again she hadn't made a grave error. Yet, she felt good about doing something for a man who looked like he could really use a little help with his life.

Yes, she was proud of her good deed for the day.

By the time Lorelei was ready to leave the store that evening, she was content with the knowledge that this would be her last night at the hotel.

Besides the big, potbellied stove in the main room of the store, there was a smaller version in the back that had a wide, flat lid, perfect for making hotcakes and warming pots of canned food.

She would be quite comfortable living there, and would be her own security. The past several nights, she had worried herself to sleep because of the store. What would she have gone through if it had been stacked to the ceiling with supplies?

Thank heavens, now she wouldn't have to find out.

The bell jingled, and she sighed wearily. She had put a sign in the window denoting that the mercantile would not reopen for another week. As nice as it was to know people were actively seeking to do business, she was just too tired to muddle through another long introduction and explanation.

She walked into the main room, tucking a stray tendril of hair behind her ear, which joined numerous other recalcitrant strands. A spur rowel jangled on the uneven flooring. "Oh, hello, Chad."

"Evenin'. 'Pears you've done a heap of work 'round the outfit."

Lorelei's spirits brightened. Someone had actually taken notice of her hours of hard labor. "Why, thank you. It's not exactly the kind of thing I normally do, but I must say, I have learned a lot in the past few days."

Chad tucked his thumbs under his suspenders and looked around at the clean counters, tables, windows and shelves. However, his eyes were on Lorelei when he replied, "Looks nice. Real nice."

Her cheeks pinkened. She knew what she looked like, after a sleepless night and a full day's labor, yet he had paid *her* a compliment. "Th-thank you, again. What brings you by today? Uhm, I have not had time to place your order." She brushed enough dust from her skirt to form a gray ring around her on the floor, and her nose twitched uncertainly.

"I aimed to see you."

"Me?"

"Yes, you, pretty lady. Why'd ya reckon otherwise?"

Lorelei blushed. "I am surprised, is all."

He stepped closer and wiped a smudge from her cheek. "You ain't got no notion how comely ya are."

Flustered, and just a little nervous, she embarrassed herself further by giggling. Then she cleared her throat. "I really do not think . . . I mean . . . we hardly know each other."

He immediately backed off a step or two. "Didn't mean ta make ya skittish. Honest." His voice lowered.

He gazed intently into her rounded eyes. "Just givin' ya fair warnin'. You're really somethin', an' I aim ta know you a whole bunch better."

Lorelei was at a loss for words. She had never dreamed of being courted out here in the wild west. How her father would love to see this. "I am flattered. I truly am."

Chad added, "But?"

"I cannot make any promises. It is true, you know, I hardly know you, and there are so many things to take care of here. I don't see how I'll have time for a personal—" There was a deep glow in his blue eyes that caused her to hesitate.

Chad stood rigidly by her side. "So, I might's well hang it up pronto. That what you're meanin'?"

His disappointment was so strong that she felt it, too. "Yes. No. Oh, I don't know. I guess that meeting . . . someone . . . was the last thing I expected to happen when I came to Durango."

His stiff features softened. "Can I call on ya, then?"

She sighed and fluttered her thick lashes. "I suppose it would not be so terrible."

Laughing, he put his arm around her shoulders and walked with her to the door.

While she locked up, she couldn't control the thoughts that raced unfettered through her mind. Why, when Chad touched her, did she suddenly start comparing him to the cowboy? Most disturbing of all, why didn't her spine tingle whenever Chad stood near?

She berated herself for even thinking such things. At least around this man, she felt that she could control her feelings, instead of experiencing the wild, runaway sensations that always seemed a part of her encounters with Mr. Holt Dolan. Chad was every bit the gentleman, too, which was something she couldn't bring herself to believe about Holt.

"Whyn't I herd ya home? Or is that gettin' too personal?"

She had almost forgotten that he was waiting. "I would like that." And surprisingly, she *was* pleased to be in his company. He had certainly bolstered her flagging spirits.

She gave him a covert once-over beneath her lowered lashes as she fumbled with the key. He was a fine figure of a man. Shorter and more slender than the cowboy—Oh-h-h! She bit the inside of her cheek. Chad was right here by her side, and she couldn't keep her mind from that . . . that . . . man. What was the matter with her?

Chad offered his arm, and she was about to take it, when a commotion erupted in the middle of the street. People were suddenly running up and down the boardwalks, ducking into doorways and hiding behind stacked barrels.

"What is happening, Chad? Why is everyone running?"

He pointed just as she looked for herself. Two men stood in the middle of the street, facing one another. Both wore holsters strapped to their hips, their arms held away from their sides, hands hovering just above the deadly weapons.

She sucked in her breath and stood transfixed by the macabre scene. She had read about the infamous gunfight, but had never believed something so horrifying could be real and not just some overzealous reporter's imagination.

A movement down the street distracted her. A woman and her small daughter emerged from a millinery store. The lady reached for the little girl's hand just as the child darted for the street.

Lorelei gasped. The girl was in the line of fire. Should the gunfighter facing in that direction miss . . . She shouted, "Stop. Go back."

The mother rushed forward just as the two adversaries slapped their hands to the butts of their pistols. From out of nowhere, a man in a black vest and hat ran to place himself between the woman and child, and the gunmen.

Lorelei's knees went weak. Her hand grasped at her throat. The first shots cracked the air. The man was Holt. Holt Dolan.

Chapter Four

On his way from the livery stable after checking on his Morgan stallion, Holt was brought up short by the increased activity on the streets. His gut constricted, and his mouth felt like it had suddenly been stuffed full of cotton. He had seen enough gunfights in his thirty years to recognize what the flurry of excitement represented.

His keen gaze settled on the little girl at the same instant he heard a woman's terrified shout. Without another second's hesitation, he dashed toward the toddler and bore her to the ground as the gunmen drew and fired.

Chad had drawn Lorelei into the mercantile's recessed doorway. She clung to him, her eyes wide and filled with horror as her gaze riveted on Holt. An explosion rent the air. Then another, and another. She cringed and covered her ears. Too late. Much too late. The impact of lead rending flesh reverberated through her head.

Townspeople slowly began to emerge from other

hastily procured havens of sanctuary. Lorelei's legs shook, but she walked to the edge of the walk. She took a deep breath and nearly gagged on the acrid stench of gunpowder. Holt and the little girl were still down. Neither form had moved so much as a muscle.

Blood rushed through her veins at near blinding speed. "Dear Lord, let them be alive," she silently prayed. Surely such an unselfish act of bravery couldn't go for naught.

Then, in a blur of movement, she watched as the young mother rushed to grab up her child, who in turn wrapped her tiny arms about the woman's neck. Surprisingly, though, the little girl was not crying. She laughed and pointed to the long form still stretched out in the avenue.

Lorelei gasped. She had unknowingly descended into the street and stumbled over a wagon rut. Her heart thudded madly when Holt slowly arose, grinned and dusted himself off. Then a heated flush stained her pale flesh as the attractive mother leaned up to kiss Holt's cheek.

"My God, did ya ever see the like? That was some shootin'. Drilled him right through the heart, first shot."

"What?" Lorelei started and spun around to find Chad had followed her. She had willed the gunfight out of her mind in her concern for Holt and the child. Chad's reminder caused her arms to wrap protectively about her waist. She had studiously avoided looking toward the middle of the roadway, not wishing to know the outcome of the ghastly confrontation.

Chad's blue eyes glittered with barely suppressed

excitement. She noticed the tension in his usually relaxed form. His fingers twitched in what she guessed was a reflex action to the gunfight.

She shuddered, then reluctantly followed the direction of his transfixed gaze. Nausea churned her stomach. A small cry of terror escaped her trembling lips as her gaze fell on the dead man lying, in what almost seemed a peaceful repose, not ten feet in front of her.

Her knees buckled. She thought she might fall, but Chad quickly grabbed hold of her arm and pulled her against his strong, young body. Grateful for the support, she hid her head on his shoulder.

"There now, pretty lady. It's all over. No harm done."

Bile choked her. All trace of color drained from her face. She strained away from him. Her throat was so dry that she croaked, "No harm done? No harm? How can you say such a detestable thing? There is a man lying *dead.*"

"Yeah, and wasn't it something? That other hombre can sure shoot."

Lorelei took another step back, unable to believe her ears. What was the matter with people out here? Did they have no respect whatsoever for human life?

Then Chad looked into her glazed eyes and placed a comforting arm about her shoulders. "Hey, I'm sorry. You're really upset, ain't ya?"

She sniffled and pulled a delicate lace handkerchief from her reticule. He gently turned her around, and they were about to step up on the boardwalk when a prickling sensation feathered across the nape of

Lorelei's neck. A darted glance over her shoulder gave proof to the fact that someone was, indeed, watching her.

Holt Dolan stood a few feet away, a scowl wrinkling his dark features. His eyes pierced her, causing her step to falter. When his scorching gaze dropped to the arm draped so possessively over her back, her flesh seemed to sizzle from the heat directed there.

Confusion rocked her to the core of her being. Why did he appear so disgruntled? And was that a look of disappointment she saw? Why? She shook her head and walked on. What should she care, anyway, what the cowboy thought of her, or her friendship with Chad? She swallowed carefully. Besides, the queasy sensation gurgling in her stomach was becoming more and more insistent.

Sensing an anxiousness in Chad's behavior as he politely awaited, she stepped from beneath his arm, though she felt weak and bereft without his support. "Please, Chad, you go on. I have forgotten something inside the store."

People milled around them. One man muttered, "This has got to stop," as four more men lifted the dead gunfighter and carted him unceremoniously away. Tension gripped her when the dead man's gun dropped from his lifeless fingers and a young boy ran to retrieve it. She gulped, twice, hard. She needed to be alone.

"There is no need for you to wait. I will be perfectly safe," she pleaded.

Chad had been casting furtive glances toward the saloon across from the store, and she had a suspicion that was where the victorious gunfighter had adjourned to brag about his feat of derring-do. So she was not surprised when he licked his lips and made a feeble attempt to sound disappointed. "Well, if you're sure. I, ah, do need to see a man. . . ."

"Good evening, Chad."

He grinned. "Yeah, see ya, pretty lady." His spurs jangled merrily as he tipped his hat and spun around to hurry across the street.

She shuddered and turned toward the mercantile. Her head spun like crazy, and she grasped for the nearest rail as she mentally berated every man who carried a gun. Why? What was so fascinating about weapons? Frank had been caught up by the madness, too. A shiver quaked her spine as she remembered how his hands had caressed the long, cold barrel of his rifle, and the almost sensuous way he polished the wooden stock.

There had even been times when she had accused him of loving his firearms more than he could possibly care for a mere woman. A knot formed in her stomach. And just look where it had gotten *him.* Her thoughts solidified her decision to not stock firearms or ammunition of any kind in the mercantile.

She swayed again. Suddenly, a strong arm wrapped about her waist. The shock that rippled through her body informed her even before she looked that Holt Dolan had come to her rescue. Unsure of what to expect when she gathered the courage to glance into his eyes, she was surprised to find tender compassion. His voice rumbled with understanding when he told her, "You look a mite peaked. Here you go, just hold on to me."

He led her to the door, took her key and unlocked it. She gave him a watery smile, which quickly faded as she covered her mouth with both hands.

"Want me to come in with you?"

She shook her head and ran. Later, when she came back to the door, it was closed and the key was in the lock. Holt was gone.

Finally, she walked over to sit on the window ledge. Men and women alike wandered the street as the sun shone its last brilliant rays through the glass. The warmth felt good to her chilled flesh.

Leaning her head against the sill, she sighed, long and dejectedly. She was still shaken from the gunfight, and her chest constricted painfully whenever she recalled the sight of Holt Dolan running directly into the line of fire. It had felt like her heart dropped clear to her toes before shooting up to lodge in her throat.

An inner warmth spread from her lower belly outward. Of all the men standing nearby, *he* had been the one to risk his life to save the child. The same overbearing oaf who had brashly stepped forward to defend her honor, who had considerately assisted her into the store when he knew perfectly well she was about to be ill. He had even been willing to stay with her, for heaven's sake.

There was definitely more to the man than she had at first imagined. Quite a lot more.

Holt Dolan sat in the Mother Lode Saloon nursing his third beer. His belly felt as if a dozen snakes were slithering through it. It was always that way, after a gunfight, whether he was involved or not. He took a deep breath and succeeded in eradicating at least a few of the crawly creatures.

Through the dirt- and grime-stained window, he kept an eye on Abbott's Mercantile. The nearly empty glass twirled in his hands. Stupid woman. Was she planning to wait until midnight to navigate the streets? Didn't she know that after something like a gunfight, the town would be restless, nervous? No telling *what* could happen to a woman alone. . . . Then again, thank God she *was* alone.

One of his hands dropped to his silver buckle. There was still an ache in his gut that even the drink couldn't dissolve. He had thought the wind had been knocked out of him when he and the child had fallen, but it had been nothing compared to the blow he had experienced as he turned and found Lorelei standing with her head on the kid's shoulder.

He downed the remainder of the beer in one gulp. It was warm and burned his gullet. Damn! It seemed nothing could distract him from thinking about the way she had leaned against the kid, and how the other man's arm had curled around her, as if staking his claim.

The mug slammed so hard on the table that a fleck of foam clinging to the rim splashed on his wrist. Curses rained softly from his lips as more unwanted memories flooded his mind. His stepmother. His wife. He pounded the table. He needed another drink. Fast.

Why were ladies of quality and good breeding always finding him lacking? Even the snooty Miss Abbott. He had vowed a long time ago that he would not go through the pain and heartache associated with women of their—ilk.

The door to the mercantile opened, and Lorelei stepped into the light of the kerosene street lamp. The tender spot in his stomach throbbed. Hell and damnation! He couldn't sit here and watch her head out all by herself.

When the swamper set a fresh beer on the table, he looked at it longingly, then raided his pockets for a coin. Flipping it to the old man, he said, "It's on me," and hurried through the swinging doors.

Meanwhile, Lorelei fumbled the key in the lock. Oh, why had she waited so long? Full darkness had long since fallen while she sat and daydreamed, and now, she admitted, albeit grudgingly, she was afraid.

She had taken only a few steps down the walk when a shadow loomed toward her from the street. Gasping, she raised her parasol and threatened, "Do not come any closer."

A deep rumbling laugh caused her to bristle with a new emotion.

"I am warning you."

"Warning me of what, Miss Abbott?" In a heartbeat, he jerked on the wrist holding the ineffective weapon and forced her arm to her side. "Do you have any notion of what you're doin'?"

She hissed, "*You* again. Why—"

His iron-hard fingers curled even more tightly around her fragile bone, cutting off her retort more quickly than if they had wrapped about her throat. He dragged her down the walk and into the dark, empty space between the mercantile and the local newspaper.

She tried to catch her breath as he shoved her against a wall, then wrinkled her nose. For heaven's sake, the man had been drinking.

Before she could comment on his apparent transgression though, she found herself pinned in place by his hard, lean body. The breath she had been about to expel caught in her throat. Her heart thumped wildly.

It was aggravating to discover the roiling emotions she experienced were due more to excitement than fear, even though he glowered menacingly at her, an easy fact to discern now that the moon had risen in all of its full glory.

"Where's your sense, woman? Hasn't anyone told you it's dangerous to be on the streets alone, especially at night?"

She gasped with outrage, but exhaled quickly when her breasts came into contact with his solid chest. "Y-yes. I believe you mentioned it the other evening. And my father has taken care to impress upon me the need to be cautious."

Holt felt his chest collapse when their bodies connected. For a minute, he forgot what he was yelling about. His gaze was drawn to the moonbeams flickering in her bonnetless hair like a million sparkling diamonds. Suddenly, the bluster evaporated, and the biggest word he could think of to utter was "Oh."

At least he knew she was aware of the danger. Then his anger roiled to life again when she had the temerity to smile. Was she making light of the situation, of his concern?

"I wish to hell you'd paid attention, then. Blood was drawn today. Men get restless. They might . . .

could—" He suddenly leaned closer. He couldn't help himself. Their thighs touched. She stared intently into his eyes, as if taking notes of his every word.

"Aw hell!" He bent his head and kissed her.

Lorelei was too stunned to react quickly. From the way he had looked at her—almost as if he hated her—a kiss was the last thing she had expected.

His lips were firm and moist and ignited tiny sparks in her lower belly. Blood gushed through her veins with such force that she felt dizzy and was grateful for the support of both the building and of Holt's sturdy frame.

She had been kissed before, but never had her legs threatened to give way. His tongue teased and tantalized. He leaned into her until they were pressed together from chest to knee. Her body responded with a shuddering yearning that set off an alarm in the back of her mind. She was fast losing control. That could not happen. Not now.

Holt felt her tension. He eased the kiss and regained his senses enough to take a deep, ragged breath and pull away, cursing his stupidity for succumbing to the temptation in the first place. Hadn't he learned his lessons yet?

Lorelei could have died from shame when her traitorous body swayed toward him, like a moth caught in a forbidden flame. Oh Lord, if he noticed, or had the audacity to say anything. . . .

"My apologies, ma'am."

She sighed. That was better.

Then he snatched her hand and hurried from the shadows. "We'd better get you to the hotel." Before he managed to do something even more foolish, he thought.

Grateful for, yet wondering over, his unpredictable switch in disposition, Lorelei stumbled along as she tried to keep up. "You will not have to . . . worry . . . again."

Trying rather unsuccessfully to get his raging emotions under control, he replied, "Oh?"

"Y-yes. I am moving into the mercantile."

He stopped so abruptly that she thudded against his back. "Are you serious?"

"Quite," she huffed, confused anew by his behavior. She had thought he would think the news wonderful.

"Look, woman. Look around you. What do you see?"

She frowned and peered over his shoulder. Two men staggered down the middle of the street. Here and there, hard-looking men leaned against a post or rail. Down the way, a rowdy cowboy spurred his horse up on the walk in front of a saloon, shouting and waving a bottle in his free hand.

Lorelei gulped. "Well . . ."

"How can you even *think* of livin' down here by yourself? I *assume* you'll be alone. You want the same thing to happen to you that happened to John?"

Her eyes widened as she jerked her hand free. "What are you talking about? What does my uncle's death have to do with anything?" And to herself, she fumed, *And what makes him think I would not be living alone?* But she didn't have the nerve to ask him *that* face to face.

Holt shook his head. What, indeed. Hell, why was he

so all-fired concerned about the woman? *He* certainly couldn't be expected to take her to raise. He had a ranch to see after, and enough work to keep him busy for the next twenty years.

There wasn't time, or reason, to enlighten a full-grown, hard-headed woman as to the risks of living in the center of the wildest street in a boom town if she didn't already know of them. Any child could see it was foolhardy and dangerous.

"Never mind. Just do what you want." But his gut churned as he tried to keep from looking at her. There was something about the lemony freshness of her smell, the sweet-tart taste that still lingered on his lips, and the tingle in his belly from the press of her full breasts that threatened to drive him crazy.

He sighed with relief when they finally arrived at the hotel. Her dark eyes cut into his soul as her gaze searched for a sign as to what brought on his disgusting behavior. And disgusted was a perfect word to describe the way she made him feel every time he allowed her to tempt him, every time he gave in to his damned desires. Holt growled, "Good night," before he turned and stalked from her aggravating presence.

Bewildered, Lorelei stood on the steps and watched him leave. She touched her tender lips and felt an unwelcome moistness fill her eyes. Her chest constricted at the thought that he seemed truly concerned about her safety.

Holt Dolan had to be the most exasperating man she had ever met.

* * *

Clifton Abbott refolded the telegram and absently tapped the edge of the missive against the desk top. The sharp ticking sounds coincided with the swinging pendulum on the massive grandfather clock in the far corner.

He chuckled. How he would have loved to have seen Enders' face when his sassy daughter accosted his right-hand man on the streets of Durango.

Robert had been certain he had been found out, but Lorelei had only been on an errand of mercy, as it were, offering the emaciated man a job so that he could afford to buy a decent meal or two.

Clifton laughed, a deep, rumbling that shook his huge belly. That was his Lorelei– taking in helpless strays, rooting for the underdog. Robert Enders, helpless. Clifton wiped tears from his moist eyes.

Then he sobered. A frown wrinkled his thick brows. He hoped she wasn't getting along *too* well. That event was not in his plans—not at all. A knot of worry lodged in his heart. What would he do if she actually got that damned store going again? Surely she wouldn't decide to stay on in that godforsaken no-man's-land called Colorado, would she?

His aching fingers crumpled the telegram.

Lorelei cursed under her breath, then blushed profusely as she struggled with two heavy bags the next morning. They bumped up and down the steps. She tripped when they caught on uneven or splintered boards in the walk. At the same time, events of the previous afternoon and evening rioted through her mind. Apparently, she had even forgotten requesting Mr. Endsley report for work that morning, because she dropped the bags and looked up in surprise when the cadaverous form stepped out of the doorway leading into her mercantile.

"Oh! Oh, my. Is it ten o'clock already?"

"Yep." His gravelly voice held a note of irritation.

She sighed and unlocked the door. At least she wouldn't have to worry about making small talk just for the sake of conversation with Mr. Endsley around. When she reached back for the bags, he had them in hand. She sighed with relief. "Thank you. Thank you so much."

Reading the question in his eyes as he glanced from her to the cases, she explained, "I am moving from the hotel." The minute she saw his frown, she anticipated his thoughts and snapped in her defense, "Do not say a word. I am aware there might be a bit of danger involved, but it can not be any worse than the hotel. At least here there are locks on the doors and these walls are quite sturdy."

"You have a gun handy?"

She stiffened. "I most certainly do not. I hardly think there will be cause to use a weapon, for *any* reason."

He shrugged and cast her a we'll-see-about-that look as she stood imperiously in the middle of her empty store. Her chest heaved with disgruntlement. Men. They were *all* exasperating.

Feeling stifled and frustrated, she needed time to herself. "Mr. Endsley, I have several more bags at the hotel. Would you be so kind as to fetch them for me?"

The frown was still on his face as he shrugged and

left. She nibbled at the edge of her lower lip. It seemed all she encountered lately was disapproval. But she couldn't help the little niggle of pride and accomplishment that stiffened her aching back. She was making her own decisions now and would stand by them, whether they be right or wrong.

Smiling, she lugged the bags into the storeroom and began unpacking while humming along to a piano tune drifting over from the nearby saloon. She felt good. Everything would be fine.

"Damn it, Tony, I've been hangin' around here for five days now." Holt rubbed the back of his neck while he paced in front of the grimacing clerk.

"Have you telegraphed Denver, Mr. Dolan?"

"I did that the first day."

"Oh? Uh, what did you find out?"

"The bull was delivered to the stock yards and supposedly left on the first train west." Holt threw his hands in the air, and quickly stepped back when he almost deplumed an old lady's bonnet. "My pardon, ma'am."

The woman scowled and turned to her husband, a grizzled little man who took one look at Holt's brawny frame and smiled ingratiatingly. "Quite all right. Quite."

Holt choked back a grin when the lady impaled the old man with her ferocious glare. He had a feeling the couple's trip on the Denver and Rio Grande Railroad would be a tad frosty this morning.

At least his spirits had lifted. Seeing the hat reminded him of Lorelei's flowered bonnet and her deft handling of that wicked parasol.

He thoughtfully rubbed his chin. Maybe he could find something interesting to do with the rest of the day after all.

"So long, Tony. Guess I'll just have to check back again tomorrow."

Holt grumbled as he left. Damn it, surely there was a way to trace the bull. Maybe if he kept the young clerk upset, Tony would badger someone else down the line, and so on, until *someone* found out what in the hell was happening.

He jauntily picked his way down Main Avenue until he glanced up and saw a tall, thin man wearing an apron that wrapped about his narrow form twice, sweeping the porch in front of Abbott's Mercantile. Holt's eyes narrowed to dangerous slits.

There was something about the man's efficient movements that caused Holt to approach with caution. "Who are you?"

A pair of pale green eyes seemed to stake Holt in the street, reinforcing his suspicion that this was no ordinary flunky. The man's growled answer of "Who wants to know?" was clipped and precise.

Holt stepped up onto the walkway. Their eyes met at a level. "I'm a frie—an acquaintance of Miss Abbott." When the other man's eyes darkened and measurably softened, Holt had the strangest sensation that the fellow knew him, that maybe they had met before. Naw. He would have remembered this man.

He nodded toward the broom. "You work for Lor—Miss Abbott?"

"Yep."

"Since when?"

"Day 'fore yesterday."

There was a discernible twitch to the man's mouth that Holt found irritating. Then a faint rustle near the doorway drew both men's attention, and they turned to find Lorelei watching them.

"Mr. Dolan?" Her dark eyes flashed. Heat suffused her face when she recalled their last encounter, and she patted her cheeks. "It certainly is a warm day, is it not?"

Holt cleared his throat as he, too, recalled the feel of her soft lips and warm, slender body. A sudden gust of wind dried the sweat on his neck. "Seems cool to me."

She flushed an even deeper shade of red, if that were possible, and opened her mouth to give him a well-deserved piece of her mind. Then she noticed the suggestive question on Mr. Endsley's face and snapped her jaws closed so hard her teeth clicked.

Holt had the curious desire to reach out and see if the lock of hair falling down the back of her long, sensuous neck was as silky as it looked. His fists clenched. "Well, I suppose you went ahead with your plans?"

Her eyes darted to her skirt, where she fussed with a wrinkled pleat. "Y-yes. It is almost like home."

He rocked back on his heels. "You've been busy, then."

"Yes." Fidgeting from one foot to the other, she fervently wished she could forget the taste of his lips and how her body had responded to the hard length of his. Even now she experienced the strangest sensations in her breasts. Though she had always considered herself well able to handle any man who made advances toward her, she had, literally, never run up against anyone quite like Mr. Holt Dolan.

Dust rose into the air in a furious flurry as Endsley wielded the broom. Holt stifled a cough. Hell, he should leave. There were other ways to spend his time. He could sit alone in his room, or drown his troubles in warm, tasteless beer at the Mother Lode, or he could . . . stay right where he was, in the company of a beautiful—he licked his dry lips—voluptuous female, especially when she was quiet and subdued for a change.

He drew himself up and walked past an open-mouthed Lorelei into the darker interior of the mercantile. It took a moment for his eyes to adjust. "You know, you ought to put another window or two in this place." He knew she had followed him, for he caught the faintest whiff of lemon and . . . dust.

Lorelei bit the soft inside of her mouth in an effort to refrain from flailing him with a sharp retort. It wasn't as if she had not had the same thought a hundred times herself in the past few days, but it angered her to have him march in and declare what she *ought* to do.

Then he sauntered on through the store and into the back room, now her living quarters. Of all the gall. That was *her* private place. *Hers.*

The shy embarrassment she had felt upon seeing him again after what she now thought of as "the kiss," fled the instant she charged after him, shouting, "Just where do you think you are going? You have no right to . . ."

As soon as she trailed him inside the room and around the corner, far removed from curious eyes,

Holt turned. He grinned at her flushed features and sparkling eyes. Now this was the Lorelei Abbott he looked forward to confronting. His own eyes deepened to the color of a billowing storm cloud as she stopped only inches away, caught off balance by his abrupt halt.

"So, you're really goin' to do it?"

She was caught staring at his strong jaw and impudently jutting chin. She blinked. "Pardon me?"

His arm swept around the room, indicating the cot and a makeshift closet, even as his gaze devoured her peaches-and-cream complexion and soft, pouting lips.

"You're really goin' to stay here, aren't you?"

The sudden coldness in his eyes set her belly aquiver. All she could do was nod.

Chapter Five

Lorelei suddenly found herself face to face with Holt. Only a scant inch separated them. Her breath came in short huffs from running after him. His arms lifted and encircled her in a firm, but gentle, embrace.

Instinct demanded she push him away, but her arms were trapped between their bodies. The impulse soon faded when she discovered just how good it felt to be cradled against him. With one deep breath, she was assaulted further by the alluring smell of leather and soap and a distinct, pleasing aroma that was his own special masculine scent.

Finally she sighed and relaxed, and Holt pulled her even closer. But rather than kiss or fondle her, he just held her. He found himself entrapped by her soft womanliness. It had been a long while since he had held a woman thus; an even longer time since he had *wanted* to be so close to someone who didn't belong to the persuasion of the girls who worked the rooms above the saloons.

His chest constricted. The ache in his gut forecasted that he should tuck his tail and run while he still had the chance, but he could not bring himself to release her. A helpless sensation invaded his arms and legs, like he was powerless to keep from touching, holding, protecting her.

He mentally shook himself. God, what had come over him? Without removing his arms or allowing distance between them, he looked into her upturned face. He hardly recognized his own voice when he rasped, "Where is your family? How could they let you come all of the way to Durango by yourself?"

Lorelei blinked. Her black eyes took on a decided gleam. In a way, it was nice that he sounded concerned, but for a moment she had thought . . . She tilted her head and gazed into his incredible eyes. What had she thought? Licking her lips, she pressed back against the bounds of his arms, unwilling to speculate on such absurd notions.

Besides, it began to rankle that he questioned her actions as if she were nothing more than a child. Her voice was huskier than usual when she replied, "I will have you know that I am perfectly capable of taking care of myself." She had the grace to blush when his cocked eyebrows reminded her of the run-in with the two drunkards.

"And my father has complete confidence that I will make the correct decisions as to handling my life." Her eyes lowered, unable to hold contact with his, afraid he would read the lie in them. Her father had confidence all right—confidence that she would fail—again. He most likely expected her to return to Boston at any time.

"What of your husband?" Holt's arms tightened slightly. "Does he trust you, too?"

"I-I have no husband."

"So I figured. You're too high-tempered and bossy to suit most men's tastes."

His smug grin infuriated her. "How dare you! High-tempered? Bossy?" She struggled, but was unable to pull away. She was chagrined to realize that her efforts were only half-hearted, at best, and she wasn't *really* angry. Evidently she affected him in much the same way he bothered her.

His eyes were scintillating beneath their heavy lids, and she went weak all over. What was it about the cowboy that caused her to behave so irrationally?

"Oh, I dare plenty." His arms were like steel bands encompassing her. Their bodies lightly touched. Lorelei's eyes widened as tremors jolted through her slender form.

Holt swallowed down curses as undeniable proof of his desire for the woman burgeoned beneath the flap of his trousers. He watched her eyes turn to black liquid. As her resistance eroded, his hands splayed across her back, roving sensuously up her spine and over her delicate shoulders. He couldn't resist the temptation a moment longer and gently threaded his fingers into the soft hair pinned at the nape of her neck.

It was even finer than he had imagined, softer than silk. He was tempted to free the long tresses and sift his hands through their length at his leisure. He hardly recognized the huskiness of his own voice when he startled himself by asking, "Why do you wear it pulled back so tight?" The heels of his palms cupped the underside of her jaw. "I bet it's long and thick and falls in waves down your back."

Lorelei shivered. His deep, seductive voice was mesmerizing. She swayed into his broad, strong length. Her nerve endings came alive. He felt every bit as hard, yet comforting, as she remembered. Her own body turned hot and cold at the same time as another shiver quaked from the top of her scalp to the tip of her toes. An unfamiliar pressure began to build, deep inside, like lava surging and subsiding, then surging again, within the walls of a steaming volcano.

Holt's head lowered until his warm breath teased her trembling lips. Her arms stole about his waist, and her hands pressed against the flat of his back. She reveled in the feel of hard tendons and sinew beneath the soft flannel of his shirt. When his lips grazed her mouth, she stood on tiptoe so that he could reach her more easily.

The front door slammed. Heavy boots clomped through the store. "Miss Abbott?"

Her forehead dipped against Holt's chest as she gasped for breath. She could feel the rapid pounding of his heart. Relief warred with a sense of utter disappointment as she backed slowly away.

Holt let his head fall back until he grimaced at the cracked ceiling. "Damn!" His hands dropped to his sides, fingers curling into frustrated fists.

Lorelei willed her shaking legs to support her as far as the doorway. "Mr. Endsley? Did you need me?"

The hired man stood in the middle of the large room, surveying the tables and shelves. "Wagon outside with a load of goods. Sent it around back so we could take inventory first." As if realizing he might have overstepped his bounds, he lowered his eyes. "If that's what you want."

"Yes. Thank you, Mr. Endsley." She watched as he turned and went back to his sweeping. Inventory? Now, what would Mr. Endsley know of that?

Pounding from the back of the store drew her attention away from the scrawny man, and she scurried, still somewhat breathless, to open the door. A short, balding man in a heavy blanket-type coat stood beside a heavily laden buckboard. Another younger man sat on the wagon.

"Howdy, ma'am. Smithers, down at the freight office, said ya wanted this stuff right away."

She nodded, grateful that she had taken the time one afternoon to make arrangements for the supplies to be delivered as they arrived.

While the men unloaded the crates and stacked them inside the door, Lorelei paced back and forth. She had noticed Holt's absence when she came back through the storeroom and couldn't help but fret over why, and how, he had disappeared so quickly. Had he been as shaken by their encounter as she?

Later, after she had the boxes prepared to open the next day, and after she had dismissed Mr. Endsley and asked him to come back early tomorrow, she slowly wandered into the area of the storeroom that was her own private hideaway. There were so many things to think about, not the least of which was Holt Dolan's ability to turn her whole world upside down. Her mind had been in a riot of confusion all afternoon.

Suddenly she stopped, dead still, one hand on her breast, as she listened intently. She could have sworn . . . Her head cocked to one side. There it was again, kind of a deep-pitched growl. Her stomach knotted, and her mouth felt suddenly as dry and scratchy as sandpaper. She had been positive the store was empty when she locked the door.

Fear overrode her unrest. She grasped for the trusty parasol propped at the foot of her cot. Holding the unwieldy weapon in one hand and her bulky skirt in the other, to mute the swishing of her petticoats, she walked stealthily toward the noise. It seemed to come from behind the draped sheet that formed her closet.

She took a deep breath, gathered her courage and charged through the small opening. Eyes rounded with surprise, she came to a tottering halt an instant before the parasol swung downward. Her lips twitched with relief. Pent-up breath hissed from her lungs. It was Holt, asleep and tilted back against the wall, supported only by a chair's two spindly legs.

She held a hand over her throbbing heart. She had been terrified, and it was all his fault. If he hadn't warned her over and over about the dangers of living in here alone . . . a wicked glimmer suffused her eyes as she stared down upon the unsuspecting man.

His black hat slanted forward, concealing most of his face. A decided shame, she thought, as she took a step forward. And his long legs dangled just inches off the floor, the black, handmade boots appearing scuffed and worn below the dark denim cuffs of his pants. Probably scratched from kicking dogs and children with his nasty attitude, she mused.

Her heart fluttered and her skin prickled with chill bumps. Oh, but she had seen first hand another side to the cowboy recently. There was a gentle, compassionate nature hidden beneath that crusty exterior.

Another gurgled snort startled her. The arms, crossed over his chest, jerked. All was quiet again. She wondered if anyone had ever told him he snored? An ache built in the pit of her stomach. He had found out that *she* wasn't married, but what of *him?* Was some beautiful woman—naturally she would *have* to be beautiful since he was so handsome—waiting at home? And where *was* home?

She shivered. Just what did she know of this man? Here he was, in her room. It was nearly dark. He had scared ten years off her life. And yet, she found herself drawn to him in a way that was even more terrifying than any physical threat could ever be.

She sighed. No, she did not feel that he was a menace of any kind. After all, he had saved the life of that young girl. But there was too much at stake to waste time swooning over something that could never be. The important focus to her life right now had to be proving to her father, and to *herself,* that she could run this mercantile, and do it successfully.

Yet she couldn't help the little skip in her heart when she looked at his lean, virile frame. He snorted again. A mischievous grin curved her lips. She poked the tip of the parasol beneath one of the suspended chair legs. All it would take would be one little jerk.

Before the plot could be put into motion, the chair banged to the floor. Lorelei jumped, but the parasol received a yank that catapulted her right into the grinning scoundrel's lap. She stammered and fluttered her hands, then found her lips quieted by a long, deep kiss. Her fingers settled on a huge expanse of flannel- and leather-covered chest. Her flesh and bones disintegrated into the consistency of warm butter.

"I've been waitin' to do that for hours. Thought you never would finish all your little chores."

Her languid eyes took on a new sparkle. *"Little chores?* I will have you know—"

"Please, have pity. I can't take another fit of temper right now." He shifted uncomfortably beneath her, then pushed back his hat. A lock of coal-black hair fell onto his forehead, swinging just above his arched, black brows.

Lorelei's gaze fastened on the appealing sight. She almost giggled aloud. Women in Boston would kill for such beautiful brows, and here they were, wasted on a *man,* for heaven's sake. But, oh, what a man.

While she speculated over his outstanding good looks, Holt castigated himself for allowing such a prickly situation to develop. Under normal circumstances, he would take every advantage of holding a beautiful woman captive in his arms. But Lorelei Abbott was far from normal, as were the circumstances.

He had been aware of her the moment she attacked his resting place, had watched the conflicting emotions of fear, puzzlement, and something he couldn't place a name to, play across her mobile features. An undeniable sense of attraction seemed to draw them together.

And that made him wary. Why had he been fool enough to stay after Endsley interrupted them earlier? Was he so weak that he had no control whatsoever over his mind, or body? The predominant answer seemed to be *yes,* and he smothered an agonized groan.

All it took was one touch from her delicate hands to set his body afire with a yearning that should never be, replacing his dreadful memories with a longing for something special, not forbidding. God, help him!

Suddenly, he pressed his nose to hers and asked, "Would you like me to stay and 'protect' you tonight?"

Her heart thrummed so rapidly that she was afraid he would hear and recognize just how appealing the idea was. "Ah, I do not believe that will be necessary."

He leered at her. "Maybe not necessary, but it could be fun." A wolfish grin curled his lips, and he patted the thick layers of skirt and petticoats covering her behind.

She huffed indignantly. With awkward, self-conscious movements, she struggled to remove herself from the too-familiar position on his lap. A red stain colored her cheeks. She should have moved much, much sooner.

Whatever had happened to her good sense and moral upbringing? Although she did not remember her mother, she had a suspicion that that particular parent was moaning in her grave. And her father? Heaven only knew what *he* would do if he caught her in such a compromising situation. Probably shoot first and ask questions later.

Holt hadn't missed the sudden apprehension in her black eyes, or the curious pout to her lips. She was the loveliest thing he had ever seen, even in her disheveled state. And those eyes. A man could lose his soul in their dark depths.

He quickly jumped to his feet, remembering he'd begun this misadventure, because he needed her off of his lap before he completely embarrassed himself, in more ways than one. He had to get away—and stay away—from this woman. He shook his head, reinforcing his hard-won conviction. He couldn't survive the pain. Not again.

Being relatively untutored in the wiles of men, for all of her worldly ways, Lorelei nevertheless accurately assessed the consternation in Holt's incredible eyes. Somehow, it appeared, their positions had been reversed. Wasn't *she* the one who should gather her composure about her, like a huge protective cape, and run?

Holt backed toward the door. He was almost intimidated by her suddenly secure and infallible attitude while he teetered on the edge of a deep chasm.

"Take care of yourself. If you have any trouble . . ." The sentence trailed into silence. What could he suggest? As soon as that damned bull arrived, he'd be gone, and she would be on her own, anyway.

Lorelei was of mixed emotions. She prayed he would leave quickly and give her a chance to put her thoughts into perspective once again, yet she did not want him to go at all. Her body and mind seemed to draw her in different directions.

"Yes? You were saying?" Her face flushed a deep red. She was only prolonging her agony.

He cleared his throat. "Nothin'. Just hope you don't have problems. But I'm sure you'll be fine, as you've assured me so many times."

She cocked her head and eyed him quizzically. "Thank you. I am glad you finally realize that."

He didn't like the knots that tied his gut. No, he

realized no such thing. Deep down, he feared for her. Durango was too dangerous for a young, beautiful woman on her own. But what could he do about it? He had tried his best to get her to see reason. She refused.

"Good-bye, Mr. Dolan."

He hesitated. A frown drew his brows together. She had said *good-bye*—not good night. Had she read his mind? "Good night, Lorelei, and good luck."

Silently, he added, *I have a feelin' you're goin' to need it.*

During the next few days, Lorelei welcomed the arrival of more crates and goods, and especially the long, exhausting hours spent stocking shelves and cupboards. It was the time she spent alone, without the shadowy presence of Mr. Endsley and his running monologues of "Yep" and "Nope" and "Guess so," that found her suffering long moments of deep melancholy.

She had told herself that she could forget any feelings she might unaccountably harbor toward Holt Dolan in the time it took to snap her fingers. Well, she had snapped them forty times a day for half a week, and the ploy had not worked.

No man had ever affected her like this before. Not even Frank, when she had tried so hard. . . . A shudder racked her body. At least Holt distracted her from worrisome thoughts of the past. Every night she was besieged with dreams of the cowboy and awoke the following morning tired and frustrated. It was annoying. She wasn't used to feeling irritable, or snapping at people who innocently inquired about the store.

So, she was very happy when Chad provided a pleasant diversion one morning just after she unlocked the door.

"Good mornin', pretty lady." The rowels on his spurs spun noisily as he walked inside and looked about the store with wide, admiring eyes. "Hey, the outfit looks just dandy."

Lorelei's chest expanded with pride. "I think the room seems smaller with just the merchandise that has already arrived."

She watched with delight as his gaze flicked over the glass case containing perfumes, jewelry and mirrors. On the nearby shelves were lace, fans, hair pins, parasols and an assortment of muffs lined in silk or velvet.

Her own eyes shone as they passed over a table loaded with linens, silk, wool, calico, gingham, muslin, serge and denim. In one corner were rakes, shovels and plows. Another contained bags of flour, sugar, rice and beans.

"And there is so much more to come. Only a fourth of what I have ordered has arrived. I can hardly wait to see what the store will look like when it is filled from top to bottom."

He smiled. "It'll be a sight, sure 'nuff."

Before he had a chance to ask, she said, "And a box of your tobacco arrived yesterday."

"No kiddin'. I'll take the whole box."

"The *whole* box?"

"Sure."

She shrugged her shoulders and went behind the counter. It seemed strange that he should want so much at once. Why, she had yet to see him use any. But then she remembered, he was *out* of tobacco.

A soft sigh escaped her lips. She had forgotten, too, how pleasant and unthreatening his company could be. There was none of the tension or fluttering stomach she associated with Holt's presence.

After collecting Chad's money, she invited him to sit down and share a cup of tea.

He held up his hands. "Thanks, anyway, but I really gotta go." Then his blue eyes twinkled as he winked. "Don't think I make a habit of turnin' down pretty ladies. I'll be back real soon if ya throw in a homemade cookie or two."

She beamed when she remembered that a real, honest-to-goodness cook stove, to replace the potbellied one in her room, should arrive any day. Why, she might invite him to share an entire meal. Coyly she replied, "I will see what I can do about that someday."

He grinned engagingly and turned to leave. "Will ya be gettin' any winter coats? It's colder'n a skinned jackrabbit outside of a mornin'."

She walked him to the door and looked toward the distant mountain range. It was cloaked in a myriad of colors ranging from dark to light green, brilliant gold to rusty orange. The sight nearly stole her breath away every time she gazed outside. And sometimes, when the wind blew just right, she could smell the pines.

The fact that she was beginning to feel a real sense of belonging was apparent when she answered Chad with the conviction of a woman who knew her business and would be around to manage it forever. "I expect more supplies by the end of the week. Check back then."

Chad nodded. "Reckon I will. 'Cordin' ta the old-timers, this'n could be a hard winter."

She gulped. Winters were severe in Boston, but back there she had a huge, cozy fireplace and servants to chop wood and bring her hot cocoa. And a man to hitch the team and drive her about town, cozily wrapped in a warmed blanket. As much as she enjoyed her life today, it was intimidating to think that she was really alone.

She followed Chad onto the walkway and suddenly tripped over a broken board. He took hold of her elbow. "Careful. Ya all right?" When she assured him she was, he continued, "Thanks for orderin' my tobacco. Would ya mind goin' ahead and sendin' for more? I'll take whatever ya get."

Her shock was evident. "More?"

"Like ta keep plenty on hand." His eyelids drooped, hooding his blue eyes from her searching gaze.

"Well . . ." Something caused her to glance toward the street. Her tongue became as clumsy as her feet. Holt had materialized, as if from nowhere, and was glaring at her. She frowned. When he finally stalked forward, her heart skipped a beat, then hammered double-time.

She had thought never to see him again, at least not after the way he had left the other evening. It had seemed as if they both had made an unspoken, yet mutual, agreement that their lives would continue much more smoothly without the complication of their involvement with each other. Involvement? It was hardly likely.

But her eyes sparkled. The flesh on her cheeks and neck felt as if it were suffused by a thousand tiny pin pricks. He was here. Holt had come back. Why?

Chad's eyes narrowed when Holt joined them. Holt's scowl deepened. Chad condescended to speak first. "Howdy, Dolan."

Holt tipped his hat in Lorelei's direction, then growled, "Chad."

Lorelei's excitement over seeing Holt deflated quickly. She looked from one man to the other, feeling like a fat mouse caught between two starving beasts.

What was going on here? The two men apparently knew each other, but their antipathy was as palpable as a heartbeat. Only one glance at Holt's black hair and flashing gray eyes put her in mind of a beast, all right: a big, dark lobo wolf. She could even imagine the hair on the back of his neck bristling.

Suddenly, a warm tingle slid down her spine. An improbable, but conceivable, thought occurred to her. Were the men jealous, over her? Surely not. Then again . . .

When Chad had come to the mercantile this morning, she had assumed the reason for his visit was to pick up his tobacco. But he never *asked.* She had *told* him it was there. Perhaps he had only wanted to see *her.*

Her lower lip trembled. And though there were times when Holt acted distant and forbidding . . . well, he seemed to like her good enough when he kissed her. Unconsciously, she gnawed on the tender flesh inside of her cheek.

Holt then captured her undivided attention when he said, "Haven't seen you around lately, Chad. What have you been up to?"

The younger man's hand dropped from Lorelei's elbow and came to rest on his belt, just inches above his pistol butt. His face was so stiff it looked to Lorelei that it might crack into tiny bits when his lips moved. "None of your business what I do, Dolan." His eyes narrowed. He wouldn't look directly at Holt. It seemed he had completely forgotten anyone else's presence when he glanced across the street and followed the progress of two lovely ladies as they moved from window to window, shopping.

Then he looked contritely back to Lorelei and answered, "Just been hangin' 'round. How 'bout you?" And this time his eyes bored into Holt like a .45 slug.

Holt shrugged and shifted his weight to the balls of his feet. He, too, gazed meaningfully at Lorelei. "Waitin' on a train, is all."

Chad fidgeted, clamping his fingers around the packaged tobacco as a heavy-set Mexican rode past on a lathered paint and slanted him an almost imperceptible nod. Finally, he excused himself. "Well, hate ta leave so *soon.*" He placed significant stress on the last word, then leaned over to give Lorelei an unexpected peck on the cheek. Over her shoulder he glared at Holt. "Got business to tend to. Don't forget that order, pretty lady."

Beneath the cold, blue shards of Chad's eyes, she noticed a glimmer of some indefinable emotion when they rested upon her. Whatever had been bothering him must have passed. She smiled sweetly. "I most certainly will not . . . Chad."

She pronounced his name with a warmth she had never felt before. This was all so exhilarating. For the first time in her life, there were two men acting—well, she did not know exactly *how* to describe their behavior. *Strange* was the best she could come up with at the moment, but she still reveled in the feeling.

"What did *he* want?"

Lorelei jumped at the snapped inquiry. Holt looked absolutely livid. She nearly clapped her hands with glee. What fun! "Why, I hardly think it is any of your business, Mr. Dolan." In that respect, she totally agreed with Chad.

"Tell me!" His fingers curled around her upper arm like giant claws. She tried to squirm away. He seemed unaccountably ferocious, and it was easy to imagine him gnashing his teeth and snarling as she became his next victim.

"H-he only bought tobacco. Why?"

His grip loosened, and she took a deep, steadying breath. She had actually experienced a tremor of fear. Perhaps she had been mistaken. Surely mere jealousy could not cause such a vicious reaction, not even from the intractable Holt Dolan. Again, she wondered just what there was between him and Chad.

Holt released the breath that he felt like he had held ever since encountering Lorelei with Chad. Damn it to hell! He had *vowed* to stay away from the vixen—couldn't—and now look what had happened. He had made an ass of himself; that was what.

But how could he have predicted the jolt to his gut when he saw the younger man touching her; and Lorelei, smiling like some calf-eyed . . . He shook his head. What did it matter? She was free to be with anyone she wanted. And she was perfectly correct. It *was* none of his business. Was it?

He was unable to help it, though, when he growled, "Stay away from him. Do you hear me, woman? For your own good, stay the hell away." He spun on his heel and literally stormed down the street, spewing clods of dirt in his wake.

Lorelei stared at his broad, muscled back, her face a muddle of bewildered confusion. Rather than try to sort through everything that had transpired during the past two minutes, and cause her poor head to throb even harder, she sighed and walked back into the store.

Once behind the closed door, though, she allowed herself one small tantrum. Her eyes blazed. She clenched her fists. Who did that cowboy think he was, telling her what to do, or who she could see? What right did he have? What right?

Chapter Six

Holt pulled his sorrel stallion to a stop on a ridge overlooking his ranch headquarters. Indecision tore at him as he stared down at the one-story log home surrounded on three sides by a wide veranda. How he loved to sit back in the handmade rocker on the porch, with his feet propped on the railing, leisurely surveying the huge double barn, pole corrals, and nearby traps knee-high in grass.

But now he was leaving again. He wanted to stay. Yet an overwhelming urge demanded he return to town.

The Morgan horse had needed exercise, and Holt had come home with the intention of staying several days. The ranch was his haven, where he usually enjoyed a nice, quiet, peaceful existence. But not today.

Striking a match down the seam of his denims, he cupped his hands protectively about the tip of the long, thin cheroot. With one deep drag, the tip of the cigar glowed red, and the tension in his neck and shoulders eased a bit. If only the turmoil in his mind could be assuaged as easily.

Damn it! Damn her! Without a doubt, it was Lorelei Abbott causing his unrest. He sighed and shifted in the saddle as the horse stamped its feet.

At least he was leaving with the knowledge that everything was in order. The corral was ready for the bull. He closed his eyes and inhaled deeply of the cheroot. Tony had given him that one piece of good news just before he'd ridden out of Durango that morning. His prize-winning Hereford, Sir Dominick the III, had been located in a holding pen somewhere along the tracks, apparently none the worse for wear, and would be shipped on the next available car.

Thank God for small favors. Once the animal arrived, there would be absolutely no excuse to remain in town—not even for the headstrong, opinionated, delectable Miss Abbott.

With a determined nod, he nudged his horse down the rocky slope toward Durango. Peace settled over him like a protective poncho. Another day, or two at most, and he would be home. A calm smile meandered across his lips.

Half an hour later, he was certain his blissful moments had literally been the calm before the storm. Taking the round-about way back to town, he had just ridden into a thick stand of piñon pine when his horse threw up its head and snorted. Holt's legs reflexively clamped against the saddle just in case the stallion decided he wasn't through kicking up his heels. The animal had been full of vinegar after spending several days in a small enclosed stall and had tested Holt's skill during the ride to the ranch.

Suddenly, a pair of buzzards squawked and flapped

their wings off to the right of the road. Holt watched as they half hopped, half flew down the lane, evidently too full to fly, he surmised. Searching warily through the sharp-needled branches, the hair on the back of his neck began to prickle. His legs felt like lead weights as he hesitantly dismounted, tied the horse, and began to thread his way through the undergrowth into a narrow clearing.

The stiff fall breeze caused a limb to creak overhead. Holt's nerves were so taut that he jumped at the unexpected sound. Flies buzzed nearby—lots of flies. The crescendo of noise increased when he walked past a large boulder.

He stopped abruptly. At first all he saw was a scuffed boot. Cautiously, he moved farther around the rock. He suddenly felt as if a contrary mule had kicked him in the chest with both hind feet.

A man lay sprawled on his back, arms and legs flung akimbo, sightless eyes staring into the bright sun. Holt's gut churned. It almost appeared the man had three eyes. A round, blue-black hole was drilled smack in the middle of the unfortunate fellow's forehead.

Holt shuddered. God, he had come to Colorado Territory to get away from gunfights and death. His rigid form sagged. Violence followed wherever he went. It was a fact of life. So, why couldn't he accept it as such?

Off to the side, another inert form caught his eye. He walked over and discovered the broken, mangled body of a dog. The red coat had been sleek once, almost sienna in color, with unusual black markings on all four paws and a patch of white in the center of its chest. From the looks of the swollen underbelly, she had been nursing a litter.

He shook his head and returned to the dead man. A shame, that's what it was. The whole scene was a damned shame.

As he glanced once more at the body, he began to notice details he had missed before. The man's gun was still in its holster. The expression on the frozen face was one of surprise. Either someone had come up on the fellow quickly, or he had been murdered by someone he knew—possibly even a friend. Friend? Sure.

While building a travois to take the body back to town, Holt couldn't help wondering what connection the dog had with the shooting. He kept his head cocked, listening for any sound of pups. Nothing. And he had seen no tracks.

What in the hell had happened here?

Several days later, Lorelei was on her knees near the front window unpacking a crate of straw and silk hats. As she set aside adornments of feather plumes, ribbon and lace, she noticed a buggy pull up to the hitch rail.

The sight of Chad climbing from the shaded interior caused her eyes to round with wonder. It was a Chad she had never seen before, wearing a new Stetson hat atop his neatly trimmed hair. A fawn-colored jacket covered his usual cotton shirt and suspenders, and he was minus the ever-jangling spurs. He looked quite dapper, indeed.

A bright smile lit her face when he headed toward her. Although Holt's warning rang a weak bell in the back of her mind, she had only seen Mr. Dolan once since the day he had made that so-called threat, and then he had just popped in and out, enraging her further because he seemed to be checking up on her.

What an infuriating man he was. She was quite capable of drawing her own conclusions about people, and as far as *she* was concerned, Chad was every bit as nice, maybe even more so, than the bossy Holt Dolan. She dusted off her palms, dislodging bits of broken straw, as if emphasizing the credibility of her decision.

"Mornin', pretty lady."

Lorelei's cheeks turned bright pink. She knew better than to take Chad's compliments *too* seriously, but it made her feel good every time he called her "pretty." Somehow, the dirt beneath her nails and her soiled skirt didn't seem quite as disturbing, or distracting.

"How are you, Chad?" She started to mention that no more tobacco had come in, but bit back the information. Maybe, as she had once suspected, he wasn't there on business.

"Just dandy." He glanced nervously to the half-empty crate, around the store, and finally at the waiting buggy. "Shore is a pretty day out yonder."

She had already taken note of the beautiful fall morning. The air was warm and the sky such a brilliant shade of blue that she squinted whenever she looked out-of-doors. "It is a perfect day."

"Too nice to hole up inside, don'tcha think?" He had his hat in his hands, twisting the brim around and around through his fingers.

Lorelei sat back on her heels, her head cocked questioningly to one side.

He met her eyes and grinned. "Ain't used ta askin' ladies ta step out for rides."

A sudden warmth pervaded Lorelei. "Why, Chad,

are you asking *me?"*

"Yes'm, shore am. Ya prob'ly ain't seen much of Durango, or the country. Reckon I couldn't blame ya much if ya turned me down. This's all kinda sudden, even for me."

She was quite taken aback. On the one hand, there was *so* much to do in the store. But, then again . . . She looked longingly out of the window. Oh, how she would love to be outside, to see first hand the rest of the town and some of the gorgeous mountains and meadows she had only glimpsed from a distance.

"I even packed us a lunch."

"What?" He had spoken so softly, she wasn't sure she had heard him correctly. She pretended to hide a cough when she noticed the red tint that crept over his cheeks.

But he repeated, "Got us a basket of food. If ya decide ta go, we could stop along the road somewheres an' have us a . . . a . . . picnic."

Lorelei wondered what he suddenly found so fascinating about the warped flooring, but when she said, "I would love to accompany you," his eyes shot up, as if to make certain she was serious and not making fun of his request. "Really. I would like to go with you."

While Chad stood in apparent disbelief, she retrieved her cloak, just in case the weather should take a turn, and called into the back room. "Mr. Endsley, I will be out for a few hours." She glanced over her shoulder for a confirmation on the time they might be gone. Chad nodded.

Before she could turn around, Endsley walked out carrying a load of canned goods. "What's that you said, miss?"

"I am leaving with Mr.—er, Chad, and will be back

in a few hours. Do you mind watching over things here?"

"Nope."

She sighed. "Oh, good. I shall—"

"Nope. I can't."

"Oh. Oh! Why not?"

"You said we'd work this morning. Didn't mention the afternoon, too."

She blinked. "Well, I just thought . . ." She drew in a deep breath and gave a curt nod. "Very well, perhaps you are right." Her disappointment was evident, but soon her lips curved into a smug grin. She really wanted to go on this outing. With determination edging her voice, she announced, "We will just lock the doors and call it a day."

Robert scowled. "Maybe you oughtn't—"

"Just leave what you are doing, Mr. Endsley. And plan on spending all day tomorrow. That is, unless you have better things to do."

She felt slightly annoyed with herself for aggravating poor Mr. Endsley. It wasn't *his* fault that she had decided to play hooky from work.

However, there was no chance for her to make an apology before he slammed the box on the counter, nodded, and shouldered past Chad and out of the door.

"Whew! Shore riles quick, don't he?"

"He never has before." She glanced toward Chad, then steadied her gaze when she thought she saw his eyes blaze and then narrow as he watched her hired man. But when he looked at her, all she saw was warmth. Mentally, she shrugged, wondering where her mind was going.

Lorelei smiled and asked, "Are we ready?"

He held out his arm. "You betcha."

She placed her hand on his sleeve and was dismayed when her first thought centered on how much more slender he was than Holt.

The horses trotted briskly out of town. Lorelei's face was flushed with pleasure as tendrils of hair tickled her cheeks.

Chad handled the lively team with finesse, and offered to teach her to drive. "Please, no. I would much rather watch the lovely scenery. I never realized how big and wild and . . . solitary . . . it is out here."

"It's that, ain't it?"

They rode in companionable silence for some time, until he turned the horses off the main road and onto a less traveled set of tracks that led to the top of a gradual rise.

Lorelei sat up straighter and grasped his arm when they reached the top. Spread out before them was a wide, rolling meadow. A narrow creek meandered in front of a grove of golden aspens. Their round leaves shimmered and quaked in the gentle breeze.

To the west was a thick line of oak trees, also bedecked in fall finery of varying degrees of rust and yellow. It was beneath the shade of these trees that Chad drew up the buggy. The creek gurgled over smooth gray rocks and created a happy atmosphere.

Lorelei clapped her hands together and gazed about with delight. "Thank you, Chad, for bringing me here. This is wonderful."

Though it was fall, there was still a variety of color from thick shrubs with white flowers and feathery plumes, to wild rose bushes with their round, red hips visible in the bright sunshine. It was a time of change—of leaves, of colors, of people—as even now Lorelei felt she was different from the person she had been a month, or a week, ago.

The contrast of rugged mountains rising into the heavens and vast meadows stretching as far as the eye could see was breathtaking. As Lorelei helped with the blanket and basket of food, she could hardly keep from stopping what she was doing every once in a while to just stare at the beauty of it all.

Chad chuckled. "Here I got all gussied up, thinkin' ya wouldn't be able to keep yore eyes off *me.*"

She blushed and covered her embarrassment by gingerly lowering herself onto one corner of the blanket. The grass crinkled beneath her knees, and she giggled. She hadn't giggled in years.

Glancing from beneath her thick, fringed lashes, she noticed that Chad was suddenly still, his slim body taut, his head slowly turning so that he could study their surroundings. His right hand rested competently on the butt of his pistol.

She drew in her breath. "What is it? Is something wrong?" Visions of huge bears, or slinking mountain lions, filled her head. Until now, she had concentrated on only the beauty of the outing, completely disregarding the fact that this was still an untamed land.

Then an image of a black lobo wolf flashed across her mind. She shook her head. Fear shivered down her spine. "Chad?"

Finally, he relaxed and leaned back against a tree. "Wasn't nothin'. Just thought, maybe, someone was watchin'." He shrugged and opened the basket.

"What'd ya like first? Got fried chicken, cheese, rolls." He sniffed appreciatively. "Bread's still warm."

A large, thin-bladed knife suddenly appeared in his hand. He cut off a huge chunk of the white, crusty delicacy.

Lorelei's mouth watered as the aroma of yeast and flour wafted to her nose. She took one tasty nibble, then another. Her eyes rolled heavenward. "Delicious. Where did you get all of this food?"

He licked his fingers and cocked his eyebrows in a manner that seemed altogether too familiar, and it wasn't Chad whom she remembered making the gesture. She took a big bite of the bread. Oh, well, the thought wasn't worth cluttering her mind with on such a lovely afternoon.

Chad continued to lick his fingers. "Know a couple cooks 'roun' town."

From the gleam that lit his eyes, Lorelei got the impression that the "cooks" he "knew" were probably young and pretty and very amenable to his rakish charms. She grinned. Just as *she* was quickly becoming fond of the boy . . . man. Now, what had caused her to think of him in terms of "young" and "boy"?

She chewed on her lower lip until he passed her a piece of crunchy chicken.

"Say, looky here. A jug of wine," he exclaimed.

Lorelei laughed when he twirled the tip of his short moustache. He was fun. She enjoyed his playful teasing. And he had yet to even try to hold her hand.

Her eyes scanned the fluffy clouds floating above them. She would be willing to wager last year's bustle, which was now out of style, thank heavens, that if she had come out into the country, all alone, with Holt

Dolan, he would have already . . .

Chad handed her a glass of the dark red liquid. She nearly dropped the wine when their fingers brushed. *Stay away from him, woman. Stay away.* The warning rang through her ears.

But Chad only smiled and touched the rim of her glass with his. She nodded. There was nothing to be afraid of. Not with Chad. Her teeth ground together. How dare Holt Dolan intrude on her pleasant interlude! How dare she *allow* him to do so! And with that thought, she shoved him entirely from her mind.

"Chad, where are you from? I mean, before you came to Durango." She held her breath. There was that look again. No. No, it was gone. Holt's warning was causing her imagination to run wild. That was all.

He took a long sip from the wine, then stretched full length on the blanket with his face to the sun and sighed. "I've been so many places, it's hard to remember 'em all."

Well, that certainly didn't tell her much. "Where is your family?"

"Not many left."

This time she was positive. A dark look suffused his eyes, *and* his face.

"Only one I see's a *brother.*" The word was spit from his mouth as if it were something extremely distasteful.

Lorelei felt a sudden kinship with Chad. All she had was her father. "Do you see him often, your brother?"

He grimaced. "Sometimes."

Concern etched her face. "It does not sound as though you like your brother." And it seemed to her that he had to really concentrate to keep his twitching fingers from clenching into fists.

His eyes wouldn't meet hers. "Now, I wouldn't say that."

She picked at a chunk of cheese. "I only have my father, and I miss him terribly." She was surprised to feel the moistness in her eyes. Yes, though she'd had to fight for her independence, she knew that in Clifton's own way, he had her welfare at heart, and she loved him for it. She would write and tell him so, soon.

Suddenly, Chad rolled off the blanket and got to his feet. "Reckon we oughta head back."

She hid her surprise, and disappointment, beneath a flurry of activity as she replaced the remnants of their meal inside the basket. "Y-yes. I guess it is late."

His back was to her as he rustled through the back of the buggy. When he turned around, to face her, he grinned and held out another basket.

Her eyes widened, and she took a step backward. "Oh, I dare not eat another bite. Really."

"Take it. It's a present."

"For me? Are you sure?"

Now she really did become flustered. No one besides her father had given her gifts in years.

"Look inside."

Finally she held out her hands. He seemed so pleased with himself, and so excited, that the feelings soon became mutual.

The basket was heavy, and she almost dropped it. "Oh, dear." There were faint scratching sounds coming from inside. Her eyes flickered up to Chad as she knelt on the ground, but she couldn't resist throwing open the lid.

"Whadaya think? Like 'em?"

Two small, warm bodies, connected to two very wet

tongues, tumbled from the basket into her lap. Lorelei laughed and hugged them to her breast. "They are precious. Wherever did you find them?"

Chad leaned down to scratch the puppies behind their floppy ears. "Just found 'em around. Somethin' must've happened to their mammy. Look starved, huh?"

Her hands roved over the tiny pups. "Poor things. Look at their little ribs. It is a wonder they are still alive."

He clucked his tongue and left to store the baskets. When he returned, he handed Lorelei and the pups into the buggy. "Guess it's lucky I found 'em."

She smiled as the dogs snuggled into the warm folds of her skirt and looked up at her with huge, adoring eyes. One of her hands rested on each furry body, and she could feel the rapid beating of their little hearts. "What are you going to do with them?"

"Remember? They're yours, as my gift."

She had already opened her mouth to protest when he turned his head, his voice muffled, as he stated, "You have ta take 'em. I don't have a place. An' I couldn't stand thinkin' of 'em all alone, maybe dyin'."

Lorelei swallowed and glanced at the now sleeping pups nestled trustingly against her. They were so pitiful. It was a miracle they were even alive, or that Chad had happened to find them.

The tension in Chad's body communicated itself through the warming of her own senses. How could she not take the poor little tykes? This *man,* sitting beside her, was so caring and compassionate. She would gladly do it for *him,* if for no other reason.

There, finally, she had been thinking in order again.

When she glanced up, he was looking at her. She smiled.

Holt stood in the shadow of the Denver and Rio Grande depot as the couple passed on their way into town. His piercing gaze noted Chad's arm draped possessively across Lorelei's shoulders.

Silently, he cursed long and loud. So, she had decided to ignore his well-intentioned advice. Fine. He just hoped she was prepared to suffer the consequences.

Though he tried to remain indifferent, he couldn't keep from watching as they drew up in front of the mercantile. His upper lip curled at Chad's dress coat and the fancy buggy. It was just like the boy, putting on airs to attract a pretty woman.

His curiosity overrode his disgruntlement, though, when Lorelei leaned out of the buggy and handed something to Chad. He tried, but couldn't make out what it was from that distance. Then he shrugged his shoulders. What the hell difference did it make?

Quite a bit. When Chad laughed and followed her inside, Holt felt as if he had been gored by the damned bull that had finally arrived that afternoon. How long would the boy stay? Were they kissing? Did she respond with the same degree of passion that still ignited his insides whenever he thought of the times he had taken her soft, pliable lips beneath his own?

A movement down the street drew his reluctant attention. The coroner walked across the road, reminding Holt of his grisly discovery. He cursed under his breath and pushed away from the building. To take his mind off the dead man, and Lorelei and Chad all cozied up together, he'd go check on his stallion.

He'd be leaving Durango at first light, taking the Hereford bull to his ranch. And he would stay there, too, doing the things that were *really* important. Who needed the hustle and bustle and dangerous excitement that came with remaining in town—around Lorelei Abbott.

It had been dark several hours when Holt finally emerged from the saloon. He had fully intended to get rip-roaring drunk to celebrate his last night in Durango. But, damn it, no matter how much he drank, he only succeeded in becoming sullen and bitter. Eventually, the friends he'd started the evening with had left one by one in pursuit of more gratifying pleasures.

A burning sensation in his stomach snaked lower. He could still smell Darla's cheap perfume on his shirt. His teeth ground together until his jaw ached. Even Darla hadn't sparked his interest, or that part of him that now jumped to life as he stared toward the mercantile. His body was damned traitorous, that's what it was.

A long, dejected sigh deflated his lungs. He stuffed his hands into his pockets and crossed the street, nonchalantly sauntering past Abbott's toward the newspaper office. He darted a quick glance through a shutterless window—stupid woman, didn't she know better than that?—and caught the dim glow of a lantern flickering from the back room. Her room. Where she slept.

Very clearly, he remembered the feminine way she had fancied up her little corner with a guilt-framed mirror, a bright plaid quilt for the cot, and . . . He chuckled, suddenly recalling the yards of calico cloth draped over the privy door. If anything could take his mind from thoughts of her . . . in bed . . . that touch of feminine frippery was it.

He didn't realize he had stopped in front of the window until a series of grunts and noises penetrated his consciousness. A shout from the alleyway caused him to freeze in place.

"Hey! Get away from there! What are you two . . . ? Wait. No, put that down!"

At the sound of a shot and a cry of pain, Holt flew into action, drawing his own gun as he raced along the side of the mercantile, sticking to the concealing shadows.

Two bulky forms loomed in front of him. They stood over Ed Tremaine, the newspaper's night watchman. The larger, heavier-set shadow pointed a pistol at Ed's slumped figure. Holt aimed and fired. The gun flew from the huge man's hand as Holt's bullet shattered his arm.

The smaller shadow muttered a Spanish curse and whirled to face Holt. Before Holt could redirect his aim and fire another round, he saw a bright flash and felt a searing sensation along the inside of his right thigh. By the time he got off another shot, the two dark forms were racing around the back of the building and out of range.

Curious spectators began to peek into the alley. Holt yelled for some of them to come get Ed and take him to the doctor. He pointed in the direction the two men had run, and more bystanders followed, although Holt held out little hope they would find the men, even with one of them being wounded.

Blood trickled down Holt's leg. Limping painfully, he felt his way along the pitch-black side of the mercantile. All of a sudden, he paused, sensing something in the blackness. He reached out. All he encountered was chipped paint and splinters. He sighed and started moving again. The events of the evening were getting to him. Must've been the beer.

Finally reaching Main, he grabbed hold of the nearest post to rest. A huge lump lodged in his throat when he searched out the doc's office, several blocks away.

A slight movement from the window snagged his blurry attention. Knowing it had to be Lorelei, he cocked his brows and slanted her what he considered a cocky grin, though he couldn't tell if his lips even moved. He reeled and clutched the post more securely.

The door slowly opened, and he watched Lorelei, in a thin gown and robe, inch her way toward him. He called out to reassure her. "Evenin'."

Her pale face shone as clearly as if it were a full moon gradually revealed by drifting clouds as she neared. His insides burned when he was able to distinguish the curves and depressions of her voluptuous figure as she pulled the robe more tightly about her.

"Wh-what was all of the shooting about?" Lorelei's voice cracked with fear.

Holt swayed in her direction, even as his fingers dug into the hard wood like sharp talons. "Don't know really. Ed Tremaine was shot. And . . . I . . ."

Lorelei came closer. Concern for Holt was etched

deeply between her knitted brows. Her eyes devoured his muscular frame from the crown of his black hat, over his form-hugging shirt, to the shiny dark stain on his trousers. She gasped "Oh, my heavens, you've been hurt!"

He grinned when her usual, precise, perfectly enunciated words ran together. "S'all right. Just a scratch."

But he had to admit to a feeling of relief when she pried him loose from the post and tugged his arm over her shoulders to help him inside. He felt the strength in her slender form, and his pride and admiration for Lorelei Abbott soared until he seemed to glide just beneath the ceiling.

She gently led him into the back room and ordered that he sit in the chair. After that deed was accomplished, her eyes took on a feverish glow as she paced and began to wring her hands, especially once she had seen the blood more closely.

"I must go find a doctor. You could bleed to death." She turned and frantically held her hands out, palms toward Holt in what was supposed to be a soothing gesture. "Stay right there. Do not move." She knew she was babbling, but couldn't seem to help herself. And her face flushed with color when she noticed the delicate location of the wound. Oh, good heavens!

She drew in a deep breath and rushed past Holt. He groped for her wrist and caught her with surprising strength.

"No. Don't go." He gulped, ashamed at his weakness. He felt like a small boy, needing someone close to him while he was sick and injured.

"It's not serious. I can tell you what to do."

Her free hand once again clutched at the neck of her gown. Panic fairly leapt from her dark eyes. "No! I can't! I've never been near a gun . . . gunshot. . . ." A shudder racked her slender form as she tried in vain to free herself from his iron-hard grasp.

"Please."

Her eyes refused to meet his as they darted wildly about the small room. Finally she looked at him, helplessly, like a mouse stilled by a predator's hypnotic stare. Her chest swelled to near bursting. He wanted her to stay. He needed her. And leaving him was the farthest thing from her mind. "All . . . all right. I'll try."

Unaccountable relief flooded Holt's taut body, and he slumped back into the chair. "Good girl. First, just put some water on to boil."

A weary sigh hissed through his clenched teeth as he ran trembling fingers through his hair, knocking his hat to the floor. He didn't even notice. He stared at Lorelei's back, long and hard, before he unbuckled his gun belt and hooked it over the back of the chair.

When she turned around after setting a large kettle of water on the stove to heat, he took a deep breath and straightened his back. A wicked sparkle emanated from his light gray eyes. "Next, we need to get these pants off."

She visibly paled. "P-pants? Off?"

"Can't do much with them on."

His voice sounded like a deep, rumbling growl. Lorelei shivered. That was exactly the way she wanted to keep him—clothed—and ineffective.

Holt bit back a groan. God, she was beautiful when she was flustered and agitated. He suddenly felt much better. The wound was painful, but not serious. The dried blood made it look worse than it was. Of course, he was weak. "I really could use some help."

Pin pricks of light, like bursting stars, shone from Lorelei's eyes. She was scared to death that he might die if she didn't lend assistance, yet was terrified to touch him. She had never seen a man without his pants on, nor one so coated with blood stains. Her heart hammered fitfully against her breast, and she lifted a trembling hand to her throat.

"Ahem. Are you goin' to stand there gawkin' all night, or are you goin' to give me a hand here?"

"Wh-what?"

Holt stood up to pull down his britches and swayed precariously. Righting himself, he tried to unbutton his fly; but his hands shook, and he couldn't control the movements of his fingers.

Embarrassment turned his face a rusty red that almost matched the color of the stains on his pants. "Sorry, Lori, I can't do it." His deep voice shook as he looked toward Lorelei with glassy eyes.

Before, he had been joshing with her. Now he was deadly serious.

Chapter Seven

Lorelei blanched. Her throat went dry. "Y-you can't?"

Holt's features were wan and drawn, and he sat back down so hard that the chair nearly toppled over backward.

She rushed toward him and steered his elbow to a small table that could be used for support in case he started to slide. Her hands fluttered above his waist like a pair of hummingbirds seeking nectar.

Though he tried to grin, she noted the waxen pallor of his skin. She swallowed and tentatively reached down. Her knuckles grazed his flat stomach, and she felt the muscles there jerk and ripple. All of a sudden, her light-weight gown and robe became hot and heavy. Sweat beaded her body. But she forced herself to continue with the chore like the intelligent, competent woman she so devoutly professed to be.

When she discovered a clinging barrier of light cotton beneath his trousers and she no longer touched bare skin, she sighed with relief. Thank heavens for underdrawers.

He blinked heavy lids. She thought she had never seen more seductive eyes in her life.

Once all of the buttons were unfastened, she leaned back and ran her tongue over her bottom lip as she pondered the next dilemma. "Can you stand up again, for just a minute? I need to slide your p-p-trousers down."

He nodded, leaning heavily on the rickety table, and lifted himself enough so that she could pull the denims off his hips. The material had dried to the wound, and when it rubbed over the raw flesh, he sucked in his breath.

Tears pooled in Lorelei's eyes. She would have given anything not to have hurt him. As the pants dropped below his knees, it was her turn to gasp. Blood had soaked into the cotton drawers, turning them a dark red around the wound. Nausea churned her stomach. She closed her eyes. This was her first close-up sight of a gunshot wound—and she hoped it would be her last.

Then, knowing there was still much to be done, she pulled herself together and got up to dip a clean cloth in the warm water.

Holt muttered under his breath when she placed the cloth against the injury. It had started seeping with the removal of his pants.

Instead of crying out in sympathy, as she was so tempted to do, or offering useless pity, she ordered, "Hold the pad in place while I take off your boots."

His white teeth flashed, then disappeared all too quickly. "Yes, ma'am."

Once he was unclothed down to his balbriggans, she stood with her hands on her hips, gnawing at the insides of her mouth until the sensitive flesh was raw. Then, with determination and resolve furrowing her forehead, she knelt between his knees. Her hands shook only slightly as they reached toward the top button of the underwear. Again, she contacted flesh lightly coated with short, wiry hair. Droplets of perspiration pooled on her upper lip.

She had thought she was getting pretty good at unfastening men's clothing, but the stitching on the buttonhole was tight. Eventually, though, after a good deal of fumbling, her trembling fingers accomplished the chore. Her eyes rounded, and heat coiled through her insides when she felt a hardness beneath her wrists that had been absent before.

Holt's voice sounded like dry leaves blowing in the wind. "Why don't you . . . cut . . . it off." God, he couldn't stand her touching him like that, there, another second.

"Wh-what?"

He grimaced. "The drawers. Cut the leg off just above the wound."

"Oh. Of course." Her face flushed crimson. Of course, the drawers. What else could he have meant?

The stormy gray of his eyes softened to a color that reminded her of baby bunnies. Her heart constricted, knowing he was in pain and yet she seemed more concerned with her own sensibilities than with what was important, tending to his wound before it became infected.

At least the bleeding had stopped, and she could see

that the wound was a long, jagged furrow that luckily was not very deep. With a quivering stomach and shaking knees that had nothing to do with the sight of raw flesh, she found a knife in a scabbard on his belt and dipped the blade in the now boiling water.

It was none too easy cutting the tight material from his slim, corded leg. The wound was high on the inside of his thigh, and it brought her into close proximity to . . . well . . .

Holt figured he was being unduly tortured. God, he couldn't keep his eyes off her hands. They were too close. . . . Her fingers were so soft, so soothing, so . . . tantalizing. No matter how hard his mind fought what her hands wrought, his body reacted of its own accord.

Finally, unable to endure her teasing ministrations, no matter how well meaning, a moment longer, he took the knife from her hand. "Let me." Hell, his manhood was so stiff and swollen that she was only inches from . . . One slip and . . .

She cleared her throat. Thank heavens his eyes were directed somewhere besides the back of her head, or her clumsy fingers. Leaning back to straighten her humped shoulders, she immediately missed the warmth that radiated from the sheltering cocoon his body had provided.

He smelled wonderful, like old leather and bourbon and spicy soap. His scent produced sensuous sensations that she gave up even trying to deny.

When he finished cutting around the circle of his leg, he groaned and gave her a silly grin. "Done."

She tentatively took hold of the uneven edge of material and began to peel it down, tugging gently at the congealed crust atop the wound. Again his muscles involuntarily quivered. She held her breath, trying desperately to avoid hurting him.

Finally, the material pulled free. She sighed, and had to swallow several times before she could speak. "The warm water helped to loosen the scab." Shaking her head, she thought, *What an inane thing to say.* Her mind wasn't functioning clearly for some strange reason.

He nodded and released his death grip on the chair. His knuckles were white, and his fingers ached when he uncurled them. "Thanks."

She held another clean, wet cloth. "This will hurt, but I need to cleanse the wound."

He moaned and nodded. "Go ahead. I'm ready for—anything."

His wicked wink caused her to hesitate, yet gave her the confidence to proceed with the gruesome task. As gently as possible, she rinsed his torn flesh, then dabbed away the blood coating the remainder of his upper thigh.

Her breathing came in rapid little gusts as she smoothed the cloth over the taut skin enveloping hard tendons and supple sinew. Every once in a while a curly black hair entangled her fingers, and her heart leapt into her throat.

Then she nonchalantly attempted to look up. Her hand gradually slowed its movement. His eyes met hers, their gray depths fairly smoldering. She jerked the cloth away as if his skin had suddenly become as hot as a burning coal.

Holt cleared his throat. "That feels real good, Lori."

With the back of her hand, she swiped away a strand of hair stuck to her cheek. Lori. No one had ever shortened her name like that before. And the way it sort of rolled over his tongue, in that long drawl . . . She liked it. Very much.

And as she really looked at him, she noticed for the first time the pale lines winging from either side of his eyes. He was a man used to the out-of-doors—rough, tough, strong, dangerous. If it were possible, he was suddenly even more appealing and attractive.

She dropped the cloth and jumped to her feet. One more minute kneeling in such a compromising position between his long, slender legs and . . . She *had* to get away.

However, Lorelei soon returned, carrying a dark bottle of light-colored powder. "The medicines have not arrived yet, but I have some alum. It should do nicely on your wound." Sprinkling on a good amount, she then covered it with a clean pad. She tore a long strip of cotton to bind it in place, then knelt in front of him again.

One arm was on either side of his leg as she wound the material over and under his firm thigh. When she went under, she had to lean forward. Her breasts would brush his knee, and she felt an electric tingle that set her insides all aflutter.

Holt watched her from beneath hooded lids. Besides being thoroughly aroused, he was captivated by her extraordinary beauty. With her eyes downcast as they were, he noted her long, long lashes. They were mostly pale, the color of her hair, except the tips, which were dark brown and gave the impression of two unfolded fans spread against cheeks the color and texture of ripe peaches.

He inhaled the familiar traces of her fresh scent and let his head fall against the back of the chair as he slumped down to give her better access to the wound as she wound higher and higher.

At last, proud of the neat bandage she had wrought, and hardly realizing what she was doing, Lorelei leaned back and placed her palms on his knees. One hand rested upon cotton, the other on warm, bare skin.

That did it! Holt lurched to his feet, toppling Lorelei over backward in his haste. He took several deep breaths and turned his lower body aside as he hastily reached down to help her rise. "Sorry."

He frantically scanned the room for any excuse to hide himself away and luckily remembered the calico-covered privy. "Ah, excuse me for a minute, will you?"

She noticed the direction of his gaze, and another deep blush colored her face. "Certainly."

Unsteadily, he made his way forward, waving away her offer of assistance. If she touched him again, he was uncertain of what he would do. Just as he reached for the latch, he heard a scuffling sound from the other side of the door. He frowned. What in the hell? He jerked the door open. If it were rats, they were sure big ones.

Holt fell back in surprise when one red ball of fluff and one brown tumbled onto his bare feet. Side-stepping first one way, then another, he yelled, "Toss me my gun. Quick!" Damn. Why had he taken it off in the first place? Trying to impress the lady, he reasoned.

Lorelei gasped, "I most certainly will not," and quickly ran to retrieve the two gamboling puppies. She held them up against her chest and nuzzled her nose into the soft fur. Her brow crinkled as she glared at Holt.

"Just because you do not like puppies, does not mean you have to murder the poor little things."

He shook his head. "Puppies?"

She sniffed indignantly. "What else did you think they were?"

Visions of huge outhouse rats, and no telling *what,* still rioted in his head. "Well . . ." He expelled a long breath. "Puppies. How in hell did you wind up with *puppies?"*

She couldn't believe that a man such as Holt Dolan didn't like animals. Sometimes it was hard to judge character. "Chad gave them to me. When we went on a picnic this afternoon."

His eyes narrowed. "Did he, now." Holt's gut churned. Among other things, he didn't care for the easy manner in which she bandied about the terms of "Chad" and "we" in the same breath.

Before he could scold her for ignoring his warnings about the young man, Chad, the floor suddenly began to dip and sway beneath his feet. Dizzy and weak, and unwilling to have Lorelei see him in such a state, he turned into the tiny, dark cubicle, hurriedly lit a candle, and closed the door.

Lorelei stared in open-mouthed disbelief, then shrugged her shoulders and placed the pups on the floor. Why should she be surprised by his rude behavior? One would think she would be used to it by now.

When the puppies whimpered and began to sniff

around the floor, she scooped them up again and headed toward the back door. "Oh, no. You are going to learn when to go outside, understand?"

By the time she and her charges returned, Holt had lowered himself halfway onto the cot.

"Wait! You can't lie down. You mustn't stay here."

He grinned rather foolishly and collapsed. "Won't stay long. Need rest. Feel . . . rode hard . . . put up wet."

Scowling, wishing she understood even a little bit of his cowboy lingo, Lorelei plucked at the heavy arm draping over the side of the narrow bed. "No. Please. Go home."

She knew he was hurt and weak, knew he was at the end of his enormous strength, but she couldn't help the expression of guilt that stole across her face as she glanced about the room. They were definitely alone, not counting the puppies. It was wrong. He could not be found there. But as his arm fell from her grasp, she also knew there was no help for it. He was there to stay, at least for a while.

As she was about to turn around, his hand lifted, and his fingers closed over her wrist. "Don't go." That was all he said before his head rolled to the side.

Dark smudges stained the thin skin beneath his eyes. His mouth was drawn into a fine line, even though he slept. She tried to free her arm, but he held on firmly. Finally, she sighed and leaned over to catch hold of the chair so that she could drag it next to the cot.

Sitting there, she had nothing better to do than stare at his exquisitely handsome face. Hints of bristles darkening his usually clean-shaven cheeks lent him an almost innocent, boyish quality. That he did not wear whiskers, or a moustache or long sideburns, was in itself an oddity. Most of the men she had seen in the West grew at least one, or a variety of all three.

She sighed, glad for the opportunity to study at her leisure his high, chiseled cheekbones; that smallish, aquiline nose; and the strong, yet somehow quite sensuous square jaw. Whenever she looked at him, he nearly took her breath away, and the same physical phenomenon seemed to be occurring at that very moment. Oh, yes, she liked what she saw.

And she liked the *man,* even if he didn't like puppies. Then her eyes widened. Whatever she was feeling for Holt, it had started with a spark that leapt into a flame that burned brighter and more intense with every encounter.

Would it last? Or would her feelings for him diminish with time just like every other project she had tired of and placed aside?

She reached over and pushed a stray lock of ebony hair from his damp forehead. Her fingers sifted through the crisp, thick layers like one of her customers would weigh a length of pure silk. She shivered. What was wrong with her all of a sudden? Why, the man looked silly, lying the full length of her bed, with his vest and shirt and undershirt extended in various degrees down his narrow hips above one bare leg, and one clad in such tight-fitting cotton that it might as well be.

But there was nothing silly about the rush of emotion that swirled inside her breast until she was afraid of swooning from lack of breath. She had never felt this way with a man before, experienced this excitement and overwhelming desire—and fear—until her muscles ached with tension.

She unconsciously wound and rewound her cold hands and fingers. Her senses were going crazy, and she didn't know what to do to control them. Most distressing of all, though, was the notion that perhaps she didn't want to try.

Lorelei shifted uncomfortably in the chair. What a strange dream. She wriggled her head. Her cheek rested against something soft and smooth that smelled similar to her father's cowhide sofa. One of her hands lay on a fine, spring mat. The fingers of her other hand entwined with long, bony objects that were cool and rough to the touch.

She wrinkled her nose. Something tickled her face. Her eyes blinked open, closed, then opened wide. She tried to lift her head; but her braid was caught, and there was a tingling ache in her back. As her mind began to blearily function once again, a large smile spread across her face.

"Go ahead. Grin. I feel like a damned rug." As much as he hated to, Holt unwound his fingers from Lorelei's hair.

Able to move her head at last, Lorelei gradually, reluctantly, raised herself from his chest. Every vertebra in her back snapped and popped. She groaned, stretched like a contented kitten, then grinned again as her eyes greedily scanned Holt's virile form.

One puppy lay curled in the middle of Holt's belly, the other at the apex of his thighs. The pair of gray eyes that latched hold of her amused black ones appeared quite disgruntled.

Trying valiantly to smother a giggle, and failing miserably, she plucked the ball of red fluff from his stomach. "Freda, what a naughty girl." She placed the dog gently onto the floor and reached back to remove the brown pup. Her hands hovered in midair.

A deep rumble vibrated throughout Holt's long body. She stared. It was the first time she had heard him laugh. And it was entirely too dangerous for a man to possess such a gorgeous smile.

"Go ahead. Take the thing. Just be mighty careful." He leered wickedly.

Her eyes rolled. That was all she needed—for him to make her even more nervous. Then her lips quirked mischievously as she fooled him and lifted the animal by the scruff of its neck. Holt murmured something that sounded like "coward," and she glared at him as she cuddled the puppy to her breast. "Don't worry, Sissy. The nasty man won't hurt you."

A loud guffaw broke the suddenly strained silence. "Freda? Sissy? What kinda names are those for pups?"

She attempted to stiffen her back, but found the effort much too painful. "It just so happens I named them after my two best friends back home."

Holt chuckled. "Your friends have cold noses and sharp little teeth?"

She blushed at the teasing glint in his eyes. "Of course not! Freda has reddish hair. Sissy has brown."

"Oh, sure, now I can see the resemblance."

Lorelei was tempted to haul off and hit the big oaf, but suddenly remembered he was a wounded man.

Contritely, she asked, "How does your leg feel this morning?"

He yawned and stretched, raising the tail of his shirt until only one thin layer of material concealed his lower anatomy. She focused on the white bandage and attempted to keep her gaze averted from his long, muscular leg. She lowered her lashes to mere slits and darted swift glances anyway. He had awfully pretty knees.

Looking guiltily away from the bare expanse of flesh, she met the shimmering pools of his deep gray eyes. Their warmth seeped throughout her body, and she soaked it up like cotton absorbed water—or blood.

She shuddered. It had just penetrated her consciousness that Holt could have been killed last night. The horrible thought literally robbed her of breath. Somehow, some way, this man had become very dear to her. Her eyelids fluttered shut. No, it wasn't possible. She was just lonely, and maybe a little frightened because she was away from home and friends. Holt had stepped in to protect her at a time when she was exceedingly vulnerable. That was all. She had no "feelings" for him. Not really.

Able to take a deep breath at last, she remembered that he still had not answered her question. She took advantage of the respite to scoot the chair a ways from the cot. "Your leg, does it hurt?" Her voice was thin and quavery. She inhaled sharply. Heaven forbid that he realize the effect he had upon her senses.

"Can't feel a thing." His voice was deep, almost gruff. And he lied like a bandit. His nerve endings were so sensitive that he could feel her every move before she even made it.

God, she was beautiful. He had lain awake, watching her sleep for hours, it seemed, mesmerized by thick lustrous lashes outlined by smooth, creamy cheeks unadorned by powder or false color. His stomach growled. And she smelled good enough to eat.

Hearing the telltale gurgle, Lorelei was embarrassed by her lack of good manners and hospitality. The man was probably starved. "Are you hungry?" She frowned at the ferocious gleam that suddenly suffused his eyes and inched back farther.

"Famished," he muttered. Feeling suddenly weak, he let his arm dangle off the side of the bed. One of the pups waddled over and nudged its wet nose into his palm. He pushed it away, too engrossed in imagining what Lorelei could do to slack his hunger, to pay attention to the animal. Besides, he had never had a pet of his own, and didn't really know what to do with the annoying creature.

A sad smile twisted his lips when he recalled all of the strays his half-brother used to drag home. And when one of them died, the boy was devastated. Come to think of it, those were the *only* times he had ever seen his brother show any form of emotion. Anyway, Holt had decided then that there was too much unhappiness as it was, to expend such grief on an animal.

Flustered by the wistful expression on Holt's face, Lorelei decided it would be best to get away from the enthralling man and fix him something to eat. As she started to rise, she found her wrist still encompassed within his strong grasp. At the same time, she accidentally stepped on the puppy.

The startled animal yelped in pain. Lorelei tried to lift both feet at the same time. Holt tugged her arm in a well-meaning effort to help. The next thing she knew, she was dumped onto the small bed.

Holt's breath whooshed from his lungs, but his arms instinctively wrapped around her to keep her from rolling off and onto the hard floor. She clutched frantically for a solid handhold, which turned out to be his big, broad shoulders.

Not a sound stirred the air. No one dared move. Even the puppy had stopped its pitiful whimpering. Lorelei's breath clogged in her throat. Her breasts smashed flush against his chest. Her legs straddled his narrow hips. Obsidian eyes stared into smoldering gray ones. She could almost imagine wisps of smoke surrounding them like a thick fog.

Holt cocked his thick brows in a most rakish manner and grinned. "Hhm-m-m, breakfast? So soon?"

Chapter Eight

Lorelei squirmed in an effort to move off of Holt. How could she have been so clumsy? Her heart beat a staccato rhythm against her breast as his fingers spread along her spine. Lethargy seeped through her bones. But she had to get up. There were things to be done.

Holt's breath hissed between his teeth as he inhaled sharply. Her sporadic movements only tended to arouse an ache in his gut, and groin, that was fast throbbing out of his control. "No. Don't move."

Lorelei instantly obeyed as his eyes delved into hers. Blood boiled through her veins. Her body flushed with heat from the roots of her hair to the tips of her toenails. Her nipples contracted, and she was mortified when Holt's breathing quickened.

Even through two layers of thick cotton, a pulsating bulge lengthened and grew hard near the apex of her thighs. A pinpoint of fear was literally erased from her mind, though, when she realized what it was, and that old maid Lorelei Abbott had caused such a reaction in a man made of solid muscle and steel strength.

A certain glow of confidence suffused her insides. She had never been so attracted to a man before—had never experienced such a sense of need.

Holt's hands moved to her sides, where they soon began a slow, sensuous exploration of the taut muscles in her neck and back. As she began to relax, her head dipped lower. He kissed her forehead, her cheek, and nibbled gently, fleetingly, at the tender flesh on the side of her throat.

Lorelei gasped when his moist tongue flicked the lobe of her ear. No man had ever kissed her there. She became achingly aware of every tiny area where their bodies touched. His fingers worked magic, loosening the tension that had consumed her every conscious thought and movement since he had entered her room late last night.

Her head turned, almost imperceptively, until her lips brushed his. She moaned, ever so softly, as his mouth took hers in a kiss that devoured her very soul. Her bones melted to mush. It felt as if her body molded against every contour of his hard length—breast to chest, belly to belly, thigh to thigh.

Lorelei wriggled and slid atop his lean body. She couldn't help it. Her nerve endings itched. Suddenly, his hips arched at the same time she felt his hands inch along the bare skin of her back. Bare? Dear heavens, her nightdress and robe must have ridden up without her noticing.

Another niggle of doubt assailed her. She could call a stop to this. It wasn't right for him to touch her like that. Or was it? When the warm pads of his fingers massaged the length of her spine, it felt good. *Too* good.

She could barely remember her mother telling her, like in a fairy tale, that one day a man would come along to trust and love, and Lorelei would know that it was *right*. Her feelings now took this beyond right, to heavenly.

His tongue sought for and gained entrance to the moist depths of her mouth. A curl of desire ignited and spiraled throughout her nether regions until she quivered uncontrollably. Her own fingers hesitantly, unexpectedly drifted from button to button down the front of his vest, then his shirt. When she remained thwarted from reaching his chest by the clinging layer of his undershirt, she became almost frantic in her efforts to pull up the soft cotton.

"Hold on, Lori. Raise up a tad. There we go."

His voice was low and husky in her ear. She shivered when his warm breath teased the extra-sensitive flesh at the base of her neck.

Holt quickly shed the rest of his clothing and then surprised her by tugging her nightgown and robe over her head. She trembled, completely exposed to his rapt gaze. Her eyes blinked closed, unable, unwilling, to see what might be revealed in those smoky depths.

"Ah, Lori, you are some kinda woman. You're perfect. Gorgeous."

Her stiffness eased beneath the breathless tones of his voice. She did not doubt his sincerity, for she felt the thunderous beating of his heart, was seared by the heat of his skin and, finally, read the truth in his eyes when she gathered the courage to look up.

His arms wrapped about her in a gigantic bear hug. She thought her rib cage would be crushed until he released her just enough to turn onto his side, but still keep her pressed full length against him.

"God, you feel good." The thick mat of black hair on his chest tickled her breasts. He caressed her silky smooth flesh with rough and calloused, yet exceedingly tender, palms. "You taste good, too." His head dipped to capture her lips.

The myriad of sensations that engulfed her body went straight to her head. Her eyes drifted shut. She clung to him, then impulsively began to explore his shoulders and back. Her hands slid tentatively, innocently, sensuously, over smooth flesh stretched tautly across rippling layers of sinew and muscle.

All at once, Lorelei drew in her breath. Her roaming fingers encountered a hard, ragged ridge just above his shoulder blade. Leaning slightly back, she found another, inches to the left of his flat male nipple.

Aware of her horrified scrutiny, Holt buried one hand in the thick mass of blond hair tumbling loose over her shoulders and brought her face close to his. "They're nothing."

"B-but the scars—"

"Are long since healed. Kiss me, Lori. Please?"

How could she resist such a plea? Fleetingly, she marveled over what was happening to her. She lay in bed, in the early morning, naked in Holt's arms, and was reveling in it. Yet, she hardly knew the man. Where was the guilt, the shame, she had expected to feel?

When his hands gently cupped her face, her questions evaporated like the fresh morning dew. The emotion that erupted from the roiling pit of her stomach lodged like a wad of cotton in her throat. Pressure expanded her chest until she thought it might burst. Her ears rang with the excited throbbing of her heart.

She wanted him to touch her, to kiss her, to show her how a woman should feel when a man made tender, glorious love to her. And *that,* she realized, as her hands smoothed soothingly, lovingly, over his body, was the real key to her dilemma. He was so exquisitely gentle with her. He led, tempted—never demanded—and she acquiesced oh, so willingly.

Her body hummed with unfamiliar sensuality under his skillful ministrations. If he stopped now, she was afraid she would wither and die, like a new bud without the life-giving sustenance of a spring rain.

Holt bent and took the rosy tip of one lush breast into his mouth. Her soft moan knotted his stomach. His loins burned with need. God, he wanted this woman. He couldn't remember ever experiencing that gut-wrenching desire to take, yet to give, and keep giving, until she was his, and his alone.

Lorelei's long, slender leg was supple and sleek beneath his fingers. The inside of her thigh was as soft as velvet. He kneaded the smooth flesh there until she writhed against his manhood. Quickly, he drew her leg over his hip and pulled her femininity to the throbbing proof of his need, which urgently nudged, seeking entrance.

"Do you want me, Lori?"

She whimpered. Her body spasmed. The ache between her thighs was the most pleasurable, painful, sensation of her life. She knew exactly what she wanted, yet was afraid to admit to being so wanton. Did she *want* him to continue? Did she *want* him to make love to her? "Oh, yes, Holt, please."

The time for question and apprehension slipped

away as he shifted his hips and slid deftly inside her. She gasped, but when he suddenly hesitated, her body began an instinctive, steady, rocking motion that impaled him farther. Soon the slight pain turned into a sequence of small eruptions and explosions, much like a pine knot bursting from an intense lick of flame.

Her every nerve ending pulsed. Perspiration beaded her body, to be cooled by the brisk morning air.

For a miniscule second, Holt hesitated. A virgin? Lorelei Abbott? She seemed so world-wise and mature. Competent and . . . How could he have known? Something warm, and almost liquid in feeling, coursed through his chest. A silly grin crinkled his face and glowed from his eyes.

Soon, though, through a possessive haze of tenderness, his body took control of his mind as he, too, moved with a slow, even rhythm. But as her inner muscles contracted about him, he found himself clutching her tightly to his chest as they surged to the ultimate height of pleasure together, completely.

Their breathing came in ragged gasps as they lay as one, warm and exhausted, entwined in a sated embrace. Moments drifted by like fleeting seconds until Holt felt light, butterfly touches on his lips and eyelids and down the crooked ridge of his nose. A sheepish grin curved his mouth. "It was broken once. Maybe twice. Don't remember."

"Such a beautiful nose. It possesses character."

Her voice was deep, huskier than usual. His body responded instantly. He chuckled as feeling returned to his limbs. He had never felt so drained, so . . . so . . . wonderful. "Character, huh?"

"Uhmm." She felt him move inside her and nuzzled

her nose into the hollow of his shoulder. The shudder that rippled the length of his fine body brought a delighted sigh from her lips.

There was the strangest ache in her chest when she looked up at his rugged features. And it was good to see the color had returned to his handsome face. Last night his pale, strained appearance had frightened her almost more than the sight of his wound.

Wound. The scars. Who was Holt Dolan? What kind of life had he led to bear such signs of violence and danger? Her finger traced the puckered edges of the small, round indentation on his shoulder. She experienced an irrational rage at the unknown person, or persons, who had dared to harm this wondrous man.

Wondrous? How could she think to know that? The more she learned about Mr. Dolan, the more confused she became. Then a slow smile stole across her lips. Oh, yes, wondrous. He made her feel so exquisitely feminine, so wonderfully alive. Her body tingled and quivered with pleasant anticipation as his hands continued to caress her.

Holt, himself, was in a languorous daze as he stroked her moist, silken skin. His chest rose and fell in deep heaves as he fought to resume a normalcy of breath.

But he fought his feelings of satisfaction and well-being to mentally castigate himself. He had always taken pride in the control he maintained during his encounters with women. Until now. There was nothing about the last thirty minutes or so that came anywhere near what he would call "control." And he didn't like the sense of drifting, of having lost charge of purpose, that caused him to feel soft and fuzzy-headed.

There had to be a reasonable explanation. He had

been under a lot of strain. Hell, he could have been killed last night or from the tender location of the wound, deprived of his manhood. He had just needed to reaffirm that he was truly alive and well and capable of performing as a man. Lorelei was nothing special. Any woman could have given him the same unutterably intense . . . yeah, any woman.

So, why couldn't he bring himself to release the vixen and get up and on about his business? He was burning daylight and should already be at the ranch, instead of lying here, in her bed, lazy and contented.

"Are you hungry?" Lorelei's voice came out in a hesitant squeak. She remembered full well that aspersions to breakfast had begun the liaison in the first place.

Liaison. The word, and its illicit connotations, created a sharp pain in her chest. But why? Surely she didn't desire a deeper relationship with the man, did she? He was belligerent, rude . . . tender. . . . A tear pooled in the corner of her eye, spilled over, and trickled aimlessly down her cheek.

Holt saw the wayward droplet and blocked its path with his finger. He traced the apple of her cheek, the indention of her face, the firm jawline and cupid's bow shape of her lips. "What have you got to offer?"

She blinked. "Wh-what?" Dear heavens, hadn't she given him *everything?*

"For breakfast. What have you got?"

"Oh." This time, he wanted food. Why was she suddenly disappointed?

It was mid-morning before Holt left the mercantile.

As he opened the door to let himself out, Mr. Endsley walked in. The two men eyed each other warily before Endsley tipped his hat and squeezed on inside.

Holt went out, but stopped on the walkway to glance back over his shoulder. Strange sort, that Endsley. Quiet. Somber. But Holt could have sworn he had just seen a flicker of amusement in those hard-bitten eyes.

Then Holt shrugged. Naw. Because he felt better than he had in years didn't mean that everyone else shared the same sentiment. Besides, Endsley's face, or eyes, would shatter under the strain of a smile, he was sure.

Stuffing his hands into his pockets, he whistled all the way to Dr. Foster's office. Damn! What a morning. What a woman. All of a sudden, he had an urge to charge out to the ranch and build the new corrals, fix the sagging barn door, repair the porch steps—all of those things he had put off while concentrating on building his cattle herd and mending borderline fences.

Holt stopped and shook his head. Hell, he was almost so far gone as to picture two rocking chairs in front of the fireplace.

Finally, he glanced up and saw that he was standing stupidly in front of the doctor's place. The door was ajar, so he walked on in. The sound of heated voices drew him toward the surgery.

"Gol durn it, Doc, I'm gonna live, unless ya keep on pokin' me like that."

"Shush up, Ed. Let the good doctor do his job."

Holt recognized the voice of the owner of Durango's newspaper, Miss Catherine W. Romaine. He had seen her around town; an intelligent, feisty woman, who had been one of the first business people to arrive in

Durango when the town was little more than rows of tents or clapboard fronts.

"Well, I for one am fed up with the lawless element in our fair city. It isn't safe for man nor beast to walk the streets," stated the mayor.

Holt entered the room just in time to be the recipient of the mayor's practiced scowl.

Dr. Foster nodded toward Holt and pulled the sheet over Ed's bare chest. "Something's got to be done, that's for sure. Either that, or bring in another doctor, or two. Frankly, I can't keep up with all the work anymore."

Ed raised his head off the examination table and looked directly at Holt. "There's the man that saved my life. If it hadn't been for Dolan, those two scoundrels would've drilled me dead center for sure. Thanks, Holt. I owe you."

With four sets of eyes staring toward him at once, the knot in Holt's bandana became suffocatingly tight. "Just happened to be there at the right time, is all."

Catherine Romaine crossed her arms over her ample bosom and lifted her chin at a haughty angle. "Don't be so modest, Mr. Dolan. You have certainly done more than your share of good deeds for the people of Durango during the last few weeks. I hope we continue to be so fortunate for a long time to come."

Holt hunched his shoulders and found an interesting splinter in the floorboards. How he wished he had gone straight to the stable. He and the bull would be well down the road to home by now if he hadn't taken the time to check on Ed.

Then a pang of guilt lodged in his chest. He shouldn't have waited until morning. He should have come on to

Doc's last night instead of allowing Lorelei to take him in. Or he could have at least gotten up and left early this morning when he first awoke to find her and her damned dogs draped all over him.

But no, he had let lust and desire rule his better judgment. Judgment? What judgment? What was left of his good sense had stampeded from his mind the first moment he had laid eyes on the woman. He had no business allowing her to get so close. It would eventually do nothing but cause her pain.

"Mr. Dolan? You do agree, don't you?"

Holt's head jerked up. Everyone was staring at him, and Miss Romaine more intently than before. "What?"

She shoved her spectacles more securely in place on the bridge of her nose. "I just stated that what the town needs is a competent person in charge of enforcing the law."

The mayor hooked his pudgy thumbs into his vest pockets and thrust out his mounded chest and belly. "Quite right. A good sheriff would handle the ruffians and riffraff burgeoning the gutters of Main, spilling forth from the bordellos—"

"We get the idea, Mayor." The doctor ran roughened fingers through his thinning hair. "Just whom do you intend to rope into that exalted position?"

Everyone looked at Holt. His mouth opened, but nothing came out. Trapped. That old feeling—the one he thought he had left behind when he came to Colorado—welled up until he nearly choked. It had always been that way, whenever the inevitable caught up with him.

But no, he had a choice. This town, these people, were not his responsibility. They were *not!*

Finally, he took a long, deep breath, controlling outwardly the emotions roiling in his gut. He swallowed, and said, "Givin' a man like me the job of sheriff would be like turnin' a lobo loose with a flock of lambs."

Catherine placed her hands on her hips and looked him up and down. "We know all about you, Mr. Dolan. We know exactly what we'll be getting."

Ice-cold fingers ran down his spine, and Holt had to fight to keep from shuddering. Why should he be surprised? He pulled a cheroot from his vest pocket, but took his time in lighting the tobacco. The next move was still theirs to make.

Mayor Hennesy nervously cleared his throat. "Ahem, uh, we have known of your, er, reputation, for quite some time. That is why we—I mean—you would—"

Doc Foster grunted disdainfully and interrupted, "Most men around town respect you. The ruffians give you a lot of room. They'll think twice about breakin' the law if you're sheriff."

Miss Romaine actually smiled. "And we have seen what you have done since you came to Durango. You have helped a lot of people."

Holt snorted. "Sure." All he had tried to do was mind his own business and start his life over again.

"You saved my life." Ed's head dropped back to the table, as if the effort to add his say had sapped his remaining energy.

Catherine nodded. "And Jenny Summers. You didn't have to pull her from the line of fire during that horrendous gunfight the other day."

The mayor puffed out his chest as if he were someone of considerable importance and had something notable to say. "You are the only man for the job. What do you say?"

Holt glanced quickly around the room. Expectation glowed in their eyes. He felt sick to his stomach and took a long drag from the thin cigar. "Sorry, but I can't help you. I've got a ranch to run. Whoever you hire will be a better man than me."

When the doctor finally noticed Holt's blood-caked trousers, Holt waved aside the man's concern. His initial intention to have the doc check out his wound had lurked uneasily in the back of his mind since he had entered the office, but he suddenly realized he trusted Lorelei. She had taken exceptional care of him, and he felt as if he could read her every thought and emotion when he looked into her guileless face.

Strange. He normally didn't trust anyone. Now he decided to place his faith in a woman? Strange was a mild description of the emotion that nearly knocked the supports from under him.

Dismayed by the direction his thoughts had taken, Holt turned and left with an air of casual nonchalance, though all the while he wanted to bolt from the room. Besides, he couldn't stay to hear the arguments, for he could tell from the expression in Miss Romaine's and the mayor's red faces that they objected to his refusal, vehemently.

By the time he reached the porch and had closed the office door behind him, he was trembling like a broken limb caught in a wind storm.

No, he couldn't do it. Not again. Not ever again.

It was noon by the time Holt was ready to leave town. He rode the Morgan stallion down Main Avenue on the way to the railroad pens to pick up his bull.

He meant to keep his gaze focused straight ahead, but as he drew abreast of Abbott's Mercantile, his eyes shifted of their own volition. There was a movement from the shadows in the window. She came forward until he could see her. Beautiful. All gingham and lace, her hair pulled back again in that tight bun.

God, he could still feel its cornsilk softness as it dangled onto his chest. He rubbed his fingers together as if to fondle a long, wavy tress. When their eyes met and locked, he could not get his breath.

He didn't even feel the horse slowing and hesitating, unused to its master's slack attention. Why? Holt thought. Why now? And what right did he have? He would only hurt her, or worse, as he had all of the other women in his life. But there was one thing he could never deny—she was something special.

Lorelei gasped at the sharp stab of emotion suffusing her breast as she stared back at Holt. He sat in the middle of the street, atop the most beautiful red horse she had ever seen. Sunlight outlined the pair. Heat waves shimmered and spun around them until she was nearly blinded.

She loosened the stiff top button gouging her neck. Warmth seeped into her pores and radiated to the center of her being. Whereas before she had felt chilled, she was now assailed by the uncanny need to shed a layer or two of clothing.

His chiseled features etched themselves into her mind. His high forehead and straight, thick brows. The bump in his nose. Those incredible, sensuous lips. Oh, yes, those lips that had driven her nearly frantic—was it just that morning?

Her fingers traced her own mouth, still tender from the long hours of passion and searing kisses. They felt different—fuller, more sensitive. *She* felt changed, too, inside and out, in mind as well as body. There was a warmth that permeated clear to her soul. Warmth that had been missing from her life for a long time.

Her eyes slowly widened when she saw Holt sternly shake his head and urge his horse into a fast canter down the street. The notion that she might care for him, really care, was disturbing. Did he, perhaps, feel the same?

Then the crushing reality of her idyllic morning slammed into her as the sun reflected from the pearl handle of his pistol. She shuddered. What did she know about him, after all? He carried a gun with practiced ease and grace. He was gallant and attractive. And represented everything she had learned to despise in a man.

The muscles along her stomach quivered. Her chest constricted. She knew one other thing. She could very easily do more than just care for the man. He had barged his way into her heart. When she was least suspecting and had her guard lowered, he had come into her life like a raging storm. He brought to the fore so many conflicting emotions that her head was constantly spinning. But she would get over it. Like she had so many other times, she would conquer those feelings.

Though she tried to clamp her mind closed on the memory, Frank forged his way inside. Lorelei shivered as chill bumps coated her flesh. Frank. Again. Her eyes misted. Could she now, at last, face the truth?

She and Frank would never have been married—no matter how hard she tried to escape the fact. If he had not been killed, he would have called off the ceremony the next day.

Her arms wrapped about her waist. Dear heavens, he had found someone else. She had suspected it, but still insisted, to herself, and to everyone else, that he loved her. The truth was, she had been spurned. At least he had not told her family, and she had been spared that embarrassment.

But something inside her had chilled that day he'd told her so callously that the wedding was off and then gone merrily on his way to hunt with his friends. Cold. Ice. She had not allowed herself to feel so strongly for a man since.

She sighed and closed her eyes, holding her lids down tight. That *something* was beginning to thaw. She felt all squishy inside at the sight, or thought, of Holt Dolan. Even now, her breasts felt achy and heavy, and the insides of her thighs prickled with imagined sensation.

Her eyes popped open. She had made a mistake in choosing Frank—another mistake in a long list of errors in judgment. Was Holt to be just one more?

Several times during the morning, little stabs of guilt had pricked her conscience. What she and Holt had done was wrong—yet there was another side to the argument taking place in her mind.

She was far from home and accusing fingers. She was finally taking charge of her life. So why allow herself to feel so awful about feeling good? It had been her decision to give herself to Holt. And it wasn't as if she would ever have to worry about the marriage bed.

Hadn't her father pointed out the fact often enough that she was nearing the "old maid" stage of her life? Who would want her for a wife now, anyway?

"What else do you want done, Miss Abbott?"

Lorelei jumped. She'd been so preoccupied with her musings that she had forgotten where she was, and who was with her. She vacantly scanned the store. "Uh, I think that will do for today. Thank you, Mr. Endsley."

She hardly paid any attention to his frowning countenance when he grumbled, "Another order of your . . . friend's . . . tobacco came in. Wonder what he does with all of it?"

Her eyes narrowed as she focused her gaze on Endsley's skeletal face. Rather than address the subject of the shipment, she questioned his pronounced slur of the term "friend." "You do not like Chad. Why?"

"Can't say I do or don't." He picked up a broom propped against the counter.

Lorelei felt like screaming. She was tired and overwrought, and Mr. Endsley's taciturn personality was beginning to wear on her. Why couldn't he ever give a straight answer to her questions? She was just about to tell him exactly how she felt when she took a step forward and instigated a sudden explosion of sound. She had stepped on a puppy's foot.

Untangling her fingers from the lacy material covering her thundering heart, she knelt down to soothe the whimpering animal's feelings. "Poor Sissy." She rubbed the tiny paw and was reminded of the moments spent last night tenderly caring for Holt.

Lorelei pulled the furry beast to her breast and nuzzled her nose into the soft down. She didn't know how long she knelt there, thus absorbed in thought, before Robert gathered the pup from her arms. He also held the other wayward adventurer.

"I'll put them in the back, missy."

"Thank you." She absently scratched the white patch of hair on Freda's red chest.

The bell above the door jangled repeatedly. At first, she did not recognize the popping sounds as they mingled with the bells. Then she saw the excited ladies leaning in the window, peering outside, and she knew. A shudder racked her body as her hands covered her ears. Gunshots! And more gunshots! Would it never end?

She took a steadying breath and scrambled to her feet to join the rest of the onlookers. But she ached, deep down in her chest, when she gazed out at the town she was growing to love.

Would she ever feel safe in Durango? Would she, could she, make it her home?

Chapter Nine

Holt was still shaking his head over the unsettling effect Lorelei Abbott seemed to have on his mind and body as he rode past the Brunswick Hotel and the sign advertising meals at all hours. There was an empty, gnawing sensation in the pit of his stomach, but it had nothing to do with hunger, damn it.

He pulled the sweating stallion down to a walk. The animal tossed its head and pranced a few more steps before complying to Holt's sharp jerk on the reins. With his attention centered on the horse, Holt almost missed the activity taking place toward the rear of the express office.

But he did notice, and the furtive movements of two men wearing long dusters, and that of a third man slowly approaching the alley leading five riderless horses, caused the hair on the back of his neck to stand on end. Trouble. He could literally smell it in the air.

Still shaken by the morning's conversation in the doctor's office, Holt was tempted to spur his stallion on and ignore whatever was taking place at the back of the building. He just started to squeeze his calves against the horse's sides when he saw one of the men pull a shotgun from beneath the long coat and climb the two steps leading up and into the office.

Holt's breath hissed through his clenched teeth. Suddenly he understood what had first alerted him to the danger. It was much too warm a day for anyone to be dressed in heavy overcoats. Stupid idiots. They deserved to be caught if they had to be that obvious.

Quickly, he stepped from the saddle and hitched his horse to the nearest rail. He grabbed his rifle from the scabbard as a backup for his pistol. A man going up against a scatter-gun needed all the help he could muster. He also mentally tallied the positions of a secluded knife and derringer.

He glanced up, then down the street, as he flattened his back along the siding near the corner of the building. Hardly anyone was about at mid-afternoon, and in a way, he was glad. Fewer bystanders would be innocently harmed.

Leaning only his upper body, he peered down the alley. All he saw was a chorus of swishing tails belonging to the waiting horses. More than likely, he thought, the handler was stationed by the back window while the other men negotiated the business inside.

The one thing that had him most concerned was the number of horses compared to the men he had seen. Five horses. Three men. All of the animals were saddled. Why the extra ones?

He immediately scanned the alley and the rooftops adjoining the building. Were scouts stationed around to protect the others as they made their escape? Perhaps there were more men already inside the express office. Holt saw nothing. Heard nothing.

Once again he looked down the street. A few ladies paraded along the walks, gazing into windows and chatting happily with friends. There was no one he could count on for help.

Taking a deep breath, he eased around the corner. He dropped the rifle to his side and pulled out his pistol, knowing that at close range, the short-barreled .45 Peacemaker would be handier to use. Carefully, but as quickly as he could move without drawing undue attention or making telltale noise, he glided toward the rear door.

He was so close now that he could hear the soft snorts of the bored horses and listen to the creak of leather as one of the animals shifted its hind feet. He smelled sulfur when the outlaw tending the horses lit a smoke. Dust clouded his vision as a sudden gust of wind swirled through the alley.

Nearing the doorway, he crouched and slowed his pace, concentrating on where he placed his feet. The boards were cracked and thin, and could easily creak, or even break, beneath his weight.

His left foot was on the first step when all hell broke loose. Someone pounded on the locked front door. A shout sounded from inside. The shotgun went off, so close to the door that it nearly deafened him.

One of the men wearing a duster burst through the exit and careened into Holt. When he saw Holt's rifle, the man spun back and fumbled for his revolver. Holt fired. The outlaw grunted and slid down the wall, his hands emptying of weapons to clutch at his belly.

Holt cleared his mind of the downed man and ducked into the office, the stock of his rifle braced on his hip, his pistol held steady at arm's length in front of him. Bullets whizzed past his head. He dropped to one knee, holding his fire until he could tell who was friend or foe.

A side window shattered as someone dove through to sure and sudden safety. Holt bent over and halfway crawled to the broken aperture, at the same time snapping a shot back toward the man wielding the scatter-gun.

Amid shouts and moans and whining lead, he poked his head up and quickly peered through the opening, but just glimpsed a denim-clad leg and boot, and barely caught the clank of spurs as whoever it was made his getaway behind the furniture store.

All at once, the front door to the express office caved inward, and several townsmen rushed inside as the two remaining masked outlaws ran out the back. Holt aimed and pulled the trigger, but the only sound was a faint click as his gun misfired. He cursed. Just when it was needed most, the damned gun refused to cooperate.

He shook his head and shrugged, then straightened and looked about the long, narrow room as mental images of his first gunfight flickered before his eyes. A slight shudder inched down his spine. He'd been young enough and fool enough to challenge a man who probably could have killed him, but the other fellow's gun had failed. Holt had won. Bile choked him. Won? That was a detached way to describe the taking of a life, wasn't it?

Damn it all, why was this all coming back to him now? He'd gone a long time without the nightmares and cold sweats associated with his early years as a gunfighter. Why did it have to haunt him now, when his life was beginning to mean something again and he had a ranch to look forward to building?

He realized that one of the express agents was talking to him. He blinked at the man's hazy outline and reholstered his gun as he sought time to put his mind in order.

". . . sure appreciate your help. Another minute and they would have gotten away with the payrolls for two of the mines."

Dr. Foster loomed over the agent's shoulder, still breathing heavily from his sprint down the avenue. "You best reconsider about that job offer, Dolan. This town needs you, and you know it."

Holt sighed and rubbed the back of his neck. He'd always felt he had a lot to atone for. Maybe he did owe it to the place he had chosen to make his home, and to himself, to see if he could pass the muster and really settle in, make Durango a safe place to live, where a man could have friends, maybe even take a wife and raise a family—something he had never thought to be able to consider again.

Finally, he looked into the faces watching him so intently. "I'll think about it." He turned on his heel and stalked toward the back door, past men fingering the broken glass still dangling from the window, by others helping a wounded agent from the floor, out the door and between men gaping at a dead outlaw.

He only stopped long enough to study the cold, set features of the man who had tried to kill him. The fellow was young, too young, in Holt's estimation, to die so violently.

As he walked away, Holt saw visions of the man's

contorted features. Something nagged at the back of his mind. That face was vaguely familiar. But though he tried, Holt couldn't place him. Probably just someone he'd bent an elbow with at a saloon, or something.

Holt shook his head in disgust, thinking what a waste of life as he hurried back to his Morgan. Shoving the rifle into the scabbard, he mounted and turned his horse back down the street.

The sun was low on the western horizon, but he rode in the opposite direction of the depot. The bull could wait another hour. Right now, he felt a desperate urge to see Lorelei, just to make sure she was safe—and to satisfy his own need to know she was there . . . waiting . . . for him.

Lorelei stared at Chad, wondering what he had been doing to be so out of breath. He had come barging into the mercantile, nearly upending two ladies haggling in the aisle over a yard of lace.

Her eyes narrowed. Still shaken over the drawn-out bursts of gunfire, she found herself embarrassed to wonder over Chad's unusual, almost suspicious, behavior. But then she ducked her head and blushed when he looked at her and winked.

"Howdy, pretty lady." When he noticed the frown marring her beautiful face, he added, "Yore a tad out of sorts this afternoon."

His insightful comment immediately changed the focus of her thoughts. She began to rearrange the hats and bonnets she had labored so painstakingly over only yesterday afternoon. "I do not mean to be. It is just . . . I did not get any sleep . . . I mean . . ."

He stepped nearer and took hold of her arm, rubbing his thumb along the soft underside of her wrist. "Hey, don't get all flustered. I was joshin'."

Too embarrassed by what she had almost let slip, she took a step backward. The rowels on his spurs spun in circles as he followed. The tense silence was broken by a sharp series of high yips as two puppies gamboled into the room that was now nearly filled to capacity with merchandise.

The furry animals slid to a sudden stop. Both growled and pounced at Chad's feet. One sank its teeth into the rolled cuff of his denim trousers. Chad just chuckled as Lorelei bent over, attempting to fend off the vicious-as-puppies-can-be-attack.

Out of breath, and red-faced, she grabbed the brown pup's rumbling body when it rocked back on short, unsteady legs, preparing to launch itself at a pant cuff already bearing imprints of tiny teeth. Before she could reach the second sprawling ball of red fur, Mr. Endsley appeared to capture the recalcitrant escapee.

Robert's deep voice cut into the thickness of the air as he shot a venomous glance toward Chad, while directing his words to Lorelei. "Sorry. Got away. Fed 'em something they didn't like, I guess."

As Endsley gathered the miscreants, Chad laughed and good-naturedly reached out to rub the puppy in Lorelei's arms before it was taken away. However, he thought better of the gesture when the pup growled and bared its teeth. "Cain't understand what got into the little bast—uh, dogs. Figured they'd be grateful to the feller what gave 'em such a good home. Huh?"

As Robert and the pups disappeared into the back

room, Lorelei shook her head. "I apologize, Chad. They were just playing."

Once again, Chad moved to Lorelei's side. He tilted her chin up and gazed raptly into her ebony eyes. "Don't matter. I came ta see you, an'—"

The door opened so abruptly that the bells clanked together quite unmusically. A figure loomed into the darkness of the room. Silhouetted by the afternoon sunlight, all Lorelei could see was the outline of a tall, broad-shouldered man wearing a wide-brimmed hat.

As the rangy form glided closer, she felt Chad stiffen. His hand dropped from her face. Her own body thrummed with delight when she recognized the black vest and blue bandana.

She quickly tamped down her excitement. What happened last night would never transpire again. They had each made that decision. It was what they both wanted, whether her newly awakened, traitorous body agreed, or not.

"Holt—Mr. Dolan. This is a surprise. I thought you left town hours ago." She gulped. Could that high-pitched, squeaky voice belong to her?

He towered before them, and she would have shrunk backward but for Chad's support. But her eyes drank in the sight of Holt's beard-stubbled cheeks and firm, thin lips. Those lips that were now drawn so tightly together. And his usually light eyes now literally blazed at her. Why? What on earth could have happened to make him so angry?

Holt's voice was a deep, vibrating rumble, almost like a clap of thunder when he spoke. "Forgot somethin'." Hell, he thought, as he stiffened his shoulders, he should have known better than to hurry to Lorelei.

She would never think to worry over *him* when she had a young, handsome man paying court to her. Damn it all!

Meanwhile, Lorelei's face turned chalk white as she wound her fingers together. Dear heavens. What could he have forgotten? The first thing that came to her frantic mind was a pair of balbriggans, but then she distinctly remembered him pulling them on over long, leanly muscled legs and hard, round buttocks. . . .

Her color returned so quickly that she swayed and felt Chad's thin arm graze the side of her breast. Like someone who had accidentally stuck a finger into a flame, she jumped aside and nearly reeled with relief when Holt's intense gaze shifted to Chad. It would have been impossible, she knew, but she could have sworn those same eyes suddenly turned the color of a bank of billowing storm clouds. The image caused her to shudder.

"'Lo, Chad."

The younger man straightened his shoulders and shifted even closer to Lorelei. "Dolan. What do you want?"

Holt splayed his hands atop the thick ridge of his gunbelt. "I came to speak with the proprietress of the establishment. Don't see as how it concerns you a'tall." He smothered a disgusted sigh. Damn it, what was the woman up to? Couldn't she see Chad was thoroughly smitten? Was she trying to lead the boy on? He hunched his shoulders to ease the taut cords in his neck. If her purpose was to spark shafts of jealousy on *his* part, it was damn sure working.

Lorelei instinctively sensed that the situation building between the two men was fast becoming dangerous.

Once, when she had thought their animosity was caused from jealousy, it had seemed cute, wonderful. Now, though, it was as if they only used *her* as the fodder to feed a wrath that was deeper and more terrible than she could ever imagine. The notion left her feeling confused, and even a little hurt.

She had just come to the conclusion that the nearness of Chad's body held little warmth when compared to standing close to Holt. And, as if the young man magically read her mind, she was taken by surprise when Chad's arm wrapped possessively about her waist. She stiffened and pushed his hand away, then felt guilty. He was, after all, about the only real friend she had in Durango.

Chad glared at Holt. "It might be my business. Me an' the pretty lady—"

Angry that they continued behaving like two dogs bristling over a meaty bone, she interrupted, "Are just friends."

Lorelei twisted free of Chad and hastily walked behind the nearest counter, refusing to be in the middle of their confrontation. Children, that's what they reminded her of—two little boys in grown-up clothing.

Looking directly at Holt, her heart tripped over itself as she asked, "Wh-what did you forget?"

He stepped back and leaned his hip against the edge of a table stacked high with cotton flannel shirts. His finger smoothed along the edge of a soft collar.

"To tell you the truth, I've forgotten," he lied. No way was he going to admit his urgent need to come back and take her in his arms and kiss her senseless one last time.

His eyes must have conveyed at least part of the message his lips refused to utter, because Lorelei gasped and gripped the edge of the counter. She darted a guilty glance to Chad, but he was busy, nervously regarding the shelf displaying men's toiletries, shaving items and tobacco.

Her eyes darted back to Holt, even as her body unconsciously leaned toward him. Her brows knitted into a deep frown when her hand traced her suddenly tingling lips. It was so infuriating, to think that even from a distance, he could dominate her senses.

Chad's attention returned quickly to Lorelei, and he shot a smug grin toward Holt as she took a tentative step forward. He put a hand on her shoulder, but she shrugged it away. When he tried to slip his arm about her waist, she twirled around, shooting him an exasperated look. "Please, Chad."

She shook her head, chagrined, when Chad continued making advances. His strange behavior was beginning to bother her. What had gotten into Chad today? He had never acted this possessively before.

Finally, Holt decided to take pity on Lorelei. He could see she truly did not understand that Chad was attempting to stake his claim and that she was unwittingly foiling the boy's every overture. He stepped away from the table and said, "Leave my woman alone. She's not interested."

Lorelei turned startled eyes from Holt, to Chad, and back to Holt. "What?"

But as Holt approached Lorelei, Chad's right hand slid to the butt of his gun. He threatened, "I wouldn't do that if I were you."

Lorelei gasped and, without even thinking about what she was doing, moved in front of Chad, blocking his view of Holt.

"Get outta my way," Chad growled.

Her eyes went wide. "No! And you take your hand off that gun right now, or leave my establishment."

Blue eyes darkened to indigo as Chad shrugged and let his arms drop. He glanced back and forth between Holt's long form, stiff and unyielding with suppressed tension, to Lorelei's huge, pleading eyes. "I have ta. He's sullied yore honor."

Color returned gradually to Lorelei's face, starting from her toes and working up her body as the implication of Chad's remark sank in. However true it might be, though, she couldn't let anything happen to Holt. She argued, "H-he's done no such thing. Why, he . . . he . . ."

She took a deep breath. "He's done nothing I have not . . . wanted." Mortified by her unexpected admission, she buried her face in her hands. How she prayed the boards beneath her feet would suddenly buckle and swallow her into the earth forever. She had never been, nor would ever be, so embarrassed.

And Holt stood there listening and watching like some great lobo wolf, waiting patiently for her to step even farther into who knew what kind of trap. Why didn't he say something? Deny Chad's accusation? But she knew the answer. He was too honorable a man to out and out lie, just like she *used* to be a proper, respectable lady. The air left her lungs in a giant heave. How much she had changed in such a short period of time.

The expression on Chad's face, when she finally dared to look, made her stomach crawl. He was crestfallen, and had such an air of disillusionment about him that she started to reach out, to reassure him that they would always be friends.

He flinched and stepped back so quickly he nearly tripped over his own spurs. His face had turned a blotchy red.

Lorelei pleaded for his understanding. "Chad?"

The frozen set to his blue eyes arrested her approach, but she still held out her hand. He ignored her appeal and turned toward Holt. "This ain't the end."

There was a sadness to Holt's voice Lorelei had never heard before as he answered, "I know."

Chad's hand fell away from his gun as he stalked toward the door. He stopped once, to look back over his shoulder. There was such an intense look of longing, or was it . . . hatred? . . . on his young features that Lorelei nearly sobbed.

When she and Holt were left alone, Lorelei spread her hands and said as if to herself, "I never knew. I always thought—" Her throat closed. She couldn't finish. Friends. That was what she thought of Chad, and had assumed he felt the same.

Holt came toward her, a look of sympathy on his incredibly handsome face.

About that same time, there was a muffled curse from the back room, and again, the pups made a mad dash for freedom. Lorelei tried to block them from Holt, to keep them from attacking, ripping his pants legs and generally causing irreparable havoc.

Her efforts to hold them proved futile as she tripped on the hem of her skirt and had to use her hands to keep herself from falling. The sound of happy yaps drew her frustrated and reluctant eyes to the excited melee.

Instead of growling and circling Holt's feet, the

puppies bounced like hairy balls, scratching at his pants legs, begging for attention. Every now and then, one became unbalanced and rolled backward, only to scramble up and leap again.

She hid a smile at the annoyed look on Holt's face. But her heart flipped into her throat, and her knees turned weak as soft butter when he finally smiled and knelt down to rub the pups behind their ears.

At that precise moment, she knew. She had lost her heart to Holt Dolan. The tough, unflappable cowboy had stolen that tender part of her that she had vowed would never be attainable to any man, ever again.

The knowledge literally knocked her legs from under her, and she flopped onto the nearest available crate. Dear heavens. What was she going to do now?

Holt straightened and glanced toward Lorelei. She stared at him with such an unusual gleam in her black eyes that he looked down to see if all of his buttons were closed.

They were. But he felt stupid and like an utter fool anyway. What had gotten into him a moment ago? He had behaved like a jealous idiot, and was both angry and sorry for his unpredictability.

He just hadn't been prepared to find her with Chad when he rushed into the store. So, what *had* he expected? he admonished himself. That she would be waiting, teary eyed, for his return? Hadn't he made it perfectly clear, just that morning, that he would *not* be back?

Holt shook himself. This was ridiculous. His coming back was the act of a crazy man. And now those damned, cute dogs were wallowing at his feet. . . .

"Get these animals out of my way. I've got to get out

of here." Inside, his gut churned piteously as he watched her face crumple. He hadn't meant to sound so gruff and callous. It was just time to leave, and he had this incredible need to do it *now!* While he still could.

Lorelei held herself in check while she gathered up the wriggling puppies. She scolded them unnecessarily when all she really wanted to do was lash out at Holt for stealing her heart, then tromping on it as if it meant nothing at all.

She wanted terribly to sit down and cry, but she held herself stiff and erect. Holt would never know her feelings for him ran any deeper than those of a clerk to a customer. He would never again breach her defenses, and she would never allow him to come as close to her as he had last night.

It was for the best, though she wished the pulsating ache in her breast would stop for just a moment. The mercantile came first. She had to remember that. The store was almost completely filled with goods, yet there were hardly any customers. All of her energy must be directed to making a success of the business. Her pride and self-respect depended upon it.

But when Holt started backing toward the door, mumbling nonsense about hoping everything went well for her, and that maybe he would see her around town sometime, she had to use every ounce of self-possession she could muster to keep from throwing herself at his feet, much like the pups had done, and begging him to stay—for a moment, an hour, forever.

As the door closed firmly behind him, she sagged to the floor, clutching the two puppies to her breast.

One thought spun through her frazzled mind. Why had he come back? Unbearable emptiness welled within her chest when she came up with no plausible answers.

Chad followed two burly smelter workers into a smoke-filled cantina, dodging a door that swung back and nearly hit his shoulder. Searching the dimly lit interior, his eyes skimmed past a young boy plucking an old, cracked guitar and over crowded tables packed so tightly together that fights broke out every time a patron tried to move a chair.

As he walked farther into the room, those sitting closest to the entrance fell silent, to resume their drinking only after he had passed them by. Even then, their voices were lowered, as if afraid to talk loudly would attract his attention.

A dark-haired serving girl, wearing a thin, soiled off-the-shoulder peasant blouse and a calf-length gathered skirt, backed away from a table where she had just gathered a tray full of empty glasses. One of the men ran a grimy hand beneath the full skirt and up her bare leg. The girl spat an oath and spun around, to come face to face with Chad.

Her eyes rounded to the size of a saucer, and her dark features turned deathly pale. The tray tipped. The load clattered to the floor. Shards of glass splattered in all directions, but the girl seemed too frightened to take notice.

Chad's lips curled back from his teeth as he roughly shoved the woman into the owner of the roving hand's lap. "Keep the slut outta my way," he hissed.

The big man gulped and nodded. The girl sat trembling, darting fearful glances between Chad and the bartender. The barkeep shook his head, and the girl stayed where she had landed, with her skirt riding high on her thighs, one breast nearly exposed by the precarious slant of her loose-fitting blouse.

Chad stood and looked unaffectedly at the exposed flesh. Then he shrugged and continued to search the cantina. When he found what he was looking for, he suddenly reached out and ran his hand slowly down the girl's chest until his finger stopped at the frayed edge of gathered cotton. Her flesh quivered. Her nipple, barely concealed by the thin material, hardened. He squeezed the tender nubin—hard. She gasped with pain.

Smiling, he whispered, "Be in my room at midnight." He stared until the terrified woman nodded. "Good."

Other women, struggling under large trays filled with mugs of sour beer and shots of rot-gut whiskey, drew in their breaths and staggered to a halt as Chad passed. He paid them no mind, and gradually, activity returned to normal.

A sneer curved Chad's lips as he surveyed the dingy surroundings. One of these days, he would go to San Francisco and buy his own damned saloon, and drink only the finest liquor. His chest expanded as he took a deep, satisfied breath. It wouldn't be long now. Another six months to a year, and he could buy San Francisco.

When he reached a round table in the far corner, he pulled a chair out from under a small, but tough-looking, miner. The miner's Adam's apple bobbed in his throat as he considered protesting the affront. One of the man's friends put a restraining hand on his shoulder and shook his head. The miner frowned, but went over to lean against the wall and finish playing out his hand of five card stud. His eyes looked anywhere but at Chad.

As if he had forgotten the miner existed, Chad straddled the chair and crossed his forearms over the curved back. Four heavily armed men glanced up and acknowledged his arrival with careless nods.

A huge Mexican, with ammunition belts crisscrossed over his massive chest, spat a brown stream of tobacco onto the sawdust-covered floor. "Wheen we ride?"

"Don't know, Jose. Didn't get the shipment yet." Chad motioned to one of the serving girls, who immediately nodded and went to fetch him a drink.

The men's attention to their cards suddenly waned. They stared meaningfully at Chad, who merely shrugged. "I'll get it. Just got sidetracked, is all."

"Good. Jose owes me enough to start my own bank after that last hand."

Chad watched in disgust as Jose twirled the tip of his stiff, curled moustache. The Mexican's beady, dark eyes bored into those of the skinny white man who'd spoken so bravely. "You want leeeve to collect, Spider? I no have pay a no-good—"

Chad slapped the table top. "All right. Whyn't one of ya kill the other an' get done with it. The rest of us got plans ta make."

The man called Spider glared at the big Mexican, then pointed a long, bony finger toward the street. "What'd the gal say hap'n'd to it?"

"Didn't get ta ask. She had comp'ny," Chad snorted.

The men slunk furtive, questioning glances at each other, as if they weren't used to anyone besting their boss at anything.

"Saw her the other day. Sure is a looker," said another

member of the gang as he sipped at a shot of tequila. He was a small, thin man, of Mexican descent, better dressed and more refined than his compatriots.

Chad gave the man a dark look. "She's a bitch, Miguel. Thought she was dif'rent, but she's no better than all the others. Whores. Try ta treat 'em nice, but women're all whores."

Jose was the one who voiced the question they were all thinking. "Why you no get the stuff today, boss? Who weeth woman?"

For a moment, Jose drew in his breath, and his hand twitched nervously as Chad glared at him. Then four heads nodded in understanding when Chad spat, "Dolan."

The last, and quietest, member of the group, a thick-muscled man with a long, puckered scar that ran the width of his left cheek from the corner of his mouth to the lobe of his ear, snarled, "I'm gonna have ta kill that Dolan. He got Mick today. Gut shot 'im."

Chad leaned across the table, spilling beer and tequila as he grabbed the front of Jack Saunders' shirt. "He's mine! Understand? I'm the one's gonna take care of Holt Dolan. No one else!"

Chapter Ten

Lorelei dusted off the last can on the shelf. The fact that she had cleaned the same shelf and everything else in the store the day before yesterday made little difference to her. Since the confrontation between Holt and Chad over a week ago, neither man had returned to the mercantile.

She hadn't realized until now how much she missed having them around—Chad for his friendship, and the way he teased and made her laugh, Holt because . . . because of the warm way he made her feel inside, because . . . he was handsome and brave and she admired him, and because she . . . loved him.

Wandering over to plop down onto the stool Mr. Endsley had built to use behind the counter, she touched a finger to her mouth. After all this time, she could still feel the imprint of Holt's lips where he had kissed her. Heaven help her, she went weak-kneed every time she thought of the sight of his gorgeous bare body the morning they had made . . . love.

He was so lean and hard and had muscles *every-*

where. And the way he had smiled at her—the way his lips quirked up on that one side. . . .

Where had he been? Was he really going to his ranch and never coming back? Would he never kiss her again? The very thought of not seeing him settled her into a state of depression that she might never shake.

She shivered and hid her face in her hands. When a few moments had passed, she took a deep breath and resolved that she would not let herself fall into the doldrums.

With a defiant shake of her head, she looked around the customerless store and almost retreated again. What was wrong with the mercantile? Why weren't people buying from her? She had stocked everything a person could use or want. If she didn't start seeing some return on her expenses . . . No, she would *not* think about that. Not now.

When Robert emerged from the back room, she called him over. "Mr. Endsley, what are we going to do? We are lucky if one or two customers come into the store a day." She looked out at the bustling streets and the people literally bumping into each other along the boardwalks.

Robert's dour expression softened when he leaned against the counter and gazed at her sad face. He rubbed his chin. "Well, missy, I've given it some thought. Were it me, I believe I'd go next door to that newspaper. Folks seem to set a big store by what they read and see in the durned thing."

Lorelei snapped her gaping jaw closed while Mr. Endsley gave his advice. It was the most she had ever heard him say at one time, besides being a wonderful idea. In fact, she couldn't believe she hadn't thought of it herself.

She also gave the man a long, hard look, as she found herself doing too often. What was there about him that was not as it should be? The question seemed to plague her. Was it the guarded look in his eyes? His dignified manner, so belied by his bumbling actions and speech? She shook her head, knowing the answers were beyond her comprehension—for the time being.

All of a sudden, she jumped down from the stool and threw her arms around Robert to give the startled man a big hug on the way to fetch her reticule. She was going to quit worrying and do something positive for a change.

However, her excitement was short-lived as she walked out of the mercantile and turned toward the newspaper. Mentally counting the remainder of her funds, she hoped advertising was not too expensive.

She straightened the bodice of her dress and patted her hair by the reflection from the window. Then, taking a long, deep breath, she marched down the stairs and across the alley to step boldly into the news building.

A fairly tall woman, maybe just an inch or two shorter than Lorelei herself, turned from a huge oak desk that literally dominated the otherwise small office. Lorelei glanced past the woman. The editor must have either stepped out, or was working in the back.

"Good morning." With ink-stained fingers, the woman tucked a loose strand of reddish-brown hair behind her ears.

Lorelei stared at the lady's unimpressive features—she had a thin nose and mouth and bland brown eyes.

Yet there was such an air of confidence and self-possession about her that Lorelei felt intimidated. "Ah, I . . . need to speak with the editor . . . but if he is not available, I can come back."

"I'm the editor. What can I do for you?"

"Oh. Oh!" A woman? Lorelei knew her bemused expression must appear comical, but she couldn't seem to help it. She smiled. "I am Lorelei Abbott. I own the mercantile next door, and would like to see about placing an advertisement in your newspaper."

As Lorelei gave the details of what she wanted, she couldn't keep her eyes off the editor. And her father said women didn't have heads for business. Just wait until she wrote and told him about *this*.

"Excuse me. Is there something amiss?"

Lorelei realized the woman had caught her staring and flushed with embarrassment. She knew how *she* felt when people came into the store and found out a *woman* ran the establishment. It was quite demeaning.

"I am so sorry. But, it is unusual to find a woman in charge of a business, and I . . . am terribly pleased to meet you."

The editor put her pen down and held out her hand. "Me, too. Name's Catherine Romaine."

Lorelei took the proffered hand and pumped it vigorously, until with a shaky giggle, she released it. "Sorry again."

Catherine smiled and came out from behind the desk. "How've you been doing? Can't say I've heard much about you, or the mercantile, lately."

Sadly, Lorelei said, "Business is not so good. That is exactly the reason I came to you."

Catherine rubbed her hands together. "Well, I'll do

my best. Let's see, maybe we can come up with a fancy, eye-catching design."

"Wonderful!"

A gunshot reverberated from the street. Lorelei jumped, then glanced, disconcerted, toward the stalwart editor, who was drawing on a slip of paper and never even moved a muscle. She questioned, "Doesn't it scare you, to have a gun fired almost in your front door?"

Catherine shrugged and reached inside a desk drawer for her Smith and Wesson. "No, I'm not afraid, as long as I have my own protection."

Lorelei nearly choked when the woman patted the cold piece of iron almost fondly. Before she could vent her abhorrence of the weapon, Catherine snorted and complained, "Better get used to it if you're going to stay in Durango."

Color flushed Lorelei's cheeks. Holt Dolan had used almost those same words when she had first arrived. She twined her fingers in the folds of her skirt to keep from thoughtfully chewing her abused nails.

The editor's eyes narrowed. "Wouldn't have to see to our own justice if we had a decent sheriff, but the mayor hasn't figured out a way to persuade the man, yet. He will, though, or at least he better. We have to have some law enforcement, fast as the town is growing. . . ." Catherine's thoughts seemed to trail off as she stared through the filmy window.

Lorelei shuddered as another shot sounded, this time from much farther away. She turned anxious eyes to Catherine. "It seems as though you have a certain man in mind. Will he not take the job?"

"Doesn't appear too interested. He was a bit wild in

his younger days, from all I've heard and read. Even tamed a town once, before he went back East. But he's made a good man. Holt is just what Durango needs."

"H-Holt? Are you talking about Holt Dolan?"

"Why, yes, of course. Do you know him?"

"Well . . . we have met." Lorelei had to bite her tongue to keep from plying the woman with a million questions about Holt. Wild? Tamed a town? She thought of the gun he wore low on those slim hips. He must be quite good with the weapon.

Her heart sank to the pit of her stomach. They wanted Holt to be sheriff. He would be in constant danger—could be killed, just like Frank. But then she remembered his confident, easy manner. She had lost her heart to a man who put on a gun with no more thought than donning an overcoat.

"Miss Abbott?" When Lorelei turned startled eyes on the editor, Catherine blushed. "Forgive me. I didn't know if you heard me. But do you think you could help us talk to Mr. Dolan? *Anything* you could do . . ."

Lorelei's eyes burned. "Wh-what could *I* possibly do?" She tried to swallow, but found her throat terribly dry. Several ideas crossed her mind as to *what,* indeed, she might do to persuade Holt, and they all caused a riot in her lower belly. Heat surged through her body. Her face flamed as red as the handkerchief she had hastily stuffed into her reticule just that morning.

Catherine's alert, brown eyes noticed Lorelei's discomfort, and she waggled her brows. "I didn't mean for you to seduce the man. Just bat your eyelashes and, you know, get his attention. Soften him up a little, then mention how badly we need him."

Again, Lorelei's cheeks felt hot as a poker. Need

him? Oh, no, she could *not* say *that*. "Please, Catherine, I would rather not. Getting the mercantile on its feet is my only consideration at the moment." And keeping herself *on* her feet.

Lorelei's eyes darted toward the door. She had to leave before her mind went completely daft. However, when the editor frowned, Lorelei conceded, "*If* the opportunity arises, I might"—she gulped—"bring the subject up."

Catherine beamed. "That's more like it. Now, you go on and skedaddle home, because I think I just saw our man tying his horse to your hitch."

Lorelei's stomach turned a flip-flop. "What? Now? H-he's here?"

"I can't say for sure, but it looked like him. And don't you worry. I'll bring over a sketch of the advertisement before I run the next edition."

Unable to make her feet move, Lorelei gave the woman a sickly grin. "Well, then, I guess I should be going."

Catherine nodded and sat behind her desk, her attention turned to matters of running a newspaper. Lorelei forced herself to open the door, walk out and close it softly. She dared a glance toward the mercantile. Sure enough, there was a beautiful red horse tied in front. Then she looked the other way, sorely tempted to run up the street and hide and never come back.

No! she argued. As a grown woman, she was capable of handling the situation. Hadn't she been depressed for a week because she thought she might never see him again?

But she had made such a fool of herself when they were last together, actually admitting her feelings right in front of Holt and Chad. Her knees began to twitch. She had never professed to being uncommonly brave.

Holt tied the Morgan to the rail in front of the mercantile. He tilted his Stetson to the back of his head and sifted his fingers through his flattened hair. What in hell was he doing here?

He had no more than turned Sir Dominick into a small, grassy pasture, and vowed to get to work on the broken boards in the hay loft, when he found himself saddling his horse and riding hell-bent-for-leather into town.

For over a week, he had tried to get back into the peaceful routine of the ranch. When he sat in front of the fire at night, instead of a satisfied tiredness enveloping his weary body, he experienced a disquicting loneliness that kept him irritated during the day and sleepless at night.

He brushed the dust from his trousers as he stepped onto the walkway in front of the mercantile. Snow already covered the high peaks surrounding his homestead. Since he and his neighbor had helped each other get their winter hay stored, things were pretty much under control around the ranch. But even as he entered the store, it grated on his nerves that he was there, in town, to see Lorelei. What had come over him? Why had he left the one place he most wanted to be, now, and forever?

Holt shrugged, unable to find a satisfactory answer to his dilemma. He found Robert Endsley standing by the counter, and had warily greeted the man and tiptoed through a muddle of squirming pups, when they both noticed Lorelei slowly walk to the door, reach for the latch, then turn and scurry down the boardwalk. The last thing they saw was the flare of her skirt as she ducked into the alleyway.

"Well, I'll be." Robert scratched the top of his head, his fingers pushing aside his thinning hair.

Holt doused the beginnings of a smug grin and dug into his pocket. Pulling out a half eagle, he handed it to Endsley. "Why don't you take the mutts for a long walk." Then, surprising even himself, he bent and rubbed the pups behind their floppy ears.

Enders looked at Holt, at the money, and frowned.

Of course, Holt noticed the scrutiny. "No need to worry. I just want to talk to Lor—Miss Abbott, alone, for a while."

After long seconds of staring Holt directly in the eye, Enders held out his hand. Then, in keeping with his part, he bit down on the coin before flipping it in the air and bustling the pups from the store.

Holt found himself wondering over the man's protective nature concerning Lorelei, but he had a gut instinct Endsley could be trusted, and was glad to know there was someone else looking after her.

As soon as Endsley was out of sight, Holt went over to lock the front door. After that chore was completed to his satisfaction, he hurried through the piles of goods and into Lorelei's private room. He had just reclined on the bed, stretching his arms over his head, using his palms for a pillow, when he heard a key grate in the rear lock.

He watched, barely breathing, as Lorelei slipped through the door. She darted a quick look toward the main room, then rested her forehead on the thick pine portal as she heaved several deep breaths.

Just as she turned to enter her quarters, he drawled, "You're not tryin' to avoid me, by any chance, are you?"

Lorelei screamed, dropped her reticule, and clutched frantically at her pounding chest when she saw who was in her room, and where.

Her voice was a reedy whisper as she stammered, "Wh-what are you d-doing here?"

He cocked an amused brow. "Answer *my* question first."

Color returned to her face faster than a fat jack-rabbit could run from a hungry wolf. "I-I don't know what y-you are talking about. I am not avoiding any-one. I-I need to . . . to . . ."

From the smile on his arrogantly handsome face, she knew he wasn't believing a word. "Oh, all right. If you are so smart, and know I don't want to see you, then why not respect my wishes? Why come into my room like . . . like . . ." She stomped a slippered foot. "What will Mr. Endsley think, for heaven's sake?"

"I gave him a well-deserved afternoon off."

"I beg your pardon? How dare you? You have no right."

His hand snaked out and snatched her wrist. He jerked, and she fell forward to land with a bone-jarring thud astraddle Holt's stomach. Air whooshed from his chest. The end of his nose touched the delicate tip of hers. Though the distraction was great, he fought to concentrate on her angry words.

She was right. He had no rights where she was con-cerned. Didn't want any. His eyes shifted from the curve of her cheek and her full, pouting lips, to the cracked ceiling, giving thanks that she hadn't fallen an inch or two lower, before he glowered at her.

He attempted to move to a more comfortable position, but stopped immediately when the pointed tips of her breasts nuzzled against his chest. To keep his mind from delving into the pleasures her tempting body offered, he dredged up a feeling of indignation at her accusation.

What was she up to? Was she trying to trap him into saying something stupid? Maybe into making a commitment? Though the bulge between his legs throbbed with his need of her, he would *not* be led around by the . . . nose. He did not want, or need, a permanent woman on his hands, especially now.

Lorelei was suffering almost as badly, if not worse than Holt, lying atop his lean, muscular body. Blood surged through her veins as hot as a bowl of chili at Mr. Torres' restaurant. Finally, she sighed. "What do you want? Really?"

His mind went crazy, listing everything he would like to have from her. But he was amazed at the words that blurted past his lips. "I'd like for you to go to dinner with me."

The toe of his boot scraped the floorboards as one leg dangled over the cot. Damn! What had possessed him to make that fool invitation? Hadn't he just decided it was a mistake to be here in the first place?

Her eyes narrowed. "That's all?"

"That's all." Yes, that was all. And then he would bring her back and ride to the ranch for all he was worth.

Relief flooded her, and a disappointment she had to fight to control. Dinner. Did she dare? Before she had a chance to think rationally, she found herself answering, "That would be nice."

Then she thought of the disturbing conversation with the newspaper woman. "Why are you back in Durango? I thought you were going home, to your ranch."

Though Holt was unaccustomedly excited that she had accepted his invitation, her question sobered him immediately. Indeed, why was he back? And how could he explain it to *her* when he couldn't satisfy his own curiosity concerning his unpredictable behavior. Sometimes his insides felt like he was being torn in a hundred different directions.

Lorelei watched as changing emotions flickered across Holt's face. Was he seriously planning to become the sheriff in Durango? Had he only come to purchase supplies? Her heart thumped against her rib cage like a child beating a drum. Or had he, perhaps, come back to see *her?*

No, she dare not hope. Besides, if he did choose to use his gun, to take lives, there could be no future for them. But a niggling ripple of anticipation eroded the core of her hardened heart. What if he really had feelings for her? Could she turn him away so easily? Deny herself the pleasure of being near him—loving him—whenever possible?

Holt ran his hands up Lorelei's arm, marveling at the fineness of her bones. She was tall of build, independent in nature, and yet, so fragile. "You know, I went home, then realized I couldn't stay."

Lorelei's heart skipped a beat, then another. Her breath clogged her throat.

"Yeah, I forgot to pick up grain for Dominick."

She finally swallowed what seemed like a rough-skinned watermelon. Even as her chest caved inward, grating against her backbone, she tried to convince herself that it was ridiculous to feel so devastated. What had led her to expect more?

"Who?" Her voice came out in a husky whisper.

"The bull. The reason I stayed in town so long in the first place." He gritted his teeth. It took every bit of his willpower to keep from admitting that *she* had eventually taken precedence over everything, including his prize animal.

He shifted his hips in an unsuccessful attempt to erase any evidence of her power over him—his body, and his mind.

Lorelei cleared her throat and shivered as tingles ran the length of her arm. Even knowing that she meant nothing to the man, she liked it when he touched her—too much. "Ahem, I better get ready if you still want to go to dinner. Wh-what time did you plan to come by for me?" Sensing he was close to backing out of the invitation, she forged directly ahead. She needed that time—any time—with him.

Holt couldn't help but laugh, though it sounded constrained, even to his own ears. He loved her shy sensitivity, and the way her nose was the first part of her beautiful body to turn red when she blushed, and—Good God! When had he started thinking of Lorelei using the descriptive connotation of "love"?

No, no! It was a slip of the mind. He hadn't meant it literally.

Then he looked into the black, black depths of her eyes. Or had he? Was that the reason he couldn't stay away from her? Why he didn't have a moment's peace when he wasn't with her?

His stomach knotted. His heart thundered until he felt his chest would explode. The wound throbbed, though it was nearly healed, unconditionally reminding him that the woman meant trouble, in more ways than he was willing to consider at the moment.

Suddenly, he set Lorelei off of his lap and jumped to his feet. He had intended to stay right where he was until time to go eat, and if that time had come after a few hours spent making beautiful love, so much the better. But the turn of events dictated he make a hasty exit. And it would prove that he damn sure *could* leave her, any time he wanted.

"Uh, I'll stable my horse around back. Be ready in half an hour."

A puzzled frown furrowed Lorelei's brow as she nodded her acceptance of the *order* at his retreating back. What on earth had gotten into the man? She had just decided that this would be a perfectly good time to broach the subject of his taking the sheriff's job, and he decided to up and leave on a second's notice.

Men!

Holt took Lorelei to Delmonico's for supper. He had packed a dark brown corduroy coat and gray vest in his bed roll, and the landlady at the boardinghouse had pressed them both for him.

As they entered the restaurant, Lorelei immediately noticed that almost every woman in the crowded room cast surreptitious glances in Holt's direction. She sighed. Why not? He was gorgeous. His hair was only a little darker than his coat, and his eyes perfectly matched the shiny vest. And those trousers hugged his lean hips and long, muscled legs like a second layer of skin. She had to really concentrate to keep her eyes averted from the subtle outline of his masculinity.

She couldn't help the feelings of pride and superiority to be seen in his company, yet had extremely unladylike urges to scratch out the eyes of any woman who dared to gape at him. She fanned her lace handkerchief in front of her suddenly warm face and neck.

Holt handed her into a chair, all the while gazing with rapt admiration at her form-fitting, pale blue gown. How he longed to remove the damned fichu, or whatever that piece of material draped about her neck was called. It completely blocked his view of what he could tell was a low, scooped neckline.

With her back turned to him, he used the opportunity to glare at the men openly ogling her. The next person who so much as raised his eyebrows was going to get a mouthful of knuckles.

His eyes greedily roamed down her back, noting the smooth, delicate outline of soft material against even softer flesh. His fingers itched to slide down and caress the shape of her corsetless spine. And with that knowledgeable observation, he decided she was even smarter than he thought. Sometimes, he didn't understand how a woman could take a good breath hitched into one of those awful contraptions.

His eyes once again rose to survey the dining room. Benevolence overcame him as he studied the rest of the fellows present. Poor devils. He had the most beautiful woman in town on his arm. They knew it. He knew it. Let them look. Tonight she was his.

He hesitated, then acknowledged, yes, by damn,

tonight she belonged only to him. An empty sensation sank into his chest and belly. Just tonight? Somehow, someway, he wanted more. And as her eyes gave him another thorough once over, he hung his hat on the back of his chair and blessed his lucky star that he had spent the two bits on a bath and shave.

When he took his seat across from her, he was nothing but smiles and charm. It was important that Lorelei have eyes for only him.

The waiter approached, and Holt ordered a bottle of wine to start their meal. The special was steak, potatoes and gravy, and green beans, including apple pie for dessert. He was afraid it would be too heavy a meal for a lady, but Lorelei nodded her avid approval.

In fact, Lorelei's mouth literally watered as the young man read the contents of today's special. Compared to the little meals she knew how to prepare herself, steak and potatoes sounded heavenly, and filling.

Holt poured the wine and handed her a glass. Their fingers touched when she reached out, and his lingered until she had a good hold on the stem. The sensation of his rough calluses sliding across her smooth skin sent shiver after shiver racing down her spine.

The quivering she could stand. It was when she happened to glance into his eyes that she knew she had made a mistake. A pleasant meal was not the safe outing she had thought it would be. She felt as if she were sitting naked across the table from him, so intense was his gaze.

Light from the chandelier flickered over their table. Holt's features wavered near, then seemed to fade. Lorelei found herself leaning forward. His lips quirked and brows slanted in that certain way that caused her stomach muscles to flutter.

All of a sudden, she blurted out the first words that came to mind, which had been on the tip of her tongue since the evening began. "I met Catherine Romaine, the editor of the newspaper, this afternoon."

She nearly choked on a gulp of the wine. His eyes had narrowed. He was frowning at her.

"I know the lady." Holt felt as if he had swallowed a rattler and it was slithering through his insides.

"She seems like a very nice person." Lorelei reconsidered mentioning the prospect of his becoming sheriff. After all, she hoped he would not take the position.

Then, as if her thoughts conjured the woman, Catherine swooped upon their table. "Why, good evening, Holt. And Miss Abbott. How nice to find you both together." Her voice lowered as she leaned toward Holt. "I don't suppose Lorelei's asked you whether you've given the mayor's proposition more thought?"

Lorelei's hand fluttered in front of her breast, then fell into her lap, where she gripped the soft chiffon skirt until the material crinkled between her fingers. "No. No, I have not."

Holt sank into his chair. So that was why Lorelei had so readily agreed to join him tonight. The two women had conspired against him. She was planning to use her many feminine wiles to cajole him into becoming Durango's next practice target.

He smiled up at Catherine, if you could call the merest twitch of his lips a smile. "No, she hasn't gotten around to it, yet, Catherine. But, how very . . . pleasant . . . to see you again."

Lorelei's smile felt frozen on her face as she glanced

between Holt and Catherine. If only she'd had the chance to say her piece first, before Catherine happened along. It was easy to surmise, from Holt's stiff features, that the evening was ruined. His face was completely blank. She could read nothing of his feelings.

She did not notice when Catherine left. The waiter brought their plates, but the few bites she put in her mouth tasted like sawdust. The hunger she had experienced earlier in the evening now churned like sour milk in her stomach.

Holt just barely took her arm as they left the restaurant and immediately walked toward the mercantile. The brisk pace did not allow time to stargaze, and she was at a loss for anything to say that would put the mischievous sparkle back into those pale gray eyes.

Holt felt incapable of speech. He was angry over the idea that Lorelei could stoop so low as to betray him. Though why he had expected better of her, he couldn't say. It brought back all of the unpleasant memories of his wife. And, too, a bitter taste was left in his mouth because his well-laid plans for the evening seemed to have trailed in Catherine Romaine's wake as she'd made her grand exit from Delmonico's.

Lorelei had also turned reticent, and he was unable, and maybe even unwilling, to put the evening to rights again.

When they reached the door to the mercantile, Lorelei had to hunt through her reticule for the key. Her fingers didn't want to function. Finally, Holt took them from her. She flinched when his fingers brushed hers. The sensual tingling that had suffused her in Delmonico's seemed to have vanished as quickly as a morning fog on a sultry day.

Holt sighed. Damn it all, why had everything gone wrong? But as he put the key into the lock, the door pushed open of its own accord. His body stiffened. He suddenly grabbed Lorelei's shoulders and shook her as he demanded, "Wait right here. Don't come inside until I call you. And if there's gunfire, run like hell!"

Chapter Eleven

Lorelei stood outside and waited, her hands clasped tightly together, her heart in her throat. Her mercantile. What had happened inside? How had the door gotten open? Holt had locked it himself when they left to go eat. Images of the worst possible scenarios flashed across her mind.

Bumps and thumps and mumbles and curses drifted through the open doorway. Several times, she started to run inside, but remembered the fierce shake Holt had given her. She shifted her weight back and forth from one foot to the other. One more minute, that was all he would get.

Just as a light flickered to life inside the store, she caught sight of a lone figure illuminated in the doorway of the saloon across the street. Chad. He lifted a hand and flicked the brim of his hat in a mock salute. She blinked, but when her eyes reopened, the entrance was empty. The hair along the back of her neck stood on end. The swinging door was perfectly still. Had she only imagined him?

She clutched her cloak more closely about her shoulders and flinched as Holt called her name. His voice betrayed his own anxiety, and she wondered how long he had been waiting for her.

As anxious as she had been to enter the mercantile, she now went in slowly, taking cautious steps as she scanned the mess littering the floor. Everything that she had spent hours stacking and folding was strewn over the floor or dumped in front of the stripped shelves.

It felt as if she were in a daze as she walked about the aisles, stepping over shirts and blankets and canned goods. Of all the things she could have imagined happening, such as running out of money or having to sell the place, this was the last thing she had expected.

Someone had come into her store, her home, and touched everything she owned. Not only had they touched, they had destroyed, and she was devastated. All of her hopes and dreams were dependent upon her making a success of the mercantile. Now her entire inheritance was demolished.

"Whoever did this must have seen or heard us comin'. Looks like he left in a hurry." Holt failed to hide his disgust as he looked around the room.

Lorelei turned to look at Holt. His craggy features were shadowed, then highlighted to a deep bronze by the lantern he held at arm's length. Thank heavens he had been with her tonight. If she had come back alone, and found the intruder still here . . . or what if she had been here, and whoever it was had come in anyway?

She returned to the front to search through the items scattered around the counter. Shaving mugs and brushes, wallets, belts, tobacco, soap and toilet water were strewn on the floor. All of the breakables were smashed, the liquid soaking into the dry wood. As she contemplated the cost of the damage, and what it would take to replace everything, her stomach twisted.

The more she looked, though, the more puzzled she became. "Nothing seems to be missing."

Holt, who had been following her with the light, sat down on the stool. He, too, looked perplexed. "What about a cash box?"

"That was the first thing I checked." She walked over to a lady's hatbox and pulled out a tin wrapped in silk ribbon. "There was nothing in it, anyway. Business has not been—" she stopped abruptly, unwilling to burden him with her problems.

Holt got up and stepped across a fragrant pool of something-or-other. A horrible sense of foreboding tautened his nerves. He had found the mercantile in much the same disarray when he'd discovered John's body. He rubbed the back of his neck where a nagging pain seemed to have suddenly settled. Thoughts of finding Lorelei, injured, bleeding, perhaps even dead, like her uncle, were more than he could bear.

He cursed under his breath. His mind had just been made up for him. He would take the job of sheriff, if for no other reason than to protect Lorelei. He would find the man who did this—and bring down John Abbott's murderer at the same time.

Lorelei lifted her skirt to step over a pile of broken glass and walked slowly toward Holt. She felt as if she were dreaming, and that when she awoke, everything would be right again.

But it was not a dream. A sense of outrage flooded

her being. How dare someone do this to her. How dare they break into her store, her home, and wreak such malicious havoc. Under the circumstances, she thought she had borne up fairly well so far, but when Holt's sympathetic gaze engulfed her, and he opened his arms, the moistness in her eyes turned to rivulets of tears as she rushed to him for the comfort she needed, craved.

Her arms crept around his waist, and her hands pressed into his tautly muscled back. His heart thudded rhythmically beneath her cheek. He was solid and secure, and she felt safe for the first time since stepping into the mercantile.

Holt held her tight against him. His hands rubbed up and down her arms and back, creating a friction that warmed him, as well as her. He bent and nuzzled the top of her head. Funny, he had always associated the scent of lemon with something tart or sour, but not anymore. Lorelei was sweet and cuddly, and he knew for a fact that she smelled faintly of lemon from her hair clear down to her toes.

When she grasped his shoulders and stood on tiptoe with her lovely face tilted up to his, he groaned. The invitation was in her eyes and lips and the sensuous sway of her body. The cleft of her thighs cupped his masculinity and he was lost—or, maybe, found.

He swept her into his arms. Two long strides carried him over to kick the front door closed, and in a matter of seconds, they stood in her room by the foot of the narrow cot. How he wished the bed was even smaller. Tonight, he wanted to be so close to her that he would feel her imprint against him forever.

When he looked back to Lorelei, there was such a tender expression on her face that his stomach convulsed. His arms wrapped around her, squeezing until she moaned.

His grip loosened so quickly that Lorelei nearly toppled backward. She smiled at the horrified look on his face.

"I didn't hurt you, did I? God, Lori, I never meant—"

Taking his sweet face between her palms, she reached up to kiss him on the mouth, effectively cutting short his apology. "Does that feel like you hurt me?"

Relief flooded Holt like the gurgling current of a full creek lapping against a stony bank. He swung her off her feet. "I'm glad, sweetheart. I'll never hurt you. Never."

Lorelei thrilled at the endearment. She felt warm and special as he held her next to him. Their bodies, though separated by layers of clothing, molded together perfectly. She wished that they could be like this forever.

Whether it was wrong or not, she was glad he was here, her haven in a world gone suddenly awry. She needed him tonight, to help her forget the mercantile and what would come tomorrow, assessing the aftermath. She needed to feel secure and, no matter the consequences, loved.

Holt pushed her coat from her shoulders with trembling fingers. It was just now dawning on him that Lorelei could have been hurt tonight if she'd been there when the intruder broke in. A deep, dark anger lodged in his soul. There was a chance that her life was in very real danger, and as he gently unfastened the buttons lining her bodice, he vowed to protect her with his own.

They helped each other from their clothes, and when they stood, naked and revealed, Lorelei stared with awe at the bare expanse of sculpted masculinity displayed as if for a private feast to her eyes and senses. He was magnificent. From his shiny, jet-black hair, to his aristocratic features, broad, broad chest, flat, ridged belly, narrow hips, and long, tapered legs, to his arched feet.

And last, but definitely not least, to that part of him jutting from the apex of his corded thighs; that part of him that pulsed with life, and nudged insistently against her bare abdomen. Magnificent did not come close to a proper description. No one word could.

Holt's voice was a husky whisper in her ear. "God, Lori, you're beautiful. Even more so than I remembered." In his dreams, she was perfection, but in real life, standing naked before him, she was a goddess. And tonight she was his, to hold and to protect and to cherish.

Lorelei shyly lowered her lashes. "I was thinking the same about you."

He lifted her and laid her on the bed as if she were made of fine porcelain. Lying down beside her, he ran his fingers through her hair, scattering pins in every direction as the long tresses fell free. Then he smiled. "No one's ever thought I was beautiful."

There was amusement in his voice, but Lorelei could tell he was truly touched from the soft hue of his eyes and the way his mouth thinned to a fine line. She felt as if liquid fire danced through her bones, and was glad she was the first to do something so memorable, so simple, for him. Perhaps he would remember *her* sometime, somewhere, in the future. With fondness? Maybe even a touch of love?

Tears blurred her vision. The future. Was there any hope that the two of them might share it? From the way he touched her, loved her, she thought it could be possible.

Holt gasped when Lorelei's hands began to move over his body like fluttering butterfly wings, touching here, caressing there. Her lips tasted and tantalized until he writhed in pleasurable agony. He groaned, "Damn it, Lori, if you ever want to torture a man, you've found the way to do it."

She teased against his flat male nipple, "Torturing is too good for you, mister. Do you give up?"

He suppressed a moan of pure defeat. Give up? Give up what? His body? His soul? His heart? His love? Damn it, but the minx already had it all.

He twisted, rolling her gently beneath him, and trailed languorous kisses from the satin undersides of her breasts to the dainty arches of her ticklish feet. He'd never enjoyed bringing a woman to the peak of pleasure quite as much as he did this one cute, cuddly, passionate creature.

Gritting his teeth when her slender fingers curled tentatively around his manhood, he beseeched, "Now who's goin' to give," as if *he* were the one in control.

Lorelei was nearly out of her mind. Her teasing had backfired tenfold. At any moment she would disintegrate into a million flaming pieces. "I give. Please, Holt. Now." As far as she was concerned, it didn't matter who gave first, because either way, they both won.

As he entered her, Holt wondered if she truly gave as much as he, but then all rational thought floated from his mind when he felt her warm sheath take him inside, to a soul-shattering depth, to the most beautiful, satisfying, experience of his life.

Lorelei bucked beneath Holt, feeling every inch of him to the core of her being. A different kind of tension began to build. She felt like a coil held taut by a thousand-pound weight, which when suddenly lifted, allowed her to spring free, to glide up and up to a mind-dazzling height.

Drifting back to earth, light as a feather, she couldn't help but smile. Then everything went black and fuzzy.

At first, Holt thought that Lorelei had fallen asleep, but as he rolled over and pulled her with him, of a mind to hold on to her always, he noticed the unusual limpness of her limbs. He frantically shook her shoulders and patted her cheeks. "Lori! Good God, Lori! Speak to me. You can't leave me. You can't."

Her eyelids fluttered. A weak hand lifted to rub at her tingling nose. Then her glazed black eyes drifted up to meet his stormy gray ones. Her voice was weak, but deep and throaty. "Hello."

A relieved grin spread across Holt's lips and shone from his eyes. "Hello, yourself. Are you all right?"

The anxiety in his voice caused Lorelei to frown. "I have never been better. Why?"

He kissed her forehead, her eyes, her nose, her cheeks and lingered for a time over her soft, moist lips. "Oh, nothin'. Just wondered, is all. I've never had a woman faint on me before. It's kinda scary."

Her eyes widened. "Faint? Me? You must be mistaken. I have never fainted—not once—in my whole—"

"I know, your whole life. You've lived so long, and experienced so much."

She sniffed. "Yes, I have."

He yawned and hugged her close, snuggling her head against his shoulder. "Go to sleep, Methuselah. We can talk later."

Dawn's first brilliant rays peeked through the cracks on either side of the back door. Lorelei snuggled her nose under the cover, delighting in the warmth radiating from Holt's large body. How nice it would be to wake up like this every morning, with the man of your dreams holding you close.

She muffled a heartfelt sigh. Holt had made glorious love to her over and over during, what had seemed to her, a very short night. If she hadn't been before, she was now, deeply, hopelessly, in love. And though it meant she might be laughed at, or even spurned, she felt it necessary to tell him how she felt. It was a secret she could not bear to keep, one that threatened to burst from her lips with wild, passionate aplomb.

Tempting as it was to stretch her cramped limbs, Holt's arms held her too tightly, and she didn't want to wake him. It would have been nice to turn over and look at him, to run her fingers through his tousled hair and kiss his eyes open; but the bed was too small, and they were wedged together like two spoons.

So, she did the only thing she could think of to *arouse* his attention. She pressed her back against his chest and wriggled her bottom into his belly and thighs. He stirred, but then his breathing became even deeper. She wriggled again. A slight bulge nudged her back.

Lorelei grinned. At least one part of him was alert and rising. Heat radiated throughout her body. She should have been ashamed of the way she behaved last night, the things she had done, what he had done to her. Her toes curled at the memory. It had seemed right, though. Felt right. And shame was the last thing on her mind.

Suddenly a hand inched forward to squeeze her breast. Fingers pulled at her tender nipple. Warm breath teased the wisps of hair curling in front of her ear. "What made you stop, darlin'? I kinda like the way you wake a man of a mornin'."

Holt's other hand splayed across her belly, tugging her more tightly against him. By now, a stiff rod poked her buttocks. She giggled. "You were not asleep at all, were you?"

"I was thinkin'."

"Thinking? You? After last night, I could have sworn you were a man of action." She bit her lower lip. Good heavens! How had she come up with the nerve to say such a brazen thing? This was not like her at all. Not at all.

Again, she felt the urge to turn and face him, but his hands caressed her so wondrously. . . . Then he rested his chin in the hollow between her neck and shoulder. She shivered as the overnight stubble of his beard teased her sensitive flesh.

Perhaps it would be best to say what she had to say with her back turned. She wouldn't have to see his face or look into his eyes to know if he was pleased or angry. When his fingers delved between her thighs, she hissed in her breath and squirmed. "Wait. I need to tell you . . . Holt, this is important. I want you to know. . . ."

"S'all right. I know what you're goin' to ask."

"Ask? No, I need to—"

"You can tell Miss Romaine that I've decided to accept the mayor's offer. I'll take the job."

For a moment, Lorelei had a hard time following his train of thought. She was thinking of something else entirely. Then she stiffened. Her stomach knotted. "Wh-what?"

He nibbled the fleshy lobe of her ear. Now that he had made up his mind, he was pleased that his decision would make Lori happy. "I'm goin' to take the sheriff's job."

She struggled to sit up and jerked the rumpled sheet with her. "Why?"

Holt's eyes narrowed. "What do you mean, why? I thought you were supposed to lure me into acceptin'. What's the matter now?"

Tears blurred Lorelei's vision. She blinked them back. "No. Catherine only asked me to find out what you had decided. I-I had hoped . . . to talk you out of it."

Thoroughly confused, he scooted up to lean his back against the wall, caring less whether he was modestly covered, or not. "Let me get this straight. You *don't* want me to take the job."

There was a pinched look to his features when she shook her head.

He frowned. "So, it's my turn to ask, why?"

She turned her head and busied her fingers smoothing out a wrinkle in the woolen blanket. "I abhor violence. And firearms." Her voice faded to a mere whisper. "And people who use them."

Holt's mouth fell open. He could hardly believe his ears. To make sure he understood, he repeated, "Let me get this straight. If I become sheriff, I'll have to use a gun and you won't have anything more to do with nasty ole me."

His entire body, inside and out, felt as if he were stretched out like a hide to dry. God deliver him from womankind. He had just about worked up the nerve to bare his soul and ask the firebrand to marry him. Now she came up with this nonsense. Damn her to hell, and back!

Lorelei blinked. Her jaw worked, but nothing came out. Her heart splintered into a thousand fragments. Couldn't he see how difficult this was for her? Couldn't he try to understand?

Holt's voice rose as he stepped from the bed to pace nude before her. "What if I told you the reason I'm taking the damned job is because of you?" He gave her no time to answer, punctuating his words by poking the air with his fist. "How about what happened here last night? Should I just disregard it and hope no one dares to do it again? And what about John? He was killed when someone broke in. Should we clasp our hands together and cry, 'For pity's sake, surely they won't come back and hurt anyone else.'?"

Lorelei quickly hid her hands beneath the covers. Drat the man! Why did he have to use logic to combat her feelings? She raised her head and stuck her chin out stubbornly. "Guns are not the answer. There has to be a better way to deal with hooligans."

Holt snorted. "Oh, yeah. Pretty please, don't rob me. Please and thank you, don't shoot me."

"You do not have to shout, or be sarcastic. I cannot help what I believe."

He searched for his discarded clothes, pulling on the pieces as he found them. When he ended up with underdrawers and a belt left over, he wadded them up and stuffed them inside his shirt before yanking on his jacket.

"I know this, lady. If you let people get away with thievery and murder, it's an even greater injustice." He put his hat on backward, but was too angry to stop and turn it around as he made his grand exit. "Good day, miss. And good-bye."

Lorelei sat perfectly still. Softly, as a wisp of smoke evaporated in a breeze, she whispered, "Good-bye, my darling." Slowly her face crumpled. Hot tears spilled down her cheeks. Sobs racked her body. When, at last, the torrent was over, she cowered in the blankets.

The door to the mayor's office slammed open. Caught napping after a long night at the card tables, Bob Hennesy nearly slid from his chair, but Holt Dolan never cracked a smile.

"Swear me in, Hennesy. I'll take your damned job."

The mayor sputtered and shuffled busily through a stack of papers. "Uh, well, that's fine. Yes, fine. But this is quite improper. We need to—"

"Get on with it, or I'm leavin'. It's up to you." Holt wormed his belt through two button holes and strapped it around his narrow waist as the mayor tried to make up his mind on which was more important—proper procedure, or getting the town a good sheriff. The sheriff won.

A few minutes later, Holt stood with his right hand upraised, taking the oath to become Sheriff of the city of Durango, Colorado Territory. Though he spoke the words between clenched teeth, he was determined to uphold each and every one of them, whether little Miss Lorelei Abbott liked it or not. Especially, or not!

While the mayor droned on and on, Holt worked up another good rage over the mercantile proprietress's stubborn, hard-headed stupidity. Surely she could see with her own two eyes what would happen if people who cared about the law and rights of others didn't stand up to those who would take advantage of the weak and the helpless.

Someone had to see that right triumphed over wrong. And a little guiltily, he remembered a time when he had ventured on the opposite side of the law. At least he had come to his senses in time. Or to be truthful, he just hadn't the stomach for the outlaw life.

"Here's your badge, young man, and may God be with you." Mayor Hennesy handed over the tin star and shook Holt's hand.

Holt took the piece of metal and pinned it to his shirt pocket. A calm acceptance settled over his features. Determination thinned his lips. Things would be different this time. Durango was another town entirely from the one he had left so long ago.

And he would make sure that Lorelei Abbott departed all in one piece.

A deep sigh deflated his broad chest. Because if she didn't leave, he would damned sure have to.

Chapter Twelve

Lorelei sat on an empty crate, daydreaming about Holt and how wonderful he had made her feel last night. But wasn't it strange how a person could feel so good one minute, then be so down another? All she could think about this morning was that she truly regretted Holt had left angry. Try as she might, through tears or smiles, she could see no other recourse to the situation.

One thing for sure, it was certainly a day for feeling sorry for one's self, she thought.

Earlier that morning, she had barely finished dressing when Mr. Endsley came to work. He had surveyed the mess and pitched in to help her right the shelves and clear the floors, then immediately begged a few days off. Exasperated that he would want to leave at such a crucial time, she had nevertheless relented and allowed him to go, without so much as hinting that his untimely departure would put her in a troublesome situation. Surely he could have seen that much for himself.

She sniffed. Perhaps it was best that she had this time

alone. It was time to face the fact that she had only herself to rely upon. Unless, of course, she decided to throw up her hands and run home to daddy.

As much as she hated to think it, that might be the answer. Boston. She dabbed at her eyes with the damp handkerchief she'd kept handy in her pocket all day.

Boston. It was a place to go. Everything in her life was a shambles. The mercantile had failed to earn any return on her expenditures. Money was running low. She couldn't keep help. Mrs. Westfield had sent another wire stating she wouldn't be back for several more weeks.

Her friends had deserted her. Chad had not come back. Catherine had all but betrayed her, although the editor certainly had no notion of what her words had perpetrated.

Holt . . . no, she couldn't think of him yet. But, then, no time would be right, would it?

Boston. The word held appeal at the moment. Her father would welcome her with open arms. He would hug her and kiss her on the forehead. Then he would say, "I told you so."

Her back stiffened. No, she could never return with things the way they were. Surely *something* would go her way—soon.

The bell above the door jangled merrily. Lorelei scowled. It wasn't right that anything should sound so happy. Not today.

A familiar jingle raked across the floorboards. Her head tilted. Why, she had just pictured his smiling face.

"Shore smells like someone's duded up real fancy in here. That be you, pretty lady?"

"Chad!" She flashed him a welcoming, watery smile

as she nearly fell from the crate in her haste to get up.

"Hey, what's the matter? Why're ya cryin'?" He reached over the counter and took one of her cold hands. A cocky grin curved his lips, though his eyes remained hooded. "Cain't say I haven't brought tears to a lady's eyes afore, but this here's ridic'ylous."

Lorelei sniffled and squeezed his fingers. "I am very happy to see you, really, but this has not been one of my better days."

He wrinkled his nose at the strong aroma of toilet water wafting around him, then bent over to rest both elbows on the counter. "So I can see. Tell me all about it. Mebbe I kin help."

She sighed. "I wish you could. At least most of the mess is cleaned up, and the shelves are—"

"Slow down a mite. What're ya goin' on about?"

"Oh, I guess you haven't heard." She sighed dejectedly. "The mercantile was ransacked last night. It took all day to put everything in order again."

Chad straightened instantly, a look of pure outrage on his young features. "Robbed? Who'd wanna do a dirty thing like that to such a special lady?"

Lorelei flushed. How wonderful to have her friend back again. She really needed to hear his exuberant voice and outlandish compliments. "I have no idea who, or why."

His body eased down into a more relaxed pose. "Well, I hope somethin' is bein' done about it."

It was hard to keep the sarcasm from her voice, but she tried. "Our new sheriff will probably take great delight in hunting down the perpetrator."

"New sheriff?"

"Oh, yes. Just this morning, our . . . friend . . . Mr.

Dolan, took up the badge." She didn't mean to sound bitter, but she had learned the information from Catherine Romaine. Holt hadn't had the nerve to come tell her himself.

Chad thoughtfully rubbed his chin. "Don't say. Does he know 'bout this?"

"Yes, he was here right—" She stopped abruptly, praying that no one would find out she and Holt had been together inside the store last night. The scandal would ruin any chance of her making a success of the mercantile, as if it needed anything else to go wrong. "Ah, he heard me call out just after I found the door, er, ajar."

"Right neighborly of 'im, ta be passin' by at that hour."

She frowned. She didn't think that she had mentioned what time the break-in had been discovered. And there was something else—that vague image she remembered seeing near the saloon.

Chad placatingly held out his hands. "Hey, I don't mean ta say nuthin' bad 'bout the new sheriff. I s'pose he'll be as good a one as any."

Images of Holt's bullet-riddled body flashed before her eyes, and she shuddered.

Chad stuck his hands in his pockets and wandered around the room. "Ya don't happen ta have any t'abbacy on hand, do ya?" He scanned the few items on the shelves.

She rubbed at her weary eyes. Her whole body felt suddenly drained of energy. "Let me see . . . it seems Mr. Endsley mentioned something. . . . I'm sorry. I just cannot remember."

Chad walked over to her. Though she felt the heat

from his body, she was suddenly chilled. But when she looked up, he smiled encouragingly.

"Do ya think it's here some'ere?"

The events of the night and the long day were taking their toll. She was so-o tired. Too tired to think straight. "I honestly don't know." Lorelei rubbed the small of her back and pleaded, "Come back in the morning, Chad. Perhaps by then I will have found it, or know what happened to it."

He backed away a step. "Ya say the hired man had it last?"

"I think so. Anyway, I promise to look for it."

He grinned and tipped his hat before quickly turning to leave. "See ya, pretty lady."

Clifton Abbott crumpled the latest of Enders' telegrams. Damn it all! What was going on out there? Why hadn't his daughter come to her senses? And what did Enders mean that her life wasn't in *immediate* danger, or that some no-account cowboy was looking after her?

Clifton pounded the shiny surface of his desk. If his business ventures weren't so pressing at the moment, he'd go to that spot-in-the-road called Durango and straighten everything out himself.

He narrowed his eyes. Hhmm. Matters in Boston could be tied up within two to three weeks. Maybe he *could* get a first-hand glimpse at just what was so fascinating as to keep that hard-headed girl away from home so long—and to also see what in the blazes Enders was trying to cover up in his tell-nothing missives.

He twiddled his thumbs on his large belly. Just who

was this Holt Dolan? What were his intentions toward Clifton's only daughter?

Four days after Holt had taken the sheriff's job—Lorelei counted the time using that means of measurement lately—she stood behind the counter, totalling another purchase. It was the third customer that day, and several more people were browsing through the store.

She helped the middle-aged woman gather her packages. "Thank you, Mrs. Mendlebaum. It was so nice to meet you. Please come back."

When the lady answered, "I will, my dear, I most certainly will," Lorelei smiled. A ribbon of happiness wound around her insides, until she was tempted to kick up her heels and shout with glee. Before today, she hadn't had three customers during one week.

Her spirits lifted. Swiping a strand of hair out of her eyes, she decided she was tired of feeling sorry for herself. No more hiding in the store and moping. If she was going to make her living with the mercantile, it was up to *her* to get out and see that the townspeople *wanted* to do business in Abbott's.

A glow of satisfaction pinkened her cheeks as she glanced about the busy store. There was no doubt in her mind that the advertisement in the newspaper had brought the people in. Catherine had shown her a copy of the ad yesterday, promising that it would be printed in today's edition. Any anger she had felt toward the editor had dissipated upon sight of the fancy scroll outlining Abbott's Mercantile in large, bold type. Underneath had been a partial listing of items stocked in the store.

Lorelei glanced once more about the almost crowded aisles, and there was a tightening in her chest. The change was miraculous. At a time when she had been about to give up hope, Catherine had come through and made her space something special.

Even Chad had come in again, cheering her morning. However, she had been unable to locate either his order, or Mr. Endsley.

Thinking of the hired man, she couldn't help but worry. He had been so dependable, until just lately, that she had hoped to hire him full time. But what if she couldn't count on him now that business was picking up? He could take off and disappear again at any time.

One of the women in the front of the store suddenly called out to a friend. "Oh, look, Edna, there's our new sheriff. Isn't he the most handsome young fellow you ever saw?"

Lorelei felt like a fist had clenched around her heart. She had done so well the past few days, not thinking about Holt more than two or three times an hour, except during the night, of course, when she dreamed of him constantly.

She took a deep breath and informed herself that she had business to attend to in the back, but unaccountably found herself standing behind the customers, staring across the street as Holt was stopped, over and over, to shake hands and nod as people along the avenue wished him well on his new job.

"It's so good to know there is someone who will protect us now, isn't it, Edna?"

The plump Edna waved a stubby hand. "Oh, my, yes. Why, I've been afraid to leave the house for days at a time. It's about time we had a sheriff in this town who at least *looks* like he can handle the job. Remember that last young whipper-snapper?"

The women moved off through the yard goods, leaving Lorelei alone in the window. A deep pride suffused her as she watched Holt. He really was an impressive figure. Then she sighed. Why couldn't the ladies see things *her* way? It was the use of guns that got people killed. They were just too dangerous.

She swatted at an offending lock of stray hair. Of course, in Holt's view, the use of weapons kept more people safe. Deep down, though, once she really thought about it, stronger than her hatred of firearms was her fear for Holt. If anyone stood a chance of losing his life, it was the man wearing that badge and a six-gun.

Her heart clogged her throat when she noticed he had stopped and was looking directly through the glass at *her*. She held her breath. Would he come over to say hello? Excitement bubbled unbidden in her chest, until he shrugged and continued down the street. Her chin drooped, and her heart felt as if it had torn itself from her breast to follow after him.

Then she shook her head. No! He was not going to do this to her. He had made his choice. She had made hers. If he could behave in such a childish manner, so could she—except the notion was so pathetic, it hurt. Childish. That was exactly the way she had acted. Yet she couldn't deny her firm beliefs. She had felt strongly on the matter of guns for years, and she couldn't just ignore her convictions for Holt's sake—even if he was the man she loved—would always love.

Sadly, she turned and went back behind the counter.

The short, matronly Edna was already there and told Lorelei she had found some lace that would add just the right finishing touch to the new dress she was stitching.

Lorelei's lips curled into the semblance of a smile. The business was what she must concentrate on. It could be fun, if she let it. She would have to make it exciting and invigorating just to keep her sane.

Well after dark, Holt made his rounds of Main Avenue. He looked into one of the rowdier saloons, surprised to find it calm, with most of the patrons involved at the card tables or watching the games, rather than bellied up to the bar.

He hooked his thumbs in his gun belt and wandered on down the street. He was doubtful that fear of a new sheriff in town had quieted things down, but was, nevertheless, grateful that his first few days on the job had gone smoothly.

Except for that one brief moment he had spied Lorelei looking out her window. She had been watching him, and he was certain he had seen the same desperate longing on her face that he had been feeling since the morning he had stormed from the mercantile.

Damn it! He still couldn't bring himself to talk to her for fear he'd rave and rant all over again and try to pound some sense into that hard, gorgeous head. He didn't know what was worse—seeing her, or not seeing her. Either way, she was driving him crazy.

All at once he stopped and looked around, startled to find he had walked all the way to the depot. He stuffed his hands in his pockets and scuffed the toe of his boot into the dust as he continued on.

But a feeling of unrest settled between his shoulders, and he glanced around as the shadows swayed and shimmered with the cool breeze. The sliver of moon cast just enough light to lend an eerie kind of glow to the darkened, outlying buildings and the railroad cars side-railed nearby.

After nearly a quarter of an hour spent checking locked doors and visiting with Tony, he worked his way across the tracks to look toward the river. The Rio de las Animas—the River of Lost Souls. It was an adequate description of the way he felt tonight.

Holt turned and started back, ready to walk the east side of Main. He had just come even with a cluster of small juniper trees when he thought he heard a noise. He stopped and tilted his head. A moment later, he heard a low, moaning sound.

Drawing his pistol, he stepped carefully through the fragrant trees. A groan came from near his left foot, and he quickly spun cocking the hammer as he did so.

A patch of white beneath low-hanging branches caught his eye, and he cautiously moved toward it, nearly tripping over a pair of boots belonging to a pair of long, thin legs. He then heard another, softer, moan. Holt bent low, straining to see, and finally discovered the form of an inert man lying facedown in the rocks and dirt.

Keeping his gun at the ready, he quickly moved to the fellow's head. Dark splotches marred the back of the man's shirt, and when Holt felt for a pulse, his fingers came away dark and sticky with blood.

Holt reholstered his gun and knelt down, striking a

match along the seam of his trousers to get a better look as he carefully turned the man over with his free hand.

Suddenly, the fellow's arm lifted, and his fingers wound around Holt's wrist in a surprisingly strong grip. He whispered, "Miss Abbott. . . ."

Holt rocked back. What? "Lorelei? Are you talkin' about Lorelei Abbott?" Fear knotted his gut. Was she in danger, too?

"Watch . . . after . . . her. . . ." Then the man went limp.

Holt held the match lower and recognized Endsley, Lorelei's hired man. Pressing his fingers to Endsley's neck, Holt was relieved to find a weak pulse. Afraid to leave the man, Holt hefted the long, thin form over his shoulder.

Thinking furiously, wondering what the man's cryptic message could mean for Lorelei, Holt made his way as quickly as possible over the rocky, uneven ground. Once he reached the edge of town, he went down the back alleys to Doc Foster's.

After several loud, rapid knocks, a grumbling, night-shirt clad doctor cracked the door. Holt immediately pushed it open and barged inside. "Sorry to get you out of bed, Doc, but I've got a man here in pretty bad shape."

The doctor lit several lanterns as he led the way to the surgery. When he told Holt to lay his burden on the table, the sleepy glaze was gone from his eyes. "What happened to him?" the doc inquired as he washed his hands in a basin.

"Don't know. He was hidden under some trees near the depot. It's a wonder I found him at all."

As the doctor peeled off Endsley's shirt, silence

settled over the room. After a few minutes, he walked over to the medicine cabinet and returned with several bottles and a jar of ointment. "These are knife wounds. None of the main arteries were severed, but he's lost a lot of blood. Do you know who he is, or if he has any family?"

Holt nodded. "He's a drifter, works down at Abbott's Mercantile." He frowned, wishing he could have just one minute to talk to the man. Then a terrible thought struck Holt. He had always been afraid for Lorelei, but what if he never had the chance to find out what Endsley was trying to tell him. "Doc, is he goin' to make it?"

The doctor wiped his bloody hands on a towel. "Can't say just yet. But it's a good sign he's lived this long."

Holt paced the floor at the foot of the table. His eyes flicked to the door and back several times. "There anythin' I can do to help?"

Dr. Foster looked meaningfully at the unconscious man. "I can take care of him. You've got plenty to do."

"Well, then, I'll check back in the mornin'."

Holt didn't receive an acknowledgment as the doctor bent over one of the nasty gashes on Endsley's back. He quietly let himself out and hurried up the street.

Several doors away from the mercantile, he slowed, approaching cautiously. Most of the surrounding buildings were dark, including the store. The only light shone from the newspaper office.

He stepped up on the walkway and peered through the store window. Too dark. He tried the door. Locked. Walking to the end of the porch, he started down the alleyway between the mercantile and the paper. The scar on his thigh tingled.

He stopped beside the only window along that side of the building and gave the sash a push. It didn't budge. A harder shove. Nothing.

Reaching the rear corner, he stopped long enough to search both ways down the alley, then checked the little lean-to where he'd stabled his stallion one night not so very long ago. Everything seemed in order. Yet he couldn't shake that uneasy feeling.

As he edged toward the back door, he thought he saw a movement, but couldn't be sure. He leaned against the sideboards and slipped soundlessly to the nearest step.

Using only the toes of the soles of his boots, he went up that one step, then the second. He reached for the latch with one hand while drawing his Peacemaker with the other. The door swung open. Holt silently cursed.

Holt lunged through the doorway, and a long, hard, yet slightly flexible, object batted his head. His hat flew off. The thing hit him again. His right hand slammed into the doorjamb, and his numb fingers loosened their grip and dropped the gun.

His arms automatically lifted to ward off the blows as he was struck again and again across the back of his neck and shoulders. Deep, rasping breaths came from the left. When the hail of wallops finally began to diminish, he dove down in an effort to tackle his assailant.

His arms wrapped about a pair of shapely calves. A surprised shriek and a whoosh of breath tickled his ear as they fell. He twisted a long, bent object from one limp hand and groped for the other before he could be attacked again. His fingers grazed a soft, feminine mound. Good God! "Lorelei?"

There was no answer. He started to rise. Suddenly, her one free arm and two long legs pummeled him, but there was little strength behind the swats. At last, he managed to capture both slender wrists and throw his heavy leg over her thighs. "Damn it, Lori, stop fightin' me. It's Holt."

"I-I know wh-who you are. H-how dare y-you . . ." she wheezed, "sneak in . . . into my bedroom."

He bellowed, "Sneak? Me? What in hell was your damn door doin' open at this time of night? Were you expectin' someone in particular? Maybe I interrupted somethin'?"

"O-o-h-h! Y-you . . . you . . . man . . . you!" Lorelei would have merrily scratched his eyes out if she could only free her hands. "Let go of me! This instant."

Holt's nerve endings felt as if they were being pierced by daggers. The heat from her taut body seared his. "Oh, no, my pappy didn't raise any fools. If I let go, you'll beat on me again."

She tried to kick out. Couldn't. Her hips bucked, and she felt a familiar hardness between his thighs, so closely were they locked together. Immediately, she ceased to struggle.

He literally growled in her ear, "What did you hit me with, anyway? I can feel lumps on the top of my head."

She was tempted to retort that the lump *she* was feeling was a far cry from his hard head but, instead, calmly replied, "My parasol. And you ruined it. The brand new one my father gave me just before I left home."

There was such despair in her voice that Holt relented and freed her hands so he could cup her soft cheeks. He promised, "I'll get you another one. First thing in the mornin'."

Lorelei couldn't help but think his offer sweet, until she realized she was partially free and remembered the scare he had given her. All of a sudden she gave a tremendous shove, and he fell sideways, just far enough to allow her to roll from under him.

She leapt to her feet and ran toward the door and a semblance of light, searching, trying to find anything to keep him at bay. If he touched her again, no telling how she would react. Her heart thudded painfully in her breast. More than anything, she wanted to be held in Holt's comforting arms, but knew it would mean disaster to her firm resolve.

The first weapon she saw was his gun, lying so innocently on the floor. Her hand trembled as she reached down. Then, out of the corner of her eye, she caught sight of the battered parasol, and gratefully reached for it instead. She also remembered the puppies locked in the privy. No. The umbrella would have to do. The dogs liked Holt and wouldn't be any help at all.

Lorelei snatched up the parasol and turned, holding it out before her in the manner a fencer would wield an épée. "Stand back," she threatened. "Don't you dare come near me."

Holt had intended to leave, until issued that daring challenge. He grinned, and stood with feet braced wide apart, waiting.

Lorelei, tired from the previous battle, found it difficult to hold up even the light-weight parasol. It dipped, and she immediately brought it up, thrusting it briefly toward him. She stepped back, then forward. It dipped again, and Holt lunged. He grabbed the end and simultaneously gave the thing a jerk.

Caught off guard, Lorelei hadn't a chance to release the handle, and found herself trapped in Holt's arms. She struggled. The effort was costly. Lorelei sagged against the mat of black hair covering Holt's chest. Somehow, she guessed, during their struggles, the buttons had popped from the front of his shirt, baring the broad expanse of flesh to her fingers, which combed greedily through the thick curlicues.

It was perfect. It was right. It was . . . insane. Her head snapped up. What was she doing? She had vowed to stay away from this man. He devastated her good senses with one flip of an eyebrow or a quirk of his lips. He was dangerous.

When his head descended, she sucked in her breath, trying unsuccessfully to alleviate the flip-flopping of her stomach and to give her knees support.

"Kiss me, Lori. Please."

Please. That did it. If he hadn't sounded so desperate, or so sincere, she wouldn't have turned her face up to his. She would not have wrapped her arms about his neck so he couldn't pull away.

Just this one last time, she told herself. She needed it, to remember. The thought of his lovemaking would keep her warm in the coming winter, would refresh her in the spring, would wash over her in cool waves during the hot summer and would give her pause in the fall.

Somehow the door was closed and locked. Somehow they were by the bed. Inhibitions and anger dissipated with each tender touch. Holt's hands were gentle and arousing at the same time as he removed Lorelei's clothing piece by piece. He carefully saw to it that her silken flesh was properly adored by his lips as each inch was slowly, but surely, bared.

Lorelei shivered with anticipation as Holt untied her chemise and cupped her breasts within his palms. Her back arched, pressing her sensitive nipples against his rough calluses until the sensation ignited a thin trail of fire from her belly to the throbbing center of her femininity.

Her own hands smoothed over the taut skin encasing Holt's muscled shoulders. His shirt slid from his arms. She was awed anew by the broad expanse of lightly furred chest and flat belly. Trembling knees refused to support her when Holt stepped away to remove his boots and pants, so she quickly sat on the edge of the bed, self-consciously covering her breasts with her arms, though trying to appear calm and unaffected.

Holt joined her and gently pulled her hands away. "Don't be embarrassed by your body, Lori. You're beautiful."

Her body turned the consistency of warm mush as she melted into his embrace. He laid back on the cot, positioning her legs on either side of his hips. At first she was hesitant, unsure of what he expected; but his fingers and lips soon worked their magic, and her instincts took control.

Lorelei moaned her delight when she felt that pulsing, silken part of Holt's body join with hers. Little star-bursts of pleasure immediately jolted her senses.

Holt had wanted to prolong their lovemaking, but

he, too, experienced a sudden fulfillment when her inner muscles contracted about him. His heart swelled with an undefinable emotion as her arms and legs wrapped around his body, encompassing him in a cocoon of warmth that also filled his insides with a liquid sense of serenity.

Their breaths ragged and bodies slick with perspiration, he rolled over until they lay on their sides, facing one another. They remained silent, as if afraid a spoken word would end the peaceful moment. She brushed a lock of black hair from his damp forehead. He ran a hand soothingly up and down the ridge of her spine.

Their hearts were in their eyes, their lips, their fingertips; yet each was fearful to voice their deepest thoughts.

Lorelei's chest constricted. She knew Holt possessed too much pride to turn his back on the town.

Suddenly, she closed her eyes and took a long, deep breath. It occurred to her that the feelings she had for Holt stemmed from the man he was, and always would be. Would she love him as much if he changed? A sad moistness pricked the back of her eyes. The answer was no. She loved him the way he was, not because of how she wanted him to be.

Holt was thinking along the same path. It was disconcerting, the depth of his feelings for this woman, but he admired her indomitable spirit and courage. He knew the strength of her beliefs and could not ask her to change.

Finally, Holt leaned forward and kissed her eyes closed, no longer able to stare into those ebony pools without saying something he might later come to regret. He put his finger to her lips when it seemed she, too, wanted to speak, but was fearful of doing so.

"Rest, Lori. Just rest."

Holt couldn't believe he had slept. With all that was on his mind, he expected to lay awake for hours.

A cold nose snuggled into the crook of his neck. He shivered when her breath ruffled the hairs at the base of his throat.

Damn it, it was time. He had to go. But, first, he should tell her the bad news he had purposely avoided mentioning. "Lori? Wake up, sweetheart."

Her nose tilted upward, and for a fleeting moment, he thought he felt the butterfly softness of her lips on his chin. He gently shook her shoulder. "Lorelei? It's almost dawn. I need to get out of here, but . . .. we have to talk first."

Lorelei gradually stretched her cramped limbs. When the wiry hairs on Holt's legs and belly brushed against her, a pleasant sensation rippled across her bare flesh. Wake up? She had been trying to keep from it for the past hour. She wanted to savor this time together, to soak the feel of him into her skin, her bones, her soul.

Finally, she mumbled, "Hhmmm? Don't wanna. . . ."

Holt grinned. Damned hoyden. What he wouldn't give to wake up next to her like this every morning. "Come on, sweetheart. It's important."

Lorelei's heart thundered in her breast. Was he, perhaps, going to tell her he had decided to quit his job? Did he finally see things her way? Or did he have even more important things on his mind—like love? or marriage? Dare she hope?

She leaned up on one elbow. Long blond hair fell across her shoulder to tickle and tantalize the flesh on Holt's chest. He grabbed the teasing tresses and held them in a clenched fist.

Her eyes were clear and questioning. He swallowed. He really hated to tell her this. "Last night . . . before I came . . . callin', I discovered . . . Endsley—"

"Robert? Thank heavens. I've been so worried about him. Did he say anything about when he might come back to work?"

Holt traced the outline of her lips, stifling her questions. "He won't be back anytime soon, I'm afraid. He's been hurt—bad."

She gasped, and he held her more tightly. "Wh-what happened to him?"

"I don't know for sure. He passed out soon after I found him." Holt sighed. This was more difficult than he had imagined. "The doctor doesn't know if he's goin' to make it. I'm sorry, sweetheart, really sorry."

Chapter Thirteen

Lorelei was so shaken over the news about Endsley that Holt escorted her to the doctor's office. Her ramrod-stiff demeanor caused him to fear that she might shatter into tiny pieces with the next stout breeze.

He hadn't realized how much she had come to care for Endsley until tears had pooled in her dark eyes and spilled down her peach-tinted cheeks when he'd told her the man might not survive. At least he'd had the sense to keep Endsley's last words to himself. The warning would have only caused her more distress.

"Watch after her." What *exactly* had Endsley meant? Was he just concerned for her welfare? Or was he aware of something more sinister? From the uneasy feeling in his gut, Holt surmised it was the latter.

Cursing beneath his breath, he came to the conclusion that Lorelei had been a complication in his life lately. He damn well *tried* to see after her, but the hellcat would have none of it. "Especially if it meant toting a gun," he mimicked to himself, exasperated by her continued contrariness.

But in all honesty, he was afraid for her, and had been terrified last night after leaving the wounded Endsley at the doctor's. Damn it, what did the man know?

Lorelei was almost running by the time they reached Doc Foster's. Holt had steadily increased his pace until she was gasping for breath, but had said nothing as her trepidation also intensified. She hurried through the door Holt held open, yet stumbled to a stop in the middle of the office.

She turned imploring eyes to Holt. "I-I'm frightened. Wh-what if he is . . . has . . . ?"

"Would you like for me to go in first and find out?" Holt wanted more than anything to reach out and take her in his arms, to soothe her fears, to protect her from hurt and pain, but hesitated, thinking his offer of comfort would probably be rejected. He wasn't sure just where he stood with her, even though they had made incredible love only a short while ago.

Holt started when Lorelei reached over and clutched his arm. "Yes, I would love for you to do that for me."

He had already turned toward the surgery when she added, "But, I must do this for myself." There was a look of puzzlement on her face. "I really had . . . have . . . become fond of Mr. Endsley, even though he was . . . is . . . quite irascible at times." She smiled as a tear ran down her cheek.

Holt wiped it away just as the door to the surgery swung open. "Well, here you are now. There's a fellow in here making quite a pest of himself asking for you, little lady. Ahem, I'm assuming you *are* Miss Abbott."

"Y-yes. Can I go in now?"

The doctor nodded, and Lorelei's face broke into a wide, sunshine-bright smile. A knot formed in Holt's throat, big enough to choke a mule. How he wished things were different between himself and Lorelei.

He followed her into the room. If Endsley really was better, he needed to ask the man some questions.

Lorelei kept her lips curved in a smile, though inwardly, she wanted to weep for the pale, seemingly even thinner man. He was so still, the room, so sterile and . . . inhospitable. Her nose wrinkled at the strong odor of medicine.

Taking a deep breath, she marched over to the cot. Nothing in her demeanor gave away her fear. "Mr. Endsley, I am pleased you are . . . awake." She lowered her eyes to the immaculate white sheet spread over his nothingness, hoping he would ignore her near slip of the tongue. Dear heavens, she had almost told him she was glad he was still *alive.* Which she was, of course.

"Morning, missy."

His voice was weak and thready, as if he still suffered a great deal of pain. She winced when he asked, "How's things at . . . the . . . store?"

She grasped one of his paper-thin hands, which had always seemed so strong. Then her features truly brightened. "You were right, Mr. Endsley. Advertising was just what the doctor—I mean, just what the mercantile needed. Business has increased until I hardly have time . . ."

Her eyes narrowed as she paused and thoughtfully considered the injured man. "I need help desperately, Mr. Endsley. And Mrs. Westfield is gone indefinitely," she partially lied, though she really didn't consider it as such, as the woman kept putting off returning to

Durango, knowing Lorelei needed her.

Robert frowned. Lorelei hurried on, "I will be more than happy to save your job for you, though, if you promise to come back as soon as possible."

Endsley's eyes sought out Holt even as he nodded. Lorelei looked back and forth between the two men, noticing Robert's tired, strained features and Holt's intense, questioning gaze.

She sighed. "I suppose our new sheriff wants to talk to you, too." She fussed with the pleats on her skirt, wanting to stay, yet sensing she was expected to leave. "I-I will come back again this evening. If you wish."

When Endsley managed to curve his lips upward a fraction, she nodded, somewhat mollified. "Good." Backing quietly toward the door, she would have remained there but for him motioning Holt to see her out.

Once the door was closed behind her, she gave in to the desperate urge to stomp one dainty foot. Drat them! What secrets were they keeping from her? A perplexed expression crossed her features as she leaned back against the thick portal. What hadn't they wanted her to hear?

A sense of unease settled over her. Just what did she know about her hired man, other than the fact he had needed a job? Who was he? Where had he come from? How had he been hurt?

She shook her head, loosening the pins barely managing to control her thick tresses. She realized it would be difficult to find the answers to her questions. It was a moot point, anyway. Mr. Endsley was a nice man. He worked hard. It seemed as if she had known him for a long, long time. And she sensed there was nothing to fear—from *him,* at least.

Huffing loudly, she started for her store. How she wished she could say as much for the other man in her life. Why, was it only an hour or so ago she had thought that Holt would profess his undying love, or make some gesture of commitment? How stupid of her to imagine such a thing!

Inside the small surgery, Holt straddled the chair beside Endsley's cot. He, too, could see the strain the man exerted to stay awake. Soon, the doctor was bound to storm in and put a stop to his questions.

"Who did this to you, Endsley?"

"Enders."

Holt blinked. "What?"

"My . . . name is . . . Robert Enders, not . . . Endsley."

Holt slowly crossed his arms over the back of the chair, giving himself time to digest this bit of information. What the hell was going on? Was the man feverish, out of his head? He had thought this was just a case of an innocent man being set upon by bandits. Or was this "Enders" a lot more than he seemed? He waited as whoever the man was regained his breath to continue.

"I'm here as a personal . . . envoy . . . for Miss Abbott's father."

"Good God!"

"He was afraid . . . after what happened to his . . . brother. But the . . . missy . . . insisted upon coming."

Holt sat forward. The man's energy was almost gone. And he sympathized with Mr. Abbott's predicament. He'd been around Lorelei long enough to know that once her hard head was made up on something, it would be like pulling a dog off a meaty bone to get her to change her mind. "Any idea who attacked you, or why?"

Enders whispered, "Couldn't see. Asked about . . . tobacco. Watch . . . in . . . store." Then his head lolled to the side.

"Damn it, man, I wasn't finished. I need to know more about Lorelei." Frustration furrowed Holt's brow as he felt for a pulse and was relieved to find it stronger than it had been last evening.

The door opened, and the doctor walked in. When he found his patient unconscious again, he scowled at Holt. "You could have waited until he was stronger. I must say, Sheriff, your tactics—"

"Hold on, Doc. He was the one who wanted to talk. I hardly had a chance to *ask* him a thing."

Dr. Foster harrumphed. "Well, go on and get out of here. You can see him again tomorrow, *if* it's necessary."

Holt nodded. Oh, yes, he'd be back. And he'd find out more about why Endsley—Enders—whoever, was so concerned for Lorelei's safety. Was it because of John Abbott's death, or was there more to it?

Meanwhile, he had a lot of thinking to do. What significance did the tobacco hold? What did he need to watch for inside the store?

Holt frowned. The entire situation was becoming more confusing by the minute.

* * *

Lorelei kept extremely busy over the next few days. Customers steadily poured into the mercantile, and most left with purchases.

She had gone to Catherine Romaine and asked the cost of printing weekly specials. It was within her budget now that she was beginning to take in a little money. In several weeks, she planned a sale on the items left in stock that were of a summer, or early fall, nature.

Snow capped the distant peaks, and the wind had a winter bite to it. What she needed now was to clear her shelves to make room for items that would be necessary during the four to six months when the weather would be icy and cold. She would order extra overshoes and sheepskin coats, heavy mittens and woolen hats.

Her excitement was a tangible thing, and Holt felt it the moment he walked through the door. He had purposely waited until closing time and was satisfied to see the only customer was at the counter making arrangements to pay for a purchase.

It was disconcerting, the way she frowned upon seeing him, but he bore it stoically, as he had at the same time yesterday when he had come to walk her over to see Enders; Endsley, still, to her.

Lorelei grumbled to herself. There was the "sheriff" again. Why wouldn't the aggravating man stay away so she could concentrate on forgetting him? Didn't he know how hard it was on her—her body—her senses—when he kept appearing like this, touching her when he held her arm, disarming her with that too-knowing smile?

She turned to fetch her cloak and reticule as Holt

locked the door after the customer. She assumed he had come to escort her to the doctor's office, and she could handle that. But it was necessary to get out of these close, confining quarters before his blatant masculinity completely overwhelmed her.

However, Holt was of a mind to talk. He took her lined cloak and held on to it as he guided her back to the stool and sat her down. He tried to hide the sudden tremor in his hand when he let go of her elbow.

"Uh, before you go to see End—Endsley, there're a few questions I need to ask."

Her eyes widened. "Me? Whatever for, Sheriff? I cannot imagine that I did anything to cause such an *official* tone of voice." She indignantly cocked her head to one side, daring him to refute her innocence.

He rubbed the back of his neck in frustration over her damnable obstinate nature. "No, of course not. Just bear with me, all right?"

She finally, imperiously, inclined her head.

He sighed. "Thank you, Miss Abbott. Now, have you had any sort of trouble with tobacco? Shipments? Ordering? Anything?" He grimaced, having no idea what he was searching for, hoping she would be able to help him somehow.

Lorelei shook her head. How silly. What could tobacco have to do with anything? But she narrowed her eyes in thought. "I carry several brands. They arrive as often as twice a month, or as far apart as every six months."

She wrapped her arms about her waist and stared at dirt clods trapped between cracks in the floorboards. She experienced a faint niggle of apprehension. There was only one order that came with any regularity, and she had often wondered about it. "There is a person who has a penchant for a certain brand. Wild Bull, I believe. It comes directly from Denver."

Holt perked up. "Who? Who spends that kind of money?"

Lorelei frowned. Should she give out that kind of information? Wasn't there a rule that a store owner did not have to tell the names of her clients? No, she guessed not. Nevertheless, she was reluctant. As much as Holt and Chad disliked one another, this information could cause more friction between the two.

"Come on, Lori. Who is it?" Holt could sense her indisposition. Why?

"Chad orders the tobacco," she defended.

Now Holt frowned. Funny, he couldn't recall the boy ever smoking, or chewing, either.

Lorelei scooted off the stool and placed her hands on her hips. "Why? Why do you want to know? What will you do to him?" And now that she thought about it, where had Chad been the past few days? She had gotten used to his regular visits again.

Holt flinched at the accusation in her voice. Did she think he would string Chad up just because he used Wild Bull tobacco? Then again, if what he suspected were true . . .

"Don't worry. I don't plan on doin' anythin' to your pretty boy. Yet," he added beneath his breath. "When is the next shipment due?"

She shifted uneasily as she suddenly remembered something. Speaking more to herself than to Holt, she said, "You know, he never received last week's order.

And he asked about it. I think Mr. Endsley said he put it . . . somewhere."

Holt's stomach knotted as he held out her cloak. "We better get movin' if you're goin' to see Endsley before dark."

Her head swiveled until she was able to see out of the window. "My heavens, the sun goes down quickly now."

"Yep. Let's go." Holt's voice sounded strained.

Her lips thinned into an irritated pout as he helped her on with her coat and opened the door. "Slow down, if you please. We don't need to rush, do we?"

Later that night, alone in his office, Holt scrunched down in his chair, tilted back, and propped his boot heels on the edge of the scarred desk. He'd been thinking all evening about a package of Wild Bull tobacco, supposedly sitting on the top shelf in Lorelei's storeroom, behind a stack of canned peaches.

Enders said he had forgotten all about the tobacco, and had set the cans up there temporarily until he made space for them on the shelves up front. The box had not been purposely hidden.

Holt rested his chin on steepled fingers. Was Chad behind the break-in at the mercantile and Enders' attack? Or was it all coincidence—like another time and place?

His feet hit the ground with a thud. Lorelei should not be involved in all of this. From the looks of things, it could get dangerous, and fast.

He needed that Wild Bull. But how could he lay his hands on it without her finding out, and wondering why he wanted it? Thank God he had been able to talk to Enders privately and she had no idea of its whereabouts. That, alone, could keep her safe.

Holt's opportunity came the next morning. He *happened* to be across the street from the mercantile, watching, waiting, when Lorelei left about half an hour before time to open. She appeared to be heading for the newspaper.

A smile sauntered across his lips. Great! All he needed was a minute or two, and once the women started gossiping . . . With studied casualness he walked to the other side of the street. Edwin Brunner, the druggist, was sweeping his walk, and called out. Holt tried to ignore the man, acting as if he hadn't heard.

However, Edwin hurried to cut him off. Damn it! Holt pulled his watch from his vest pocket and snapped open the lid. This delay had better be important.

"Sheriff? Sheriff Dolan. If I may have a moment, please." The man's thick German accent caused Holt to listen carefully in order to understand his words, which further irritated the sheriff. No one ever stopped him when he *wasn't* in a hurry.

Edwin huffed, out of breath, having experienced more exercise in his short run than he got in a week of strolling about his small pharmacy. "I am so glad I caught upf wiv you."

Holt sighed. "Mornin', Mr. Brunner. What's on your mind?" *And make it quick,* he grumbled to himself. Lorelei would be back in the mercantile anytime now.

The heavyset Brunner placed a hand over his heart as

he panted, "I was delegated to make sure you received an invitation to our social Saturday night."

Holt almost snorted, but covered his nose and mouth as if stifling a cough. A social! Good God! Didn't folks know he had crimes to solve? Murderers to put behind bars? Would Lorelei be part of the activities?

Before he even knew what he was saying, he replied, "Sounds like a good idea, Herr Brunner. I'll try to be there."

The man smiled so beautifully that Holt felt guilty about wishing to rudely brush him off.

"T'ank you, Sheriff. T'ank you."

Holt tipped his hat and hurried on his way before the portly German finished an effusive farewell.

As much as he detested slinking, cowardly behavior, he found himself sneaking around the back of the mercantile. He tried the latch to the back door. It didn't budge. Damn! She would start locking her doors *now*.

After looking up and down the alley, he reached into the top of his boot and pulled out a long, thin-bladed knife. A few pokes and prods and he was rewarded with a sprung lock and an open door.

Carefully, he resheathed the knife and then slipped inside. The "storeroom" was to the left of the door; Lorelei's living quarters were to the right. He paused a moment, looking longingly toward the quilt-draped bed, the small cookstove and the calico-covered privy.

And the next thing he knew, he was mauled by two growling puppies that were quite a bit larger than the last time he'd seen them.

One jumped on his leg, snarling like it would tear his pants off. The other crouched in front of him, baring its teeth and wagging its tail. When he spoke and called their names, they pounced on him with wriggling bodies and happy whines.

As he looked down at the red and white patched pup, something jogged his memory. A body. The crumpled bitch dog. Could these be . . . ? Naw. Surely not. But then again . . .

He frowned and bent over to puppy level. "Good, Freda. Good, Sissy." With gritted teeth, he wondered whatever happened to dog names like Rags and Muffy. "You remember me, don't you? Want your damned ears scratched?"

The brown pup immediately flopped down and rolled over with its feet in the air, twisting on the wood floor while Holt rubbed its tummy. Red, as Holt took to calling it, stood off, watching, cocking its head from side to side, eager to join in the fun, yet hesitant.

Holt knelt. His knees popped, and he cursed. The pup angled its head to one side and just stared. Holt reached out the back of his hand so that the dog could get his scent. Finally it relented, and allowed Holt to give it a good rubbing. "Not as trusting as you used to be, huh? That's good. You'll make a fine protector for your master."

Then he grumbled beneath his breath and clambered to his feet. What in hell had gotten into him? He was talking to dogs now. Scooting the animals away with the toe of his boot, but much more gently than he normally would have done, he turned to inspect the storeroom.

He found the shelves, all right, and even saw the canned peaches, but they were behind stacks of crates and boxes that had evidently piled up since Enders had been injured. He stepped over one, climbed over two more and put his foot through another. All to the tune of happily yapping pups. By the time he was in front of the shelves, he was thoroughly disgruntled.

Once he had the wrapped package of what he hoped was the tobacco in hand, Holt turned to face the obstacle-strewn way back. He took a deep breath and lifted his foot to step over the first huge box. His toes had barely touched the ground, and he straddled atop the thing, when the excitement erupted.

If he had paid any attention to the pups, he might have been warned, but he had been too busy—busy stealing a damned package of who-knew-what, for who-knew-why.

The brown pup whined. Red barked. Then both bounced up and down. Lorelei walked into the room. Holt cursed.

The damned woman stopped dead still, tilted her head, and must have heard his heavy breathing because she immediately began to scream for help. He quickly tucked the small package beneath his coat and pasted a sickly grin on his face. When she continued to let out the awful noise, he shouted, "For God's sake, quit your caterwaulin', Lori. It's only me."

Her voice quavered. "Me, who?"

"Damn it, Lorelei Abbott, you know *who!*"

Lorelei promptly fisted her hands on her hips and glared at Holt.

He fumed. She acted as if she wasn't even surprised to see him thus, spraddle-legged over a crate.

"Might I inquire as to why you are in my storeroom, Mr. Sheriff?"

An answer came to mind, but Holt quickly swallowed it. No sense in riling her all over again. *Think quick, Dolan,* he ordered himself. "I, uh, wanted to surprise you."

A flicker of a smile stole across her lips, then vanished. "You certainly accomplished that, wouldn't you say?"

When he hesitated, she prompted, "And why did you wish to 'surprise' me?"

"Well, I was, uh, wonderin' if . . ." A thought struck him like a bolt out of the blue. ". . . if you'd heard about the social Saturday?" Her black eyes glittered, adding fuel to the storm brewing in the pit of Holt's stomach.

"Social? No, I had not."

A long, hissed sigh released the tension crowding his chest. Thank God! "That's why I'm here, then. Uhmm, to see if you wouldn't do me the honor of attendin'. . . . Ah, if you would like to . . . Damn it, go with me!"

Lorelei gulped. Her hands clasped together. It was all she could do to keep a straight face. "Why, sir, how could a lady refuse such a gallant . . . proposal . . . as that?"

He frowned. "Will you go, or not?"

Adopting a disinterested attitude, she shrugged. "I guess."

After a long moment of silence, he awkwardly swung his other leg across the wide box. His eyes narrowed. His breath came in short pants as he hobbled to the door. "Good. And be sure to lock this when I leave," he ordered over his shoulder as he made a hasty getaway.

Lorelei bent back her head and laughed, more loudly and longer than she had in ages. Then she did as he suggested, patted both puppies, and stood staring at the storeroom. A pensive scowl furrowed her otherwise smooth brow. Just what had he been up to?

The door had been locked. She had checked it before leaving to visit Catherine.

Suddenly, her eyes sparkled with anticipation. Was there really going to be a social Saturday night? She truly doubted it. The only reason she had accepted Holt's stammered invitation was to put him on the defensive. She had never seen such a guilty look on a man's face before.

But if there was? The sobering thought wiped the soft curve from her lips. Dear heavens, what then? She would have to spend the whole evening with him. With his arrogant, smiling face, and his whipcord lean body, and . . .

The bell jangled at the front of the store, and she gratefully shook the unsettling images from her mind—for all of two minutes.

Holt unwrapped the package. It was tobacco, all right. Pouches and pouches of Wild Bull. He emptied them from the box and stared. So what was he supposed to do with it?

He picked up two or three sacks of the stuff and turned them over. Frustration lined his features. He drew his arm back as if to sweep everything from the desk. The motion stopped in midair. His eyes literally pierced the one pouch that was different from the rest. The "bull" was a steer. Searching quickly through the rest of the sacks, he found only the one changed. Why?

He picked it up and rolled it in his hand. It felt stiffer than the rest, and he heard a distinct crinkle. He slid the drawstring open, and along with the tobacco, dumped out a folded piece of paper. The thin parchment read: SL 3 Th.

What in the hell?

Before he had a chance to ponder over the possible implications of the strange missive, Tony Shultz rushed through the door.

"Mr. Dolan . . . I mean, Sheriff Dolan, this is for you."

Holt took the telegraph from the boy's trembling fingers.

The bold type read: **BANK HOLDUP IN SILVERTON. STOP. PERPETRATORS HEADED YOUR DIRECTION. STOP.**

Chapter Fourteen

Dawn was barely breaking the eastern horizon when Holt galloped out of town. He doubted if the outlaws had ridden straight for Durango after leaving Silverton, but it was the only lead he had.

The Morgan stallion tugged at the bit, and Holt let the animal run for a ways. It did feel good to be in the open, away from the confines of town and the stifling throng of people. Whether he ran across the robbers or not, it was a perfect morning to ride.

Frost melted from the ponderosa pine needles as the sun rose higher in the baby-blue sky. Holt shrugged out of his heavy coat and tied it behind the cantle. The trail he followed switch-backed up the face of a steep hill, and though the air was still mighty cool, the sun beat down hot on his back and shoulders.

Upon reaching the crest, he reined his horse into the shade of a stand of blue spruce. He squinted as his eyes made the transition from bright to dark, but as he surveyed the scene before him, all he saw for miles on end were the conical shapes of more trees and tall mountain peaks. It was wild, rugged country, and, God, he did love it.

He removed his hat, wiping sweat from the band. From the position of the sun, it was a little past noon, and he reckoned that if the outlaws had ridden this direction, he would have cut their trail by now.

Rifling his fingers through his damp hair before replacing the Stetson, he kneed his horse off the ridge. He'd search the next valley, then head home and wire the officials in Silverton of his unsuccessful outing.

Rocks dislodged beneath the Morgan's hooves and clattered into clouds of dust in front of them all the way down the steep slope. He rode into a peaceful meadow knee-deep to the horse in grass.

Most of the aspen had lost their leaves, and the ground was a mixture of yellow and gold as it crushed beneath the animal's iron shoes. As far as Holt could tell, no one else had entered the valley for some spell.

He leaned over to get a closer look at the damp earth bared by their passage. Still no sign of tracks. Holt was just straightening in the saddle when he detected the snap of a branch and then the faint murmur of voices.

Then suddenly, like a tempest before a storm, riders burst through the trees only a hundred yards down the narrow clearing. They stopped at the same time Holt pulled up the stallion, and they all sat motionless, staring at one another.

The gang had come to a halt in a tight bunch, but now spread out in a single line abreast of each other. Holt yanked out his rifle and levered a shell into the empty chamber. He took a deep breath and adjusted the reins so that he could have some control over the horse and still be able to take aim and fire.

He started forward, hoping that it was just a group of miners on their way to Durango, yet the ache in his gut was proof that he knew better. Suddenly, there was a flash of light. The sun reflected off the piece of metal on his shirt pocket as he rode into the sun.

Damn it, from the mutters and determined faces, the riders had seen it, too. Of all the luck. He should have hidden the badge away and at least had an opportunity to get closer to the gang.

The outlaws went into action, drawing their guns, riding toward him at a dead run. The nervous jitters that had at first assailed him, all at once evaporated. He faced the odds with a calm acceptance. The deck was stacked against him, but he had survived such a deal before. If only he could have had the time to shuffle the hand a little better in his favor.

As he kicked the stallion into motion, he realized that he wasn't *afraid* to die—everyone did it sometime—but there were still important things he wanted to do. Images of Lorelei flashed through his mind, and he experienced a sharp pang of regret.

A bullet whizzed past his right arm. The jarring strides of his horse took some adjusting to, but he sighted and fired his .44-.40 Winchester. Through the thunder of hooves, Holt heard one of the leaders cry out. The man dropped his rifle, but clutched at the saddle horn with one hand and pulled his pistol with the other.

Holt cursed, admonishing himself to be more careful. Every shot needed to count.

As the outlaws drew nearer, he thought he recognized one or two of the men, but the dust rose so thick and heavy that the faces blurred until he could no longer be certain. He snapped off a shot at a huge monster of a man with a curly handlebar moustache and was satisfied to see the robber sommersault from his laboring horse.

In the back of his mind, Holt calmly wondered over the small things a man noticed during lightning-quick action. Colors, shapes, smells. A bullet snagged his shirt. He fired at another outlaw and missed. His eyes narrowed. He sat up straighter and stared at the man. An almost unbelievable ache radiated through his gut.

Then the stallion stumbled. As Holt jerked forward, his head was suddenly hammered by a blinding pain. Hazily, he watched the ground come up to meet his sagging body.

His eyes were open. His mind registered the fact that his long frame was stretched flat on the ground. He even saw a hawk soaring above him amidst puffs of white clouds. Then a dark fog blurred his vision as the storm rolled in and everything went black.

Holt blinked. It hurt. His eyes drifted closed. Think. He needed to think. Even that was painful. It felt like someone chopped at his brain with an ax. He groaned, deciding he must've spent one helluva night to deserve such a hangover. But where? When? He'd never been so drunk that he couldn't recall the particulars before.

Something important nagged at the back of his mind; but his ears buzzed, and he couldn't concentrate. All he knew was that he had to get up and be about his business. People were counting on him now, and no telling how long he had overslept.

He tried to sit up. A sharp, aching pain spiraled

down his spine. His head throbbed and seemed to spin and dip with each abrupt movement.

Gradually, he became aware of the fact that instead of reclining on a soft bed, surrounded by four moth-speckled papered walls, his mattress was composed of grass and rocks and he was hemmed in on two sides by green needles and narrow brown trunks.

Where in the hell was he? What had happened that he was alone, in the middle of nowhere?

Then his slitted eyes settled on a hazy red object. He blinked again. As his vision cleared, he recognized the blur as his stallion. The horse seemed content, munching the short, green grass that had been protected from the latest freeze by taller, yellow stems.

Every now and then the animal threw up its head and tested the wind, then cast a wary eye in Holt's direction. Holt puckered his lips to whistle at the well-trained horse, but nothing happened. He tried again and blew hot air.

Finally, a high, thin noise, not at all similar to his usual whistle, lured the stallion closer. After a lot of effort and trial and error, Holt found he could move his arms and legs. Nothing appeared to be broken, but he couldn't summon the energy to get up.

When the Morgan sniffed his chest, Holt spoke soothingly and grasped the bridle reins. He pulled the animal forward until he could reach the left stirrup. Each time he tried to rise, his limbs turned to mush, and he fell. He jabbed the horse's side so many times, he feared the animal would tire of the punishment and bolt. At last he pulled himself to his knees, then his feet. He swayed unsteadily, holding on to the saddle until the world quit whirling in dizzy circles.

After gulping several deep breaths, he gazed toward the south end of the valley, then peered north. The sight of trampled earth, a discarded rifle and an unmoving body brought his memory crashing back around him.

An odd warmth trickled down his neck. When he reached up to see what it was, his fingers came away slick with blood. Damn!

The pounding inside his head increased as he worried that the outlaws might decide to ride straight to the bank in Durango, believing the sheriff out of commission permanently.

It took a few attempts, and he almost landed face-down on the other side of the horse; but he finally planted both legs over the fork of the saddle. The effort was costly, though, for blood oozed steadily down the back of his head, and his vision once again became unfocused.

His hands trembled, but he managed to tie his bandana over the jagged wound above his ear. One last glance at the valley illicited a firm promise. Though he couldn't handle it now, he would be back for that body.

Holt's stomach knotted as he kneed the stallion into motion. He swayed and grasped the horn with both hands. As the horse plodded toward Durango, Holt had the unsettling feeling that he should be remembering something important, but the harder he tried to think, the worse his head throbbed.

Lorelei locked the door for the evening and hung up her new CLOSED sign. She peered out the window and watched the dark clouds building on the western horizon. The sun had long since hidden behind the thick layers, and she pulled her sweater together as a chill shivered down her spine.

It looked cold. It was cold. Even the river sounded sluggish, as if it wouldn't be long before ice formed along the banks.

She walked toward the back room, straightening items that had been strewn about by careless customers. Her back ached, but all in all, it was a good ache. The sale had gone well, but the customers had been almost more than a person alone could oversee.

Her body was tired and sore, her nerves shaken from mediating squabbles between usually calm and even-tempered people. Perhaps she should wait awhile before advertising another store-wide special.

She filled a basin with cool water and had just splashed the refreshing liquid to her flushed cheeks, when something scraped against the storeroom window. Her hands froze. Water dripped from her chin. Her chest tightened as she scanned the small room. Unbidden, thoughts of Catherine Romaine and the woman's trusty pistol entered her mind. She banished them in a second. No! She would never need to defend herself with a gun.

The noise came again, louder this time. She gathered her courage around her like an iron shield and stealthily crept into the storeroom, nearly tripping over a broom. Her hands groped for the handle and felt as though they became permanently adhered to the smooth wooden surface.

She did manage to pry one hand free long enough to move the scrap of cotton material serving as a curtain. She gasped. A large shadow loomed in the small square of glass, and she jumped backward, stumbling over a stack of boxes. Clumsily righting herself, she yanked the curtain away from the window and then wielded the broom like a long club.

A sigh of relief drained her lungs. The broom dipped down to the floor. A horse. Only a horse. The noise had been caused by the bit rubbing against the sideboards as it scratched the side of its head. Her shoulders sagged, and she was about to set the broom back in the corner when the horse moved and she saw a denim-clad leg attached to the saddle.

Fear again gripped her stomach until she felt weak and nauseous. Dear heavens, who? Why? What was the person doing lurking about her back window?

Minutes passed. She stood still as a stone. The horse shook its mane. Nothing else moved. Once, the leg twitched, and she thought she might have heard a moan.

A moan? She inched nearer to the glass. Her heart fluttered to her throat when she made out the horse's color. Red. Holt had a horse that—

She wouldn't take the chance that it wasn't Holt. The broom clattered to the floor as she raced to the back door. She fumbled with the lock. A curse tumbled from her numb lips. At last, the latch clicked open, and she ran down the steps into the alley. She must have held her breath, because her chest felt singed as she rounded the corner.

Her steps faltered. She swallowed a fiery breath. It was Holt! Holt—leaning against her building. Just leaning.

The longer she stood, staring, ire began to replace her earlier trepidation. Her hands fisted on her hips. What in the devil was the man up to, scaring her half to death, sitting in the alleyway, with his eyes closed, bleeding all over. . . .

Bleeding? She hurried toward the horse, which stamped its hooves and shook its head. The reins fell loosely to the ground. Holt never moved a muscle.

Some emotion, mightier than fear, gripped her breast. He was hurt. And he had come to her.

The dark stains on his neck and shirt had to be blood, although the closer she came, the more it appeared to be dried, rather than fresh. Thank the Lord!

Upon reaching the horse, she picked up the reins to make sure the impatient animal didn't make a sudden move. Then she laid her free hand on Holt's hard thigh.

"Holt? Holt, can you hear me?" Panic edged her voice. There was no answer, no movement. She squeezed his leg, nearly shrieking, "Holt! Please, wake up!"

His eyelids flickered.

Her fingers dug into the thick denim. "What happened to you?"

One of his eyes blinked open. She came close to fainting when his brow cocked at a familiar rakish angle. He licked his lips. His voice was deep and gravelly. "Hap'ned?"

"Wh-wh—you're bleeding." Her hand fluttered over his leg. Now that he was aware of her, she was afraid to touch him. Things between them were so tense and uncertain that she hardly knew what to do anymore, how to behave around him.

"Bleedin'?"

Her palms were damp as she looked at him. Dread filled her heart. He was disoriented and, evidently, unable to comprehend a thing she said. She had to get him to the doctor. This was something she didn't dare handle on her own.

Fighting back the terror in her voice, she straightened and ordered, "Sit up, Holt."

That one eye had closed, but it blinked open. "Huh?"

"Sit up straight and hold on. I am going to take you to the doctor. Do you understand?"

"Doc?"

When she tugged on the reins, the stallion lurched forward. Lorelei held her breath as Holt teetered in the saddle. She shouted, "Grab the horn!"

He automatically obeyed her command and steadied himself. Lorelei nearly cried out loud, but regained her composure and managed to keep the horse moving.

The trip to Dr. Foster's, which usually took ten minutes, seemed to drag on interminably. Every time Holt moaned, she stopped to make sure he was all right, and then felt awful when the horse moved and he became unbalanced.

Anguish like she had never known before must have shown in her features, for when the doctor answered her summons, he took one look at her face, then glanced to the horse beyond and rushed out to Holt without her having to utter a word.

"What happened here, Miss Abbott?"

Her fingers were wrapped around the reins so tightly that her knuckles popped as she opened her fist to help the doctor get Holt from the saddle. Her breath came in rapid gulps. "No idea. He was outside. Horse made a noise. Would never have known. The horse made a noise."

The doctor must have noticed her trembling hands,

for he waved away her help as he said to Holt, "Come on, boy. Slide down. I'll catch you."

By the time Holt was on the ground, Lorelei thought she would go crazy. Though she could see no other wounds besides the one on his head, it was more than she could bear to think of the suffering he must have endured.

He had been so brave and strong while she'd administered to the wound on his thigh. She had thought then that nothing could harm him. Her fear that he might someday be killed once he became sheriff seemed so far removed that even she eventually scoffed at the notion.

But he was only human. Very human. And as she had needed comforting on occasion, so he needed attention now. Her heart literally swelled to bursting. It would give her the greatest of pleasure to be there for him.

Holt's legs would not support his weight. The doctor struggled to hold him upright. Lorelei noticed the predicament and rushed to Holt's opposite side. Between the two of them, they maneuvered the injured man up the stairs and into the building.

Enders raised his head when they staggered drunkenly through the doorway. When he would have gotten up to help, the doctor frowned and shook his head. Nevertheless, Robert supported himself on one elbow and demanded, "What happened to him?"

After Holt was lowered to the other cot, Lorelei answered, never taking her eyes from the man she loved. "We don't know. He hasn't been able to tell us anything."

The doctor brought over a lantern to get a better view, then removed the bandana from Holt's head. "It's a bullet wound, but doesn't appear to be too deep. Just a lot of blood."

He started to take off Holt's clothes, checking for more injuries. "Lot of bruises," he mumbled.

Lorelei hung over his shoulder, scanning every purple patch on Holt's flesh with concern.

Enders cleared his throat. "Don't you think you better go in the other room, missy?"

As if he had forgotten her presence, Doc Foster's hands fell abruptly from Holt's belt buckle. "Yes, ma'am, you go on now. This is no place for a lady."

Lorelei's jaw dropped. She started to argue, but the doctor added, "Why don't you put his horse in my barn. I'd say it earned a good rubdown and an extra bait of grain tonight."

As much as she wanted to remain and assure herself that Holt was, indeed, not seriously injured, Lorelei knew that the men would run her out forcibly if need be. Besides, she agreed with the good doctor and knew that Holt would appreciate knowing his horse was being taken care of, too.

So, she shrugged her shoulders and muttered about "pig-headed men" as she left the office.

The stallion stood with its head hanging and one hind foot cocked, looking tired and bedraggled. It nickered a welcome as she patted the end of its velvety nose. For a minute, she studied the large beast and all of its trappings. She had ridden some over the years, and enjoyed being around horses, but there had always been a groom to take care of the more physical aspects.

Lorelei had to step lively. The horse was so eager to be put up for the night, that it nearly trod on her heels as she led it to the oversized lean-to that the doctor referred to as his barn. A lantern was lit in one corner, and the doc's horse was stabled in one of the two stalls.

Once she had the stallion enclosed in the small space, she stepped back and scratched her chin. Now what? Should she try to get the saddle off, or leave it on? And what had Dr. Foster meant by a "bait" of grain?

The big horse bent its neck and eyed her warily, even as she surveyed the situation and debated the most logical thing to do. The poor animal surely couldn't eat with that bit in its mouth, and would probably be uncomfortable wearing the heavy saddle all night.

But how did one go about removing the blasted contraptions? She pursed her mouth. Wouldn't her father have a fit if he could see her now? Young ladies in Boston would never be caught standing in piles of hay and . . . droppings. Ugh! She took a deep breath and wrinkled her nose.

Then she stiffened her spine. Her chin jutted out defiantly. Holt needed her help, and help he would get, no matter *what* it involved.

First, she closed the gate to the stall. At least the horse couldn't escape, even if she did something terribly wrong.

"All right, Velvet, what do we do now?"

The horse switched its tail, flicking Lorelei in the face. She grimaced, and scolded, "That's not the way to get acquainted." Then she grinned when the animal rolled its big, brown eyes.

She moved up to the horse's head, which she decided might be the safer end, and decided the saddle was the first item that needed removing. There couldn't be much to unfastening a piece of leather.

And it turned out that it wasn't so difficult. She only

broke three nails and one finger in the process.

The next problem was getting the huge thing off the horse's back. Since everything had been accomplished with relative ease so far, she wondered how hard it could be.

It felt like she reached forever to finally grasp the horn and the cantle. She bent her knees and pulled. It hardly budged. She took a deep breath, and yanked. It slid an inch or two. Surely it wasn't *that* heavy. She rubbed her roughened palms together, reached up again, and gave it one more good jerk. The saddle lifted free of the horse's withers and careened into her arms.

Heavy was not the word she would have used to describe the weight that caught her directly in the chest. She stumbled backward, hooked her heel in the soft dirt and hay, and fell, landing hard on her backside, the saddle in her lap.

Air literally exploded from her lungs. Unable to move, she just sat there until she caught her breath again, then wiped tears and damp hair from her face. At first, she wasn't sure but what she was trapped in the filth and manure, but she finally struggled from beneath the ungainly chunk of leather. Dusting off her hands, she looked down and decided the saddle could stay right where it was until one of the men was able to put it up.

After dueling with the saddle, the bridle was a simple chore, even when the stallion clamped its teeth and refused to spit out the bit for a time. Later, she actually smiled when she discovered a feed bag with oats already measured inside. If it wasn't a "bait," it was close enough.

A few armsful of hay filled the manger and there was

water nearby; so she figured the horse would be comfortable enough until the doctor came out to douse the light. Her bottom still stung, but she shook most of the debris from her skirt and walked proudly back to the office. She had accomplished something extraordinary tonight, and was quite happy with herself.

Upon entering the surgery, Lorelei was greeted with one of Holt's heart-melting smiles, and wondered what more a woman could ask. She walked to his side and started to take his hand when he raised it, but he shook his head. Startled and disappointed, she almost stepped back, but his fingers brushed her cheek instead.

Something crumbled from her skin. Her face turned brilliant red when she remembered swiping back her hair with her dirty hand. And he picked a piece of hay from her blouse. She thought she would die of mortification. Five minutes ago, she had been on top of the world, and within two seconds he turned her into an embarrassed, blithering idiot. "I-I . . ."

Holt had no such trouble finding words. "You're beautiful."

The doctor scowled and grumbled, "Hey, you two, there *are* other people around. Don't *I* rate a little thanks for bringing the boy back to life?"

Chapter Fifteen

Lorelei blushed at the doctor's teasing antics. She tried to move away from Holt, but it seemed he sensed her discomfort and grabbed her wrist, keeping her at his side.

Doc Foster grinned. Endsley just shook his head when she shyly met his eyes. Was her attraction to Holt so apparent that everyone could see? She tried so hard to hide it, even from herself.

Holt squeezed her hand. "I'm goin' to be fine. Just a little gouge in the side of my scalp an' a headache. If the bullet had hit anythin' softer than my head, I'd probably be dead."

He was trying to joke and ease the tension, but it had the opposite effect. She was already on edge because of the knowing look in Holt's eyes earlier, like he'd guessed the depth of her feeling, and now *he* had to admit that he could have been killed. Her body trembled from that formidable thought. She turned anxious eyes to the doctor.

"Yep. He'll be up and around in a day or two."

Then her gaze fell on Holt's naked chest, and her insides went all fluttery. She tried to convince herself the reaction stemmed from her relief. Her chest constricted until she could hardly take a breath. Where would he stay while recuperating? Here with the doctor? Should she offer . . . ? It would be tantamount to announcing . . . Disappointment at the thought he might not stay with her was a complete surprise. Did she really want him where she had to personally see to his welfare? Yes! And that knowledge terrified her to no end.

As if sensing her train of thought, Holt's eyes smoldered into hers. His voice was deep and throaty. "Sure appreciate your seein' after me . . . an' my horse."

Lorelei straightened, and a tremulous smile curved her lips. "I took off Velvet's saddle and bridle, and put out oats and hay." To the doctor she said, "I hope you don't mind, but I left the light burning in the barn."

Doc Foster nodded. "That's fine. I need to go out later and water the horses, anyway."

Suddenly, Enders closed his eyes and moaned. Lorelei would have gone to him, but Holt kept the steady grip on her arm. The doctor had already rushed over, talking low, checking Enders' wounds.

While the others were thus engaged, Holt pulled her close and chided, "Just who in the hell's this 'Velvet' you were talkin' about?"

Lorelei's eyes focused on the tip of his nose. "Why, your horse, of course."

He rolled *his* eyes, thinking first of Freda and Sissy, and now Velvet. Good God!

Seeing his reaction, she challenged, "Well, what *is*

its name?"

He colored slightly. "Doesn't have one."

Disbelief at such dispassionate treatment of his animals furrowed her brow. "What? Everything has to have a name."

"Why?"

That stopped her for a moment, but she answered quite logically, "Just because. And . . . and . . . they won't know to come when you call without a name of their very own."

Holt really tried, but could think of no sensible argument. He closed his eyes and sighed.

Lorelei thought he'd passed out and bent worriedly over him. "Are you all right? Say something."

She looked up in fright, ready to call out to the doctor, when his free hand clasped her arm. "Worried about me, huh?"

Flustered, caught displaying her fragile emotions, she sniffed. "N-n-no. Of course not." But her voice lacked conviction. She tried to back away. He would have none of it, and her face hovered only inches above his. She licked her lips.

Holt's eyes flared. Brilliant sparks suffused the dark gray. But he suddenly released her when the doctor stood up and assured Endsley that his pain was to be expected and should ease in another few days.

Dr. Foster administered a tablespoon of something that had to be ghastly tasting from the way Endsley gagged. Lorelei wrinkled her nose in sympathy.

Then Holt's fingers found the soft underside of her wrist, and Lorelei realized she should have used the distraction to place some distance between herself and Holt. But her feet refused to move. No matter how she *wanted* to feel, she *needed* to spend as much time with him as possible, under *any* circumstance.

Looking from Endsley to Holt, her face drained of color as she recalled the scare he had given her when she found him outside the mercantile. The knowledge that he could have died gnawed at her insides until she nearly became ill.

"What's wrong, Lori?"

Her eyes sought his, and she gasped at the expression she saw there. His concern and regard were vividly displayed. It should have warmed her heart, but instead, a chill shook her thin frame.

There was too much between them to return his feelings—openly, at least. If only things were different—if their expectations and beliefs were similar—if . . . Her eyes misted. So many *if's*. Too many questions.

"N-nothing is wrong. Whatever made you think there was?" Rather than give him the opportunity to come up with the correct assumption, she quickly confessed a partial truth. "I was just thinking how glad I am that you are going to be all right." She did her utmost to paste on a bright grin and adopt a happy air. He couldn't suspect how much she cared for—loved—him.

"Oh."

Was that disappointment, even hurt, she heard in his voice? Had he wanted her to say more? Probably. She had a suspicion that he wasn't a man used to showing his affections. And dear heavens, she loved him even more because he couldn't. Damn it.

Finally, afraid of what she might do, or say, if she stayed, she stammered, "Well . . . I am glad that you are—will be—" Her throat clogged. The longing in his eyes clawed at her heart. She gulped. "I-I will be back . . . t-to see you . . . and Mr. Endsley . . . tomorrow."

Then she fled the room. One more second and she would have thrown herself into Holt's arms, unmindful of the doctor, Mr. Endsley, or anyone else who cared to see. She would have professed her love and begged him for his love.

She stumbled through the night. Sobs shook her shoulders. Why, oh, why, did she have to feel so strongly against his way of life and his belief in the necessity of guns? Was she so wrong?

Holt left town early the next morning. Doc Foster had thrown a fit, but Holt had gone anyway, assuring both the doctor and Enders that he was fine after the night's rest.

And he guessed he was fine, except for the dull ache in his head. Or maybe the piercing jabs that pained his heart.

The Morgan stumbled. The spare horse balked. Holt cursed, then apologized aloud. It was Lorelei he was upset with, not the horses. Damn it, why did he have to go and lose his heart to some holier-than-thou goody-two-shoes who didn't know her nose from a rifle butt?

Who was *she* to say that her way was the only way? *He* didn't enjoy using a gun, sure as hell didn't look forward to hurting people, but sometimes it *was* necessary, especially out here in a new, growing territory. Couldn't she give, too?

By the time he reached the little valley where the shoot-out had taken place, his head had begun to throb. He winced when he looked into the bright sky and saw buzzards circling.

A nauseous sensation settled in his stomach as he imagined what he might find when he reached the body. Scavengers of all kinds roamed the mountains, and he dreaded his grisly chore. As it turned out, the cold weather had kept the corpse in fairly decent shape, and he was grateful.

Holt looked at the stiff features of the huge Mexican and vaguely remembered seeing the man in Durango, just lately. Something else teased at the back of his mind, something about the valley and the riders, something important. But the more he tried to recall whatever it was, the worse his head hurt. Finally, he gave it up. If it was important, it would eventually come to him.

The events of the previous day and night, and his premature departure from the doctor's office, took their toll. Holt couldn't believe the trouble he encountered in lifting the dead weight of the body. Even the pack horse caused problems, prancing and fidgeting at the sight and smell of the corpse.

At last, he hoisted the heavy body across the animal's back and managed to tie it down. He mounted his stallion and nudged the horse into a fast walk, suddenly anxious to return to his office to sort through the stack of wanted posters in his top drawer. Since the man had tried to kill him, the ex-bandito was more than likely wanted for other crimes.

Lorelei stood with her back to the mercantile, waiting to cross the street. She had been there for at least a quarter of an hour, and had not moved a step. If she didn't hurry and do *something*, it would be time to open the store.

She sighed and headed for the doctor's office. A promise had been given, and return she would, even if it caused a great deal of embarrassment. Last night she had made a complete fool of herself, and if Holt was callous enough to bring it up, it was only what she deserved.

The doctor was talking to another patient when she entered. He smiled and nodded toward the surgery. Her own face was stiff when she tried to return his greeting, and her stride faltered before she reached the closed door.

Deciding she was acting much too cowardly, Lorelei took a deep breath and walked boldly inside. Endsley lay in his bed. Holt's was empty. Her eyes narrowed.

"'Lo, missy."

Lorelei strolled over to Robert. To keep her eyes from straying to the other cot, she asked, "How are you feeling this morning?"

"Better."

She fiddled with the dangling tie on her bonnet. "Good."

"Out with it."

She swallowed a lump as hard as old brown sugar. "I-I beg your pardon?"

Though he kept his lips straight, there was a gleam in Enders' eyes. "When are you going to ask about that young man?"

She glanced innocently about the room. "Which—"

Then she noticed his frown and fought the urge to bolt from the room. "Oh, all right. I thought he was supposed to stay here a day, maybe two."

Enders snorted. "That was the doc's idea, not Holt's."

"Wh-where is he?" The apprehension she had felt since entering the room made itself apparent in her voice.

Robert shook his head. "Don't know. Left early this morning. Doc said he saw him ride out of town."

Lorelei was scared. What if he didn't come back? What if he was hurt worse than he thought and *couldn't* come home? Home? Again? Yes, Durango had taken on the aspects of home. She had friends here. Loved ones.

Her gaze rested on Endsley's drawn features as a totally frivolous thought took hold. What if he didn't come back for the social tomorrow night, which she had learned was actually taking place? He had asked her to go with him, after all. And if he didn't show up? Well, he had just better!

"How's business?"

She gazed gratefully down at Endsley, blessing him for taking her thoughts from Holt. A genuine smile tilted her lips. "Wonderful. I had a sale this week and . . ." Cocking her head to one side, she shrewdly eyed the man. "It was more than I could handle by myself. I will not schedule another until I can be assured you will be able to help."

His brows came together. "Did pretty good, did you?"

"Not nearly as well as I could have if you were there."

A kind of glow brightened his heretofore dull eyes. "We'll give it another try then, later."

She solemnly nodded. "Yes, we will."

Then his eyes slowly blinked closed. Lorelei gently touched his sunken cheek and tiptoed from the room. A knot of anger tightened her chest.

If not for Holt's unpredictable behavior, she would have returned to the store, satisfied with her visit. She mentally shrugged. If that was the way he was going to be, fine. But *she* would be at that social, with or without Mr. Dolan. How dare he leave town and not say a word as to when he might be back, or even *if* he would.

Perhaps it was for the best if he did stay away. Hadn't she just decided that it was better for both of them to see as little of each other as possible?

Yes. And she would stand by that resolution. She would!

Lorelei stared out the window at the low-hanging clouds. The wind was from the north, and had turned bitter cold. She pulled the heavy sweater tighter about her shoulders. A chill raked her spine, but it wasn't because of the weather.

Where was Holt? It was Saturday afternoon, and she had yet to see or hear from him. If he were still planning to take her out, wouldn't he have made an appearance sometime during the day?

She sank down on the small ledge around the window, being careful to avoid knocking over the new display of women's toiletries and accessories she had spent the morning arranging and rearranging. Deep inside, the gnawing ache that had taunted her for hours, grew into a real pain that churned her stomach. She had been worried sick for two days. What could have possessed Holt to leave the doctor's office so early? Hadn't the man any sense?

The toe of her shoe tapped a staccato rhythm against the floorboards. At the moment, the only emotions she felt like concentrating on were those of frustration and anger—anger with him for treating her so callously, and frustration with herself for allowing it to happen. If she had followed her head, rather than her heart, she would never have accepted his invitation. And the more she thought about it, the more upset she became over finding him in her storeroom that one afternoon. Her imagination drove her crazy every time she wondered what he had been up to.

Seeing nothing out of the window but depressing grays and browns, she decided to close the new curtains and lock up for the day. Most of her customers had come early anyway, making their purchases for the big social.

She had almost summoned the energy to get up and go to the door when a figure crossing the street caught her eye. It was Chad.

He was walking toward the mercantile. Her pulse accelerated. Dare she hope that he would offer a solution to her dilemma? She shook her head and berated herself. How dare she even think such a thing.

Her stomach fluttered. Conscience demanded that she not act hastily, that she give Holt more time. Yet her instincts prompted her to take whatever opportunity arose.

Sure enough, Chad came into the mercantile. The doorbell jangled until she thought the clapper would break. He grinned. "Howdy, pretty lady."

She smiled. "Hello, Chad. How are you?"

"Finer'n frog fuzz split three ways." He glanced curiously around the empty store. "Ya fixin' ta close 'er up?"

"Just about." Her fingers twisted the folds of her skirt. Conscience scolded that what she was thinking was wrong. No, she should *not* purposely maneuver another invitation to the social. Yes, it would be better to stay home rather than resort to such trickery.

"Ya goin' to that there shindig tonight?"

She gulped. "Shindig?"

"Yeah, ya know, that social?"

Her hands fluttered nervously. "Oh! Er, I thought I was, but I-I—"

"I'd be plumb proud ta walk ya over. If ya'd like ta go, that is."

Although she wondered, and felt somewhat apprehensive about the peculiar gleam in his eyes, she acknowledged the obvious fact that he had asked of his own accord. She had done nothing untoward. But still . . . "I really shouldn't. . . ."

"Please?"

The way he cocked his brow sent a warm twinge through her stomach. She did want to go, in the worst way. And people would be gathering in less than two hours. Holt had had his chance. "Well, all right, I suppose. I would love to have your company." And it wasn't really the same as the engagement with Holt. Chad was only accompanying her.

The beaming smile on his face suffused her with guilt. Her stomach literally tied itself in knots. So, if she had done the proper thing, why did she feel guilty?

Chad listened as a cuckoo clock chimed five o'clock. "I'll come back at six. That give ya time ta get ready?"

She was certain it would take at least five hours to make herself presentable. "Six will be fine."

He tipped his hat and headed jauntily toward the door. "See ya then."

Her feet felt leaden as she walked back to her room. The pretty yellow velvet dress she had chosen to wear for Holt hung on a nail on the wall. Its princess cut was sleek and flat across the front and sides. The fullness was gathered at the back and tied low behind the knees. The new style was flattering to her tall, full figure, even if she did say so herself.

All of a sudden, she fought the urge to rip the gown to shreds—to spite Holt, to spite her silly pride. But, instead, her hands smoothed down the fine fabric. It was too beautiful to destroy because of her anger at a man. She would wear it tonight, and do her utmost to look as nice as possible.

She would show Mr. Dolan that she could have a good time without him. Better, in fact.

So why did she have to search for a handkerchief to mop the flow of tears?

Lorelei was smoothing a mixture of glycerine and rose water over her hands when she heard the first knock at the back door. Butterflies flittered against her rib cage as she stopped in front of a small mirror and vigorously bit at her lips until they were a pouty pink.

Before she opened the door, she patted at the tendrils of hair pinned in soft curls atop her head, and smoothed the plush material of her dress over the flat planes of her stomach. Though she had never thought of herself as vain, she found herself desperately wanting to look pretty tonight.

It wasn't until the latch was sprung and the door was swinging open that it dawned upon her that Chad would not be knocking there. Who—?

Her thoughts died in midstream when she stared into Holt Dolan's incredibly handsome face. His tall, lean form was encased in a tailored black suit with a crisp white shirt and a string tie about his neck. She could see her reflection in the shine of his boots, and was startled by the sickly appearance of her own features.

He held out a bouquet of beautiful wild, purple flowers. Her stomach turned upside down, and she placed a hand against the door frame for support. It was a thoughtful gesture, and he had to have gone to a lot of trouble to find flowers so lovely at that time of year. For the first time that she could ever recall, Lorelei was speechless.

After all, what did one say to a man that she had jilted to go out with another? She felt the blood drain from her face and neck. Her mouth opened, but she only choked and coughed.

"Aren't you goin' to ask me in?" His gray eyes scoured her body until she felt like hiding her breasts and nether regions with her arms and hands, but she didn't possess nearly enough of the appendages to do the job properly.

Finally, she gulped and stepped back, allowing him space to squeeze inside. The room became considerably smaller and more stifling with his larger-than-life presence. She fanned a handkerchief in front of her suddenly flushed face.

"Don't you want the flowers?"

Swallowing a guilty reply at the hurt in his voice, she

reached out a trembling hand. Her fingers gripped the delicate stems so hard, she felt sap stick to her skin.

His eyes fairly sparkled as he gazed so fondly at her that perspiration beaded her forehead and upper lip. The question that had been lurking unobtrusively in the back of her mind for several seconds now screamed at her. What in heaven's name was she going to do now?

And, naturally, to add to her panic, at that precise moment, there was a loud knock at the front door. Her feet seemed glued to the floor. The soft kid leather suddenly pinched her toes and heels, making walking impossible. Her hands wrung furiously.

Holt cocked his head and eyed her with question. "Want me to see who's callin'? It's kinda late. No tellin'—"

"Uh, no! I-I can . . . I know. . . . Oh, dear." She wrung her hands and moved like her legs were made of lead.

She gritted her teeth as Holt played the big protector and followed her to the door. His warm breath blew down the back of her neck, and she shivered.

By the time she reached the front of the store, she was out of breath from trying to stay ahead of Holt. And she was frantic with worry. Why hadn't she explained things immediately instead of letting it go so far?

Her hand waivered above the latch. She could see the outline of a slim man wearing a wide-brimmed hat. Chad. What had she expected? That because Holt had shown up, Chad would conveniently disappear? Or forget that she had accepted his invitation in a pique of anger?

She cursed beneath her breath, using every foul word

she had ever heard or imagined. She was such a dolt.

Then, before she had time to react to his movement, Holt reached past her and opened the door. Chad rushed inside, stomping his feet and slapping his hands against the stiff arms of his long duster.

"Whew! That wind cuts like icicles." He rubbed his hands together and looked directly at Lorelei. It was then that he saw Holt standing in the shadows.

Chad's face went pale as a ghost's. For a moment, Lorelei thought he might be sick, but he blinked and massaged his frozen fingers even more vigorously, quickly recovering his composure. "Well, I'll be damned."

The stunned surprise that had briefly flickered in Chad's eyes swiftly altered to something unreadable. His lids hooded further expression. "What're ya doin' here, Dolan?"

Holt stepped out into the light. His right hand rested on his hip, within an easy drop to his gun. "Miss Abbott and I are steppin' out tonight. How 'bout you, Chad?"

Chad's eyes shot to Lorelei, who seemed to shrivel into a bright yellow lump on the floor. She held out her hands, palms extended to the heavens, then let her arms drop to her sides while she stared a hole into the toes of her slippers.

Lorelei thought she might throw up then and there when Chad challenged, "I'm goin' to a party. An' the pretty lady's comin' with me."

Chapter Sixteen

Holt's hands curled into fists, but his eyes were trained on Lorelei, not Chad. "What's he talkin' about? You said you'd go with me, didn't you?"

The last sentence was stated quietly. It was a demand that she explain herself. Lorelei flinched beneath his sharp glare. But before she had a chance to reply, there was a loud cracking sound from the direction of the storeroom.

Lorelei turned to stare as the click of sharp toenails digging into lacquered wood produced two puppies running full-tilt. Freda slid to a stop and circled Chad, growling. The ruff on the pup's thick neck vibrated with every threatening movement. Sissy also careened to a halt, to sit contentedly on the toe of one of Holt's boots.

When Lorelei regained her composure and called to the misbehaved animals, Holt put a restraining hand on her arm. "They're not hurtin' anythin'. Right now, there's more important matters to worry about."

She glared at him. And was she mistaken, or was that

a flicker of amusement she saw in his eyes as he watched Freda stalk Chad? Whatever she thought she saw, it was gone when his gaze riveted back to her.

The distasteful glint in his stormy gray eyes seared her, leaving behind a distinct chill. She crossed her arms over her chest in an effort to keep from shivering and revealing how much he upset her.

"Well?" Holt also crossed his arms over his chest, but in a manner that brooked no more stalling.

Chad reached down to touch the red pup, but drew back when the gesture was greeted with a snarl. "Yeah, I thought ya were goin' ta the shindig with *me*. What's Dolan doin' here?" He pointed to her hand. "Bet he brung ya them flowers, huh?" An accusing glower was directed at Holt, who appeared quite unruffled as he bent to scratch Sissy's floppy brown ears, his eyes never leaving Lorelei for a second.

She closed her eyes and took a deep breath. This was *one* of—if not *the*—most embarrassing moments of her life, but she had no one to blame but herself.

Resigned to her plight, she decided to tell the truth and get it over with. At least then she could change clothes and throw herself upon the bed to cry her eyes out in private. The two men would surely fall over themselves in their rush to get away.

She heard Holt snap his fingers and knew it was now—or never. Her eyes pleaded for understanding as she looked into two intense faces.

"This is all a huge misunderstanding." She hesitated. It was going to be harder than she thought. Her eyes sought Holt's. "I went to the doctor's office yesterday." The silence that filled the room was palpable. Even the dogs seemed to wait expectantly for an explanation.

"I-I found you gone, without a word. And, well, I had no idea whether you had forgotten . . . or if you had more important . . . or if you would be back." She sighed. There, the truth was out, sort of. It shamed her to admit how vulnerable she felt where he was concerned. She envisioned herself walking across a swampy bog, searching for the next secure foothold.

There was a slight flush to her face. She had told *most* of the truth, only leaving out the part concerning Chad. Now she turned to face him. Even in the darkened room, illuminated by only one lantern, she could see the mottled blotches creeping up his neck to his cheeks. "I am so sorry."

His eyes narrowed. She backed up a step. His voice was thick and strained. "I reckon ya'll step out with Dolan, rather'n me, then." He knew the answer. It wasn't a question.

There was something so cold and calculating about the way he spoke that Lorelei shuddered. Yet he appeared to smile at her; at least his lips were curved. Nothing about him reflected that smile, though, the way he stood poised on the balls of his feet, his eyes like icy shards.

"I-I have no other choice."

The looks she received from both men stated clearly that she had several choices, though she might not like any of them. However, in her own mind, from the moment she had found Holt on her doorstep, there had been no doubt as to her decision.

"Mr. Dolan, Holt, did ask me first. But I honestly believed . . . I mean . . ."

Chad shifted his shoulders, and she was afraid that the movement would shatter his stiffened form. "Save me a dance, pretty lady?"

She was so relieved that he wasn't going to be difficult over her blunder, that she spoke without considering Holt's reaction. "I would be happy to."

He tipped his hat almost jauntily, and backed out, with a growling Freda hastening his departure. Once the door had closed behind Chad, Lorelei was suddenly nervous at being left alone with Holt. She began to fidget with the sash that bound her waist.

Freda loped over to sniff Holt's boot, and he knelt to pet both pups. He needed the time to think and, at the moment, the uppermost thought on his mind was what a fool he was for not following on Chad's heels and leaving. The woman evidently didn't trust him, or regard him as fondly as he had thought.

She had doubted his word, and if there was one thing he'd always been with the women in his life, it was honest. Sometimes to a fault. And it had only engendered trouble and heartache.

Hell, he'd never considered it necessary to reconfirm an invitation. He'd asked her. She'd said yes. That was all there was to it, as far as he was concerned. Who could understand the workings of a woman's mind?

Well, he might be an idiot; but he had come to take her to a social, and take her he would. And after it was over, he had something important to say to her. Then, depending on her answer, he would have a better notion of how she felt about him.

As he contemplated Lorelei's wide, dark eyes and pinched features, he arose to take hold of her hands and prevent her from twisting the damned sash into something unrecognizable. His nostrils flared at her familiar scent, which went so charmingly with the lemon-yellow dress. God, she was beautiful. And he had wanted to kill Chad for thinking he could stroll in and take her from him. "Are you ready to go?"

Lorelei started. The silence had dragged on for so long that she had come to welcome it. "Are you sure? I th-thought . . ."

Though it took a great deal of restraint to keep from losing his temper and scolding her for pulling such a foolish trick, he also admired her for facing up to her mistake. "Where's your wrap? It's mighty cold."

She managed a weak smile and called the puppies to follow her back to their cubbyhole. Upon reaching her living quarters, though, she found the latch used to lock the dogs in the privy broken. Still unsure of herself and frustrated over the puppies' antics, she shook her head. What to do now?

Her eyes brightened. With hope in her heart, she entertained the idea of staying home to keep an eye on her pets.

The thought was instantly dashed when Holt walked in from the storeroom with two lengths of rope. He tied a knot in each rope that wouldn't slip off the wriggling animals and looped the other ends to the bedposts. As he stood back, hands on his lean hips, surveying his handiwork, he asked, "What're you goin' to do with them when they get grown?"

Looking at both of the darling little faces, with their tongues lolling to the sides of their mouths, eyes turned adoringly to their human friends, her chest ached. They seemed to smile at her. But the truth stared her in the face. "I-I had not thought about it. They are so cute—"

"And need room to grow and exercise. Do you take them out to play?"

She stiffened. "Of course. They are both trained to go—"

"I asked if *you played* with them, or let them run." He glanced down at the little brown dog, which stared worshipfully up at him. A tiny pang of emotion tickled his heart, but he mentally shrugged it aside. All animals were cute when they were little. *Anyone* could become attached to a pup, *if* they liked dogs.

Lorelei looked closely at the animals. They had grown so much during the past weeks. More than she had realized. *Was* it fair of her to keep them cooped up inside? But what else could she do with them? They provided entertainment and companionship. They helped to pass the lonely nights when . . . .

When what? she asked herself. When Holt wasn't there to keep her warm and loved? An inner heat turned her face bright red. Her voice quavered. "Wh-what do you think I should do?" As much as she loved the little beasts, she wanted to do what was best for them.

Holt cursed himself for saying anything. He had upset her, and that was the last thing he wanted to do. Picking up her woolen cape, he helped her into it before replying, "There's no hurry to *do* anything. Just give it some thought."

A sadness overcame her as they left the mercantile and walked the few doors down to the empty building where the social was being held. And as they walked, her depression intensified, until she couldn't hold in her guilt any longer. "I hope you will forgive me. I would never have accepted Chad's invitation if I had thought . . ."

Even in the bitter cold, her cheeks flamed. It hurt her

to lie, and she didn't do it well, even if she told the *partial* truth. "I guess I was so angry, that I—"

"Wanted revenge? Even if the wrong was unintentional?"

They were outside the doorway now, waiting for the families in front of them to enter. A warm glow spilled into the darkness. She swayed toward him and hissed, "How was *I* to know that you'd be back? You just disappeared, *after* the doctor warned you not to."

Holt's stomach muscles quivered as a delicious warmth seeped into the deepest recesses of his body. By damn, whether she would admit to it, or not, the woman had been worried for him. It had been a long time since someone, anyone, had been concerned for his welfare, and it felt surprisingly good.

Except . . . He took off his hat and touched the tender area behind his ear. It was concealed by a thick pad, held in place by a strip of white cloth encircling his head. The throbbing ache that had hounded him for two days, made him wonder if perhaps Lorelei and the doctor had been right. Of course, it had been necessary to recover that body, but one more day in bed probably wouldn't have hurt.

Holt ducked his head when her gaze found his bandage. "I don't look real great. Hope you don't mind being seen with a—"

"With a very handsome gentleman." As they stepped inside, she took off her cloak, with Holt's gallant assistance, and shyly glanced into his silver-flecked eyes. "Shall we forget what happened earlier and begin the evening anew? I truly am most sorry."

Although Holt wasn't normally one to "forget" anything, he'd make an exception for Lorelei. He was still reveling in the discovery that she cared about what happened to him. And he could understand her insecurity. Hadn't he experienced a lifetime of it himself?

In keeping with Lorelei's suggestion that they start over, his deep "Forget what?" earned him a tender smile, which he returned tenfold. He offered her his arm as they entered the huge room. Bright banners concealed the plain board walls. Ribbons of every color crisscrossed the high ceiling and were tied off with large, draping bows.

Lorelei could hardly contain her excitement now that she and Holt seemed to be getting on better. She had never seen so many families gathered together under one roof, all dressed in their Sunday-go-to-meeting best, as she had heard it so eloquently described. Her gaze wandered from one end of the room to the other. Nowhere was there the elegance and trappings of Boston, but the simplicity struck a chord deep in the core of her being.

At the north end of the room was a raised platform, where several men were tuning hand-hewn instruments. She grinned as she noted the varying ages and costumes of the band members. The gray-haired gentleman in coveralls, plucking the fiddle, looked to be ninety if he was a day. A freckle-faced boy, with a patch on the knee of his Sunday pants, was strumming the banjo. He was pushing, maybe, ten.

Directly across from the entrance were ten or twelve long tables covered in red and white checked cloths and piled high with everything from cookies to steaming tortillas and huge bowls of punch. As she watched, several ladies brought over more dishes and uncovered them. Her stomach grumbled appreciatively.

Tugging on Holt's arm, she whispered, "Was I supposed to bring something? No one told me."

He patted her hand. Her eyes were big black diamonds sparkling up at him, and his heart skipped a beat. "Don't worry about it. You can make up for it next time. This is a very informal get-together. If you can bring something, fine. If not, it doesn't matter. Everyone's here to have a good time."

Lorelei relaxed slightly, thinking over his casual use of the term "next time" and pondering its implication. *Would* there be a next time? With him?

She moved her skirt out of the way as two young children used her as a shield to hide from another, even younger girl. Then she noticed that in the south end of the building, several older girls were supervising a large nursery. Pallets had been made for babies and children too small to join the activities.

A soft sigh escaped Lorelei's lips. Once, she had dreamed of having a husband, and children, but at the ripe old age of twenty-one, she doubted anyone would want an old maid. Her eyes slanted toward Holt. And a used old maid, at that. Still, she had no regrets over her decision to give herself to him.

She wasn't bemoaning her fate. Her life had been good; she had her father, the mercantile, and . . . Again she glanced at Holt from beneath the thick fringe of her lashes. If only she hadn't learned, first hand, what she would be missing. If only she hadn't met Holt and fallen in love.

As if sensing her gaze, he looked down at her and grinned. Her stomach lurched. His even teeth flashed white against the dark tan of his cheeks. "Would you like something to eat?"

Bedazzled by the change that crept across his already extraordinary features, she could only nod. He led her to the tables, now literally groaning beneath the weight of the mounded food. It was difficult to choose from all of the wonderful-looking goodies. She piled a plate with a thick slice of ham, deviled eggs, potato salad, beans, and bread hot from the oven spread with blackberry jam. She even managed to find room for a slice of currant pie.

Holt's plate was buried under a mountain of fare, too. If he added one more item, a landslide of food of every description would surely hit the floor. But he risked adding cornbread and sorghum syrup.

Lorelei witnessed his mouth watering, and laughed when he licked his lips. He shrugged and grinned sheepishly as they headed for two empty chairs to enjoy the feast.

Halfway through the meal, Lorelei sensed someone watching her. She looked at Holt, but he was busy licking sticky syrup from his fingers. Hiding a grin, she glanced around the room, but everyone seemed occupied with their own doings. Finally, she shrugged. It had probably been someone like herself, just looking to see who was there.

A little later, after they had returned their empty plates and the band had begun to play, Lorelei saw Chad. He was in the company of a thin, dark-skinned, raven-haired man, dressed in tight-fitting black pants and a short jacket of the same black material. A wide, red sash circled the man's lean waist.

The pair made quite a contrast because of Chad's light complexion, but Lorelei's gaze kept returning to the Spaniard. There was something cold and sinister about the man. Her instincts hinted that young, sweet Chad was out of his league with such a companion.

Holt had been visiting with the mayor, but when he saw the direction of Lorelei's gaze, and realized that Chad had, in turn, spotted her, Holt excused himself and strode swiftly to her side. He made a gallant bow and held out his hand as the band paused between numbers. "Would the lady care to dance?"

Having watched the other couples with a longing eye, Lorelei was pleased that Holt wanted to dance. In keeping with his teasing air, she simpered and placed her hand lightly in his, trying to ignore the jolt of heat that immediately raced up her arm. "The lady would be honored, kind sir."

As he took her in his arms, she was stunned by the sensation of his stimulating touch. She had forgotten the power he unknowingly wielded. Or, perhaps, from the sparks flaring in his eyes, he was aware, and had been as shocked as she.

Holt held her close, waiting for the music to begin. When he glanced toward the band, he grinned at the sight of the old man passing a jug. When they resumed playing, the eerie whine of the fiddle intoned a slow waltz.

Lorelei stifled a groan and tried to subtly remove her hand from Holt's and leave the floor. Her stomach was doing crazy things, and she suddenly felt a little dizzy. But his intense gaze coiled around her, staking her to the floor.

He was, she imagined, like a cobra hypnotizing its prey. She stood, riveted, until he began to sway to the lilting rhythm. Their bodies fit together perfectly as

Holt swung her effortlessly across the sawdust-covered floor. She had known he possessed grace and style, but was surprised to find that he danced so divinely.

The fingers of his left hand entwined with hers. Those on his right splayed across her lower back, their warmth radiating throughout her body until her blood flowed as swiftly as a raging torrent. Her eyes closed. All this as a half dozen couples in gingham dresses and starched shirts and string ties swirled past. Dear heavens.

The suggestive movement of his hips caused her heart to beat in time with the music. She glanced up and locked eyes with him. She licked her dry lips. His gaze followed the path of her tongue and scorched the curve of her mouth. She moistened her lips again, and his eyes sought hers.

Though he held her no more closely than propriety demanded, Lorelei shivered with every rhythmic caress of clothing. They swayed and dipped. Their thighs brushed. She nearly swooned when he guided her into a shadowed area of the floor and pressed his pelvis to hers. Her eyes widened. Dancing aroused him, too.

His lips flicked the lobe of her ear. "Don't you wish we were home in bed, naked?"

Before she registered what he said, she moaned and quite honestly answered, "Yes."

All too soon the music ended, and they were back under the lights. Her breathing was too rapid. He held her in place for a moment longer than would have seemed necessary. She bit back a smile. In more ways than one, men had it "harder" than women when it came to hiding their desires. She covered her blazing cheeks with her palms. Wicked. That was what she was—wicked—for even thinking such a lustful thought.

Holt saw the revealing gleam in her eyes and grabbed one of her hands, intending to keep her on the floor for the next dance. A hand touched his shoulder. Startled, he spun, his free hand dipping automatically for the gun he had checked at the door. When he saw it was Chad, he relaxed slightly—but only slightly.

Most of the younger man's back was presented to Lorelei. He grinned at Holt, though the gesture never reached his blue eyes. "Cuttin' in."

Holt looked at Lorelei, hoping she would refuse. She didn't. But he still held her hand, reluctant to let her go. Damn it, there was something he should remember. . . . But as he glared at Chad, his head began to throb unmercifully.

He blinked and shook his head, then glanced hastily around the room. Several of the closer couples were staring now. Sighing, he released Lorelei and stepped aside, out of the way of the other dancers, but to a position where he could still keep an eye on the pair.

Lorelei watched Holt recede from her vision over the top of Chad's shoulder. Though she was thrilled that Holt seemed displeased with sharing her, she was, nevertheless, thankful for the opportunity to talk with Chad. She smiled. "Does this mean you have forgiven me?"

His lips curved as he squeezed her hand. "Shore. I understand, I guess."

Lorelei tried to shift her weight, to place more space between her body and Chad's. The muscles in his arms were inflexible. Her eyes darted about the crowded room. She didn't want to cause a scene, or mention her discomfort to Chad, if he wasn't aware of how closely they danced. She had already embarrassed him once that evening.

She peered anxiously about the spinning dance floor. Chad had led her to the center of the room, and she could barely see through the crowd of moving bodies. Finally, when she did finally spy Holt, he was busy talking with several of the townspeople. She sighed with relief.

Now was as good a time as any to speak candidly with her friend. "Chad, who was that man you were with earlier?"

His eyes narrowed, and he missed a step as another couple bumped them. Lorelei stared at him, wondering if he had stumbled—and why. Even the blue of his eyes had suddenly deepened.

"Which man I seen a lot o' folks tonight."

She bit her lower lip. He was being purposely obtuse, and she knew it. "The one in the black suit."

His grip on her tightened. She squirmed until he finally loosened his arms. "Black, huh? Must've been Miguel Martinez. Why?"

Lorelei hesitated, unsure of how he would take her meddling. She looked him straight in the eyes. "There was just something about him that—." She stopped in mid-sentence. The laugh she emitted was shaky. "Perhaps I'm being silly, but I think you should stay away from that man."

Chad's eyes widened. He seemed shocked. "Ole Miguel? How come?"

What could she say, after all? She didn't know Miguel what's-his-name. It was only her woman's intuition that caused her suspicion. She shook her head. His arms closed again, pulling her more firmly against him. "I-I do not . . . Oh, never mind. You probably think I'm crazy."

"No-o-o." He prompted, "Go ahead and tell me. I wanna know what ya think."

He was so sincere that she decided to go ahead and say her piece. If he wanted to heed her advice, he could. If not . . . "I just didn't like the looks of the man. I hope that you will have no more to do with him."

Chad pursed his lips, seeming to seriously consider her words. "Could be right. Don't reckon I know 'im all that well." He winked. "Little narrow 'tween the eyes, ain't he?"

Lorelei nodded vigorously at the aspersion usually reserved for dumb or deceptive horses, and was relieved when Chad laughed. As the dance ended, he swung her into the same alcove where Holt had guided her earlier. She was suddenly pressed against the length of his slender body.

"Chad, don't. You're scaring me." She put her hands on his shoulders and pushed, struggling to get away.

His grin was a mere slash across his grimly set face. "Just one kiss, pretty lady. Figure ya owe me that much."

Though she continued to squirm, Lorelei was faced with the realization that she deserved the treatment she was receiving. She had led Chad on, then let him down in a most ungracious manner. It all could have ended in a very dangerous situation between Holt and Chad, and it would have been no one's fault but her own. Perhaps, if she let him take one kiss. . . .

"Let the lady go." The words snapped like the sharp tip of a bull whip, yet were spoken softly.

Chad loosened his hold, but refused to release

Lorelei. She pushed ineffectually against his chest. The young man was deceptively strong.

"Never did like ta share, did ya?"

Holt's face seemed set into a frozen mask. Only his eyes spit silver sparks of fire. "You'd know, if anyone would."

Lorelei continued to push against Chad, becoming more and more disturbed that neither man appeared aware of her presence. But as her initial panic eased, she pieced together disjointed fragments of their conversation. The two had known each other, a long time before *she* had come into their lives, it seemed.

Chad's laugh was a nasty, guttural sound that stood the hairs on the nape of Lorelei's neck on end. "Yeah, guess I would, at that."

"You goin' to let her go, or not?" Holt waved a hand in front of his eyes as a blinding pain stabbed the top of his head. There was still something hovering in the back of his mind, as yet unattainable.

Lorelei had never seen such an expression of . . . was it rage? . . . on Holt's features. He looked dangerous, lethal . . . like a completely different man than the one she knew and loved. A shudder racked her spine.

Upon feeling her tremble, Chad looked down. His arms slowly fell to his sides. Softly, he said, "Sorry, pretty lady."

She backed away. There was something in his eyes then, a sadness, regret. And she felt it, too. Somehow, she sensed things would never be the same—for any of them.

Chad's brow tilted at a cocky angle, and a rakish grin slanted his lips as he pushed back his hat. He was the Chad she remembered, yet he wasn't.

To Holt, he said, "It's about over."

Holt quickly grabbed Lorelei's elbow. Jerking her back to the safety of his side, he nodded. " 'Fraid so."

As Chad turned on his heel, the rowels of his spurs spinning furiously as he swiftly departed, Holt's eyes never left his back.

Lorelei, perplexed and indignant, spun toward Holt and demanded, "I want to know what's going on here, and I want to know *now,* damn it!"

Chapter Seventeen

Holt shrugged and started to walk away. Lorelei caught his arm. "Oh, no, you are not going to leave without explaining this . . . antagonism . . . between Chad and yourself. You know each other well. Correct?"

She was met with silence. Her voice rose. "Well, is it?"

He mumbled, "Yes. I've known Chad a long time."

Lorelei nodded. All right, at least she had gotten that much from him. Encouraged, she added, "And have you always hated each other?" She warded off a shudder. Hate seemed a mild description of the underlying emotions she sensed between the two men.

Holt shook his head. "Not always." His voice was flat and devoid of feeling. "Stay out of it, Lorelei. It's not your concern."

His tone warned her against further questions.

"B-but—" The man had turned his back. Ooohh! How aggravating. The entire situation was getting out of control. Why couldn't the two men at least be friends, given her feelings for them?

She frowned and slanted her eyes surreptitiously toward Holt. The stubborn set of his shoulders deflated any hopes she might have had. As he had reminded her, it wasn't really any of her business. If they needed to fight out whatever it was bothering them, so be it. If they killed each other in the process . . . Dear heavens, she wouldn't be able to bear it.

"Well, as far as I'm concerned, the evening is over." She whirled and stalked to where they had left their wraps. Frustration tautened her features as she fumbled into her cloak. She wanted no part of Holt or Chad or anyone. Home. She was going home.

When she stepped outside and started walking toward the mercantile, she was surprised to realize that the *home* she pictured in her mind now wasn't Boston. It was her little cubbyhole of a room, and the puppies waiting to welcome her when she returned.

It seemed strange, but she hardly ever talked or thought of Boston anymore, except for her father. He was the *only* person she missed. And it was becoming glaringly apparent that she never thought of Boston and home—together.

Lorelei clutched her cloak tightly about her shoulders as the wind whipped at the long folds. Her feet turned to icicles in her light-weight slippers when she was forced to stop and adjust a loose lacing.

The night shadows crept beside her as the gusts of air moaned through the alleyways and creaked into loose shutters. For the first time since leaving the relative warmth and safety of the social, she recognized the foolishness of her impulsive behavior. Suddenly, the dark recesses about her appeared to loom nearer, and she accidentally tied a knot in her laces.

She felt the vibration of the boards on the walk beneath her. The air froze in her lungs. Lorelei nearly tumbled head over heels as she saw a large form silhouetted by lanterns that flickered along the avenue.

She recognized Holt, and some of the tension holding her rigidly erect drained, even as something elemental blazed in her heart. Of course he had left the social to come after her and see her home safely. Why had she thought he might do anything less? He was, after all, the most honest, trustworthy, maddening individual she had ever had the misfortune to know.

But he had made her so-o angry. He was also close-mouthed and extremely hard-headed.

She drew herself up and stormed down the walk, treading carefully to keep from tripping over the dragging laces. As her steps naturally slowed, she could hear him following close behind. Her breath quickened. It became an internal battle to keep from glancing over her shoulder. If he happened to be *very* near, she would probably turn to him with outstretched arms.

Lorelei's legs trembled. Her mind was a jumble of confusion. Upon reaching the mercantile, instead of going directly to the front door, she slipped into the alley and hurried toward the back. She heard his footsteps and knew Holt continued to follow her because her shoulders ached under the pressure of his eyes boring into them.

When had she ever been so attuned to another human being? Would she ever be again? Despair, and a deep emptiness, weighted those same tingling shoulders, for there was only one answer. No.

The key failed to turn the lock, probably because her hand shook so badly. Tears of frustration, with herself, and her life, burned the backs of her eyes. When she was finally able to push inside, she shivered again, but this time from the cold wind that drafted beneath her skirt.

Suddenly, her shins scraped something hard. She stopped, trapped by the cot in front and Holt behind her. Now, what was the bed doing by the door? She clutched at her cloak, her eyes rounded with fear. Had someone broken in again? Were they still inside?

Then a happy whine reminded her of the pups. She breathed easier, realizing the dogs must have worked as a team to drag the bed across to the bag of trash she had forgotten to set out earlier in the day. Although it was a relief to find her animals were the culprits, the mess they had made was enough to dishearten even the hardiest of souls. What else could go wrong tonight?

Paper and debris were strewn over a five-foot-wide area, and gusted even farther as the wind howled through the open door as Holt entered the room. He closed the door behind him, and a husky laugh vibrated through every nerve ending in her body. She started to turn and scold Holt for following her, but the sight of Sissy's brown face wreathed by white cotton packing material, caused a chuckle to escape her tautly compressed lips.

Soon, she and Holt were both laughing and holding their aching sides as the dogs cowered with wide, guilty eyes beneath the end of the lopsided bed. She collapsed near the head of the cot, and Holt sat down close beside her, since the two iron legs at the foot had been bent and now tilted at a dangerous angle.

Holt took one of her hands and warmed it in his larger, rougher, tender one. His thumb circled her palm, and she felt chill bumps erupt clear down to the soles of her feet.

"Looks as if you could use some help cleanin' up in here."

She nodded. "It's your fault, you know. *You* were the one with the bright idea of tying them to my bed."

He innocently inclined his head. His warm breath whispered over the sensitive flesh on her nape. "I thought the thing was stronger than that."

She wasn't sure what he meant, until she saw the wicked leer in his smiling gray eyes. Remembering several moments of energetic exertion they had shared on the spindly cot, she blushed and used the hem of her cloak to cover her face.

When Holt pulled her into his embrace, she was incapable of resisting. Her body yearned for his caress, and felt as tightly wound as a spring on a heavy wagon, ready to uncoil at his slightest touch.

But he did not assuage her throbbing need. He did not reach beneath the cloak to fondle her overly sensitive body. He only stared into her wide, imploring eyes. She whimpered and moved closer.

His hands cupped her shoulders and held her at arm's length. "God, Lori, don't look at me like that or I'll never get this said."

She blinked. He wanted to talk? Now? When all she wanted in the world was to feel his flesh against her, feel him deep inside, moving, a necessary part of herself.

Stretching forward, her fingers unbuttoned his coat. Her palms smoothed against the silky fabric of his vest. She shifted as his arms sagged until her lips nuzzled the soft flesh of his neck above the stiff collar. Her tongue darted out to lick the underside of his chin.

Holt groaned and summoned every nuance of willpower he possessed to push her gently back. His fingers bit into the soft material of her cloak and gown. "Damn it, you're drivin' me crazy."

She slipped wayfaring fingers between two buttons on his crisply starched shirt. "Good." Rather than being shocked by her brazen behavior, she realized her new-found boldness was just another expression of her love. And it gave her a tremendous boost of self-esteem to think she could cause *him* to experience a few anxious moments.

"No," he sighed. "Not good. I need to talk. Now. Tonight."

A long-suffering murmur of disappointment deflated her lungs as she straightened to sit primly on the edge of the cot, facing away from him, hands clasped tightly in her lap. She couldn't look at him. "All right. If you must." She tried to hide the hurt his rejection had dealt, but her lower lip quivered.

Until . . . the thought occurred to her that perhaps he had followed her because he wanted to explain his unusual relationship with Chad after all. Hope brightened her expression.

Holt used the tip of his index finger to turn her stubbornly tilted chin toward him. His hands cupped her cheeks, so she had no choice but to look him directly in the eye. He willed himself not to shake, not to demonstrate how terrified he felt. It was a risk he took tonight because the rewards could be so damnably rich.

"Ahem. This isn't goin' to be easy. I never thought to say these words again." His breath was ragged as he inhaled. "I love you, Lorelei Abbott."

Lorelei's heart raged like a wild demon against her rib cage. He had said, "I love you." Happiness surged through her like water erupting from a burst dam. She loved Holt, and now she found out that he returned her feelings. It was just too good to be true.

She could only stare at him.

"Will you do me the honor of becomin' my bride?"

Silence hung in the air. Holt held his breath.

Lorelei couldn't get a breath. A proposal of marriage had been the last thing she expected to hear from him tonight. She searched his face, but all she found was a tense watchfulness as he waited for her to say something—anything.

Her sparkling black eyes scoured the dear breadth of him, from his strong features, sturdy chest, capable hands, lean waist, tapered thighs, blue-black revolver. . . . It was as if a bubble had burst, so quickly did her elation revert to despair.

Moisture blurred her vision as his hands insisted she look once again into his eyes. There was question and hurt in their gray depths. She couldn't keep him waiting any longer.

Her chest burned, and her throat felt raw as she rasped, "I-I wish I could . . . more than anything, I do."

"But?" His voice was low and strained. The muscle on the side of his jaw jerked as he struggled for control.

It felt as if Lorelei's world was collapsing around her. The evening had taken so many turns that her senses were reeling. And now . . . She had never felt so bitterly tired and weary of soul.

"I am sorry, but . . . I cannot accept your—" she

choked on a sob and managed to keep it from escaping—"proposal."

His hands fisted, then dropped to where his fingers dug into the corded muscles of his thighs. "For God's sake, why not? What we have together is special, wonderful."

He could not believe she had turned him down. He had seen the love in her eyes, felt the uninhibited passion in her lovemaking. She would never respond in such a manner if she didn't care—a lot!

Lorelei felt as if she had swallowed a jagged piece of metal. "W-we are too different. Are so opposite in our beliefs." Her eyes drifted to the oiled leather holster. "On so many things."

He took in the direction of her gaze and demanded, "It's the gun, isn't it?"

She nodded, ever so slowly, sadly, averting her coal-black eyes from him altogether.

"Is that all?"

When she looked at him questioningly, he repeated, "Is that all there is standing between us? My wearing a gun?"

Again she nodded, thinking *isn't that enough?* Her eyes pleaded for understanding, though her heart knew he would not.

Holt sighed. "I love you, Lori, but I won't give up my job, or the gun. I would give my heart, my soul, my life, for you, but what I'm doin' is important to too many people." And the most important person was one Miss Lorelei Abbott. Whether she liked it or not, he was going to keep her safe.

He rubbed the back of his neck and stood up to pace the confined space between the bed and the door.

Thoughts of five years ago still tore at his gut, and this job offered a hope of salvation, of helping him to live a normal, peaceful life. This time *he* begged for understanding. "They need me here now, and I have to do this."

His eyes were so haunted that Lorelei took a step toward him. Her hands ached to smooth the deep creases from his forehead, but her arms were immobilized. Surely her heart would splinter and break if she so much as twitched a muscle.

Should she confess that she loved him, too? Or hold her silence? Would it ease his pain, or make it greater?

He was right, just as she was right. So, what should she do? How could she bear it if he were killed, or killed someone himself? She had known her refusal would be best, and now had no choice but to make certain that they part now, before they were both hurt past redemption.

A bleak future flickered before her, beckoning, haunting. Images of herself old and gray and alone. She felt a tear trickle a lonesome path down her pale cheek. "I really am sorry."

Holt stopped directly in front of her, causing her to bend her neck backward to see his face. His breath caught at the pain he read in her fathomless eyes. But he also saw her stubborn determination.

His own fists clenched. There was no use in trying to talk sense into the woman tonight, but he was damned if he would give up. They were perfect for each other. He loved her. She *would* be his.

He came to the decision, then and there, to bide his time—to give her a chance to think things over. He did not bestow his heart lightly, and it was encouraging to watch how hard she fought to keep from giving in.

A smile curled around his insides. It had taken him a long time to admit or acknowledge his love, but that was what he truly felt for the hard-headed hoyden. Oh, yes, she would agree to marry him, as surely as he knew that he was leaving her frustrated and on fire with desire.

With that thought spurring him on, he shrugged as nonchalantly as possible, as if her refusal was no more important than her telling him she was out of sugar or bacon. It was small retribution on his part to see her eyes widen and her mouth open to form a round "O" of denial as he crossed over to the door.

Lorelei jumped to her feet as Holt flung a casual "See you around" over his shoulder. He pulled the door shut behind him before she could think of anything to stop him. There were things she needed to say—to explain.

How dare he just walk out on her like that. Was that any way to show he cared? Couldn't he give her a chance . . . ? Did she really want one? No. Yes.

She stamped her foot so hard that it caused a toe to cramp. The puppies whimpered. Her hands splayed over her hips as she glared at the animals. "Well, hell."

It was the second time in one night she had uttered a curse, and she wished it could make her feel better. Her eyes brimmed with tears as she untied the pups and began to clean the mess they had made. She tried to smile as they turned the chore into a tug-of-war, but it took too much effort.

Finally, she wadded up a scrap of cloth and threw it, then cursed beneath her breath because it didn't go nearly far enough. She hurled it over and over again until she doubled over and gave in to broken-hearted sobs.

By the time she moved the bed back to its original location, she was totally exhausted. Maybe—just maybe—she would be able to sleep without thinking, or dreaming, of Holt; of never becoming his wife, or ever bearing his children. Maybe?

Lorelei stood pensively in the window, as she so often did of late, hoping to catch sight of Holt as he passed down Main Avenue. It had been over a week since the social, and the night he had asked her to marry him.

Oh, she had *seen* him. He had even been into the store. And she had felt like a wooden statue, unable to show her true feelings. A helplessness, as if she had no control over the events in her life, seemed to pervade her soul. She didn't like it. Not one little bit.

Once, he had come by to purchase a heavy flannel shirt. He had stood so close behind her as she searched for his size that the hair on her body stood on end, as if magnetized to his large frame. It had taken every bit of her self-control to keep from whirling and capturing him in her embrace.

She scowled out at the beautiful day. Not even the crisp mountain sunshine could take her mind from the way her body ached whenever she saw Holt, from how her insides throbbed at night when, in her dreams, he held her– loved her.

Then yesterday, he had sauntered in to purchase licorice. She had been mesmerized by the erotic movements of his lips as he sucked on the stringy candy. A droplet of juice had pooled in the corner of his mouth. She had even swayed forward, tempted to kiss it from the enticing curve of his lips. But his tongue had flicked out, running slowly, sensuously, over that area of firm, moist flesh until her bones had turned the consistency of hot porridge.

Was it normal for a woman's body to crave a man's touch? Or was there something terribly wrong with her? She traced her lower lip with her index finger, thinking of the other men who had come into the mercantile during the past week. None of *them* had set her heart aflutter, or made her so tongue-tied and flustered that she couldn't remember her own name. Several of the fellows had flirted outrageously, but it was Holt she wanted. Only Holt. Always Holt.

She moved away from the window and closed the door. Business was slow. Now would be the perfect time to visit Catherine Romaine. Perhaps an advertisement for a fall sale would keep her occupied enough that thoughts of Holt could not intrude upon every waking minute of every day.

She sighed. The nights . . . she could not control.

Anguished determination settled over her features as she marched over to fetch her reticule. Yes, another huge sale lasting, perhaps, the rest of her life should do the trick.

But when Lorelei entered Catherine's office, no one was about. She waited, tapping her fingers on the edge of a cluttered desk. Finally, she peered into the smaller printing room.

Catherine was there, bent over with her back to the door, setting copy. The fluttering hem of Lorelei's skirt must have caught the woman's eye, for she slowly straightened, placing her hands in the small of her back and groaning as she did so.

"Sorry, didn't hear you come in." She came over to stand near Lorelei. "Let's go in the office. I need to get away from the press for a while."

Ink smudged the tip of Catherine's nose, and Lorelei dabbed at it with her handkerchief. "No wonder I never see you. There must be more happening in our little town than I have been aware of lately."

Catherine snorted. "Murder and mayhem is running out of my ears."

Lorelei blanched. The editor had unwittingly reminded her of just how much danger threatened Holt. The thought was terrifying, yet, at the same time, she was pervaded by a certain sense of security, knowing that a man of Holt's caliber was responsible for protecting the town.

Suddenly, her eyes widened. It was true. And if *she* felt such safety in his presence, how could she condemn him for upholding the law and making everyday life more peaceful for other innocent citizens?"

"Lorelei, honey, you all right?"

Lorelei shook her head, focusing somewhat glazed eyes on the editor. "I wish I knew the answer to that question."

Catherine laughed. "Uh oh. Been one of those days, has it? Well, tell me what's on your mind."

Lorelei sighed and began to tell Catherine of her plans for another sale. "I want a really special advertisement, something that will appeal to everyone."

Before Catherine could comment, an old man clomped past the door, only to backtrack and stick his head inside. "Mrs. Romaine, they's a fire down to Simpson's livery. Thought ya might wanna know." Then he was off again, as fast as his hobbling gait would propel him.

Lorelei marveled at the quick look of excitement flushing Catherine's face. The woman snatched a pen and notebook, and together they turned to see more people in the street, all hurrying south toward the blaze. Already, a heavy haze of smoke hung in the air.

The two women ran to the door and looked down the avenue. Concern etched both their features. Though Lorelei was new to Durango and the West, she had witnessed enough fires in Boston to know the threat one posed to people and property alike, especially in a hastily constructed community where more buildings were made of wood than brick, even her own store.

When she saw the editor glancing nervously between her and the fire, Lorelei told her, "Go on, Catherine. I will meet you back here later."

As Catherine rushed on, Lorelei went to the mercantile. It would be a long time before the fire could burn that far, but she needed to reassure herself that everything was all right. Then she, too, started toward the fire, drawn by her own curiosity and a sense of concern for those people with businesses near the livery.

Yet her steps were hesitant. Holt would be there if he was in town. She wasn't ready to face him—not now.

As she drew near the stables, she was relieved to find that the worst of the blaze was over and contained to just the livery. Townsmen had formed bucket brigades and were soaking the sides of the buildings closest to the fire. The pharmacy had been saved, also a dry

;oods store owned by one of her competitors, and she vas glad.

She saw Holt, and her heart skipped several beats. Ie was coated with ashes, and sparks and burned holes n his shirt. His face was nearly black with soot, but she vould have recognized him anywhere, from any listance—he was that commanding a figure. And uddenly, seeing him in such a state, came the ınwelcome thought that guns were not the only hazard ıe, or any of them, faced. Life itself was fraught with langers of all kinds.

Holt looked up the avenue then, and Lorelei shrank nto the afternoon shadows. When he had to stop and lirect the men just arriving from the smelter and mines vhere to lend a hand, she hurriedly headed back to the ıewspaper. Her help wasn't needed, and the ladies who ıad been pressed into service were being replaced by he new men.

Lorelei clasped her hands together, berating herself or acting like such a ninny. What had happened to her ıard-won confidence and courage the past few days?

Ten minutes later, she was kneeling in front of a tack of papers Catherine had pointed out, in hopes of inding ideas and designs for her advertisement. She ook a deep breath, and after staring into space for a ew minutes, began to sift through the papers, one by ne.

She needed to concentrate on her store. Right?

Soon, surprisingly, with everything else on her mind, ime began to literally fly by as she read through the laily editions.

It seemed that Catherine had moved to Durango ery soon after the town's inception. The people of

Animas City, the editor's former home, had turned the railroad away, so the major investors had bought land six miles farther west and developed a town plot, naming it after the Mexican city of Durango.

A warm tingle ran through Lorelei. So much had happened here in such a short time. She was, in reality, a part of the beginning, a part of the growth. A deep feeling of pride took root that she might make a contribution, might make a difference.

As she settled down to absorb every tiny bit of information she could, she began to notice a pattern of events. It was subtle at first, but then she could almost flip through thirteen or fourteen copies and find the same headline. A bank was robbed in Animas City. A payroll had been taken in Silverton.

Dates began to stand out. Strangely enough, most of the thefts had occurred within three to four days after shipments of goods arrived from Denver. She probably wouldn't even have noticed if the mischief at the mercantile hadn't happened just a few days after the latest supplies were delivered.

She sifted through the latest periodicals and experienced a slight disappointment. Nothing had been reported of any robberies during the last week, so that completely disrupted the mysterious chain of events. Oh, well, it wasn't as if there was anything significant about the information—but it had been fun, for a while, to set her imagination free.

Rising stiffly to her feet, Lorelei dusted off her hands and then her skirt. She decided to leave and come back later, but was forestalled when a bedraggled Catherine rushed through the door. The odor of smoke hung around the editor like a hazy cape. Soot clung to the woman's cloak and bonnet. The paper she placed on the desk was limp and torn along one edge.

"Well, it's out, but the structure wasn't salvageable. It'll smoke for days."

Lorelei coughed. Ashes sifted over Catherine in a white cloud as the woman shrugged from the coat and turned her tired brown eyes on Lorelei. "How'd you do? Come up with any ideas?"

Lorelei shook her head and held up one of the newspapers headlining a recent theft involving a nearby mine payroll. "I forgot to look at the ads, because—"

The front window shattered. Glass spewed into the room. Static gunfire cracked from the street. Lorelei and Catherine ducked to the floor. "Get behind the desk," Catherine shouted. "Stay down."

Another bullet smashed through the thin windowpane and thunked into a chair. Lorelei crawled as fast as her hands and knees would propel her, disregarding splinters and dirt clods as she went.

Above the resounding commotion, she heard a drawer creak open and looked up just as Catherine pulled out the large pistol. "Catherine, no! You mustn't!"

The other woman shot her an exasperated glance. "Our bank's being robbed, and by golly, if I can do something to help, I'll damn well do it." She kept her head down, but crept toward the broken window. "My life savings are over there. *I* can't afford to lose them."

Lorelei crouched behind the thick oaken desk. Until recently, violence seemed far removed from her little sphere of life, but as another bullet dug into the wall in back of her, she shivered with fright, realizing just how tenuous life could be, whether you went looking for trouble, or were an innocent bystander.

She covered her ears when the report from Catherine's gun reverberated through the small room. Then the editor shouted, "Got one of the thievin' bastards. Whoopee!" The gun spat again, and Lorelei disgusted herself by grabbing the thick desk leg and hiding her head.

Shame settled upon her shoulders like a fifty-pound anvil as she watched Catherine bravely defend her life's work, while *she* huddled like a scared rabbit, allowing someone else to fight for her.

Lorelei's courage resurfaced. Blood flowed hot through her veins. Her fingers and toes tingled as she pried her stiff arms from the desk and began to inch forward. Gradually, she made her way to Catherine's side, though she couldn't help but flinch every time a bullet whizzed past.

"Watch out! Here they come!" Catherine yelled and stood up in the window, taking aim on a group of riders whirling their horses in circles and shooting in all directions. One of their members was on the ground, trying to mount his badly frightened horse, but he was hampered by the bulging saddlebags he carried.

An outlaw facing the newspaper building must have seen or heard Catherine, for Lorelei saw his gun swing in their direction. She froze as she stared down the long, seemingly endless barrel.

A sudden surge of energy pumped through her, and she threw herself against Catherine, knocking the woman to the floor just as fire blossomed from the blue-black instrument of death. The bullet tugged at the shoulder of Lorelei's cloak. Catherine grunted as she hit the hard floor with Lorelei landing on top of her. "Gawd, honey, did you have to do that? I could've handled the . . ."

Lorelei shook her head. Catherine's words became indistinguishable from the roaring in her ears. As they were falling, Lorelei had seen images and vague movements from the corner of her eye. Now she stiffened and blinked, wondering if what she had seen was true. But when she was able to rise up enough to peer through the splintered glass, the street was empty. She rubbed her eyes and frowned.

The leader—he had to have been the leader of the gang—had swung aboard his horse and motioned the others to follow him out of town.

She could have sworn the man was Chad.

Chapter Eighteen

Holt poured a bucket of water over a horse's singed leg. The animal had been trapped in the burning barn, but he had managed to drag the terrified creature as far as the doorway before the roof collapsed.

Damned dumb animals, he thought, as he gently ran his hand over the slender leg. Even if its stall was a wall of flames, a horse would run back into it. Some sense of security they possessed.

Gunfire startled Holt. The horse flinched and whinnied with fright. Holt motioned for a boy standing nearby to take over caring for the animal, then took off at a run up the street.

He hadn't gotten far when a group of riders bore down upon him. Their guns were blazing as they fired indiscriminately at anyone who got in their way.

Holt leaped from the middle of the avenue and dove behind a wide post. A hail of bullets peppered the wood. He winced as a long splinter gouged into his neck. Snapping his gun from its holster, he leaned out and took aim at a rider deftly spurring his horse to a faster pace from the center of the gang. The fellow's hat was drawn low, and a bandana covered the lower half of his face. Bulging saddlebags hung over his shoulder.

For a split second, Holt's eyes connected with those of the outlaw. He hesitated—long enough for the man to bump his mount into that of one of the other riders—long enough that Holt's bullet took down that other man instead of the one for which he had aimed.

Then the gang galloped by, sending clouds of dust roiling into the air. Holt choked and waved a hand in front of his face, but was unable to get off a shot without endangering townspeople who were beginning to run into the street.

Holt glanced toward the outlaw writhing in the dirt. To a man standing on the boardwalk, gawking open-mouthed, Holt hollered, "You there! Fetch Doc Foster." The observer stood there, a blank expression on his face. Holt snapped, "Hurry!"

Finally, the man blinked, nodded and rushed down the walk. Holt went slowly toward the wounded man, kicking aside a smoking pistol lying within inches of the fellow's twitching fingers. Bending down, he examined the injury. It was high on the left side of the outlaw's chest, and his dark eyes were already glazing.

Holt shook his head. The man was dying. But before he could rise, the outlaw gripped his arm.

"Git 'im. Boss . . . set me up. Partner . . . too." The fingers bit like talons into Holt's sleeve. "Damned dog. Ya gotta git the boss."

Sitting back on his heels, Holt frowned. Set-up? Dog? What the hell? "I'll do what I can, but you have to give me a name. Who is your boss?"

The hand that gripped his arm fell limply to the dust.

Holt cursed. He was talking to a dead man.

Though he suspected who the outlaw boss was, he had no proof. There were a lot of people in and around Durango who were thin, of medium build, with blue eyes. God, he prayed he was wrong.

Suddenly, his head ached unmercifully. Damn it! What had taken place in that valley? Sometimes, like now, he could almost remember. Almost.

He sat on a nearby step to await the doctor and reloaded his pistol. Then he rubbed his throbbing temples. Visions of his half brother and similar scenes from a town a lifetime ago insinuated themselves insolently into his mind. How could things have gone so wrong? And why now, in the place he had chosen to make his home?

Seemingly from nowhere, old Marshal Tucker's leathered face appeared in his mind's eye. Holt shuddered. He hadn't thought of the man in years. Deceit. Treachery. Murder. It had all happened then and appeared to be recurring all over again.

Images of his father, stepmother and younger half brother flashed brightly, then faded. They'd been a perfect, happy family once, until circumstances forced Holt to leave home an outcast.

To this day, he found it hard to conceive that his own father had thought him capable of stealing from the family business. No matter that the evidence pointed to him, his father should have trusted—believed—in his son.

So the authorities had found his watch chain in the office. His watch chain. It could have been lost at any time. He had spent a lot of hours there, working. But the damnable thing, and what hurt the most, was that *he* hadn't had the chain, or the watch, in his possession. He had loaned it to his brother.

Sure, it was possible the boy could have lost it, too, but Holt had had enough doubts not to mention it to the constable, his father, or the stepmother who had raised him like her own.

As it turned out, no charges were filed, but with the threat of scandal hanging over his family, Holt had moved west and immediately fallen in with an unsavory bunch. Then Marshal Tucker had entered his life, took a shine to a lonely, frightened youngster, and turned him into a confident, capable man. A man who didn't look for trouble, but who could handle it if necessary.

And then one day, the half brother turned up. It seemed to Holt that everywhere he went, his brother followed. The boy had been spoiled and headstrong, and Holt had always given him the benefit of the doubt when he got into trouble, which happened more often than not.

Even when Marshal Tucker had been gunned down from behind while making his rounds one evening, Holt never suspected his brother—until he started his own investigation, and bits and pieces of information pointed toward his relation. Still, there was nothing conclusive.

Rather than dig further, when he received the news that his father had suddenly passed away, Holt had gone home to straighten out the business and to help his stepmother. His brother didn't bother.

Holt started when Dr. Foster tapped him on the

shoulder. "You all right, son?"

"Ah, yeah. Fine." He nodded toward the body. "He's dead."

The doctor looked at Holt's pale face, then covertly scanned his muscular body. Finding no apparent wounds, he replied, "Yes, I could see that."

Embarrassed by being caught daydreaming when there was serious trouble awaiting his attention, Holt stood up and dusted off the seat of his trousers. His shoulders ached, and he shifted them beneath the stiff denim shirt. He had the strangest sensation in his back. . . .

All of a sudden, he whirled and stared directly into the blackest pair of eyes he had ever encountered. The breath left his lungs with the force of a hard wallop to the gut.

Lorelei stared back. She had been frozen in place ever since Holt had stepped from behind the pillar into the path of the outlaws. She had been terrified that he would be killed before her very eyes. He hadn't even heard her screaming for him to run, or hide, or do whatever it took to save himself. Oh, no, he had stood tall and proud and unafraid.

The lump she swallowed scratched her throat. At the last moment, when she had thought he would surely be trampled by the stampeding horses, he had fired back. The nearest outlaw fell. Her heartbeat had accelerated, and then the strangest sensation had made her feel almost calm. She had actually felt pleased that Holt had shot the other man before being run over himself.

And who had been the first to the wounded man's side, the first to send for the doctor? Holt! He was quite a man—courageous, stalwart and compassionate. Her insides glowed with pride and a special kind of warmth. The more she learned of him, the more she admired him.

Her palms turned clammy and cold as she took a step toward Holt. Words failed to describe the emotions she felt toward him. "Are . . . are you all right?"

Holt nodded, observing Lorelei's pale features and the broken pane of glass forming a backdrop as she moved out of the shadows. He saw a tear in the puffy material capping her shoulder. Fear tautened his stomach so hard that he nearly bent double as he realized how close the bullets had come to causing her injury—or worse. God, what was she doing out here in this raw, uncivilized country?

Lorelei should be back East where she belonged, hosting tea parties, knitting, whatever well-bred ladies did with themselves. He could have lost her today, in less time than it took to draw his gun.

"What in the hell are you doin' here?" The gruffness in his voice caused him to flinch. But, damn it, she didn't have any business putting herself in danger.

Lorelei blinked. She wanted nothing more than to run to Holt, to take him in her arms and feel his vibrant flesh beneath her fingers. She needed to know for herself that he was all right and that it was really her reflection she saw in his eyes, his musky scent she inhaled.

But she didn't reach out. Instead, she shrank back in wonder at the vehemence of his glare. She stammered, "I-I . . . was only going to—"

"Don't you know better than to walk out in the street

durin' a gunfight? Don't they teach you to stay clear of trouble in New York, or Philadelphia or . . ." Damn it, she had to go home where she would be safe and he wouldn't have to worry himself crazy.

"Boston!" Lorelei clipped out the name. During a moment of insanity, she had contemplated telling him of her fears, of the confusion she had felt. She might have even admitted how very much she loved him. But his demeanor now forbade such revelations of the soul.

Suddenly, her spine stiffened. How dare he treat her as if she were nothing more than a headstrong child. "If you care to look, the outlaws have been gone for some time, and I am perfectly capable of standing anywhere I please. This is my town, too, you know."

Holt sighed, glancing up and down the avenue. Of course, she was right. The town was quiet. People were milling about the street or huddled in small groups in front of their businesses. A crowd had gathered in front of the bank.

He rubbed the back of his neck. Damned idiots. Most of them shouldn't be here either. For that matter, what was *anyone* doing here? How did one go about listing the perils to be encountered just walking down the streets of this brash, young community?

His eyes turned hard and cold, deepening their gray hue to the color of billowing smoke. Maybe they should all look at things from Lorelei's perspective. Guns were dangerous. Always had been. And it never failed that innocent people were the first to be hurt.

He had been a fool to ask a fine woman like Lorelei to live in this untamed wilderness. Her life would be in constant jeopardy. The fact that she had turned down his proposal of marriage was proof of her vast intelligence.

Holt pushed his hat to the back of his head, exposing a new crease in his forehead. He hoped she would try to understand what he had to say. "No, this is not your town. You don't belong in Durango."

Lorelei leaned weakly against the side of the building. Her fingers gripped the edge of a protruding board until splinters gouged her flesh. Of course she belonged. Durango was her home now. She truly loved her work, her friends, and . . . Holt. Why was he acting so self-righteous all of a sudden? Acting as if he wanted to be rid of her?

A deep sigh hissed between her teeth before she argued, "Say what you will, but my home *is* here. You cannot intimidate me, or force me to believe otherwise."

He stalked forward and stopped so close that she pressed against the siding to keep from touching him. His face was near enough that she felt his breath on her cheek. Her knees trembled.

"Oh, yeah? Who is it that hates guns and needless killin'?" He motioned to the dead outlaw.

She slanted her eyes in that direction and had difficulty swallowing.

"Who believes life can flow right on by without things like that happenin'? Or that there's no reason to defend against it, if it does?"

She opened her mouth to tell him that she'd had a change of heart, to admit there was something to *his* philosophy, too. But she strangled on the words as Holt placed his hands on either side of her head and just stared into her eyes.

When she thought he might lean down farther, perhaps even kiss her, he suddenly pushed himself away, muttering, "What the hell. Do as you damned well please." Then he turned and walked away.

Holt strode quickly. He couldn't, in all conscience, do anything else. If he stayed another moment, he would have yanked her into his arms and begged her to be his forever.

The hell of it was, it was too risky. He thought about the night he and Ed were wounded. Ed had been certain the two men were trying to get through the window opening into the mercantile's storeroom. Then Enders was attacked. And another break-in. There was a connection to Abbott's Mercantile and Lorelei, he just knew it. No two ways about it, she had to leave Durango before she ended up like her uncle John.

While Holt walked and cursed, Lorelei stared after him, her mouth agape with exasperation. Her eyes widened when he suddenly stopped and slammed his fist into a hitching rail, but then glittered with a sort of appeasement when he cradled the offended hand within the circle of his other arm.

Served him right! Who did he think he was, anyway? Throwing her words back in her face and then leaving without giving her a chance to defend herself.

Doubt about her sensibilities began to plague her. Perhaps she didn't know her own mind. It seemed the very foundation of her being had been turned topsy-turvy lately. All because of one damnable, hard-headed, extraordinary man.

But she didn't know what to think of him now. She

could have sworn the man had asked her to marry him—even said he loved her once. So why was he turning her away? Ordering her to leave? What had she done to cause his hateful outburst?

The days dragged by, long, boring days. A tired, dirty Holt was unsaddling his sweat-caked horse in the barn behind Dr. Foster's place. He and a dozen men from Durango and the surrounding mines had ridden hard on the trail of the bank robbers, but had come up empty-handed.

Holt bit the inside of his cheek and cursed. How could five or six riders just disappear? Whoever led the pack was pretty damned clever.

Frustrated and discouraged, he was on his way to the boardinghouse to clean up when he suddenly stopped, tipped the brim of his hat and muttered, "Good day." His eyes never quite reached those of Lorelei Abbott's.

Lorelei paused, nodded, then walked on until she could duck into the recessed shelter of the bank entrance. Then she turned and peered back down the walk.

Her mouth was so dry that she could barely swallow as she gazed longingly after the sheriff. *Good day,* indeed. How good could it be when the man you loved to distraction acted pained to grant you a civil greeting?

She ground her teeth together and literally stomped on up the boardwalk. The breeze she created as she hurried nearly chilled her to the bone. He had ignored her for over two weeks. Two weeks! And never once during all of that time had he stood still long enough to give her a chance to talk to him.

It was always "Good day," "Pleased to see you," or some such drivel, and then he rushed on his way as if remaining within speaking distance would contaminate him with some horrifying disease.

Well, two could play at that nonsense.

A mischievous twinkle shone from her eyes, the first light of life she'd experienced in ages. Perhaps she could create a game of her own. If being near her was so dreadful, then the man was due for a good dose of unpleasantness.

Something else nagged at the back of her mind. Seeing Holt in trouble the afternoon of the robbery had scared the image of Chad riding in the center of the gang of outlaws completely from her thoughts. Even when she and Holt had talked later, she had forgotten to mention it.

She stiffened. Holt *had* to have seen Chad, too. Why hadn't he mentioned it himself, or thrown up her choice of friends? Was it possible she was mistaken? She didn't think so.

The next day, Holt stood beside his horse, currying the animal's thick, red hide. The stallion snorted when he dug down too hard with the brush's stiff bristles. "Sorry, fella." He turned the horse loose and forked hay into the manger.

Holt leaned against a rail and recalled what he had thought of the elusive outlaw gang's leader. Clever? Yes. But Chad was more than clever. He was mean and conniving and used his innocent little-boy looks to his advantage, and everyone else's detriment.

Holt kicked the biggest rock he could find as he walked down the alley. Why couldn't he have seen through the boy years ago? Why had it taken so long? And now, was it too late?

Only one thing was clear in his mind. Until he could get Lorelei out of town, she mustn't know of his suspicions concerning Chad. In the first place, she probably wouldn't believe him, and secondly, she might make a slip and get herself into worse danger.

"Good morning, Sheriff. Did you and the posse catch the . . . thieves?"

The condescending tone of the voice he'd been aching to hear couldn't disguise the rich timbre that caused Holt to stop in mid-stride. His dry, red-rimmed eyes literally drank in the vision perched on the end of the porch.

Her long blond hair hung like a bright cape around her slender shoulders. The plain brown dress accentuated every curve and swell on her delectable body, better than any fancy gown could pretend to do, to his way of thinking.

"Mornin', Miss Abbott. No, we didn't find them." Heat suffused his cheeks as he rubbed at the stubble that probably made him look like a desperado, himself.

Damn, he had been so lost in his thoughts that he hadn't paid attention to where he was going. Naturally, he'd ended up at the last place on earth he wanted to be—Lorelei's front door.

Lorelei's heart thundered in her ears. He looked so handsome, just like the cowboy she ran into upon her arrival at the Durango depot. There was even the same exasperated expression on his craggy features. The dark shadow on his lean cheeks and the shaggy locks of hair that curled over the edge of his bandana invited, no insisted, that she run her fingers . . .

When Holt saw her arm rise, he side-stepped out of reach. He didn't know what she had intended, but he was dirty and smelly, and as much as he longed to step up and take her in his arms and never let go, he mustn't do anything to encourage her.

He growled, "Why don't you hurry and go back to Baltimore, or Richmond, or wherever?" His gut churned at the irony of the situation. Once, he had almost begged her to marry him, vowed she would be his. And now that she seemed to be coming around, returning his feelings, he had to push her away. It was a cruel form of torture.

"Boston!" Lorelei curled her fists beneath the folds of her skirt. Then, though her eyes were mere slits, she smiled sweetly. "Why must you keep insisting I leave? Durango is my home, whether *you* like it or not. I have a business, and friends, and I happen to . . . love . . . it here." She tilted her head. At first she had thought he was teasing about getting rid of her. Now she knew better.

"Even with all of the guns and gunfighters, and the killin'?" He grinned. She knew that he knew how she felt about violence. He'd like to see her argue with that.

Lorelei saw her chance. Now she could tell him—

"Morning, Sheriff, missy. Was hoping I'd find you both today."

The frown that had wrinkled her brow upon being

interrupted was immediately wiped clear when Lorelei saw Robert Endsley coming up the steps.

"Mr. Endsley!" Impulsively, she gave the man a hug. "It is wonderful to see you up and about." She stepped back and scrutinized the walking skeleton. "Did Dr. Foster give you permission . . . I mean, you look fine, but . . ."

The pink tint that colored Robert's cheeks from Lorelei's unexpected embrace did more to give him life than any two large steaks with brown gravy. He stuck his hands in his pockets and shifted uneasily from foot to foot. "Uh, the doctor released me yesterday. Said I was ready to go back to . . . doing anything I wanted, long as I took it easy for a while."

Lorelei noted his brief hesitation and immediately commented, "Well, I certainly hope you have come to resume your position at the mercantile. I need your help."

His taut body relaxed before her eyes as he whispered, "Thank you, missy. I was afraid you had hired someone else."

Holt stood to the side, listening, watching. Though it relieved his mind to know that Enders was back, the man was pale and weak and would be in sorry condition to defend Lorelei if it came to that very soon.

Maybe, she could just go home for a little while, and come back when things calmed down. No, he mentally castigated himself. She wasn't cut out for this kind of rough life. And it would be years before Colorado Territory was settled enough to be considered "safe."

Lorelei had surreptitiously kept an eye on Holt during her exchange with Endsley. She could tell that whatever he was thinking had caused him to puff up, as if ready to berate her with more of his insightful nonsense. Taking Robert's arm, she quickly guided him into the store. "Good-bye, Sheriff. So nice to visit with you. We must do it more often, don't you think?"

Holt opened his mouth, but her back was turned.

Enders glanced back over his shoulder. "I wanted to talk to you, too, Dolan. You saved my hide. I owe you."

With a giant shrug, Holt replied, "Just doin' my job." And with a conspiratorial nod toward Lorelei, he added, "I'd say we're even."

Enders rolled his eyes as Lorelei gave his arm a jerk.

Holt sighed and turned toward his office. Now was as good a time as any to go through more wanted posters.

First, though, a short nap might be in order. He'd never felt so tired, in mind, body and spirit.

Later that evening, just before dusk, Holt stumbled along, making his rounds. He had yet to get a minute of rest, let alone sleep. What with one thing or another, he had been kept busy all day. He stepped from the pharmacy doorway and bumped into a soft, feminine form.

"S'cuse me, ma'am. Wasn't watchin' where I was goin'."

"My heavens, Sheriff Dolan, perhaps you should purchase a pair of spectacles. This is becoming a habit."

Holt grumbled a few unintelligible oaths. This was

the third, or was it the fourth? time today he had literally *run into* Lorelei Abbott. One more instance of the firm swell of her bosom brushing against his arm, or another whiff of her fresh, womanly scent, and he would go completely, stark-raving mad.

Already, his hands clenched into tight fists to keep from grabbing at her luscious body. His groin ached as shifting his stance did little to ease the throbbing fullness straining his trousers.

A muscle jerked the length of his jaw. "Maybe, Miss Abbott, if you tended to business instead of roaming the streets, you wouldn't suffer this problem. Or have you found a new interest?"

"Ooohh! You . . . you . . ." Lorelei swallowed the rest of her retort. She mustn't show how much his insufferable attitude bothered her. Until this moment, she had done an admirable job of remaining cool and unruffled during their *encounters*. And so she would continue to be, though she sent up a prayer for additional patience.

She gritted, "You know better than that, Mr. Dolan."

"Do I? It's been a long time, Lori."

His voice was a husky whisper that sent shivers racing along her spine. He was beginning to really annoy her now. He wasn't playing fair. "Thank you for reminding me just what an uncouth cad you are, Sheriff."

He tipped his hat at a jaunty angle. "My pleasure." God, he had forgotten what a spitfire she could be. How could he manage to live without her now that he had finally found her? She was the first woman he had known who gave better than she got. He fought to hide the trembling that quaked throughout his body, just as he resisted the urge to pull her to him and take her right there on the street.

But fight he did. "I'll let you be goin' on your way, ma'am, unless you came to see if I'd care to warm your cold, lonely bed. In that case, I'd—"

His head jerked to the side with the force of her blow. As he watched her march down the walk, he rubbed the tingling imprint of her fingers on his cheek. Admittedly, he had deserved the slap, but at that particular moment, he would have been willing to say, or do, anything to get her out of his reach. And it had worked, thank God. Now all he had to do was figure a way to get her out of town.

". . . stupid beast. Fiend." Lorelei stomped back to the mercantile, unaware of Holt's watchful gaze, then closed the door behind her.

"Ooohh! Men!" she screamed at the empty room, which suddenly became filled with the clatter of sharp toenails and worried yips as the puppies raced to see what had upset their master.

She knelt and hugged the animals to her breast. Tears began a slow, steady trickle down her cheeks. The game had turned ugly. Instead of being pleased by the aggravated looks Holt sent her, she was experiencing pain. Too much pain.

And if she was to judge from his words and actions, he truly must not care for her anymore.

Perhaps she *should* leave Durango. Her heart would surely break if she stayed.

Chapter Nineteen

"It takes a different breed of man to forge out new territory and make a fresh start. And he needs a strong woman by his side."

Lorelei nearly choked on a bite of mashed potato. Catherine had invited her to dinner, and the conversation had been bland enough—until now. How they had ever gotten on the subject of the strange quirks of men and the women they found attractive, Lorelei would never know.

"Catherine, have you seen Mrs. Watkins' imported—"

"Take your man, Mr. Endsley, for example." The editor waved her fork in the air, then tilted the tines downward to spear a crispy chunk of chicken. "He's the strong, silent type. That kind needs a witty woman who's not afraid to do the talking for him."

There was a dreamy, wistful look in the woman's eyes, and Lorelei wondered, not for the first time, if Catherine had designs on poor Robert. She had paid an inordinate number of visits to the mercantile lately, ever since Mr. Endsley had returned to work.

"But do you not think—"

"And then there's Holt Dolan, a loner if I ever saw one."

Lorelei gulped, then smugly recalled the offer of marriage he had extended at one time. A loner? Maybe. But not by choice.

A queasy sensation wormed into her stomach. The half-eaten forkful of peas slithered down her throat. No, he wasn't alone because he wanted to be, but because she was an insensitive, headstrong—

"He needs a tough, but caring woman, who'll help turn that ranch of his into a warm sanctuary for him to come home to. A woman who—"

"Catherine, I smell something burning. Didn't you mention something about rolls warming?"

When the editor jumped up from the table to see to the bread, Lorelei took her first good breath in what seemed like hours, rather than just a few minutes. She didn't want to hear about the kind of woman Holt *needed;* she only knew that at one time, he had *wanted* her, and she had made the mistake of her life.

If only she had seen things then the way she did now. If only she had given him a chance—taken the time to sit down and talk over their differences. If only . . .

"If that don't beat all. It wasn't the rolls burning; it was a sticky bun left over from breakfast that had been pushed to the back of the oven."

Catherine offered Lorelei a piece of the bread. Her appetite had deserted her, but she took one of the golden-brown puffs anyway. Usually the yeasty aroma of fresh-baked bread was enough to set her mouth to watering, but thoughts of Holt had replaced her desire for food.

She craved the sight of him. Longed for his touch. Memories of his crooked smile caused her fingers to poke through the flaky crust of the roll.

"My goodness, honey, are you all right? Is there something the matter with the bread?"

Lorelei focused her gaze on her friend's concerned features. "N-no. Everything is fine. I was just thinking—"

Catherine snapped her fingers. "Excuse me for interrupting, but I've just got to let you know, before I forget. Mr. Redman's oldest son, Ralph, has a crush on the Johnson girl. Yes, indeed."

Lorelei sighed and slapped a knife full of butter on the crushed roll. It looked to be a long evening.

Almost a week after the demoralizing dinner with Catherine, Lorelei stood inside the warm mercantile watching huge flakes of snow forming soft drifts over four inches deep in the middle of Main Avenue.

It had been dark outside all afternoon, and the day had seemed to wear on forever. Mr. Endsley had used the slow business as an opportunity to escape early before Catherine Romaine could corner him at the usual quitting time.

And with the thought of quitting, images of hot vegetable stew and a slice of sourdough bread, spread thick with butter and chokecherry jam, drew her footsteps toward the door. She might as well close the store and start supper.

Lorelei had no more than reached for the latch when the door suddenly swung inward. A huge form rushed inside, bringing along a cascade of cold, wet snow. Side-stepping, she barely managed to avoid most of the icy crystals when the person shook like a big bear, sending a spray of droplets over half of the entryway.

Gray eyes locked onto her as she shoved the door closed against the blast of cold air. She self-consciously wiped her hands down her skirt and backed behind a table piled high with fur caps and winter mittens. "Wh-what are you doing here?" She bit her lower lip, hating herself for sounding so breathless and whiny.

Holt had been asking himself the same question with every step he took toward the mercantile, and had yet to come up with a good answer. He blamed it on idiocy, or that he was a glutton for punishment. Anything besides the truth—that he couldn't stand not seeing her, being near her, for another second.

"Needed some ammunition for my rifle." Uh oh. He knew he'd said the wrong thing the minute the words slipped past his mouth.

Lorelei ran the palm of her hand along the soft, velvetlike texture of the hats. Without blinking, she smoothly answered, "I thought you knew that I don't stock guns or ammunition."

He waited for the outburst, for the tirade he knew was coming against the use of guns. And he waited. "Uh, guess I forgot." Actually, bullets had been the first excuse to come to mind when she wanted to know why he was there. It was a logical mistake. A man always needed ammunition.

Then, all of a sudden, the fallacy of his reasoning became blindingly apparent. Yes, it was logical. It was a sign of the times. And it was a damned shame. There were some good points to Lorelei's reasoning. Too many people refused to take the use of weapons, or the destruction of lives, seriously enough.

All the while he was thinking, his gaze caressed Lorelei like satin sliding over silky skin. No matter how often, or how long, he looked, she was even more beautiful. She appeared almost angelic, with her blond hair cascading down her back, wearing a long white sweater.

Lorelei was thinking similar thoughts concerning how wonderful Holt looked. His coat hung open, and her gaze delved into the vee of his shirt, devouring the sight of crisp black hairs curling above the stiff fabric. She could imagine them twining in soft springs around her fingers.

Her gaze slowly crept upward, drinking in the strong column of his neck, where she knew the skin to be soft and very sensitive. His jaw was still a bit too firm. His lips, ah, those lips.

And then her eyes locked with his.

She wondered if he could read the happiness and excitement she felt at seeing him again written there for the world to see. For no matter how hard she tried to deny it, and she gave it her best effort, she loved him with all of her heart and felt like a spring blossom shut away from light and water without his life-giving sustenance. All it took was just one look, or one touch, and she was alive again.

Holt was drawn forward with the same sensation of helplessness that a moth had to feel as it flew into a flame. Only the corner of the table separated them. He reached out to run his fingers over the smooth apple of her cheek and then on into the soft wisps of hair tucked behind her ear. God, how had he stayed away so long?

He had never admitted to needing anyone in his life, but he *needed* this woman so-o badly. . . .

His upper body swayed forward. Somehow, as if of the same mind, they both took a step to the side. Nothing separated them. They swayed together, thighs melding as her sweater mated with his coat.

Her cheeks burned red when his hands cupped her face, a color that she knew suffused her entire body. She felt warm and . . . gooey . . . inside, like thick chocolate fudge just before it was ready to pour from the pan.

This was what she had dreamed of, yearned for. It was almost as if her thoughts had conjured him. Except the feel of his hands was real. Very real.

In silent agreement, as if they were both afraid of breaking the spell that seemed to control their actions, they gave consent with each sultry look and tantalizing touch. The sweater was cast aside. His coat fell to the floor.

Holt rasped, "Just a minute, sweetheart."

Lorelei moaned her displeasure as he stepped out of her reach, but sighed contentedly when it took him only seconds to lock the door, close the shades and flick a blanket to the floor. Then he was there, in the circle of her arms, his hands urgently searching her body, as if to reassure himself that she was the same woman he had loved so long ago.

He, too, had longed for this moment, and was afraid that something would happen yet to spoil it. He wanted to move slowly, gently, so as not to frighten her with his anxious movements. But with each caress, his exploration became more frenzied. Items of clothing were hastily thrust aside.

Lorelei languished under the tender ministrations of his mouth. And where his lips couldn't reach, his fingers took control. She writhed with blissful pain, aggressively fondling him in places she had never ventured before. His need heated the length of his manhood and nearly seared her inquisitive fingers. She thought the fire igniting her lower belly would surely consume her.

At last he picked her up and knelt down, laying her on the blanket as if she were a priceless jewel. His eyes shot silver sparks as he memorized every inch of her ivory-smooth form.

Lorelei felt as if his gaze ignited tiny bonfires along her nerve endings. There wasn't a square inch of flesh that didn't tingle or pulse with anticipation. Impulsively, feverish with need, she reached between their bodies and guided him to that secret place that only he had known. "Please, Holt? Now?"

The softly spoken plea was all Holt needed. It still seemed like everything was happening in a wonderful dream world, and he dreaded the time he would open his eyes and find reality. But for now, he hoped the fantasy lasted a lifetime.

He entered her with one swift stroke. Her petal-soft flesh enfolded him within its velvety warmth. He rode her with fierce urgency. She bucked beneath him like a wild filly, proud and determined to have her way. They drove as one to the heights of the heavens and descended ever so gently, as if on the back of a winged Pegasus.

Two breaths came fast and furious, until gradually, their heartbeats resumed a semblance of normalcy. But instead of feeling relaxed and sated, Lorelei was tense and uneasy. Holt, too, experienced a tightening in his gut, as he instinctively sensed something was about to happen—something ominous. His arms held her fast. His heart ached with tender dread.

"I love you, Holt." Lorelei spoke in a soft whisper.

Holt stiffened. His chest constricted. It was the first time she had voluntarily said the words first. He could hardly breathe for the pain they wrought.

Dear God, he loved her as life itself. Could he ignore the threats hanging over her? Impossible. His insides literally ripped apart, but he remained silent, pretending not to have heard. The backs of his eyes burned as he blinked several times in rapid succession.

The only consolation he would give himself was that it was for her own good. Hell, but he was a righteous bastard.

Lorelei dared not breathe as she waited for Holt's response to the words it had taken all of her pitiful amount of courage to utter. Would it make enough of a difference? Could their relationship return to the way it was before? Before she had treated Holt so callously?

The minutes passed, silently. Tears of pain pooled in her eyes. Pain and rejection. She tried to convince herself that he hadn't heard, that she had spoken too softly. But his body couldn't lie, and she still felt the contractions of his muscles beneath her cheek.

He had heard—and understood. He simply had no answer, no desire to renew the commitment he had once offered so generously, only to be brutally denied. Only now did she understand how terribly he must have hurt.

She sniffed, using every ounce of control she possessed to keep from breaking down and blubbering like a baby. Her fingers remained splayed across the lean firmness of his chest and rib cage, until she began to move her hands slowly, tenderly, memorizing the feel of him.

Her chin trembled only slightly as she sat up and reached for her sweater, wrapping it around her like a protective shield. She had no regrets over the love-making just shared, but felt extremely exposed, vulnerable. She had *wanted* it to happen, in the worst way, and he had obliged.

Though he now knew how she truly felt about him, and could possibly use that knowledge to cause her a great deal of pain in the future, she was glad she had been honest, as he had once been.

She flinched when Holt's trembling hand reached toward her cheek.

"Lori, I—"

"No, don't say anything." Her breath rasped raw in her throat. "Please, just get dressed and leave." The plea was caught on a sob as she gathered her own clothing.

Holt felt he had no other choice but to follow her wishes. If he tried to explain his reasons for behaving like such an ass, she would either make light of his fears, or demand to become even more deeply involved. Either way, it was a nobody-wins situation.

God knew, he didn't want to be sheriff of Durango forever. He dreamed of settling down on his ranch, of raising horses and cattle, and one day, a family. And the only woman he could imagine by his side was Lorelei Abbott.

Maybe, if they both lived through what was to come, and if she ever spoke to him again, she would understand and forgive his actions. Maybe.

Before he left, Holt looked back over his shoulder. Lorelei was huddled in the middle of the blanket, clutching her sweater and dress to her breast as if they were life lines.

For a fleeting moment, he was tempted to say, "What the hell," and go back. They could get through this somehow. But a sudden vision of her crumpled body lying in a pool of blood, like John Abbott's, firmed his resolve.

He straightened his back and reached for the latch. As he let himself out, he noticed the two pups sitting side by side in the entrance to Lorelei's room. Their big brown eyes appeared so knowledgeable and their expressions so solemn that he hesitated.

Then he did something that was to his way of thinking, a foolish, sentimental thing. He turned and blew Lorelei a kiss. The brown pup hung out its tongue, panting, but Holt could have sworn the reaction was a smile. He muttered an oath as he let himself out the door.

Lorelei heard the door close, but couldn't muster the energy to move. She wondered what had taken Holt so long to leave as the pool of tears that had been collecting behind her eyes began to overflow. Finally, she allowed herself to give in to the overwhelming urge to cry.

Once the pain in her chest had lessened, a listless pall settled over her. But soon, the sounds of the storm raging outside increased, and the draft on the floor chilled her empty body.

She reached for her scattered items of clothing and clumsily dressed. Catherine Romaine's voice droned in the recesses of her mind "Holt Dolan needs a strong, loving woman." Over and over the litany repeated itself, until she pounded her fists on the nearest unopened crate of goods that had just arrived that afternoon.

Strong. Loving. If the truth be told, she was neither of those. She was weak and selfish and had proven those traits time and again since her acquaintance with Holt had first begun. From day one, she had made one mistake after another. And for the life of her, she couldn't imagine what had prompted him to propose marriage to such an immature half-wit.

The more she thought about it, the more she realized the hindrance she would present to a man in Holt's position. Though she'd had a slight change of mind, she still didn't fully agree with his adherence to guns as a way of life.

And though she liked Durango, and what she had seen so far of the countryside, she had never been on a ranch before, or lived anywhere other than in a large city. Perhaps everything that had happened tonight was a blessing in disguise, for them both.

She sniffed and took a long, somewhat trembling breath. As she had decided so long ago, it was best they not see each other again. She would give him up in the hopes that he would find someone better suited to his needs.

Using the crate for support, she pushed to her feet. It slid beneath a nearby table, and she bumped her head against the hard pine planking as she righted herself. Everything had turned against her it seemed, even inanimate objects. She finally stood and walked as far as her cot before crumpling into a sobbing heap.

Soon her arms were filled with furry, wet-tongued puppies. She asked them how she could ever survive seeing Holt with another woman clinging to his arm, but they offered no answer. Damn Catherine Romaine!

At half past ten the next morning, someone pounded on Lorelei's front door. She knew the time because she had been glancing from her clock to the street for two hours, wondering what was keeping Holt. He should have passed on his rounds an hour ago.

The pounding became more insistent. Freda and Sissy whined and barked until Lorelei covered her ears and shouted. "Go away. The store is closed."

The throbbing in her head kept time with the incessant knocking. For a person disinclined to having headaches, the one she experienced that morning was a dandy. She sighed. Now that she was learning the western jargon, would there be any need for it?

"Lorelei! Open this door! I know you're in there, girl."

The red pup growled. The brown one circled Lorelei's legs as she canted her head to the side. That voice was awfully familiar. She shook her head, which she immediately regretted. No, it wasn't possible. Not in Colorado Territory.

"If you don't open the door right this minute, I'll break it down . . . or send for the sheriff."

Lorelei couldn't care less if the entire building fell down around her head, but she couldn't have Holt showing up. He was the last person she wanted to face, for *he* would know why her door was locked, and why her eyes were red and puffy, and her nose running and shining like a beacon announcing, "See Lorelei. She's been crying all night. All because of you, Holt Dolan."

Suddenly she whirled and ran for the door. As she yanked it open, her father stumbled through, his fist still upraised. The two puppies darted around his legs, snapping at his trousers.

Lorelei stood with her mouth agape as she watched her rotund parent lift his feet in quite a spritely manner. Then, before he had a chance to dance out of her reach, she launched herself into his arms. He was so solid and secure and loving, and her daddy. She held on to him for all she was worth.

"Damn it, daughter, what has happened to you since you've come to this godforsaken place?" Clifton Abbott hugged his daughter, then set her back, patting her shoulder and huffing through his heavy jowls.

Lorelei sniffed and bent down, grabbing the puppies by the scruffs of their necks to keep them from doing her father more damage. Then she looked him in the eyes, all innocence. "Why, Daddy, I have no idea what you are talking about."

She couldn't tell him the truth, she just couldn't.

From the corner of her eye, she saw Robert Endsley peeking through the open doorway. His long legs appeared several inches shorter, hidden as they were behind the drifted snow.

"Mr. Endsley?" Her eyes slanted from her blustering father to the guilty-looking employee. "I thought today was your day off."

Enders walked gingerly into the mercantile and discreetly closed the door. He, too, glanced nervously toward Clifton Abbott. "Uh, well, yes it is."

"So, what are you doing here, especially on a day

when nobody in their right mind would venture outside?" She glared pointedly at her father.

And it was precisely the reason why she had chosen this day as the perfect time to secret herself away from people in general and lick her wounds in private. Everyone was entitled to a day, now and then, to feel sorry for themselves, weren't they?

And so she kept wary eyes on Endsley and the looks the man and her father tried discreetly, but to no avail, to hide. "Well?"

Robert took off his snow-covered cap, sending a shower of tiny wet drops to soak into the floor. "I, uh, was worried."

She frowned. "About what?"

"Why you hadn't opened the store."

Suspicion took root in the back of her mind. "And how would you know that, since you were supposed to be resting, or staying inside out of the cold?"

"Ahem. I . . ."

Clifton stepped forward, to the accompaniment of a pair of deep-throated growls. "Do something with those damned beasts, girl. Since when did you start keeping pets?" His jowls jiggled. "These used to be new shoes." He pointed accusingly to the tiny tooth marks marring the shiny leather.

Enders' face brightened as he reached for the puppies. "I'll take them."

From her kneeling position, Lorelei shook her finger at the tip of his nose. "Oh, no. Something is going on here, and I want to know what! Now!"

This time she was sure of the guarded glances the pair gave each other. "Daddy?"

Her father looked around the store, at the floor,

everywhere but at his disgruntled daughter.

"Mr. Endsley?"

The employee lifted his shoulders in a "What can I say?" shrug when Clifton shot him a questioning look at Lorelei's use of the strange name.

Lorelei let the pups go, giving them silent permission to wreak what havoc they would on her father, or Endsley, either. She stood ramrod straight, with her hands fisted on her hips, glowering between the two men.

Finally, Clifton sighed and untied the sash about the waist of his coat. "All right." He glanced apologetically toward Enders. "She'll have to know sometime."

"Know what, Daddy? I swear, if you do not tell me what—"

"Lorelei, this man is Robert Enders. He has been my right hand for fifteen years."

"Sixteen next month, sir."

"Yes, yes. Quite right. Now, where was I?"

Lorelei's eyes narrowed dangerously. "Let me guess. You sent Mr. Ends—Enders?—after me. He has been spying on me all this time. I bet you've known every little thing . . ." She gulped. Dear heavens, surely not even Mr. . . . whatever, knew *every* thing. ". . . I have done, maybe even before I did it. Am I right?"

The pained, hurt expression on Enders' face did little to assuage the anger boiling from deep inside Lorelei. She had thought there was a fondness growing between them, too. But now all she felt was betrayal.

Clifton shifted his shoulders uncomfortably and nodded. "That's fairly close. But he hasn't been *spying*, as you so delicately phrased it. I asked him to keep you safe, because you are my only child. Is that so terrible?

Should I not be expected to worry about you?"

Lorelei acknowledged there was some truth to his words. He had a right to a father's concerns, just as she had often worried over him in a manner that only a daughter could understand. But seeds of doubt and distrust had been planted.

Had Enders stopped at watching out for her safety? Or had he done more? Far, far more.

Had the mercantile prospered under her direction, or had Enders, at her father's request, orchestrated the success? It had been Enders' idea to advertise in the newspaper. What else had he done behind her back?

Suddenly, her shoulders slumped. She turned her back on the startled men and scuffed disconsolately into her bedroom.

All this time, she had been so proud of her achievements, for sticking with the store and working hard to build it into a thriving, prosperous business. And now she found out her accomplishments amounted to nothing.

Was she still just "daddy's little girl"?

Chapter Twenty

After her father and Enders left her alone, Lorelei decided not to open the mercantile at all that day. She spent the time unpacking crates and restocking the nearly empty shelves. The task usually gave her a great deal of pleasure, for it was visual evidence of how well the business was doing. Today, however, she had a hard time mustering enthusiasm, and the work eventually became a chore.

She counted the hours and minutes until it was time to go to bed, then took the puppies outside. The first smile of the day cracked her lips when both animals plopped belly first into the snow and buried themselves to the tips of their noses.

Once she had tucked herself beneath three layers of heavy quilts and blankets, she thought she would at last find peace. But even her best-laid plans went awry. She tossed and turned, rolled and fidgeted until she gave up and just stared into space.

She was counting the rows of narrow boards traversing the ceiling when she heard the pups crawl out from under the cot. First one growled, then the other. Thinking they wanted to play some more, she reached down to give them another good-night pat and discovered their hackles raised and their little bodies taut and quivering.

"What's the matter, girls? Can't you sleep, either?"

The puppy she was touching at the time snarled. Lorelei stiffened and held her breath. Something was definitely wrong. Then she heard a noise. It sounded like something scraping at the back door.

The red pup ran to the foot of the bed and began to bark. The brown puppy stayed by Lorelei's feet as she sat up and searched for her slippers. By the time she managed to still her trembling hands long enough to slip on her robe, both dogs were scratching and yapping at the oaken portal.

Lorelei was frightened. This was far from the first time she had heard noises at her doors or windows, but tonight was different. There were too many things going on, dangerous things, for her *not* to be afraid.

Her voice squeaked. "Who's out there? Holt? Is that you?"

She cautiously approached the door on legs that felt as weak as soft butter. A muffled curse drifted through the cracks. She heard a muted thud.

Reaching to the side of the door frame, she wrapped her fingers around a thick handle. She had long since replaced the useless parasol with a heavy shovel. Now she could give someone a good, sound whack, rather than watching them double over with laughter as she threatened them with her flimsy umbrella.

With the would-be weapon held protectively in front

of her, Lorelei leaned toward the door and was greeted with blessed silence. It suddenly occurred to her that she hadn't heard anything from outside since she had called Holt's name. Perhaps mention of the sheriff had scared whoever it was away.

She straightened and took a deep breath, deepening the timbre of her voice to sound less hysterical. "Sheriff Dolan? I was expecting you an hour ago."

Her chattering teeth were about to give her away as she pressed her ear to the portal. Sure enough, she heard another muted mumble, then the sound of footsteps crunching through icy snow.

The pups whined and looked at her expectantly. She let out the breath she had been holding and sank to her knees, drawing the dogs into her lap. "Good girls. We did it. We scared them away."

Tears streaked Lorelei's face. "We did it."

At the same time Lorelei was crawling back into bed, with her trusty shovel propped close against the headboard and the puppies curled at her feet, Holt was in the barn saddling his horse. The town had been quiet. Almost too quiet. His nerves were strung so tight that he felt he would come unwound at the first inopportune moment.

He needed to get out of Durango for a while and get his thinking straight, something he had been unable to do for far too long. He was going home to his ranch.

In no particular hurry, he kept his stallion to a sedate pace as they rode through the night. Just as he topped the rise overlooking the peaceful valley harboring the headquarters of his spread, the Rocking D Ranch, dawn broke the eastern horizon.

Tints of pink and lavender and orange colored the edges of the few clouds banked against the mountaintops. He took a deep breath and released it slowly. God, how he loved it here and longed to sit on his porch and take in the beauty surrounding him with nothing more important on his mind than whether it was time to feed the chickens or to turn the bulls out with the cows yet.

He rode down and circled the house and barns and corrals, satisfying himself that it had all weathered the latest storm in good order.

So, why did he feel a sudden restlessness? What had caused the tingling in the back of his neck, and the new ache in his gut. Something was wrong somewhere.

Looking over his shoulder toward Durango, he couldn't ignore his instinctive urge to return.

Holt spurred his horse into a steady, ground-devouring lope and rode into town a little past noon. He pulled the stallion to a perfect slide stop, then looked all around before settling back into the saddle. His instincts seldom failed him, but it seemed his quick ride back had been for nothing.

Maybe not for *nothing*. He had a better sense of himself now, and was certain that the time he had taken to think while in those serene surroundings had done him good. The decisions he had made concerning his job and Lorelei were right. And now he could concentrate on what had to be done.

"Mornin', Sheriff."

Holt looked down to see the young clerk from the

depot standing at the edge of the street. "Howdy, Tony. How're things goin'?"

"Real peaceful."

Taking off his hat, Holt wiped droplets of sweat from inside the leather band. "I was goin' to come look you up later. When's the next shipment of dry goods due in from Denver?"

The young man looked surprised that the sheriff would be interested in such mundane things as dry goods. "Came in day before yesterday. Why?"

Holt jerked up. His gray eyes narrowed to thoughtful slits. "What's that you say?" He ignored the exasperated expression on Tony's face.

"The train brought supplies Tuesday. Day before yesterday."

Before the boy could repeat the question *why?*, Holt had kicked his horse into a dead run down Main Avenue. Mud and snow splattered in all directions. Riders and pedestrians alike scattered in his wake.

"Lorelei, come back to Boston with me. I'm getting up in years, you know, and need my only family near." Clifton Abbott set his bag on the lopsided hotel bed.

Lorelei sighed. She couldn't remember how many times her father had been on his death bed during the past years. Whenever he wanted her to bend to his will, he used guilt, and plenty of it.

"Daddy, you are fifty-one years old. You will not be leaving this world in the next few months, and that is all I'm asking for. Give me until next summer. By then the mercantile should be debt free, and I will feel better about leaving."

She sighed. That look had come over his face again. The one where he only heard what he wanted to hear, and he was definitely not listening to her now.

"Why stay? What is there for you here? Several eligible young men have been asking about you. Even young Thomas Fairchild. You remember him, don't you?"

She scowled. Oh, yes, she remembered little Tommy, with the roving hands and overbite.

Realizing that the argument could turn into an all day bout, Lorelei decided it was past time to return to the mercantile. Mr. Ends—ders would be hungry and ready for lunch. Thanks to her father's mule-headedness, she was half an hour later than she had said she would be.

She gave her father an affectionate kiss on the cheek. "See you for dinner, Daddy. We can discuss this later."

But as she strolled down the boardwalk, avoiding icy patches of packed snow, she determined to keep the subject more pleasant during the evening meal. And her decision to not mention last night's prowler had been a good one. Clifton Abbott would have personally escorted her to the next train out of town if he had but known.

The more she thought about her father's usual high-handed means of persuasion, the angrier she became. He and Holt Dolan had a lot in common lately, the way they both treated her like a wayward child who needed constant supervision. He just *had* to give her more time.

She had worked hard on the mercantile. And it was

entirely possible that *she* had turned it into a good business *all by herself.* Enders may have suggested advertising, but she had supervised the designs and the wording. And the window displays were all her creation. Plus the special treatment she gave every single customer. Why, then, was she still plagued by doubts since learning about her father and Enders' conspiracy?

Distracted by her thoughts, Lorelei failed to notice that the door stood ajar as she entered the store. She absently closed it behind her and yanked at the tip-ends of the fingers on her gloves. Why had her father chosen to come to Durango now when everything in her life was such a mess?

Suddenly, she caught her breath when something in the middle of the floor, where it should have been clear, caused her to trip and almost fall. "Why not?" she muttered, as she released the air. What else could go wrong?

Lorelei bent to jerk whatever it was out of the way. Her fingers clasped wool trousers. They covered an inert leg. Her fingers went limp, and the thud of a leather boot heel striking wood vibrated the length of the boards.

A scream bubbled deep in her chest and worked its way up her throat all the while her eyes scanned the body up to Enders' still face. A smear of red soaked the gray-brown hair behind his right ear.

Sound never escaped her mouth. A rough hand clamped her lips against her teeth so hard that the tender flesh tore. She nearly gagged on the taste of her own blood.

Panic overwhelmed her when a hard body pressed aganst her back, but she continued to struggle.

"Easy now, pretty lady. Don't wanna have ta hurt ya."

Lorelei's chest constricted. She choked on her fright. Chad! She would have recognized his voice anywhere. Her friend. The man who robbed the bank. Who tried to murder Holt.

Something cold and hard nudged the side of her neck.

"I'm gonna take my hand off'n yore mouth. All I want is a few answers. Understand?"

All she could think about was the gun. He threatened her with a *gun.* Her knees went weak. She probably would have fallen, but he had yet to remove his hand from her face.

Chad's words finally sifted through to her numbed brain. Answers? To what? Why? What did *she* know about anything that would be of interest to an outlaw?

At last, she nodded her head. She wouldn't scream. Who would hear? She had foolishly blundered into the store, unaware of the danger, and closed the door behind her.

Chad gradually removed his hand. She attempted to edge away, but he kept a firm grip on her arm, with the gun pointed at her left breast.

"Don't try anythin' stupid, less'n ya wanna end up like yore friend there."

She gulped as her stomach churned violently. "Is . . . is he dead?"

"Don't reckon. The fella's got nine lives. Shoulda kicked over the first time."

Her initial gripping fear gave way to stark, heart-rending terror. Evidently Chad had been the one responsible for nearly killing Enders several weeks ago.

Her hands clenched into fists. She was such a fool. Whatever had happened to her usual good sense? Why hadn't she seen the vicious streak in the man before? She had actually been so gullible as to believe that he was sweet and shy, and had thought him a dear friend.

Suddenly her eyes scanned the store. Something else was wrong. Something missing. Then she remembered. The puppies! Though Chad had seemed to like the little animals, she would put nothing past him now.

A spot of red flickered in the corner of her eye. Without appearing to look in that direction, she kept her lashes lowered and found both dogs partially hidden behind a crate underneath a nearby table.

A trembling sigh passed through her bruised lips. They had become very precious to her, always listening quietly to her many woes, never passing judgment. Hopefully, they would be smart enough to stay where they were, no matter what.

Chad's fingers dug into her arm. "Where is it?"

Lorelei blinked, genuinely confused. "I beg your pardon? Where is what?"

He shook her. "Don't play dumb with me. I want that tobacco. Now!"

She shook her arm. He still wouldn't release her. Tobacco? He was always after that awful stuff. Her brain clicked. Hadn't Holt also asked about tobacco orders once? She had mentioned Chad. Faint hope flared in her eyes, to be quickly dashed. That had been the last she'd heard of it. Surely Holt would have brought it up again if he had found out anything.

Stalling for time as she pretended to be thinking, her eyes searched the shelves where the tobacco was stored. There were only a few pouches left, and none of what Chad wanted. She honestly couldn't remember putting any up this week. "I-I never received tobacco. At least not the kind you ordered."

With a cruel twist, he bent her arm. "Yore lyin'. It was on the train. Now tell me, damn you!"

She stammered, "En-Enders might—"

"If ya mean that gent with the chunk out'n his skull, he don't know nuthin'." His sour breath fanned her cheek. She winced and tried to turn her head, but couldn't. "That just leaves you."

"Tr-truly, I have not seen it. If I had, it would be on the shelf."

He chuckled as if he were enjoying her torment. "Huh uh. Nice try, pretty lady. Ya better spit it out, 'fore ya ain't so pretty anymore."

"Please. I wish I could give it to you. I really do." Lorelei could have screamed when her voice quavered. He seemed to relish her fear, and it frightened her all the more.

"Wh-why are you doing this? I thought we were friends. If you leave n-now, I promise I will—"

"Sic yore boyfriend, the high and mighty sheriff, on me. I know."

"N-no. I wouldn't do that."

He backed her up against the wall and trapped her there with the weight of his body, leaving the hand that had gripped her arm free to explore the more tender areas of her body. Lorelei gasped with pain and outrage when he squeezed her breast.

"Reckon I know what ole Holt'n you been up to. Yep. Yore thicker'n thieves. Haw! Haw! Only *I'm* a thief, 'n ya won't give me the time o' day."

Lorelei gulped as she sagged against the rough wall, trying to melt out of his grasp. She felt his knuckles scrape her skin. He was unbuttoning her dress. Dear Lord, help her! She raised her hands to fend him off, but he dug the barrel of the pistol into the hollow beneath her chin.

"Huh uh. If'n ya want me ta stop, ya gotta tell me what ya did with my package."

"You have to believe me. I haven't seen it!" Her voice was a high-pitched wail. The flesh on her body literally crawled under his painful touch.

At Lorelei's cry, the puppies ran from beneath the table, creating a terrifying din. At the same time, the front door swung open, silhouetting a large, powerful form.

Holt! Lorelei nearly fainted with relief. While Chad's attention was momentarily diverted, she shoved, hard, in an effort to run past the madman. But Chad was too agile and quick. He grabbed her about the waist and held her, kicking and squirming, as a partial shield in front of him.

"Well, if'n it ain't the fine sheriff come to rescue the pretty lady. Been wonderin' when ya'd show up."

"Hello, Chad. Figured I'd find you here." Holt's gun was in his hand. He kept it there as he walked farther into the room.

Lorelei stopped struggling. She sucked in her breath. What if Holt stumbled over Enders? Chad would kill him the instant his guard was down.

But Holt was more alert than she had been. He stopped just before he would have fallen over the unconscious man's legs. His jaw hardened. "Up to your old tricks again, I see, leaving a trail of bodies everywhere you go."

Chad's arm squeezed into Lorelei's waist until she feared he would cut her in half. "He ain't dead yet. Might could use 'im, if'n I have ta."

Holt's eyes scoured over Lorelei, searching for signs that she had been harmed. When he saw the gaping bodice of her dress, exposed even beneath the heavy folds of her cloak, the hand holding his pistol jerked. But his voice remained unusually calm. "It's over now. You might as well let the woman go."

Holt suddenly trembled. His temples throbbed unbearably. Seeing Chad with the gun in his hand, pointing it first at Lorelei then at himself, brought back scenes from a too-vivid nightmare. He had ridden down a peaceful valley. A group of riders came toward him. One of the men fired. Chad. Chad had shot him that day. He swallowed, feeling suddenly nauseous.

"Over? Not by a damned sight. You ain't dead *yet,* big brother," Chad snorted.

For a moment, Lorelei didn't realize exactly what Chad was saying. She was too intent on watching Holt. He had never looked so ferocious and menacing, but there was something else in his eyes, too. Something deep, and very sad.

"Sorry to disappoint you. Guess you'll have to try again." Resignation and despair soured Holt's words.

Chad cocked his brows and grinned, then seemed

almost triumphant. "I'm gonna do more'n that. This time I'll have it all."

Absorbing every nuance of the conversation, it slowly registered in Lorelei's bemused brain that Chad had called Holt his *big brother.* She was so stunned, and quiet, that she didn't even realize Chad had released her.

Dear heavens. Brothers! And they were calmly discussing killing each other as if it were an everyday, mundane occurrence. Her eyes never left Holt as he put his gun back in its holster.

Holt eyed Chad warily. "Not here. We'll go someplace where innocent people won't get hurt."

Enders stirred and groaned.

Chad barely glanced in the injured man's direction. His eyes glittered with unsuppressed excitement. "By the river, behind the blacksmith's."

There was no expression on Holt's face. His voice was flat. "All right."

"Half an hour?"

"Fine."

Chad directed a malicious glare at Lorelei. "Be thinkin' 'bout that package, pretty lady. *We* ain't done yet, either." Even though the puppies growled and snapped at him, he bent and gave them each a scratch behind the ears.

During the next few moments, a dozen images flashed before Lorelei's eyes. The two ladies standing in the open doorway, shrinking back as Chad elbowed his way through. Her father's scowl as he stood behind them, peering into the darkened mercantile. Enders sitting up, holding a hand to his head. The puppies jumping and running everywhere at once.

And Holt. Holt's long strides covering the distance between them. His arms, wrapping around her as she sobbed uncontrollably into his heavy sheepskin jacket.

Sounds intruded upon her numbed senses. Someone shouted, "Gunfight. There's going to be a gunfight." The puppies whined pitifully at her feet. Her father mumbled incoherently as he helped a groaning Enders to his feet.

But the only thing she really paid attention to was Holt whispering in her ear. "God, Lori, I was so afraid."

Then he held her at arm's length and scanned her trembling form from head to toe, trying valiantly to keep his eyes from returning over and over again to her open bodice.

Lorelei blushed and tried to refasten the buttons, but her hands shook too badly. Holt pushed her fingers away and finished what she had started, though he visibly jerked each time his knuckles brushed her flesh. Through all of that, his eyes never left her face. "Are you all right? Did he hurt you?"

She shook her head. It was impossible to talk around the constriction in her throat.

Then her father was there. He shoved Holt aside and hugged her to his massive chest. His voice was unnaturally gruff. "Who was that man, Lorelei. And for that matter, who is this?" His chins quivered in Holt's direction.

It was Enders who answered. "Sheriff Holt Dolan, sir. I believe I mentioned him in my wires."

Clifton eyed Holt warily. So this was the man who

had helped Enders look after his daughter. He had to admit he liked the cut of the fellow. He stared thoughtfully between Lorelei and the sheriff, then shifted so he held Lorelei on his left side, and extended his right hand. "I believe I owe you special thanks, Sheriff."

Holt blinked. Who did the old geezer think he was, manhandling Lorelei that way? He had a violent urge to yank her away from the old man, but controlled his temper long enough to grit out, "I couldn't imagine why."

Clifton was unflappable, and a little amused. "For helping Enders watch out for my only daughter, and for keeping her safe from rapscallions like the one who just stormed out."

Holt gulped. Lorelei's father. God! He wiped his palm on his pant leg and reached for the hand that was, luckily, still offered.

Her father's mention of Chad reminded Lorelei of something very important, and unpleasant. She turned imploring eyes to Clifton, and to Enders, who had just ushered all of the remaining bystanders from the store.

"Daddy, could I have a few minutes alone with Holt? Please."

Clifton blustered for a second, but couldn't argue with her moist, pleading eyes and earnest features. "Oh, all right. But Enders and I will be waiting outside the door."

She gave him a watery smile and watched until the two men had closed the door behind them. Then she turned to Holt.

He was staring at Freda, the red pup, his shoulders hunched, a naked expression of pain on his face.

And Holt was hurting. Damn Chad! Damn his brother for the evil and destruction he had caused. It seemed today was his day to remember—things better left hidden in the recesses of his mind. While looking at the puppies, Holt had recalled the outlaw he shot during the bank robbery. The man had mentioned a partner and a dog, and Holt suddenly remembered the red bitch he had found lying close beside a body over a month ago. If what the dying outlaw had said was true, then Chad had to be responsible for another murder. Probably over the damned dog.

Chad had conveniently found the pups and given them to Lorelei. The red pup looked exactly like the bitch, black feet, white patch on the chest, and all. Well, it seemed he had just solved several cases at once. Damn, Chad.

Lorelei watched the play of emotions run the gamut across Holt's weary features. It seemed natural to reach out and put her arms around his waist. She breathed in the scent of leather and fresh outdoors and a virile male aroma singular to Holt. With her chin tilted upward, her eyes locked with his. "Chad is your brother?"

He nodded. "Half brother."

"Why didn't you tell me before?"

"Didn't seem important."

She bit back an angry retort. Wasn't important? The man had asked her to marry him, and didn't feel it necessary to mention his outlaw-murderer half brother? "Y-you aren't going to meet him, are you?"

"Have to."

Now she *was* angry, and refused to hold her tongue any longer. "Of course you *do not have* to. Deputize someone."

He shook his head and looked as if he expected her to understand. "I'm the only one who can take him."

Desperation gripped her heart as she clutched at his arm. "Perhaps he won't be there. He may have run off when he left here."

Again Holt shook his head.

"Why not?"

He sighed. "Because this is the way it has to be. The way we've both known it would end."

Lorelei backed away from Holt. Hurt poured from her eyes. "Why? I don't understand. You are brothers, for heaven's sake. How can you do this to each other?"

His voice was raw with emotion. Unable to watch Lorelei's stricken features, he turned his back. "Because of envy. Jealousy. We were both guilty of it. Love. Hatred. Anythin'. Everythin'."

He rubbed a hand over his eyes, then pinched the bridge of his nose. Taking a deep breath, he continued, as if once he started talking, he couldn't stop. "I was seven years old when my mother died. She wasn't a very loving woman, so I never really knew what I'd missed until a year later when my father married Chad's mother. Surprisingly enough, even during the time she was pregnant with Chad, Emily collected a lonely little boy beneath her wing and treated me as if I were her own. When Chad was born, I figured things would change, that I would be shunted aside and replaced with the new arrival. It never happened. She still gave me all of the love and attention I ever needed.

"Yet in the back of my mind, I always knew she wasn't my *real* mother. I envied Chad for having both parents and the closeness I never felt a part of."

A hoarse laugh erupted from his throat. "And all the

while, Chad was jealous that *I* was our father's first-born. He thought I would always have first claim to the business, our home, everything. But our father loved us equally. He divided the inheritance between us. It wasn't good enough for Chad. He wanted to be *first*. He wanted it all.

"Don't get me wrong. Chad and I loved each other. It was fun havin' a little brother taggin' after me. But as we grew older, everything became a competition."

There was a long pause, as he remembered and resurrected old hurts. Lorelei's heart went out to both of the young boys. She swallowed and blinked back tears of compassion as Holt drew in a ragged breath and began to speak.

"Anyway . . . somethin' happened . . . and I had to leave home."

"D-did Chad have something to do with your leaving?"

He shrugged. "Maybe. I'll probably never know. Don't want to, really."

Lorelei moved to stand close behind Holt.

"Anyway, several years later, I was working in Kansas, and who showed up, but Chad. It's been like that ever since. Wherever I went, he eventually followed."

Lorelei sensed there was a lot he'd left out of the story, but also knew she couldn't push for the rest. Not now. "So, here you are."

"Yes, here we are."

Her hand rubbed down the length of his broad back. She stated with more conviction than she felt, "You won't be able to meet him."

Suddenly, Holt whirled. Lorelei was taken aback at

the misery she read in his eyes.

"Haven't you heard a word I've said? I have to do it. There's only me. If I don't, the killin' will go on and on. Good God, Lori, if I hadn't come in when I did, he *might* have killed you, too. I'll take him down, if for no other reason than that."

Lorelei's eyes rounded to the size of silver dollars. Her hand clutched her throat. Her voice was reed thin. "You cannot use a gun on your own brother. I-it would be . . . inhuman."

Holt tugged his hat down firmly, and walked to the door. Looking over his shoulder, he answered, "You can bet I'm not feelin' very . . . human . . . right now. When I meet Chad, and *if* I live, I'll have lost a brother, and the woman I love more than life itself."

Chapter Twenty-One

After Holt left the mercantile, Lorelei stood alone in the middle of the floor, feeling as if her insides were being ripped to shreds. She thought she had felt pain before, but it was nothing compared to the all-encompassing ache spreading throughout her body, focusing in the region of her heart.

Slowly, like a bent-over old woman, she walked to the door. Her father and Enders stood in the street, watching as the saloon across the way emptied of patrons. Miners, cowboys, store owners, everyone was in a rush to be the first down the hill to find a good location to view the gunfight.

Before Lorelei had taken her first step off the walk, Catherine Romaine rushed to her side. "I just heard that Holt and Chad are squaring off. Come on, honey, if we don't hurry, it'll all be over."

If only that were true, Lorelei thought, as in a near state of shock she allowed herself to be led along with Catherine, Enders and her father. The last place she wanted to be was watching Holt and his brother shoot at each other, but she *needed* to be there. In some unfathomable way, she felt responsible.

Clifton Abbott saw the haunted expression on his daughter's face. "Lorelei, are you sure you want to see this? You and I could wait at the mercantile. Enders will tell us—"

"No, Daddy. I w-want to go."

A sense of desperation gripped Lorelei. Her steps quickened. Clifton Abbott labored to keep up as they descended the last slope to the Rio de Las Animas. As had happened with Holt, the English translation of the River of Lost Souls made an indelible impression on Lorelei.

She stumbled over loose stones and gnarled roots concealed amidst dried and dying weeds. Seeing the number of people gathered along the riverbed, she clutched at her father's arm. What was the matter with everyone? Had they *all* gone mad?

Her gaze darted over the myriad of weathered faces. Anticipation glowed from their eyes and emanated from their nervous stances. They appeared anxious for *anything* that would break the monotony of their day.

Her breath caught in her throat when she finally saw Holt. He was motioning a raucous group of men, already well into their cups, to move out of the line of intended fire. Her heart warmed, remembering his condition to Chad that they go where innocent people would not be injured. But with so many bystanders, any stray bullet . . .

Her mind went suddenly blank when her eyes met Holt's. It was as if he had felt her gaze, for he stared directly back at her. She gulped down a breath of air as her father's arm tightened reassuringly around her shoulders.

Holt. He looked so lost and alone. His cheeks were hollow, his eyes pale and sunken.

The crowd murmured. Chad sauntered cockily down the bank about a hundred yards away. He grinned as he stopped to joke with a couple of miners. Others were taking odds on who would be the faster, and he had the nerve to bet an eagle on himself. Lorelei gritted her teeth. He must be awfully confident to wager ten dollars.

As much as she hated to admit it, she feared Holt was right. Chad had to be stopped. And of all the people in Durango, who was there to do it *but* Holt? Who else possessed the courage and grit to stand up to his half brother?

Her heart literally ached for Holt. She was sure that deep down, he still loved the young boy who had idolized him years ago. How he must be hurting now. Then a horrible thought struck her. What if Holt wasn't able to pull the trigger?

Fear knotted her insides. For the first time, she considered the very real possibility that Holt could die that very day. From the look in Chad's outlaw eyes, she doubted he would feel the same compunction against killing Holt. In fact, he was still smiling, acting as if he welcomed the chance to once again be the winner, to be "first" in everyone's eyes.

Lorelei stood on her tiptoes trying to see above the heads in front of her. She had to get Holt's attention. Needed to tell him she understood and that he must prevail, no matter the cost.

No matter the cost. Had that thought really come from her? Sanctimonious Lorelei Abbott? She guessed so. Everyone had to pay a price to survive in the world—some more than others. And now that she had lost Holt, whatever the outcome of the coming battle, her own debt would be high indeed.

She suddenly ran forward, dodging through the flannel-shirted men talking and gesturing toward Chad and Holt. She *had* to get to Holt, to explain. Too many people blocked the way. Elbowing and squirming, she made it to the front edge of the crowd, only to be jerked to a stop when Enders grabbed her arm.

It was a good thing he held her, for the scene before her was enough to set her to shaking so hard she could barely stand.

Chad and Holt stood off by themselves on a flat area of ground near the water's edge. They faced each other, separated by thirty feet of pebbled sand and ice.

Holt's legs were spread and he braced himself on the uneven ground, arms akimbo, his right hand only inches from the butt of his gun. He squinted at Chad through a heavy haze that hung above the river.

Chad seemed looser and more relaxed than Holt. His fingers curled and flexed as his hand hovered above his quick-draw holster. There was a sadistic curve to his lips as he taunted, "Reckon this's it, big brother."

Lorelei held her breath. Chad seemed so sure of himself, possessing no remorse that he would soon do his utmost to bring down his own kin.

They were close enough that Holt could hear Chad above the rush of the river, but at a distance that he couldn't read the expression on the boy's face. However, the face wasn't what he was concentrating on. It was the glittering blue eyes that held his attention.

"I wish things had been different." Holt's voice was

low, but carried on the brisk breeze.

Chad shrugged. "Ain't got no regrets. Reckon Mama'll see to it ya git a rip-snortin' burial. She always did like you best."

Holt's strained features turned chalk white. He wedged his right foot more firmly between two slippery stones.

Lorelei shook her head at the sadness of it all. Her eyes shifted between the two men. Their profiles seemed chiseled in stone as they stood perfectly poised, bodies taut as tightly strung wire.

The tense quiet was disturbed by the blur of two arms dropping downward. Lorelei cringed. She had known it would happen eventually, but was not prepared for the suddenness of it all.

The faint mumble of voices behind her faded. The quiet was almost deafening as the scene unfolded before her eyes with slow-motion detail. Holt's knees bent as he crouched and drew. Chad's lips thinned into a feral snarl. The glint in his eyes was maniacal.

Their hands rose like flickers of lightning. She flinched as twin explosions reverberated in her ears. A puff of dust burst from the left side of Chad's vest. He reflexively fired another round. Holt spun to one side, but gradually turned back, his eyes riveted on his brother.

Both men stood with smoking guns. An acrid stench drifted over the crowd inching closer down the slope. Lorelei breathed a huge sigh of relief. It was over. They had missed.

She started to step forward. Enders held her back. Chad's lips sagged. His gun dropped from his hand. His eyes were wild and full of question. Then he sank to his knees and fell forward.

Lorelei's hands clenched together over her heart, trying to still the incessant thudding. She waited, time seemingly suspended, for Chad to get up and dust off his clothes. He would wink and grin and tell her everything had been a joke. Wasn't it a good one?

But he didn't move. There was an anguished groan that caused the hair on the back of her neck to stand on end. She jerked her gaze from Chad and saw Holt, a trickle of blood dripping down his arm, stumbling toward his brother. Her heart stopped in mid-beat. It felt as if her chest was caving in upon itself.

Unaware of what she was doing, Lorelei clutched at Enders' arm, her nails digging into the thick leather jacket until he winced and clasped her fingers in his.

Holt knelt beside the motionless man. Gently, tenderly, he rolled the body over. Holt's head was bowed, his chin resting on his chest. Tears rolled unheeded down Lorelei's cheeks as she saw Holt reach out a hand that shook so badly he could hardly close Chad's eyelids.

Then he picked his brother up off the ground. He staggered, and Lorelei instinctively stepped forward. But when he faced her, and turned his gaze to her, he appeared to look through her.

If she lived to be two hundred, she would never forget that moment. His cheeks were lined with damp streaks. The expression in his eyes was empty, like he had died inside. She was consumed by love and compassion, but was at a loss as to what to do about it.

She reached out her hand, but he turned his back and walked away. Walked away. He had meant what he said at the mercantile. He was lost to her forever.

Dry sobs shook her frame as her father joined her and Enders. Clifton wrapped a large, comforting arm around her shoulders and helped her back up the hill toward the store. Enders and a strangely subdued Catherine followed close behind.

The next day, Lorelei sat behind the counter while Enders checked the unopened boxes left in the storeroom. Customers had filtered in singly and in groups, and the only topic of conversation had been yesterday's gunfight.

She blinked her eyes and covered her ears. If one more person said another word about their "wonderful" sheriff . . .

All she had been able to think about yesterday afternoon and evening, or this morning, was that if things had been different between herself and Holt, she might have been able to be there for him, to ease some of his pain.

And she *did* want to be with him, not for just an hour, or a day, but for the rest of her life. There would never be another man for her like Holt. He must have known that once, too, but at the time, she had been so blind and hard-headed that she wouldn't have recognized the truth if it had bitten her on the ankle.

So, now what could she do to make it up to him? How could she *prove* her love was sincere? Would he want her even if she succeeded? Would he care that she tried?

So many things had happened since he had proposed. And when she had finally told him how she felt, he had either been deathly silent, or tried to talk her into leaving town.

She nibbled at her lower lip. How could he have had a change of heart so quickly? Her mouth quivered. Perhaps he had decided she was too shallow and stubborn to be deserving of his love. If *that* were the case, she could hardly blame him.

Enders came from the back carrying a small box. He held it out to her. "Mayhap a piece of maple sugar candy would sweeten your day."

Her eyes widened. How glib of tongue Enders had become since his association with the lady editor. "Why, thank you, Enders. Anything would be worth a try."

She took a small bite of the confection and held it on her tongue, allowing the sugar to melt and enliven her taste buds with the delicious maple flavor.

Strangely enough, she did perk up, whether because of the candy or Enders' solicitous company, she wasn't sure. She had come to rely more and more upon her father's friend lately.

"Look at the pups, missy. Wonder what they've found."

Lorelei glanced over to see Freda and Sissy digging at a box under a table of neatly folded blankets. Neat, except for one. As she walked toward the table, her cheeks flushed at the memory of what had transpired there on the floor—was it just a few nights ago, or a few years? She quickly refolded the blanket, but instead of replacing it on the table, held it in her arms.

Enders was on his knees, pulling out the box. The puppies, however, were more interested in a tiny gray mouse that had taken refuge between the box and the wall.

Robert grinned and started to push the carton back. "Mayhap, you should trade one of the dogs for a cat."

She smiled and shook her head, then said, "Wait. We might as well open the box. No telling what's in it." She swallowed a guilty lump as she recalled it sliding beneath the table *that night.* It wasn't like her to misplace anything that had to do with the mercantile.

Enders slit the top open with his knife, pulled out a small pouch and gazed pointedly up at Lorelei. The tobacco. She and Enders and Chad and Holt had all stood within inches of the stuff.

She knelt beside Enders and bumped against the gun strapped around his narrow waist. As he dumped the contents of the box onto the floor, she caught herself wondering why she hadn't even flinched at the abrupt contact.

But she didn't dwell on the gun. Her attention focused, instead, on the sacks of tobacco. She blushed at the explicit picture of the Wild *Bull.* Funny, she had never noticed it before.

Hiding her sudden embarrassment, she cleared her throat and asked, "I wonder what there is about these pouches that could cause so much trouble?" She flipped several of them back and forth between her hands. "They look like plain sacks of tobacco to me."

All at once, her fingers went numb. The packages fell unheeded into her lap. When Chad had first come into the mercantile, so long, long ago, he had mentioned that her uncle kept a supply of Wild Bull for him. Her arms wrapped about her stomach at the thought that insinuated itself into her brain. Chad. Her uncle's death. Instinctively, she knew the two were connected.

Whatever was in these pouches was important enough that Chad had been willing to take Uncle John's life to get it. And she also suspected that Holt had come to the same conclusion much earlier.

Then she thought of her father, resting at the hotel, and pictured his worn, wrinkled features. This latest piece of information would remain her secret—hers and Holt's. Clifton had mourned his brother's loss for a long time, and had just recently put his grief in the past. There was no point in bringing it up again.

Dear heavens, but Chad had made a fool of her. A burning sensation in her stomach worked its way up her throat. He had used her. Played upon her trust for his evil gains. She had taken his easy smiles and compliments to heart, at one time comparing him in a more favorable light to Holt. But what really ate at her soul, was that she had called him her friend.

Her hands clenched into fists. If the man weren't already dead, she would be tempted to—

"Are you all right, missy?" Robert turned too-shrewd eyes upon her as she clambered to her feet.

"I, ah, yes, I'm fine. I just need to freshen up before we go to the sheriff's office."

She was about to turn her back to the door when a flicker of movement caught her eye. She swung around just as a small man, clad in black clothing, disappeared inside the saloon across the street.

She stood for several minutes, waiting to see if he would reappear. There had been something familiar . . .

Heavens, she admonished herself. How silly of her to be so suspicious. She had barely gotten but a glimpse of the person. Besides, how many people did she know who frequented the bar? It was just her overactive imagination.

Holt Dolan sat behind his desk, boot heels propped on the corner, arms folded across his chest. His hat dipped low over his face. To anyone looking in from the street, it would appear that Durango's infamous sheriff was fast asleep.

But Holt was wide awake, and had been for two days. If he tried to sleep, nightmares startled him back to full consciousness.

He had buried Chad that morning, quietly, to avoid the public display that had surrounded the gunfight itself. Through all of the uproar, he kept telling himself that what he had done was right, unavoidable. Yet knowing that did not make the deed any easier to live with.

He continued rethinking the words Chad had spoken before the gunfight. "Reckon Mama'll see to it ya get a rip-snortin' burial."

Holt pinched the bridge of his nose. Chad hadn't even known that his mother had passed away two years ago, just after Christmas. What a damned waste!

Even worse than the loss of his brother, though, was having to comprehend the fact that whatever had blossomed between himself and Lorelei had been laid to rest with Chad.

God, when he had turned to her that afternoon, with his brother in his arms, his heart hanging on his shirt sleeve, she'd had the strangest look in those ebony eyes.

He'd been afraid to probe their depths too deeply, afraid of what else he might see there. She had started to raise her hand, and he had turned away, like the coward he was, unable to bear her condemnation.

Not that he hadn't deserved it. What woman could live with a man who had the gall to meet his own flesh and blood, face to face, in a gunfight? Hell, hadn't Lorelei said as much herself?

Gall. That's what it had taken, all right. But he'd had no other choice. Better him than some name-building bounty hunter. Or hardest yet, if he'd had to watch Chad swing from the end of a rope on some gallows in some nowhere town.

One thing gave Holt peace of mind. Chad had lived long enough to whisper three words—words that echoed in his head until he thought he would go mad. "Thanks, big brother."

Chad had died with dignity. For that, they had both been grateful.

Holt rubbed the bandage on his upper arm. Chad had been so cocky and sure that Holt couldn't help wondering if his brother had purposely missed. But then again, Holt had been pretty damned sure of his own self. Maybe Chad had forgotten, after all those years, who had taught him to draw.

The office door swung open. Holt shifted his hat to the back of his head. "Come on in, Enders."

A glimpse of a gingham skirt swishing behind Enders brought Holt's feet thudding to the floor.

Lorelei repressed the urge to run to Holt and smother him in a motherly embrace. He looked so drawn and haggard. That errant lock of black hair was plastered to his forehead, and her fingers curled into the palms of her hands.

She also noticed the disarray of his desk. A map was spread across the scarred surface, along with scraps of paper and several pouches of tobacco, similar to those in the box she and Enders had brought.

Holt looked from the carton Enders had laid on his desk, to Lorelei, and back to Enders. "What's that?" Although he asked the question of Enders, his eyes kept straying to Lorelei. God, she looked beautiful. Pale, maybe a little thinner, but beautiful, still a sight for sore eyes.

With his back to Lorelei, Robert glowered at Holt. "Look for yourself. Missy . . . Miss Abbott, and I, found it. Thought you should see."

Lorelei's heart nearly sang with happiness at just being near Holt. The past two days had seemed like two years, she had missed him so terribly. She had hoped that by coming to him, bringing the box of tobacco, it would prove that she was trying to help, offering her support. But she couldn't tell from his actions whether he was pleased, angry, or if he cared at all.

Holt's voice cracked as he looked into the box and pulled out several pouches of Wild Bull tobacco. "Where did you get this?" His nerve endings felt little shocks wherever Lorelei's eyes touched his body. She had that strange look again—the one that caused the muscles on his stomach to contract, and his groin to quicken.

"It was shoved under a table somehow." Robert crossed his arms and glared down at the sheriff, well aware of the fact that the younger man had yet to pay him a bit of attention.

The sheriff's hands trembled as he felt each sack one by one until he found a pouch with a picture of a steer on the cover that crinkled suspiciously. When he found what he was searching for, he yanked open the string and plucked out the folded piece of paper.

Lorelei and Enders frowned and repeated Holt's earlier question in unison. "What's that?"

The sheriff unfolded the missive and read: LA Fr 4.

He gave it to Enders, who looked it over carefully, a puzzled expression wrinkling his lean face. "So, what is it?"

Lorelei looked over Enders' shoulder, read the missive, and then studied the scraps of paper on Holt's desk. If she wasn't mistaken, she had seen one like it amidst all the jumble. At last she found it and held it up. "SL 3 Th. What do they mean?"

Holt rubbed his jaw. One brow cocked at a rakish angle. "I suspect it's a message of some kind telling . . . Chad . . . and his gang . . . where there's a bank or safe ripe for the taking, and when."

Suddenly, Lorelei's eyes began to sparkle. "You may be right. I was looking through the older copies of the newspaper one afternoon, when I thought I'd found a pattern to some of the holdups around the area. They seemed to be connected to the arrival of goods at the mercantile. But then several weeks passed, with no reported robberies, and I disregarded it as a too-fertile imagination at work."

She shifted her weight from one foot to the other and spoke faster. "Remember when Chad came around so often, asking for the tobacco, and we couldn't find it?

That was the time the robberies seemed to stop. These messages were for him. When they stopped, he did, too."

Holt grinned. "You're pretty smart, for an Easterner."

Heat suffused Lorelei's face and body as Holt raked his arm across the map, clearing away anything that blocked his view—except the two coded messages and the wire he had received from the Silverton authorities. He studied the map and the papers in his hand, then looked up triumphantly. "Look at this. SL 3 Th. It was a Thursday evening when I got word the Silverton bank had been robbed. That's got to be the answer. Whoever sent this was telling Chad and his gang to hit the Silverton bank at three o'clock on Thursday. Somehow, when this message was lost, they found another way to send the information."

He held up the second slip of paper. "I'd bet money this one says to go to Las Animas Friday at four o'clock."

A puzzled scowl wrinkled Enders' brow. "But that's tomorrow. Think the rest of Chad's gang has been alerted to the time and place?"

Holt refolded the paper and put it in his shirt pocket. "There's only two, or maybe three, left to worry about. Without Chad . . . they'll probably move on to easier pickin's."

Lorelei moved to the side of the desk. "What about the person sending the messages? How will you find out who it is?" It was hard to describe the feelings she experienced, working with Holt to solve the mystery of the messages. It was fun, exhilarating and exciting, all at the same time, and she was proud of herself for being able to contribute something.

The sheriff leaned back and sighed. "A wire or two to the right places in Denver, and the informant should be easy enough to locate."

An uneasy silence settled over the room. Lorelei fidgeted with a piece of lint she had discovered on her jacket. Holt stared at the map as if it were suddenly the most important single thing in the world. Enders just stared between the two stubborn people.

Finally, Lorelei sniffed and backed toward the door. Hope had welled anew with the compliment Holt had given her earlier, but now she could see that nothing she had done had changed his mind. He wanted no part of her.

Holt watched her leave. Desperation clogged his throat, and he choked. He was completely at a loss as to what to say to stop her. From her expression, she was still upset and would probably never forgive him. At least he was grateful that he hadn't broken down and made a complete jackass of himself by saying a lot of silly things that she could have thrown back in his face later.

There was a long pause before Robert spoke. "That what you're doing?"

"What?" Holt blinked and stared at Enders like he'd lost his mind.

"You looking for easier pickings?"

A tint of red darkened Holt's cheeks. "Look, I don't know what—"

"Why haven't you been by the mercantile?"

Holt shifted in the suddenly uncomfortable chair. It

wasn't because he hadn't thought about going to see Lorelei a million times a day. "Didn't figure I was welcome." Enders should have known that, as close as he was to the Abbotts'. Lorelei had probably informed them all about what a beast he was.

"Giving up, then, are you?" Enders jibed.

Holt slammed his fist on the desk. Papers rustled with the vibration the blow created. "Damn it! How can I give up what I never had?"

"Hhmmm. Not very smart, either. Mayhap she'll be better off in Boston."

The springs on the chair creaked with the sudden movement as Holt sat up. "Boston? So she's goin' home?" Wasn't that what he'd wanted? Yes, he told himself, but that had been when Chad was a threat. But the country was still dangerous, he thought. Then again, she could get run over by a runaway carriage crossing the streets in Boston, he argued.

Enders studied his fingernails. "Her daddy's trying to talk her into leaving day after tomorrow. She hasn't said yet what she's going to do." He coughed, as if divulging so much information at one time had sapped his energy.

"Well, ah, tell her—"

"Huh uh. I deliver boxes, not messages. Think about it, Sheriff. Think real hard."

Chapter Twenty-Two

"Daughter, you'd best come home. I'll go as far as to admit that you have done a wonderful job with the mercantile. You worked hard and made it into a good business. With that accomplished, you can come back to Boston, and I'll stake you to a trade. Anything you want."

Lorelei was pleased with her father's praise. It had taken a while, but she had finally come to realize the mercantile *had* thrived because of her labors and for no other reason. However, she was in limbo as to what to do with her life.

She wasn't ready to go back to Boston, but she couldn't stay in Durango, knowing she would see Holt every day and that they would never again be more than casual acquaintances. The physical and emotional strain would be more than she could handle.

"Hey, you folks heard the news?" Catherine Romaine came rushing up the walk, a pair of half spectacles bobbing on the end of her nose. She pushed them back into place as she stopped next to Enders.

Enders smiled, a real smile that changed the looks of his long, lean face to that of a very attractive man. Lorelei blinked in wonderment. Catherine's cheeks turned a pretty rose color.

Robert was the first to wonder, "What news?"

The editor puffed out her ample bosom. "Holt Dolan turned in his badge this morning. He quit, and says he's leaving town."

Why everyone turned their eyes to Lorelei, she couldn't fathom. It was *news* to her, too. All at once, her knees went weak, and she grasped the nearest post for support.

Clifton Abbott rocked back on his heels and gave Enders a searching look. "Why would he do a thing like that?"

Robert gave his head an imperceptible shake and shrugged his shoulders.

Catherine kept her eyes trained down the street. "I don't know. All the mayor would say was that he would start looking for a replacement immediately."

Lorelei hardly paid attention to the rest of the conversation after the announcement that Holt was leaving town. Why? He was—had been—a terrific sheriff.

Her heart ached worse than if it had been pierced by a dull knife. She should have gone to Holt days ago, put her pride aside long enough to say how sorry she was for him, and for Chad. She could have explained her feelings, found out his. Then, perhaps, her doubts would have been laid to rest, one way or the other.

"Well, Lorelei, what do you say now?"

Her father had read her mind, and Lorelei bristled. She resented being railroaded into making a decision.

Catherine took a step forward and pointed. "Look, there's Holt now." She fumbled in her reticule for a pen and crumpled piece of paper. "I was hoping to catch him."

All business, the editor stepped out into the avenue. Lorelei turned to see Holt riding his stallion toward them. The palms of her hands grew damp. He looked directly at her, and the force of his gaze staggered her senses. She hadn't realized how terribly much she had missed his wonderfully handsome features, or his virile, *comfortable* body.

A jealous surge of envy rippled through her stomach when Catherine garnered Holt's attention. And though Lorelei pretended not to notice, every once in a while he would sneak a glance in her direction, and her heart would skip a beat, or two. She didn't even have to *see* him look; she felt the tingling to the depths of her soul, and *knew*.

Enders moved to her side. "You going to let him go?"

Her lower lip quivered. "What else can I do? He doesn't want me."

"Funny. He thinks you feel the same way about him."

Robert turned to talk with her father, effectively cutting off any reply she might have made, or the questions that bubbled up her throat until she nearly choked. She stared at Holt. Was Enders right? Was it only a horrible misunderstanding keeping them apart?

Before she had a chance to reflect on the implications of that possibility, she caught a furtive movement from the corner of her eye. It was that man again—the one dressed all in black, who had lurked around the area for several days.

As she studied the fellow, and the sly looks he darted toward Holt, a flicker of recognition tugged at her memory. When he side-stepped into the alley, looking to the right, and then left, assuring himself that his movements had gone unnoticed, chill bumps ran over Lorelei's flesh.

He unbuttoned his overcoat and pulled out a long-barreled pistol. At the same time, Lorelei saw the wide band of red wrapped about his narrow waist. Then she remembered. He was the Mexican-looking man who had been with Chad the night of the social. The one she had thought so dangerous and menacing.

With her recognition, all hell broke loose. The hooligan stepped into the street and aimed his gun at Holt. Lorelei shouted and reached for the pistol strapped to Enders' thigh.

She had never held a gun in her life, but the man she loved was being threatened. The revolver trembled in her hands as she held it before her, the handle gripped tightly in both palms. With the muzzle pointed in the direction of the startled Mexican, she wrapped her index finger around the trigger and squeezed with all her might.

Her ears rang from the loud report. Someone yelled. People scattered every which way. She stumbled backward with the force of the pistol's kick and plunked down, hard, on her derriere.

Once, she thought she heard Holt's voice, and her heart gave a leap of joy. Another shot sounded, and another. She waited for more shouts and firing, but all remained quiet as she leaned back against the siding near her front window.

Lorelei dared a glance to where Holt had been sitting on his horse, talking to Catherine, afraid of what she might see. She released a huge sigh. The street was clear. He had been well enough to move from the exposed location.

Then she swallowed and looked cautiously across the avenue. Her breath caught in her throat. She almost strangled, for her worst fear had been realized. The Mexican lay facedown, the upper half of his body in the mud, the lower half splayed over the walk in front of the saloon.

She had taken a gun and killed him!

Then Holt stepped out of the alley. A rush of satisfaction stiffened her sagging form. He was safe and appeared to be unharmed. Thank heavens!

The elation lasted only as long as it took for the realization of what she had done to actually sink into her brain. She had shot a person, with every intention of killing him. Her beliefs and convictions, everything she had steadfastly clung to since her fiancé's death, had been for naught. When it had come to defending the life of one she loved, she had *acted* before thinking of the consequences.

Tears stung her eyes. Had she been so very wrong all that time? She hoped not. The basic principles were sound. But she could now see why Holt felt the way he did. Sometimes, there were circumstances that could not be ignored, when a person had to stand up to protect another. Deep down, she knew she would do it again but, oh, how it hurt to know she had murdered a man.

She was still plastered against the wall of the mercantile, squirming her tender bottom on the hard board planks, quaking like aspen leaves in a gale wind, when Holt's face suddenly blocked her view of the motionless man across the way. Behind Holt she could see the legs, and then the faces of her father, Catherine and Enders, as they bent over, peering at her, with strange expressions on their faces.

Let them stare. She *was* a freak, and a murderess to boot.

"Lori, where are you hurt? Can you move? Someone get Doc Foster over here!"

Lorelei winced as Holt shouted so close to her ear. She turned dazed eyes to him, then reached up to run shaking hands over his chest and arms. "I-I'm fine. But wh-what about you? Th-that man . . . tr-tried to k-kill you."

Gentle fingers pried the heavy pistol from her hand. She had forgotten she still held on to it. A collective sigh, giving the impression of great relief, hissed through the gathered assembly.

Lorelei blinked. What was that all about? Then the strongest, most comforting arms she had ever known wrapped around her, and she forgot everything else.

"You used that gun for me, didn't you, sweetheart? You really did?" Holt searched her soft, pliable body, probing and prodding until satisfied she was just stunned, and maybe suffering from a slight shock.

Lorelei sniffed. Why did he sound so surprised? Didn't he know she loved him? Of course he did. She had told him. Oh, yes, he hadn't cared. "Y-yes. I k-killed him. H-he—"

Holt's hands cupped her cheeks and tilted her head until she had no recourse but to look him in the eyes. "Listen to me. You didn't kill anyone, Lori. The man's not dead."

It was thoughtful of him to try to make her feel better, but it was no use. She had seen for herself. "B-but . . ." She heard nervous chuckles. Her father laughed outright. She shifted her sore behind and shot him a withering glance for having the nerve to find something so serious amusing.

Clifton pointed across the street. "If you don't believe him, look for yourself."

She didn't want to. Holt turned her chin, and she blinked her eyes open. Sure enough, Enders had gone over and was pulling the smaller man to his feet. Blood trickled down the outlaw's face, and she shuddered; the horrible chill that had racked her body eased. The man was cursing and trying to jerk away from Enders. He was alive! Dear God, he was alive!

Holt's arms tightened about her. The empty void in her soul was suddenly filled with the all-abiding love she harbored for him alone.

When she finally turned her eyes away from the outlaw, she noticed Holt watching her, and could have sworn his shoulders shook. He coughed, and she knew he tried to hide his chuckles. Her black eyes shot sparks at the insensitive oaf.

Holt took several deep breaths before stating matter-of-factly, "You really didn't hurt him. He wasn't knocked down by a bullet. Not directly, anyway." Then he couldn't help it; he let out a great belly-rolling laugh.

Lorelei punched his arm. "What is so funny? I almost k-killed a man, and you all think it's hilarious." Her angry gaze encompassed everyone within sight and the sound of her voice.

Finally Catherine confessed. "See the sign dangling in front of the saloon?"

Lorelei glanced warily across the street. Her eyes rounded. Men were pushing the heavy obstruction to one side or the other in order to enter or leave the establishment. She nodded, but her eyebrows came together in a suspicious frown.

Catherine pointed to Holt's hat brim. "And see that hole?"

Again, Lorelei nodded, but she had a difficult time following the direction of the conversation. Holt couldn't seem to keep his hands off her. He touched her face, her arms, and anywhere else he could reach that wasn't covered by her heavy cloak. Her body reacted, anticipating his every move. So much so, that she wished he would never stop.

His rich timbred voice sent shivers up her spine when he continued where Catherine left off. "To tell you the truth, I wasn't sure who you were aimin' for, the bad guy, or me."

The devilish glint to his eyes caused her to reconsider the term *bad.* Then it suddenly dawned on her what she had done. She yanked off his hat and poked her finger through the symmetrical opening. "Oh, no! *I* did that?"

Holt heaved a dramatic sigh. "'Fraid so. Then the bullet cut through the chain holdin' up that sign."

Lorelei felt a sinking sensation clear to the tip of her freezing toes. "And the sign hit the man." It wasn't stated as a question, but everyone nodded in unison, snickered, and broke into fresh rounds of laughter.

Catherine gasped, "You should have seen the looks on *both* of their faces. Holt ran like the devil himself had arisen straight from the depths of hell."

Holt scowled. "You moved like a pretty spry chick yourself, far as I recollect."

The editor fussed with a ripped seam down the side of her skirt. "Well, maybe. Oh, all right, I beat you to the alley, if that's what you wanted to hear."

Lorelei had just begun to feel a little better about not injuring anyone seriously when she realized she had come closer to shooting Holt than she had the outlaw. With one swift movement, she launched herself into his arms. "I'm sorry. If I had hurt you . . ." She choked. The thought did not bear completion.

Holt pried her arms from around his neck and held her back to where he could look into her eyes. "Why did you do it, Lori? I know better than anyone how you feel about guns. And the afternoon Chad—that I . . ."

Lorelei glanced at her father and Catherine. It was embarrassing to talk about private matters in front of them, but they *must* know how she felt by now. Besides, she would tell the whole world if it helped to get Holt back.

"I-I . . . love . . . you. That's all I know to say. When I saw that man pointing his gun at you, I had to stop him."

Before he could say a word, she pressed her fingers to his firm, beautiful lips. "That afternoon, when you held

Chad, and turned to me, I was so overwhelmed with emotion that all I could do was stand there. I-I . . ."

She ducked her head and plucked at a button on the lapel of his coat. "I-I thought you turned away because you d-didn't want me. You've tried so hard to get rid of me that—"

Holt's mouth swooped down to stop her anguished words. He tasted her lips for a long, sweet moment. His voice was so low and deep that Lorelei had to tilt her head to hear. "I thought you had rejected me, because of what I had done."

"Here, here, you two. That's enough of that." Clifton frowned at his only daughter as he helped the two young people to their feet. "I think, Mr. Dolan, that you and I need to have a talk."

Lorelei smiled a little sheepishly as she dusted off her skirt. "I have one more question. What was the rest of the shooting about? I only fired once and, ah, dropped out of the fight."

Holt looked to Clifton Abbott. He had wondered, too. At the time, he had been busy running for cover.

Clifton grinned. "It seems our friend across the street had himself a partner. Enders saw the culprit sneaking around the corner of the store when he turned to stop Lorelei from snatching his gun. He took the bast—" Abbott darted a look at the two ladies and grimaced—"owlhoot out of commission."

Lorelei shook her head. "But how? I took Enders' gun."

By that time, Robert had rejoined the group. He took a small hideaway derringer from his vest pocket. "I try to be ready for everything, missy. Even unpredictable women."

Lorelei blushed as her father handed Enders back his pistol.

Holt suddenly grabbed Lorelei's elbow and guided her to the mercantile door. He tipped his hat to Clifton. "Excuse us for a minute. We'll have that talk, sir, but first, I have something to settle with your daughter."

He pushed her inside the store, shut and locked the door, then pulled the curtains. When he turned to face Lorelei, his eyes were dark and glowering. He braced his legs wide apart, and held his hands at his sides, elbows bent, ready to catch her if she tried to bolt.

"H-Holt? Wh-what's this all about?" Her voice quavered. This was a side of Holt with which she was totally unfamiliar.

He devoured the space separating them in one swift stride. He poked his index finger in the middle of her breastbone. "You are not goin' back to Baltimore with your father."

Her eyes widened to the size of two double eagles. "B-Boston. I-I—"

He poked her again, backing her up a step. "You are goin' to marry me."

A tinge of anger seeped from under her trepidation and lent her the courage to stand nose to nose with the wonderful man. She prodded *him* in the chest. "Why?"

"Why?"

Her finger toyed with a dark curl peeking over the collar of his shirt as she drawled, "You heard me. Why?"

He backed into a table. "Well, I guess because I love you, more than I ever thought I could love anyone.

And because I want to marry you."

Lorelei felt something nudge her leg and looked down to see the puppies, ears cocked, eagerly awaiting her response.

She stepped into Holt's embrace, nestled her breasts against his chest and pressed her thighs to his as she wrapped her arms about his waist and purred, "That's all we wanted to know."

Epilogue

Lorelei hung over the top rail of the corral, pointing her mittened finger. "Oh, look at that pretty cow."

Holt winced as his prize *bull* ambled along the railing, the animal's dark red hide nearly obliterated by a layer of fresh snow. Icicles clicked together as the huge animal swayed its bulk from side to side.

"Better get off the fence, Lori. That bull is dangerous." He still nursed a bruised hip where the beast had pitched him out of the pen.

He forgot about the bull, though, when a sudden commotion erupted from the barn. He took off on the run to see what was the matter. Rounding the corner, he stopped abruptly in the doorway and grinned.

The two pups had treed a rooster in the rafters and were jumping and balancing on their hind legs in an ungainly attempt to reach the odd, feathered creature.

The enraged rooster craned its neck, flapped its wings and crowed its disgruntlement to all concerned as it strutted across a narrow beam, teasing the two antagonists.

Holt stuffed his hands in his pockets and glanced toward the far corner where his stallion nickered a greeting from the new paddock. His life had undergone a drastic change since Lorelei and her troops had come to the ranch. And he had to admit, it was for the better. He couldn't remember being so busy, or content, or so much in love.

He whistled on his way back to Lorelei, thinking that all was right with the world—until the sound took on a shrill note when he saw what the crazy woman was up to. Her hand was between the rails, and she was petting the damned bull right between the eyes.

"Lorelei, no!" He started to run, but thought better of it, afraid he would startle the huge beast into hurting his new wife. So, he walked, quickly, to within a few feet of the pair and whispered, because he couldn't raise his voice any louder, "Lori, step back, nice and easy."

Lorelei turned innocent eyes to Holt. "But he's so sweet. Aren't you, Snowball?" She scratched the bull between the horns and behind the ears. When she started to withdraw her hand, the animal snuffled and shifted its enormous weight forward, trying to follow her movement.

Holt groaned. "Oh, my God. Snowball?"

He couldn't believe his eyes. The damned vicious animal was trailing her around like a tame puppy dog, and seemed to enjoy it.

When Lorelei beamed him a smile, Holt's heart did a somersault. Maybe he and the bull had something in common, after all.

Her voice wrapped around him like a slow-moving current. "Doesn't he remind you of a fluffy ball, with his pretty white face and snow all over his back?"

Holt shook his head. "Whatever you say, sweetheart. C'mon, let's go back to the house. My toes are beginnin' to feel as cold as those icicles look."

Lorelei took his hand as they walked up to the log cabin. Her heart swelled with pride as they neared her new home. She loved it here on the ranch, and spent hours standing on her porch, gazing across the rolling meadows at the surrounding mountains, covered by a beautiful blanket of white.

Her porch. Her home. Her husband. If she were any happier, she would think she was dreaming. And she still hadn't discounted that possibility. It was always a marvel to her that *she* had been the lucky one to attract a man as virile and handsome as Holt.

When she had first come to Durango, she had already given up hope of developing self-respect or personal confidence, let alone marrying or having a family. Then in the blink of an eye, fate had changed her life, and it was good.

They went inside, and Holt pulled Lorelei onto his lap as he settled into a huge cushioned chair in front of the blazing fireplace. "Do you think you'll like it here, sweetheart?"

She kissed the tip of his cold nose. "I already love it."

He kneaded the muscles along her neck and buried his fingers in her long, golden hair. "It was good of your father to stay and take care of the store so we could have time alone together."

She sighed and laid her head on his shoulder. "Yes, but I still wish Enders had taken my offer of a partnership in the mercantile instead of letting the mayor talk him into your old job."

Holt nibbled the petal-soft lobe of her ear. "You left

the offer open. Catherine will badger him into accepting it, sooner or later."

Lorelei smiled. "Do you think she will ever persuade him to marry her?"

"Stranger things have happened."

She snuggled into his lap, suggestively wriggling her bottom. "You mean like us?"

He nodded, opening the buttons on her bodice, one by tempting one. "Lori?"

"Hhmmm?"

"Promise me somethin'?"

"Hhmm." She loosened his belt.

"When we have kids . . . *I* get to pick the names. Please?"